KT-494-063

PUFFIN CLASSICS

THE THREE MUSKETEERS

ALEXANDRE DUMAS (1802–70) was born near Paris, the son of a general in Napoleon's army. He received little formal education and started his adult life in a series of minor clerical jobs, which he got due to the beauty and clarity of his handwriting. But in 1829 he achieved great success with a historical melodrama about the French king Henry III. He had found his forte, and over the next ten years he wrote a series of extremely successful action-packed plays for the theatre.

In about 1840, however, he turned his vast imaginative talents to novel-writing. He was even more successful as a novelist than he had been as a playwright. Two of his books became just about the most widely read books of the nineteenth century. These were *The Three Musketeers* and *The Count of Monte Cristo*. Both were originally serialized in newspapers (which is why each chapter tends to end in a cliff-hanger) and astonishingly, both were written in the same year, 1844–45.

Dumas went on turning out lengthy adventure stories, including three sequels to *The Three Musketeers*, and such famous books as *The Black Tulip*. Nowadays, his novels are generally considered too long, which is why this Puffin edition has been abridged. In addition to his novels, he wrote travel books, biographies, reminiscences of his huge menagerie of pets, children's books — and even a cookbook! His output seems too large to be possible; and indeed he was helped by a series of collaborators, who sometimes amounted to a staff of writers. However, Dumas always supervised the work, and provided the plots, the imaginative details, and the twists and turns of the thrilling adventures.

In keeping with the man's nature as a prodigy, Dumas earned an enormous amount of money from his writing, but was extraordinarily extravagant, died in near poverty.

Alexandre Dumas

THE
THREE
MUSKETEERS

*An abridgement of the translation
by Lord Sudley*

PUFFIN BOOKS

PUFFIN BOOKS

Published by the Penguin Group
Penguin Books Ltd, 27 Wrights Lane, London W8 5TZ, England
Penguin Books USA Inc., 375 Hudson Street, New York, New York 10014, USA
Penguin Books Australia Ltd, Ringwood, Victoria, Australia
Penguin Books Canada Ltd, 10 Alcorn Avenue, Toronto, Ontario, Canada M4V 3B2
Penguin Books (NZ) Ltd, 182–190 Wairau Road, Auckland 10, New Zealand

Penguin Books Ltd, Registered Offices: Harmondsworth, Middlesex, England

This translation first published 1952
This abridged edition published in Puffin Books 1986
9 10

This edition copyright © Penguin Books, 1986
All rights reserved
Abridged by Robin Waterfield

Printed in England by Clays Ltd, St Ives plc
Filmset in Linotron Palatino

Except in the United States of America, this book is sold subject
to the condition that it shall not, by way of trade or otherwise, be lent,
re-sold, hired   ut, or otherwise circulated without the publisher's
prior consent in any form of binding or cover other than that in
which ᛫ is published and without a similar condition including this
 ᴐndition being imposed on the subsequent purchaser

CONTENTS

6 The Three Musketeers

1
THREE GIFTS

On the first Monday of April 1625, the market town of Meung was in a wild state of excitement. Many of the wealthier citizens, seeing the women running towards the High Street and hearing the children screaming on the doorsteps of their houses, hastily buckled on their cuirasses and, to give themselves an air of greater assurance than they really possessed, seized muskets or halberds. Thus armed they made for the Jolly Miller inn, where they found a dense and excited throng of people swarming in from all directions.

At that time panics were frequent and few days passed without one town or another recording in its archives some event of this kind. Noblemen were at war with one another: the King was at war with the Cardinal: Spain was at war with the King. And besides these public and private wars there were other elements which kept the French countryside in a state of almost perpetual unrest, notably thieves, beggars, Huguenots, and rabble of all sorts. The citizens always took up arms against this rabble; they often fought the noblemen and the Huguenots, sometimes even the King, though never Spain or the Cardinal. So, from sheer force of habit, on this bright April morning, hearing an uproar and seeing neither the red and yellow standard of Spain nor the Duc de Richelieu's livery, the citizens rushed in a body to the Jolly Miller inn, prepared for battle.

The moment they reached the inn, the cause of the uproar was discovered.

A young man was standing at the main gate, a young man of striking appearance. He was eighteen years of age, tall and lanky, dressed in a blue woollen doublet,

faded and threadbare, brown breeches and brown top
boots. He had a long, tanned face, high cheekbones – a
mark of shrewdness – frank, intelligent eyes, a hooked
but well-cut nose, and an enormously protruding, typi-
cally Gascon jaw. He wore the Gascon beret, decorated
with a jaunty feather, though even without it there
would have been no mistaking his origin. His bearing
was haughty and his attitude challenging; there was an
'I'm as good as you are and don't tell me I'm not' look
about him. An untrained eye might have taken him to be
a farmer's son on a journey but for the long sword which
he wore hung from a shoulder-strap and which dangled
against his calves when he walked, and, when he was
astride, against his horse's rough coat.

It was this horse, indeed, which had first attracted the
attention of the crowd. It was a Béarnese cob, twelve to
fourteen years old, with a rat tail and ulcers on its feet,
which jogged along mournfully from sunrise till sunset at
a steady speed of four miles an hour, drooping its head so
low between its knees that it needed no curb or mar-
tingale. Unfortunately this animal's good qualities were
not appreciated, so strange was its coat and so awkward
its stride. At that time all men were connoisseurs in
horseflesh, and the sight of this cob, which had entered
Meung by the Beaugency gate some fifteen minutes
earlier, caused a sensation which reflected badly on its
rider.

And this sensation was very painful to the young man
(d'Artagnan was his name) because he was a good horse-
man and realized that he cut a poor figure. And when
Monsieur d'Artagnan the elder had presented it to his
son as a parting gift our hero had groaned inwardly,
although he knew that the animal was worth at least
seven crowns and that the words of wisdom which went
with the gift were beyond price.

'My son,' the old squire had said, 'this horse was born

in your father's stables nearly thirteen years ago and has lived here ever since. Treasure it for that reason. Don't think of selling it. Let it live its normal span and die happy and respected. If you go campaigning with it treat it with the kindness you would show to an old servant. At Court, if you ever go to Court, which, of course, you're quite entitled to do, seeing who you are, be honest and above board with everyone. Always remember your rank and carry on the tradition of good behaviour which your family has been true to for the past five hundred years. This you owe to yourself and to your nearest and dearest. Stand no nonsense from anyone but the King and the Cardinal. Remember, nowadays it's only by personal courage that a man can get on in the world. If you see an opportunity don't stop to think, but seize it, or you may lose it for ever. If that fails, try something else. You've got two good reasons for being brave, first that you're a Gascon and secondly that you're my son. Don't fight shy of adventures; I'd sooner you lived dangerously. I've taught you to handle a sword: you've got good strong legs and a wrist of steel. Fight at the least provocation, in season and out, because now that duelling's illegal the man who fights shows himself to be doubly brave. I wish I had more to give you, my dear boy, but here's all I have: fifteen crowns, my horse, and these few words of advice. Your mother will give you the prescription for a special ointment which she got from an old gypsy woman, and which has the miraculous property of healing all wounds except heart wounds. Make the most of these gifts and may your life be long and happy. There's just one thing I might add, by the way; I'd like to give you an example to model your life on. Not myself, for I've never been to Court and only served as a volunteer in the religious wars. Not myself, I say, but Monsieur de Tréville, who was at one time my neighbour, a Gascon like myself, and who, as a child, was the honoured playmate of our good King Louis XIII, whom God preserve. Sometimes their childish games became regular tussles and sometimes the King got the worst of it. His Majesty remembers to this day how Monsieur de Tréville used to set about him and has as much respect for him now as he had then. Since then Monsieur de Tréville has had many another tussle; five on his first journey to Paris alone and, between the death of the late King and the coming-of-age of this one, seven more, all serious duels, not counting the various campaigns he fought in. Between this King's accession to power and the present day he's fought at least a hundred other duels, perhaps more. He's defied edicts, ordinances and decrees and see where he's got to! He's Captain of the Musketeers, in other words head of a band of dare-devil heroes who are high in the King's favour and who terrify the Cardinal, the great Cardinal, and it takes a good deal to frighten him, as we all know. Added to which Monsieur de Tréville has an income of 10,000 crowns and is therefore a very big man. He started life as you did. Go to him with this letter; do as he tells you and perhaps one day you'll get where he is.'

With these words Monsieur d'Artagnan the elder buckled his own sword round his son's waist, kissed him affectionately on both cheeks and gave him his blessing.

The young man left his father's room and went to say good-bye to his mother, who was waiting for him with the precious prescription which he was bound to need if he followed the advice of his father. The farewell scene between him and his mother was longer and more affectionate than that between him and his father; not that Monsieur d'Artagnan did not love his son, his only son, but he was a man and therefore thought it wrong to give way to his feelings. Madame d'Artagnan, being a woman, and also a mother, collapsed in her son's arms and sobbed aloud. Her son tried hard to keep calm as became a future musketeer, but his warmer feelings prevailed and he too shed bitter tears, although he turned his head away as he did so.

That very day the young man set forth armed with his father's three gifts, the fifteen crowns, the horse and the letter for Monsieur de Tréville; the good advice had been given as an afterthought.

After an uneventful journey, d'Artagnan reached Meung. Here, as he was dismounting at the door of the Jolly Miller without anyone, host, ostler or stableboy, coming to hold his stirrup at the block, he noticed a gentleman standing at a half-open window on the ground floor of the inn, a tall, distinguished-looking man with a rather scowling expression. He was talking to two other men, who appeared to be listening to his words with deference. As usual d'Artagnan presumed that he was the object of the conversation and stood listening. This time he was only half mistaken, though it was not he but his horse which had engaged the gentleman's attention. The stranger was explaining to his listeners the animal's points one by one, and his audience appeared to agree with him. And whenever the gentleman spoke his listeners shouted with laughter. The mere suspicion of a smile was enough to anger our young friend, so we can imagine how he reacted to these offensive explosions of mirth.

But d'Artagnan decided first to take stock of this insolent stranger's appearance. He looked at him haughtily and observed that he was a man of forty to forty-five, with shrewd dark eyes, a pale skin, a pronounced nose and a well-trimmed, black moustache, and that he wore a violet doublet and hose, with no trimmings except the usual slashes through which his shirt appeared. The doublet and hose, though new, appeared creased, like travelling clothes which had long been carried about in a valise. D'Artagnan took in all these details with the

speed of an acute observer, and his instincts told him
that the stranger was destined to play a big part in his
life.

The gentleman chose the very moment at which
d'Artagnan was taking stock of him and his violet doublet to make one of his most scholarly and profound
observations about the Béarnese cob. His two listeners
roared with laughter, and even he allowed the faintest
flicker of a smile to pass across his face. This time there
was no doubt of it; d'Artagnan had been actually insulted. Convinced of this he pulled his beret down over
his eyes and, aping some of the airs and graces of a
courtier which he had learnt from noblemen travelling
through Gascony, stepped forward with one hand on his
sword-hilt and the other on his hip. Unfortunately, as he
approached his enemy, his anger increased. He completely lost his head and, instead of protesting like an
insulted gentleman, shook his fist and became vulgarly
abusive.

'Hi, there!' he cried. 'Yes, you, Sir, skulking behind that
shutter! What are you laughing at? When I see a man
laughing I always like to be told the joke, so that I can
laugh too.'

The gentleman slowly lifted his eyes from the horse to
its rider, as though it took him quite a while to realize that
he was the object of this rather strange attack; then, as
there seemed to be no doubt of it, he frowned slightly
and, after a longish pause, answered d'Artagnan in a
tone of amused contempt:

'I was not talking to you, Sir.'

'No, but I was talking to you, Sir,' cried the young
man, stung by the stranger's manner, at once easy and
supercilious.

The stranger looked again at d'Artagnan with a faint
smile and, leaving the window, came slowly out of the
inn and took his stand a few steps away from him, facing

the horse. His composed look and the sardonic expression in his eyes increased the enjoyment of his companions, who were still standing at the window. D'Artagnan, seeing him approach, drew his sword a foot's length out of its scabbard.

'This horse is definitely a buttercup, or, I should say, has been one at some time or other,' said the stranger, continuing his examination and addressing his listeners at the window, without appearing to notice d'Artagnan, who, in his rage, had backed round and was now standing between him and them. 'It's a colour common in flowers but still very rare in horses.'

'One can laugh at a horse and still be afraid to laugh at its rider!' cried Tréville's pupil in a passion.

'I don't often laugh, Sir,' said the stranger, 'as no doubt you can tell from my face. But I hold to my right of laughing whenever it suits me.'

'And I won't have anyone laughing when it doesn't suit me!' cried d'Artagnan.

'Really, Sir?' said the stranger more quietly than ever. 'Well, that's quite understandable!'

And, turning on his heel, he walked towards the main gate of the inn, under which d'Artagnan, on his arrival, had noticed a saddled and bridled horse. But d'Artagnan was not the man to allow anyone to hold him up to ridicule. He drew his sword right out of its scabbard and ran after the stranger crying:

'Turn and face me, Sir! I've had enough of your damned sneering! Turn and face me or I'll run you through the back!'

The stranger turned sharply and eyed d'Artagnan with an expression of mingled surprise and scorn. 'Run me through? Me?' he cried. 'What are you talking about? Are you mad?'

Then in an undertone, as though talking to himself, he added: 'What a pity this is! This young hothead would have made an admirable musketeer. And the King always on the lookout for fresh blood!'

Hardly were the words out of his mouth before d'Artagnan lunged at him so furiously that, had he not stepped quickly aside, he would probably not have lived to make another joke. He now realized that the affair was serious, drew his sword, saluted his opponent and stood on guard. But at that moment the innkeeper and the two who had been standing with the stranger at the window fell on d'Artagnan with sticks, shovels and tongs. This created a diversion so rapid and so complete that, while d'Artagnan turned to defend himself against this rain of blows, his opponent quickly sheathed his sword and once more became a spectator instead of an actor in the drama, a rôle which seemed to become him better. But he muttered to himself:

'Hell take these Gascons! Why can't he get on that saffron horse of his and be off!'

'Not till I've killed you, you coward!' cried d'Artagnan, fighting back hard against his three assailants, who were plastering him with blows.

'Another of these swaggerers!' muttered the stranger. 'God, these Gascons are incorrigible! Well, carry on the fight then, since he insists on it. When he's had enough he'll let us know.'

But the stranger did not realize what an obstinate fellow he had to deal with. D'Artagnan was not the man to give in without a struggle. So the fight went on for another few seconds until at last d'Artagnan, in his exhaustion, dropped his sword, which was instantly broken with a heavy blow from a stick. Another blow, levelled at his forehead, knocked him to the ground where he lay prostrate, bleeding, and almost unconscious.

It was at this moment that the crowd began to collect from all sides. The innkeeper, fearing a scandal, summoned his stableboys and had the wounded man removed from the scene and carried into the kitchen, where his wounds were roughly dressed. The stranger meanwhile went back to his place at the window and stood looking with some impatience at the crowd outside. Its presence seemed to cause him great annoyance.

'Well, how's that young lunatic?' said he, turning as the door opened and addressing the innkeeper who had come to inquire after his health.

'I trust Your Excellency's none the worse?' asked the innkeeper.

'No, I'm all right. But I'd like to know what's happened to our young friend.'

'He's calmer now,' said the innkeeper. 'In fact he's fainted.'

'Oh, he's fainted, has he?' said the gentleman.

'Yes. But before he finally collapsed he staggered to his feet, turned in your direction and shouted a challenge.'

'That fellow's the devil himself!' cried the stranger.

'Oh no, Sir, he's not the devil,' answered the innkeeper with a sneer. 'I can vouch for that. While he was unconscious we searched him and found that he had only one shirt to his name and only eleven crowns in his purse. But for all that, before he fainted, he said that had such a thing happened in Paris you'd have been made to regret it at once whereas here you've got off, though only for the time being.'

'Oh! If he said that he must be some royal prince in disguise,' said the stranger coldly.

'I'm only telling you this to put you on your guard, Your Honour,' said the innkeeper.

'Did he mention anybody's name, by any chance?'

'Oh yes! He slapped his pocket and said: "We'll see what Monsieur de Tréville thinks when he hears about this!"'

'Monsieur de Tréville!' exclaimed the stranger with a start. 'He slapped his pocket and mentioned Monsieur de Tréville! Well now, my good man, don't tell me you didn't search that pocket of his while he was lying there. What did you find in it?'

'A letter addressed to Monsieur de Tréville, Captain of the Musketeers.'

'Is that a fact?'

'Yes, Your Honour, it's as I'm telling you.'

The innkeeper, who was rather dense, did not notice the effect of his words on the stranger. The latter now left the window at which he had been standing with his elbow resting on the sill and came forward, an anxious frown on his face.

'This is the very devil!' he muttered to himself. 'Could Tréville have sent that Gascon against me? He's a bit young, I know. But a sword thrust's a sword thrust, no matter who deals it. And a boy might catch me off my guard. A small obstacle can sometimes defeat a great enterprise.'

And the stranger thought for a moment. Then, addressing the innkeeper, he said:

'Look here, my good man, can't you get this young lunatic out of the way somehow? I can't in all conscience kill him. But,' he added, frowning again, 'at present he's a nuisance here. Where is he now?'

'In my wife's room on the first floor. They're dressing his wounds.'

'I suppose he's got his clothes and his bag with him and he's still wearing his doublet!'

'No, Sir! All his things are down in the kitchen. But if this fellow's a nuisance to you . . .'

'Of course he's a nuisance. He's causing a disturbance in your inn which decent folk won't put up with. Go upstairs, make out my bill, and call my servant.'

'What, Sir? You're leaving us already?'

'You know I'm leaving! Didn't I tell you to get my horse saddled? Hasn't it been done?'

'It has been done, Sir. As Your Excellency may have noticed your horse is at the main gate, all ready for the journey.'

'Well, do as I tell you then.'

The innkeeper looked at his guest with raised eyebrows as though to say:

'So you're frightened of that young whippersnapper, are you?'

But a stern look from the stranger brought him to his senses. He bowed low and left the room.

'That young scamp mustn't be allowed to see Milady,' thought the stranger. 'She'll be here at any moment. In fact she's late already. It would really be better if I rode out to meet her. If only I could find out what was in that letter addressed to Tréville.'

And the stranger, muttering these words, made his way slowly down to the kitchen.

Meanwhile, the innkeeper, who was convinced that it was the young man's presence which had decided the stranger to leave his inn, had gone to his wife's room where he had found d'Artagnan restored to consciousness. Telling him that he was in for a load of trouble with the authorities for having provoked a nobleman (for in his opinion the stranger was certainly a nobleman), the innkeeper persuaded d'Artagnan, in spite of his exhaustion, to get up and be off. So d'Artagnan, half-dazed, with only his shirt and breeches on and with his head swathed in bandages, staggered to his feet and, urged from behind by the host, went down the stairs. But on reaching the kitchen, the first thing he saw through the window was his enemy standing at the footboard of a heavy coach harnessed to two large Normandy horses, talking to a lady seated inside.

Only this lady's head and shoulders were visible

through the coach window. She was between twenty and twenty-two years old. We have already stated d'Artagnan's capacity to take in at a glance every detail of a person's appearance. He therefore noticed at once that the woman was young and beautiful. And her looks struck him more forcibly because they were of a kind entirely foreign to the southern provinces where he was born and bred. The lady was fair and pale, with long, golden ringlets which fell to her shoulders, large, blue, languishing eyes, rose-red lips and hands as white as alabaster. She was talking eagerly to the stranger.

'So, His Eminence's orders are . . .' said the lady.

'That you return to England at once, and let him know the moment the Duke leaves London.'

'And what about my other instructions?' said the beautiful traveller.

'They're here, in this box, which you're not to open till you've crossed the Channel.'

'Very well. And what about you?'

'I'm returning to Paris.'

'What! Without putting that rude young puppy in his place?' asked the lady.

The stranger was about to reply when d'Artagnan, who had heard everything, rushed into the doorway.

'You're wrong there!' he cried. 'It's the rude young puppy who's going to put you in your place! And this time I'll see you don't escape as you did before.'

'Escape?' repeated the stranger frowning.

'Yes, Sir! For I don't suppose even you'll turn tail in the presence of a woman!'

At this the stranger seized hold of his sword, but the lady quickly intervened.

'Remember the least delay may prove fatal!' she cried.

'You're right,' said the stranger. 'You go your way and I'll go mine. And let's be quick about it.'

He bowed to the lady and leapt into the saddle while

the coachman whipped up his horses. And the lady and gentleman made off at top speed, disappearing down opposite ends of the street.

'Coward! Rogue! Call yourself a gentleman!' cried d'Artagnan, rushing off in turn in pursuit of master and servant.

But the young man was still too weak to indulge in such strenuous efforts. Hardly had he gone ten yards than his ears began to throb, giddiness seized him, the blood rushed to his head and he collapsed in the middle of the street still yelling:

'Coward! Coward! Coward!'

The innkeeper walked up to him as he lay prostrate. 'Yes, he's a coward all right,' he said.

He hoped by this piece of servility to get on good terms with the impoverished young man.

'Yes, a proper coward,' gasped d'Artagnan. 'But she, how lovely she is!'

'She? What she?' asked the innkeeper.

'Milady,' stammered d'Artagnan.

And then he fainted for the second time.

'It doesn't really matter,' thought the innkeeper. 'I've lost two customers, but kept one, and this fellow'll be here for several days. So in any case I'm bound to be eleven crowns up.'

We know that eleven crowns was the exact sum still left in d'Artagnan's purse.

The innkeeper had reckoned on eleven days' illness at the rate of a crown a day. But he hadn't reckoned with his guest. At five o'clock next morning d'Artagnan got up, went down himself to the kitchen and asked for wine, oil, rosemary, and various other items needed for an ointment. Then, with his mother's prescription in front of him, he prepared this ointment and with it proceeded to dress and redress his many wounds, refusing all outside aid. Thanks no doubt to the healing properties of the gypsy's ointment and also perhaps to the absence of the doctor d'Artagnan was up and about that very evening, and next day almost well again.

Now it was a question of paying for the wine, oil, and rosemary. This was, in fact, our hero's only debt, for he had himself refused all nourishment, although, from what the innkeeper said, the yellow nag had devoured three times more than one would have thought possible for a beast of its size. But when the young man felt in his pocket for the money he found only his little threadbare, velvet purse containing the eleven crowns: the letter to Monsieur de Tréville had disappeared.

For a while the young man searched patiently for the letter, turning his breast and waist pockets inside out twenty times and more, rummaging about in his bag and delving into his purse. But when it dawned on him that the letter was really and truly missing he was seized with a further attack of rage which nearly called for a fresh supply of the spiced wine and oil. For when the innkeeper saw our fractious young friend getting excited and threatening to break up the whole house if his letter were not returned to him he seized hold of a pike while his wife took up a broom and his boys armed themselves with the sticks which they had so successfully wielded two days before.

'My letter! My letter of introduction!' cried d'Artagnan. 'Give it back or, by God, I'll run you all through like larks on a spit!'

Unfortunately one thing stood in the way of our young friend carrying out his threat. His sword had been split in two in the original fight, and this he had forgotten. The result was that when he grasped the hilt he found himself armed with a mere stump eight to ten inches long, which the innkeeper had carefully replaced inside the scabbard.

But our young hothead would probably have carried

on in spite of this setback had not the innkeeper suddenly realized that his claim was perfectly justified.

'Now wait a moment!' said he, lowering his pike. 'I wonder where that letter is!'

'Yes, where is it?' cried d'Artagnan. 'Listen, my good man! That letter is for Monsieur de Tréville and must be found. If it's not found now you may be sure he'll get it out of you later.'

With this threat d'Artagnan succeeded in bringing the innkeeper to heel. Next to the King and the Cardinal, Monsieur de Tréville was more spoken of by soldiers, and even by civilians, than any man in the kingdom.

So, throwing away his pike and ordering his wife to put back her broom and his boys their sticks, the innkeeper set to work to search for the missing letter.

'Did this letter contain anything of value?' he asked, after searching fruitlessly for some time.

'Good God! I should say it did!' cried the Gascon, who was relying on this letter to give him an entry into Court circles.

Suddenly the innkeeper, who was cursing himself for a fool, had an inspiration.

'That letter's not lost!' he cried.

'Not lost?' repeated d'Artagnan.

'No. It's been stolen from you.'

'Stolen? Who by?'

'By the gentleman who was here yesterday. He went down to the kitchen where your doublet was. He was alone in there. I'm ready to bet he stole the letter.'

'Oh! So you think he stole it!' replied d'Artagnan without much conviction. He knew quite well that the letter was of merely personal value and could not imagine that anyone would want to steal it. It was obvious that none of the guests or servants at present at the inn would have had any use for it.

'So you really and truly suspect that gentleman?' continued d'Artagnan.

'I repeat, I'm sure of it,' replied the innkeeper. 'When I told him your Excellency was Monsieur de Tréville's protégé and that you even had a letter with that great man's name on it he seemed very upset. He asked me where the letter was and went down at once to the kitchen where he knew he'd find your doublet.'

'Ha! So he is the thief after all!' replied d'Artagnan. 'I shall inform Monsieur de Tréville of this and he'll tell the King.'

Then, with a flourish, he drew two crowns from his pocket and tossed them to the innkeeper, who, cap in hand, went with him to the door. D'Artagnan now leapt on to his yellow horse and finally, after a long and exhausting ride, reached the Porte St Antoine in Paris. Here he sold the horse for the sum of three crowns, which was a good price considering that it had been hard pressed for the last stage of the journey. The dealer who bought the horse declared that he only paid this enormous sum because of the animal's unusual colour.

So d'Artagnan eventually entered Paris on foot, carrying all his worldly goods under his arm. He wandered about the streets until he at last found a room to let at a price which suited his slender means, a mere attic in the Rue des Fossoyeurs, near the Luxembourg.

After paying his deposit d'Artagnan settled himself in his new quarters and spent the rest of the day sewing on to his doublet and hose certain trimmings which his mother had unstitched from an almost new doublet belonging to his father and given to him on the sly. Then he visited the Quai de la Féraille to have a new blade fitted to his sword, later returning to the Louvre to inquire from the first musketeer whom he happened to meet the whereabouts of Monsieur de Tréville's house. When he learnt that it was in the Rue du Vieux

Colombier, quite close to his own little attic, his spirits rose, for he considered this a good omen for the success of his journey.

Finally, thoroughly satisfied with the way he had behaved at Meung, without regret for the past, confident in the present, and hopeful for the future, he went to bed and slept the sleep of the just.

2
MONSIEUR DE TRÉVILLE'S ANTE-ROOM

Monsieur de Tréville had in point of fact started life as d'Artagnan had done; that is to say, without a penny piece to his name but with a fund of quick wit, dash, and persistence. His courage, assurance, and unfailing good luck had been proof against the hard knocks for which that age was so renowned, and he had soon reached the top of that difficult ladder known as Court Favour, scaling it four rungs at a time. Louis XIII had made him captain of his Musketeers.

When the Cardinal saw the formidable army with which Lous XIII was surrounded he, as the joint or perhaps the sole ruler in France, was determined also to have his bodyguard. So like Louis XIII Richelieu had his musketeers, and these two rival powers were to be seen scouring the provinces of France and the neighbouring countries of Europe for men renowned for their skill in swordsmanship, to enlist them in their regiments. And King and Cardinal often wrangled in the evenings over their games of chess about the relative merits of their adherents. Each boasted of the courage and bearing of his men and, whilst they openly decreed against duelling and brawling, each secretly urged his followers to challenge the other's, grieving at any defeat and rejoicing wholeheartedly at any victory sustained by his own side.

Tréville had always pandered to his master's weakness, and it was to this shrewdness that he owed his long period of favour with a sovereign who has left behind him a name for inconstancy. It was Tréville's habit to make his musketeers parade in front of the Cardinal with an insolent air which made His Eminence's grey moustache curl with rage. Tréville had an excellent understanding of the warlike spirit of the age, in which men, when not despoiling the enemy, lived by despoiling each other. His soldiers were a regiment of dare-devils, unruly in their behaviour towards everyone but himself.

The King's Musketeers, or rather Monsieur de Tréville's Musketeers were to be seen in all the taverns, walks, and fairgrounds of the city. Their faces scarred from duelling, they would lounge about with their jackets unbuttoned, shouting, twirling their moustaches and clanking their swords. They went out of their way to jostle the Cardinal's guards and would challenge them openly in the streets with a smile on their lips and mischief in their hearts. Some of the musketeers would fall in these battles; then they were sure of being mourned and avenged; more often they killed their man in the full certainty that they would not be allowed to languish in prison, for Monsieur de Tréville was there to demand their release. Thus Monsieur de Tréville's praises were sung at every street corner by these men who adored him and who, hard-bitten as they were, trembled in his presence like schoolboys in the presence of their master, ready to obey his every whim and to die to wipe out the slightest reproof from their beloved leader.

From six o'clock in the morning in summer and in

winter from eight the courtyard of his house in the Rue du Vieux Colombier resembled a camp. Between fifty and sixty musketeers were always stationed there. These musketeers apparently came in relays and took alternate duty, so that the courtyard should always present an impressive display of arms and men. Up one of the great staircases filed an endless procession of toadies coming to ask some favour of the great man, of young gentlemen from the provinces, candidates for army commissions, and of footmen in different coloured liveries bringing messages for Monsieur de Tréville from their masters. In the ante-room, on long curved divans, waited the elect, that is to say those who had come by appointment. There was a buzz of conversation in this ante-room from morning till night, while Monsieur de Tréville, in his adjoining room, received visits, listened to petitions, gave his orders and, like the King on his balcony at the Louvre, had only to go to his window to survey his men on guard below.

On the day upon which d'Artagnan arrived the crowd was impressive, especially to a country lad straight from the provinces. It is true that our country lad was a Gascon and that at that time d'Artagnan's compatriots had a reputation for not being easily daunted. But it would have been a brave man indeed who could pass through the massive door studded with large, square-headed nails and not feel cold to the marrow of his bones when confronted with the seething mob of noisy, quarrelsome, boisterous swordsmen which composed Monsieur de Tréville's bodyguard.

So it was with a thumping heart that d'Artagnan advanced into the middle of this crowd, pressing his sword tight against his lanky leg, holding on to his plumed hat with one hand and wearing the forced grin of a shy country-cousin who wants to appear at his ease. Having passed one group of swordsmen he began to breathe more freely, although he realized that they were all turning to look at him. For the first time in his life our hero, who had till then thought quite highly of himself, began to feel ridiculous.

When he reached the staircase matters became even worse, for on the bottom steps four musketeers were engaged in some form of swordplay, while on the landing above stood a dozen more, waiting their turn to join in.

The game they were playing was an original one and held d'Artagnan spellbound. Of the four men fighting at the foot of the staircase one stood on a higher step than the others and tried with his sword to prevent his opponents from getting past him. All four thrust and parried with lightning agility. D'Artagnan at first mistook their blades for fencing-foils, buttoned at the tip, but, seeing the wounds inflicted, he soon realized that they were fighting with real, perfectly sharpened swords. Whenever anyone received a scratch both victim and onlookers laughed uproariously.

Though our young traveller had decided not to show any naïve astonishment, this pastime made him positively gasp. There were many hotheads in his native province certainly, but even there duelling was always accompanied by certain rites, and he had never before seen anything to equal the swagger of these four bloods, even in Gascony. He felt like Gulliver, suddenly transported into a country of fabulous giants. And he had not yet reached his goal; he had still to cross the landing and the ante-room.

There was no fighting on the landing. Here the men were telling stories about women and in the ante-room tales about the Court. D'Artagnan blushed on the landing and shuddered in the ante-room. His imagination, which was lively enough and which had made him formidable to Gascon housemaids and even to their young mistresses, boggled at these tales of amorous adventures and of prowess in the arts of love, tales made more wonderful by the mention of names famous throughout France and by the daring details with which they were embellished. Our hero's morals were shocked on the landing and, worse still, his respect for the Cardinal was outraged in the ante-room. There to his amazement he heard the policy which made all Europe tremble, and the Cardinal's private life, which so many high and mighty lords had been punished for attempting to investigate, criticized aloud. This great man, revered by Monsieur d'Artagnan the elder, was a butt for the wit of Monsieur de Tréville's musketeers, who mocked his bandy legs and hunched shoulders. Some of these gentlemen made obscene rhymes about his mistress Madame d'Aiguillon and about his niece Madame de Combalet, whilst others planned all kinds of practical jokes to play against his pages and guards. All this frivolity seemed to d'Artagnan monstrous and impossible.

And yet, whenever by accident the King's name came up in the conversation, some invisible gag seemed to bind these gentlemen's mouths. They would look round timidly as though they feared that the dividing wall between them and Monsieur de Tréville's private study might betray their indiscretion. Then some new mention would be made of His Eminence, upon which the wits began once more to sparkle and all the Cardinal's actions were brought into the hard light of day and criticized.

'These people are bound to be sent to the Bastille and hanged,' thought the terrified d'Artagnan. 'And I shall probably go with them, for the fact that I've seen them and listened to their talk makes me their accomplice. My father taught me to respect the Cardinal. What would he say if he saw me with all these pagans?'

D'Artagnan, as we know, was a complete stranger in this crowd of courtiers and had never been sent here before, so one of M. de Tréville's household soon came up and asked him his business. Our hero modestly gave his name, stressed his Gascon nationality, and asked the servant to beg a moment's audience of his master. The servant condescendingly promised to pass on this message to his master in due course.

Our young hero had at last slightly recovered his poise and now had leisure to look round him and take note of the appearance and dress of the Musketeers.

In the centre of the most lively group stood a tall, supercilious-looking fellow dressed in a fashion so peculiar as to attract attention. Though on duty, he happened at that moment not to be wearing the regulation dress coat but was showing himself off in a sky-blue doublet, slightly faded and threadbare, strapped across with a magnificent shoulder-belt trimmed with gold lace, which glittered like rippling water in the sunlight. A long crimson velvet cloak hung gracefully from his shoulders, revealing only the front part of the shoulder-belt, from which hung an enormous rapier.

This musketeer had just come off guard. He complained of a cold and coughed affectedly from time to time. It was for that reason, he said, that he had put on the cloak. He kept talking at the top of his voice and twirling his moustaches, exposing his embroidered shoulder-belt to the admiring gaze of the onlookers, d'Artagnan among them.

'It can't be helped,' the musketeer was saying. 'It's the fashion now. It's silly, I know, but there you are. It's the fashion, so one must conform. And besides, one must spend one's allowance somehow.'

'Oh, come on, Porthos,' cried one of his admirers, 'don't try and pretend that shoulder-belt was bought out of your father's allowance. I know who gave it to you; it was the veiled lady I saw you with last Sunday near the Porte St Honoré.'

'I swear it wasn't! I bought it myself, with my own money,' replied the man referred to as Porthos.

'Yes,' retorted another musketeer, 'just as I bought this new purse with the money my mistress put into my old one.'

'But it's true what I'm telling you!' cried Porthos. 'Listen! I can prove it. I paid twelve pistoles for it!'

This remark increased everyone's admiration of the belt, but it did not dispel their doubts.

'It's true, isn't it, Aramis?' cried Porthos, turning to another musketeer.

This other musketeer, Aramis, was a complete contrast to his friend, both in looks and dress. He was a young man, barely twenty-three, with a demure and innocent expression, dark, gentle eyes and downy pink cheeks like an autumn peach. His neat moustache formed a perfectly straight line on his upper lip: he seemed afraid to lower his hands for fear their veins might swell and he kept pinching the ends of his ears to preserve their delicate, shell-pink colour. He said very little and when he spoke he drawled. He was always making graceful bows, and when he laughed, he laughed noiselessly, baring pearly teeth which, like the rest of his person, he tended with care. To his friend's appeal he replied with a nod.

Suddenly the door leading into Monsieur de Tréville's study opened and a lackey called out:

'Monsieur de Tréville awaits Monsieur d'Artagnan!'

At this a hush fell on everyone and in the general silence our young Gascon made his way across the ante-room and entered the Captain's study.

3
THE AUDIENCE

Monsieur de Tréville happened at that moment to be in a
very bad temper. However he greeted the young man
civilly enough, and when d'Artagnan bowed low and
paid his respects, de Tréville smiled, for the young man's
Béarnese brogue reminded him of his youth and of his
native land, and whose heart is not softened at the
recollection of home and childhood? De Tréville then
went across to the ante-room and, signing to d'Artagnan
that he would attend to him after he had dealt with more
pressing business, called three times in a loud voice:

'Athos! Porthos! Aramis!'

The two musketeers to whom we have already been
introduced and who answered to the names of Porthos
and Aramis at once left their circle of friends and went
into Monsieur de Tréville's study.

When the door had closed behind the two musketeers
and the buzz of conversation in the ante-room had
started again, stimulated perhaps by this sudden sharp
summons, de Tréville began pacing up and down his
study, silent and frowning, passing to and fro in front of
Porthos and Aramis, who were standing stiffly at attention as though on parade. He suddenly stopped in front
of them, eyed them from head to foot and said irritably:

'D'you know what the King said to me last night,
gentlemen?'

'No, Sir,' replied the two musketeers after a moment's
silence.

'He said that from now on he'd recruit his musketeers
from the Cardinal's guards.'

'From the Cardinal's guards?' exclaimed Porthos
sharply. 'Why on earth?'

'Because he realized that his wine hadn't much body to it and needed livening up with a fresh vintage.'

The two musketeers blushed scarlet. D'Artagnan was thoroughly embarrassed and longed for the earth to open and swallow him up.

'Yes, that's what the King said,' went on Monsieur de Tréville, raising his voice, 'and he was perfectly right. The musketeers' credit has sunk pretty low at Court, I may tell you! Last night, when they were playing chess together, the Cardinal was telling the King, with a note of mock sympathy in his voice which maddened me, how two days ago you damned musketeers, you "daredevils", you "swashbucklers" – yes, that's what he called you, though sneeringly, mind you, and looking at me out of the corner of his eye all the time – how you swashbucklers had been loitering in an inn in the Rue Férou and that a platoon of his guards, on its rounds, had been forced to arrest you as disturbers of the peace. I really thought he was going to laugh in my face. Arresting musketeers! Whoever heard of such a thing! You two were among that lot. You must know about this. You were recognized and the Cardinal mentioned your names. What have you got to say for yourselves? Oh, I know it's all my fault, really. I've got a bad habit of picking my own men. Aramis! Why the Hell did you ask for a uniform when what you really wanted was a cassock? And you, Porthos, with that fine lace sash of yours! What's it for, anyway? To hang a monocle on? And Athos! Where's Athos? Why isn't he here?'

'Athos is ill, Sir, very ill,' answered Aramis, with a mournful look on his face.

'Ill? What's the matter with him?'

'They're afraid it's smallpox, Sir,' said Porthos. 'It would be a shame if it were, because it would quite spoil his looks.'

'Smallpox! A likely story! Smallpox at his age! Rubbish!

No, he's probably wounded or perhaps even killed. Now listen, you musketeers! I won't have you visiting low haunts, brawling in the streets and duelling in the public squares. In fact I won't have you making idiots of yourselves in front of the Cardinal's guards. They're good fellows, those guards, quiet and well-behaved. They'd never land themselves in such a mess and, if they did, they'd die rather than yield an inch. Turn tail? Scuttle off? Oh no! That's a thing only the King's Musketeers do!'

Porthos and Aramis were trembling with rage. They would gladly have strangled Monsieur de Tréville on the spot, but in their heart of hearts they knew that it was only his great affection for them which made him take that tone. They stood and glowered at their Captain, biting their lips to control themselves and instinctively clutching at their sword-hilts. Everyone in the ante-room had heard Monsieur de Tréville summoning Athos, Porthos and Aramis, and had guessed from the tone of his voice that he was in a rage. Now curiosity prevailed over caution and at least a dozen of the musketeers were standing with their ears glued to the tapestry, and their faces were white with fury for they had overheard every word of what was being said and were repeating to the company at large each of Monsieur de Tréville's insulting remarks in turn as it was uttered. In an instant the news had travelled from one end of the house to the other and all the men were fuming.

'Ha! So the King's Musketeers allow themselves to be arrested by the Cardinal's guards! God, what a story!' went on de Tréville. He was inwardly just as furious as his soldiers, but his voice was hard and clear and he clipped his words and plunged them one by one, like poisoned darts, into the hearts of his listeners. 'Six of the King's Musketeers arrested by six of the Cardinal's guards! That's the end as far as I'm concerned. I'm going straight off to the Louvre to offer my resignation as Captain of the Musketeers and to beg for a lieutenancy under the Cardinal. And if my offer's turned down I shall take to religion. Yes, by God, I'll take Holy Orders!'

'Well, Sir,' said Porthos, beside himself with rage, 'it was like this. We were six against six but we were taken by surprise, and before we had time to draw our swords two of our fellows had been killed and Athos himself badly wounded. You know Athos well enough, don't you, Sir? Well, he tried twice to get up and fell back each time. Even then we didn't give in but were beaten by sheer weight of numbers. In the end we managed to escape. As for Athos they thought he was dead and didn't even bother to carry him away. There you have the whole damned business. Hang it all Sir, one can't win every battle!'

'And I may tell you, Sir, I ran one of the blighters through with his own sword,' said Aramis, 'for I broke mine with my first thrust.'

'I didn't know that,' said de Tréville, slightly mollified. 'The Cardinal must have been exaggerating.'

Aramis, seeing that Monsieur de Tréville was calming down and wishing to put in a plea for his friend, said: 'Please, Sir, don't let it get around that Athos has been wounded. It would break his heart if the King got to hear of it. And his wound's really very serious; he was run through the shoulder and the point of the blade went into his chest. We're afraid . . .'

At that moment the curtain of the door was drawn aside and a man appeared. He was strikingly handsome but desperately pale.

'Athos!' cried the two musketeers in chorus.

'Athos!' echoed Monsieur de Tréville.

'You sent for me, Sir,' said Athos to his officer in a calm but rather weak voice. 'The fellows outside told me you wanted me. So I've come to report. At your service, Sir, now as always!'

With these words the musketeer stepped smartly into the room. He was, as usual, faultlessly turned out and showed no sign of having been in the wars. Monsieur de Tréville, moved by this soldierly display of courage, rushed towards him.

'I was just telling these gentlemen,' said he, 'that I won't have my musketeers risking their lives unnecessarily. The King rates courage very high and he knows his musketeers are the bravest fellows in the world. Athos, give me your hand!'

And before Athos had time to reply to this affectionate welcome Monsieur de Tréville took hold of his right hand and gripped it hard, not noticing the pain he was causing the young man, who, for all his self-control, winced a little and grew, if possible, even paler than before.

The door had remained half-open, for Athos' arrival had caused a sensation. Everyone knew that he had been wounded, although it was supposed to be a dead secret. A murmur of applause from outside greeted the captain's last words and in their excitement two or three musketeers actually peered through the chinks in the tapestry. At any other time Monsieur de Tréville would have dealt harshly with this breach of etiquette, but he felt Athos' hand clutch his convulsively and, looking at him, saw that he was about to faint. Athos, who had managed only with a great effort to conceal his pain, was now unable to hold out any longer and fell like a log to the ground.

'A doctor! Call a doctor!' cried Monsieur de Tréville. 'My doctor! The King's doctor! The best man that can be found! Call a doctor or, by God, our good Athos will die on the spot!'

Hearing Monsieur de Tréville's cries everyone burst into his study before he had time to stop them and

crowded round the wounded man. This display of zeal
and concern on the part of the musketeers would not
have helped much if the doctor had not happened to be in
the house at that very moment. He elbowed his way
through the crowd and knelt down beside the unconscious Athos; then, as all the noise and bustle disturbed
him, he insisted first and foremost on having the musketeer removed to the adjoining room. Monsieur de
Tréville at once opened a door and showed the way to
Porthos and Aramis, who lifted up the unconscious man
and carried him out in their arms. Behind them walked
the doctor and the door was then closed.

Monsieur de Tréville's study, usually so sacrosanct,
had now become a mere annexe of the ante-room. Everyone was holding forth, shouting, swearing, and wishing
the Cardinal and his bodyguard in Hell.

A moment later Porthos and Aramis reappeared,
leaving the doctor and de Tréville alone with the
wounded man.

Finally de Tréville himself reappeared. The wounded
man had regained consciousness and the doctor had
diagnosed his condition as not serious and his collapse as
due merely to loss of blood.

Monsieur de Tréville now made a sign to everyone to
leave the room. The whole company withdrew with the
exception of d'Artagnan, who had not forgotten that he
had been granted an audience and had stood his ground
with true Gascon persistence.

When everyone had gone and the door was closed
Monsieur de Tréville turned and found himself alone
with the young man. The scene which had just taken
place had interrupted his train of thought. He asked our
importunate hero what he could do for him. D'Artagnan
then repeated his name. In a flash Monsieur de Tréville
remembered everything and was once more master of
the situation.

'Forgive me,' he said, 'forgive me, my dear fellow-Gascon. I'd completely forgotten you! Well, you see how it is! An officer's merely a family man burdened with heavier responsibilities than an ordinary father. Soldiers are really mere children, but it's my duty to see that the King's orders are carried out and still more the Cardinal's.'

D'Artagnan could not help smiling at this, and when de Tréville saw him smile he realized that he had no fool to deal with. He changed the conversation and came straight to the point.

'Your father was a good friend of mine,' he said. 'What can I do for you? Tell me quickly. My time's not my own, you know.'

'Sir,' said d'Artagnan, 'I came here hoping that my father's friendship with you would get me a commission in the Musketeers. But from what I've seen in the last two hours, I realize that I'm asking a great deal of you. I'm afraid you may think I'm not qualified for the honour.'

'Yes, it's an honour all right,' answered Monsieur de Tréville, 'but it may not be quite so far above your head as you think. But His Majesty's made a strict ruling on this point, and I'm sorry to say that no man can join the Musketeers until he's first proved himself, either in some campaign, or by some act of conspicuous gallantry, or by serving two years in some other regiment less select than ours.'

D'Artagnan bowed and said nothing. The distinction of a musketeer's uniform appealed to him even more now that he knew how many obstacles stood in the way of his wearing one.

'But,' continued Monsieur de Tréville, looking keenly at his young compatriot as though he wanted to read his thoughts, 'I repeat, for the sake of my old and trusted friend, your father, I'm prepared to do you a special favour. I don't suppose you've got much money to spare after paying for your board and lodging.'

D'Artagnan drew himself up proudly as though to show that he would not take charity from any man.

'All right, all right, young fellow,' went on Tréville. 'There's no need to put on these airs with me. I came to Paris myself with four crowns in my pocket and I'd have slaughtered anyone who dared say I wasn't rich enough to buy the Louvre.'

D'Artagnan remembered that the sale of his horse had made him four crowns better off than Tréville had been. So his only reply was to draw himself up higher still.

'As I was saying,' went on Tréville, 'you'd better cling on to whatever money you've got in your pocket. But you also need to learn the accomplishments of a gentleman. So I'll write today to the Director of the Royal Academy and he'll admit you free of charge tomorrow. Don't refuse this small favour. The highest and richest in the land often ask for it and don't get it. You'll learn horsemanship, fencing, and dancing. You'll meet the right people and from time to time you can look me up and tell me how you're getting on. And if there's anything I can do for you, I'll do it.'

D'Artagnan knew nothing of Court manners, but even he could tell that Monsieur de Tréville's reception of him was merely formal and would probably lead nowhere.

'I'm more than sorry, Sir,' he said, 'not to have my father's letter of introduction to give you. I see now what a help it would have been.'

'Yes,' answered de Tréville. 'I must admit I'm surprised you came all this way without something of that sort.'

'I had a letter when I started, Sir,' cried d'Artagnan. 'And it was all in proper form. But some scoundrel stole it from me on the way.'

And he told the whole story of the Meung adventure,

giving such a lively and detailed description of the stranger's appearance that Monsieur de Tréville was completely won over.

'I agree, it's a strange thing to have happened,' he said. He thought for a moment and then added:

'You say you mentioned my name out loud?'

'Yes, Sir. I'm afraid I was a bit indiscreet. I was counting on your name to be a kind of shield and buckler for me on the journey. I confess I did take cover behind it once or twice.'

'Tell me,' Monsieur de Tréville went on, 'did this gentleman have a faint scar on his cheek?'

'Yes. The sort of mark that might have been made by a bullet grazing it.'

'He was a good-looking fellow, wasn't he?'

'Yes.'

'Tall?'

'Yes.'

'With dark hair and a sallow skin?'

'Yes, Sir. That's the man all right. How do you come to know him, Sir? Oh, if I ever catch that fellow again, and I'll get him, I swear I will, even if I go to Hell for it . . .'

'He was waiting for a woman, you say?' went on Tréville.

'Yes, Sir. The lady drove up to the inn; the fellow had a hurried conversation with her and then rode off at the gallop.'

'You didn't by any chance hear what they said, did you?'

'Yes. He gave her a box, told her she'd find her orders in it and that she wasn't to open it till she'd got to London.'

'Was she an English woman?'

'He called her Milady.'

'Yes. That's the fellow all right,' muttered de Tréville to himself.

'Oh, Sir!' cried d'Artagnan. 'If you know this fellow tell me his name and nationality. I'll ask nothing more of you, I swear I won't. I won't even hold you to your promise of making me a musketeer. I'm mad to get my revenge.'

'Put that idea right out of your head, my lad!' cried de Tréville. 'Keep well out of that fellow's way, and if ever you see him coming down the street cross over quickly to the other side. Don't go butting against that stone wall; you'll get battered to bits.'

'I don't care,' said d'Artagnan. 'If ever I see that fellow . . .'

'You're a good lad, but at present I can't do more for you than I've already promised. I shall always be glad to see you here. Later, when you're free to call on me at any time and to catch me on an off moment, you'll probably get what you want out of me.'

'In other words, Sir,' replied d'Artagnan, 'you're waiting for me to prove what I'm good for. Well, don't worry,' he added with a Gascon's cheek, 'you won't have to wait long.'

He bowed to the captain and turned abruptly to leave the room, as though the future were now his concern, and his concern alone. But Monsieur de Tréville called him back.

'Just a moment,' he said, 'I promised you a letter to the Director of the Academy. Are you too proud to take it, my lad?'

'No, Sir,' replied d'Artagnan. 'And I promise you it won't go the way the other one went. I'll see this one gets home all right, and if any man tries to steal it from me, I'll slit his throat for him.'

De Tréville smiled at this piece of swagger. He left his young compatriot at the window where they had been standing, sat down at a table and started to write the letter of introduction. Meanwhile d'Artagnan, who had nothing to do, tapped with his fingers on the window-pane and watched the musketeers leave the house one by one, following them with his eyes until they disappeared round the corner of the street.

Monsieur de Tréville finished the letter, sealed it and got up, meaning to hand it to the young man. But at that very moment to his great surprise the young man gave a sudden start, flushed angrily and, totally ignoring his host and the letter, rushed out of the study crying:

'Ye Gods! This time he won't escape me!'

'Who won't escape you?' cried the captain in amazement.

'The thief, of course,' cried d'Artagnan. 'Oh, I'll get him, the yellow rat!'

And he disappeared through the door.

4

SHOULDER, SHOULDER-BELT AND HANDKERCHIEF

D'Artagnan in his fury crossed the ante-room in three strides and sprang on to the staircase, meaning to run down it four steps at a time. But in his mad rush he collided with a musketeer who was leaving Monsieur de Tréville's apartments by a private door, and gave him such a hard butt on the shoulder with his head that the musketeer let out a yell.

'I'm sorry!' said d'Artagnan. 'I'm in a bit of a hurry, I'm afraid.' And he tried to rush on.

But he had only gone one step down the staircase

when he felt a strong grip on his shoulder which held him
back. Turning round he saw the musketeer glaring at
him, as white as a sheet. It was Athos, who was on his
way home after having had his wounds dressed by the
doctor.

'You're in a hurry, are you?' cried Athos. 'You're in a
hurry, you shove me, you say "I'm sorry" and you think
that's enough! Well it isn't, my lad. D'you think because
you heard Monsieur de Tréville laying into me this
morning that you've got a right to lay me out now? Don't
you believe it. You're not Monsieur de Tréville.'

'But I didn't do it on purpose,' answered d'Artagnan.
'It was an accident and I apologized for it. I can't do more
than that. Now please let go of me. I'm in a hurry. I've got
something important to do.'

Athos let go of him. 'Your manners are bad, Sir,' he
said. 'You're obviously just up from the country.'

D'Artagnan had already skipped three or four steps
but Athos' remark brought him up short.

'Look here, Sir,' he said. 'I may be just up from the
country, as you call it, but I won't be taught manners by
you!'

'Oh, won't you?'

'No, by God, I won't,' cried d'Artagnan. 'And if I
wasn't in such a hurry, if I wasn't running after someone . . .'

'You may be in a hurry now, Sir, but you don't need to
run to find me, you know!'

'Where shall I find you then?'

'Near the Carmelite Convent.'

'What time?'

'About midday.'

'Midday? Right! I'll be there.'

'And don't keep me waiting! I want to have those ears
of yours off by twelve-fifteen.'

'Fine,' said d'Artagnan. 'I'll be with you on the stroke of twelve.'

And off he started again like a madman, hoping to overtake his enemy who, at the rate he was walking, could not have gone far.

But Porthos was standing at the street door, talking to a soldier in the King's Guards. There was just enough space between them for a man to pass and d'Artagnan, thinking he had enough room, darted between them like an arrow. But he hadn't reckoned with the wind. Just as he was passing the wind blew out Porthos' long cloak, and d'Artagnan charged straight into it. Porthos obviously had some good reason for clinging on to this important part of his dress, for, instead of letting go of it, he drew it closer to him. The result was that d'Artagnan got entangled in the velvet folds, and when he turned to loosen himself only coiled himself tighter still.

Hearing the musketeer swear, our hero tried to get out from underneath the cloak, which was blinding him, and looked everywhere for an opening. He was afraid that he might have soiled the magnificent shoulder-belt which, we remember, was Porthos' pride and joy. But when he timidly opened his eyes he found himself with his nose glued to the middle of Porthos' back, in other words right against the shoulder-belt.

Alas! Like most things in this world which are good only on the outside, the shoulder-belt was embroidered with gold in front but plain buff at the back. Porthos, though a great bragger, was none too rich. He could not afford a shoulder-belt entirely of gold lace and had had to be content with a half-embroidered one, which explains why he had had a cold and had insisted on wearing a cloak.

'Look out! Look out!' cried Porthos, trying to shake off d'Artagnan who was nosing round his back. 'What the

Hell d'you think you're doing, running into people like that! Are you mad?'

'I'm very sorry!' said d'Artagnan, his head reappearing under the big man's shoulder. 'I'm very sorry, but I'm in a great hurry. I'm running after someone and . . .'

'Do you always leave your eyes at home when you run?' asked Porthos.

'No,' replied d'Artagnan, stung by this remark. 'And my eyes are so good that they sometimes see things other people don't see.'

Porthos may or may not have understood the point of this remark. In any case he got angry and retorted:

'I warn you, Sir, if you go shoving musketeers about you're in for a good thrashing one of these days.'

'Thrashing! Thrashing!' said d'Artagnan. 'That's a pretty harsh word, you know.'

'It's quite common among men who face up to their enemies.'

'I dare say it is! And I know now why you're so careful not to turn your back on yours.'

And our young hero, enchanted by his little joke, ran down the street laughing uproariously.

Porthos, foaming with rage, started off in pursuit of him.

'All right! Later! Later!' cried d'Artagnan. 'When you've taken off that cloak of yours.'

'One o'clock then, behind the Luxembourg.'

'One o'clock! Fine!' shouted d'Artagnan, disappearing round the corner of the street.

But he saw no one anywhere about who in the least resembled the man he was after. His enemy may have been walking slowly but he had outdistanced him all the same; he had quite possibly gone into some house. D'Artagnan inquired from all the passers-by, went down as far as the ferry, ran back along the Rue de Seine and past the Croix-Rouge, but found no trace of him anywhere. However his mad rush did him this much good, that the more he sweated the cooler his senses grew.

He now began to reflect on the events of the day. Much had happened and all of it bad. It was not yet eleven o'clock and he had already got into Monsieur de Tréville's bad books, for Monsieur de Tréville would certainly not have been pleased by his discourteous behaviour. And he had subsequently let himself in for two good duels with two musketeers, each of whom, as he realized only too well, was capable of dealing with three d'Artagnans.

It was a depressing prospect. Certain as the young man was that Athos would kill him it was only natural that he should not be greatly concerned about Porthos. But, as we know, hope springs eternal in the human breast, so d'Artagnan soon recovered his spirits and began to feel that he might possibly survive these two duels, though not, of course, without terrible wounds. With this idea of survival in his head he gave himself a good talking-to.

'What a silly, hare-brained ass I am! Why do I have to go barging into that good fellow Athos, with that bad shoulder of his which must hurt him so? I'm surprised he didn't kill me on the spot – he had every right to, and I must have given him a frightful jar. And then Porthos! Oh well, that was rather funny, I must say!'

And at the thought of Porthos he started smiling to himself again. But he looked cautiously round to make sure that his little private joke wasn't being misinterpreted and giving offence to any of the passers-by.

'Yes, the Porthos business was certainly funny,' he muttered. 'But I'm a silly ass all the same. Do people go barging into other people like that without warning? No. Of course not! And do they go peeping under people's cloaks to find things which aren't there? No, again. And he'd have forgiven me like a shot if I hadn't mentioned that damned sash of his. It was only a joke, of course, but too good a joke by half. Oh what a silly Gascon oaf I am! I'll joke myself into the grave one day. Come on, d'Artagnan, old boy, pull yourself together. If you escape this time, which is highly unlikely, you'll have to mend your manners a bit in future. From now on you must set an example; you must be a model of what a gentleman should be. One can be kind and polite without being servile. Take Aramis, for instance; look how gentle and good-mannered he is! And has anyone ever called him a coward? Of course they haven't! In future I'll model myself on him. Well, I'm damned! Here he is!'

D'Artagnan had been walking along the street muttering to himself and was now quite close to Aiguillon House. Here he suddenly caught sight of Aramis, talking and laughing with three soldiers in the King's Guards. Aramis also noticed d'Artagnan, but he remembered that the young Gascon had been present when Monsieur de Tréville had lost his temper and hated to think that anyone had witnessed so unpleasant a scene. So he pretended not to see him.

But d'Artagnan, obsessed with his new resolve to be as polite and friendly as possible, went boldly up to the four young men, bowed low and put on his most charming smile. Aramis gave him a curt nod in return, but did not smile. And all four at once stopped talking.

D'Artagnan had enough sense to realize that his presence was unwelcome, but he was still too much of a rough diamond to know how gentlemen retire gracefully when they find themselves with people whom they hardly know and whose conversation doesn't concern them. He was thinking out some excuse to get away without looking foolish when he noticed that Aramis had dropped his handkerchief and had carelessly put his foot on it. Here was an excellent opportunity to atone for his previous lack of tact. He bent down and with a flourish pulled the handkerchief from under the musketeer's foot, although the latter tried hard to prevent him. He then handed it to Aramis and said:

'You've dropped your handkerchief, Sir. And I'm sure you'd be sorry to lose a handkerchief like that.'

The handkerchief was indeed a beautiful one, richly embroidered and with a coronet and coat-of-arms in one of the corners. Aramis blushed scarlet and snatched the handkerchief from the Gascon's hand.

'Ha, ha!' cried one of the guards. 'Aramis, you secretive old devil! Don't pretend Madame de Bois-Tracy's finished with you, when the beautiful lady's still kind enough to lend you her handkerchief!'

Aramis threw d'Artagnan one of those looks which tell a man that he has made a mortal enemy. Then in his usual mild manner he retorted:

'You're wrong, gentlemen. This handkerchief's not mine, and I don't know why our friend here chose to give it to me rather than to one of you. And to prove it's not mine I'll show you mine!'

So saying, he pulled his own handkerchief out of his pocket. It was another handkerchief made of the same fine cambric, although cambric was very dear at that time. But this one had no embroidery or coat-of-arms on it, and only a single monogram, that of its owner.

This time d'Artagnan remained silent, for he realized his blunder. But Aramis' friends refused to be convinced by his protests. One of them now put on a grave face and said:

'You know, Aramis, if that handkerchief really weren't yours by rights, I should have to ask you to give it to me. Bois-Tracy's one of my best friends and I couldn't allow anyone to make trophies of his wife's belongings.'

'I didn't like the way you said that,' said Aramis. 'You're perfectly right, of course, but I didn't like your tone. So I won't give you the handkerchief.'

'As a matter of fact,' said d'Artagnan shyly, 'I didn't actually see the handkerchief fall out of Monsieur Aramis' pocket. He had his foot on it, that's all. And I thought that as the handkerchief was under his foot it probably belonged to him.'

'And that's where you were wrong,' said Aramis coldly, unmoved by d'Artagnan's attempt to make amends. Then, turning to the soldier who had claimed to be Bois-Tracy's friend, he went on:

'Come to that, my dear chap, I'm just as friendly with Bois-Tracy as you are. Are you sure that handkerchief didn't fall out of your pocket? If it did I'd have just as much right to ask you to hand it over to me.'

'I swear it didn't,' retorted the guardsman.

'Well if you swear one thing and I swear another, one of us is bound to be lying. I've got a better idea, Monteron. Let's each take half.'

'What? Half the handkerchief?'

'Yes.'

'That's a grand idea,' cried the other two guardsmen. 'The judgement of Solomon! There's wisdom in that head of yours, Aramis, old boy.'

The young men burst out laughing and, needless to say, the subject then dropped. Very soon the conversation ended and the three guardsmen and the musketeer shook hands and parted, the guardsmen going one way and Aramis another.

'Now's my chance to make friends with this fine fellow,' thought d'Artagnan, who had been keeping quiet during the latter part of the conversation. And with this good intention in mind he followed Aramis, who was walking away without paying any more heed to him.

'Excuse me, Sir . . .' he said.

'Sir,' interrupted Aramis, 'allow me to point out that your behaviour just now was not that of a gentleman.'

'Are you suggesting, Sir . . .'

'I'm suggesting, Sir, that you're not a complete ass, and that, although you've only just arrived from Gascony, you've enough sense to know that one doesn't put one's foot on a handkerchief without good reason. The streets of Paris aren't paved with cambric, you know!'

'I shouldn't try to be funny if I were you,' said d'Artagnan, who felt his temper prevailing over his peaceful intentions. 'I'm a Gascon, as you say, and I don't need to tell you that we Gascons are inclined to be testy. Even when we've done something silly we think one apology's more than enough.'

'Sir,' replied Aramis, 'I don't wish to have a quarrel with you. Thank God I'm no fire-eater. I'm only a musketeer temporarily, so I don't fight unless I have to, and even then it goes against the grain. But this time it's a serious matter; you've compromised a lady.'

'We both have, you mean,' retorted d'Artagnan.

'Why were you so tactless as to return me the handkerchief?'

'Why were you so tactless as to drop it?'

'I told you once and I tell you again. That handkerchief did not come out of my pocket.'

'Now, Sir, you've lied twice! I actually saw it fall out of your pocket.'

'Oh! If you're going to take that tone, young Gascon, I see I'll have to put you in your place.'

'And I'll have to put you in yours! Come on, Sir, draw your sword and let's not waste any more time!'

'No, no, not here, my friend! I'm not going to fight you right in front of Aiguillon House, with all the Cardinal's men looking on. No thanks! How do I know you're not a Cardinal's man yourself sent to provoke me? If I fight here, off comes my head. And strangely enough I like my head; I don't think it looks too bad on my shoulders. I mean to kill you all right. But I want to do it somewhere nice and quiet, where we shan't be disturbed and where I shan't get into trouble afterwards.'

'That suits me!' said d'Artagnan. 'But don't be too sure of yourself. And bring that handkerchief along with you, whether it's yours or not. You may find it useful.'

'You're a Gascon all right,' said Aramis.

'Yes, I'm a Gascon. And I wouldn't let fear of a scandal stop me fighting.'

'Musketeers shouldn't ever refuse to fight, I grant you. But a churchman should and must. And I'm only a musketeer temporarily, so I shall continue to respect the law. I shall be happy to meet you at two o'clock in Monsieur de Tréville's house. From there I'll take you on to some nice quiet spot.'

The two young men bowed. Aramis then went off in the direction of the Luxembourg, while d'Artagnan, seeing how time had flown, made his way to the Carmelite Convent, muttering to himself:

'Now I'm properly for it! But if I'm killed, I shall at least be killed by a musketeer.'

5

Musketeers and Guards

D'Artagnan knew no one in Paris. So he went off to fight his duel with Athos without the support of any seconds; he would have to make do with those chosen by his opponent. In any case he hoped to find some decent excuse for getting out of this duel, if he could do so without appearing weak, because he foresaw that this particular affair was bound to end disastrously for him.

He was a young and active man, and his opponent was already crippled by a previous wound; if he lost, his enemy would be doubly triumphant; if he won, he might be accused of having taken a mean advantage.

It was striking twelve o'clock when d'Artagnan reached the deserted little piece of ground beside the convent, and Athos had only been waiting there five minutes. So he was sharp on time. So far, so good; his conduct would have satisfied the most punctilious of duellists.

Athos was still in great pain from his wound, although it had been freshly dressed by Monsieur de Tréville's doctor. He was, however, sitting quite calmly on a milestone in his usual attitude of easy grace, aloof and unconcerned as ever. When he caught sight of d'Artagnan, he rose politely and came forward to meet him. D'Artagnan, not to be outdone, came up to his enemy bareheaded, and bowed low, sweeping the ground with the feather of his hat.

'Sir,' said Athos, 'I've asked two of my friends to act as my seconds, but neither of them has arrived yet. I'm surprised they should be late; they're not usually late for an affair of this kind.'

'I'm afraid I've got no seconds, Sir,' said d'Artagnan. 'I only arrived in Paris yesterday and I know no one here except Monsieur de Tréville. I only know him because my father gave me a letter of introduction to him.'

Athos thought for a moment.

'You know no one but Monsieur de Tréville?' he echoed.

'No, no one.'

'That's awkward,' went on Athos, talking half to himself and half to d'Artagnan. 'If I kill you I shall look a bit of an ogre, shan't I?'

'Not such a terrible ogre,' answered d'Artagnan, drawing himself up. 'Remember you're fighting me at a disadvantage. That wound of yours'll handicap you a good deal.'

'It will indeed. And I admit you hurt me a lot, barging into me like that. However, I'll fight you with my left hand as I've often done before. And don't imagine I shall be letting you off lightly. I'm ambidextrous. In fact it'll probably put you off a bit; a left-hander's always awkward to deal with, especially for beginners. I'm sorry. Perhaps I should have warned you before.'

'Of course not, Sir,' said d'Artagnan, again bowing low. 'It's very good of you even to mention it.'

'Not at all, not at all,' answered Athos, slightly embarrassed. 'And now let's talk about something else. You certainly hurt me a good deal when you ran into me. I can feel my right shoulder throbbing now.'

'May I make a suggestion . . . ?' said d'Artagnan shyly.

'What's that?'

'I've got a wonderful ointment for dressing wounds. My mother gave it to me and I've already tried it on myself with great success.'

'Oh!'

'I'm certain the ointment would cure you in three days or even less. I suggest we put off our meeting till then.'

D'Artagnan spoke simply and frankly. It was obvious that he was genuinely concerned for the other's welfare and not trying to back out.

'Well said, Sir, well said,' cried Athos. 'I won't accept your offer but it proves you're a gentleman. Unfortunately, the Cardinal's our master now, and if we waited three days before fighting everyone would get to know of it, however much we tried to keep it dark. They'd find out all right and stop the whole thing. What in God's name's happened to those two idle rogues, my seconds? Why aren't they here?'

'If you're in a great hurry,' said d'Artagnan, 'and would like to finish me off as quickly as possible, please don't worry but let's start without them.'

He said this with the same air of wishing to oblige with which a few seconds earlier he had suggested postponing the fight for three days.

'Well said again,' answered Athos, nodding at d'Artagnan appreciatively. 'What you say shows head as well as heart. I like fellows of your stamp, and if I don't kill you now, I hope to make your better acquaintance later. But I think we'd do well to wait for the two others; I've got plenty of time, and it's more correct that way. Ah, here is one of them, I do believe.'

At that very moment the gigantic figure of Porthos appeared, rounding the corner from the Rue du Vaugirard.

'What!' cried d'Artagnan. 'Is Monsieur Porthos one of your seconds?'

'Yes. Any objection?'

'No, no. Of course not.'

'And there's my other second.'

D'Artagnan looked to where Athos was pointing and recognized Aramis.

'What!' he cried, even more astonished this time. 'Is Monsieur Aramis your other second?'

'Of course he is! Don't you know that none of us three is ever seen without the other two; that we're known by all the other musketeers and by the Cardinal's Guards, at Court and even in the town, as Athos, Porthos and Aramis, or the three inseparables?'

'Well, Sir, I can only say you're well named,' said d'Artagnan. 'And if our little adventure gets talked about, it'll be a further proof of how much you all have in common.'

Meanwhile Porthos had come up and joined Athos and d'Artagnan. He greeted Athos with a wave of the hand;

then, catching sight of d'Artagnan, he stood and stared at him in amazement. (In the interval between his two meetings with the Gascon he had taken off his new shoulder-strap and put on his old one, and also discarded his cloak.)

'Well, well!' he cried. 'And what's the meaning of all this, may I ask?'

'This is the gentleman I've had the quarrel with,' said Athos, pointing at d'Artagnan.

'But I've had a quarrel with him too!' cried Porthos. 'I'm fighting him as well!'

'Yes,' said d'Artagnan. 'But not till one o'clock.'

At that moment Aramis came up.

'And I'm also fighting this gentleman,' he cried.

'Yes, but not till two o'clock,' said d'Artagnan, still completely unruffled, and enjoying the embarrassment of the other three.

'Why are you fighting him?' said Aramis to Athos.

'I honestly don't quite know,' said Athos. 'He barged into me and hurt my shoulder. Why are you fighting him, Porthos?'

'Me? Oh, I'm just fighting him . . . I'm just fighting him, that's all,' said Porthos, going rather red.

Athos, who noticed everything, saw a faint smile cross the Gascon's face as Porthos spoke.

'We had an argument about dress,' said the young man.

'And what about you, Aramis?' asked Porthos.

'I'm fighting him on theological grounds,' answered Aramis, signing to d'Artagnan to keep quiet about the real reason for their quarrel.

Athos again noticed d'Artagnan smiling to himself at this point. He turned to him and said:

'Is that really what you're fighting about?'

'Yes, we had a little dispute about a certain passage in St Augustine,' said the young Gascon.

'This fellow's no fool, no fool at all,' muttered Athos to himself.

'And now that we're all mustered, gentlemen,' said d'Artagnan, 'I'd like to make my apologies to you.'

At this surprising statement Athos frowned, Porthos smiled scornfully, and Aramis shrugged his shoulders contemptuously. And all three thought to themselves that it was a pity that this young Gascon should after all turn out to be so spiritless.

'Don't misunderstand me, gentlemen,' continued d'Artagnan, drawing himself up to his full height. At that moment the sun's rays shone on him and showed up the bold, clear-cut outlines of his face. 'I wish to apologize humbly in advance because I realize now that I may not be able to fulfil my debt of honour to you all. Monsieur Athos has the first claim on my life, a fact which greatly reduces the value of your claim, Monsieur Porthos, and makes yours virtually nil, Monsieur Aramis. So, gentlemen, let me repeat my apologies to you on that score and on that score alone. And now on guard, please! Let's waste no more time.'

With these words d'Artagnan drew his sword from its scabbard in the most elegant manner possible, like a courtier born and bred.

It was now a quarter past twelve. The sun was high in the heaven and its rays beat down pitilessly on the exposed plot of ground chosen as the site for the duels.

'It's very hot,' said Athos, drawing his sword in his turn. 'But hot as it is, I'm going to fight in my doublet. A moment ago I felt my wound bleeding again and I don't want to put this gentleman off by the sight of blood drawn from me by another.'

'That's most considerate of you, Sir,' said d'Artagnan. 'And I can assure you that I'd always be sorry to see the blood of a brave man like you, even if I'd drawn it from you myself. So I'll wear my doublet too.'

'Come on now, gentlemen,' said Porthos. 'Cut short the compliments. Remember Aramis and I are waiting our turn.'

'That remark was out of place, Porthos,' said Aramis. 'Speak for yourself another time. What these gentlemen have been saying does them both great credit.'

'When you're ready, Sir,' said Athos, 'on guard.'

'At your service, Sir,' said d'Artagnan, crossing swords with him.

But hardly had the two blades clinked together than a posse of His Eminence's guards appeared round the corner of the convent with Monsieur de Jussac at its head.

'The Cardinal's guards!' cried Porthos and Aramis. 'Sheathe swords, gentlemen, sheathe swords!'

But it was too late. The duellists had been caught in an attitude which left no doubt of their intentions.

'Hi, there!' cried Jussac walking up to them and signing to his men to follow him. 'Hi, there, you musketeers! Duelling again, I see. What about the edicts, gentlemen? What about the edicts?'

'So it's you again!' cried Athos resentfully, for Jussac had been one of the party which had set on him and his friends in the Rue Férou. 'Why don't you leave us alone? If we saw you fighting we'd take good care not to interfere with you. So leave us to fight, and you'll have a great deal of fun for nothing.'

'Gentlemen,' said Jussac, 'I'm very sorry but that's out of the question. We've our duty to do. So put up your swords, please, and come along with us.'

'Sir,' said Aramis, imitating Jussac's superior tone of voice, 'we'd be only too happy to accept your kind offer if we were our own masters. Unfortunately we have to take our orders from M. de Tréville, and he's expressly forbidden us to do anything of the kind. So run along now and leave us in peace.'

Aramis' supercilious tone stung Jussac to a fury.

'If you don't come at once we'll force you to come,' he cried.

Athos said softly, so that only his friends could hear:

'There are five of them and only three of us. We shall be beaten again and this time we shall have to die here. I could never face the captain after another licking.'

Athos, Porthos and Aramis at once closed ranks, while Jussac drew up his men in line.

At this moment d'Artagnan made a swift decision. It was one of those occasions which determine a man's whole future for better or worse. D'Artagnan had to choose between the King and the Cardinal and, the choice once made, to abide by it. To fight was to disobey the law, and that meant risking his head, in other words, making a life-long enemy of a minister who was more powerful than the King himself. Our hero realized all this in a flash and yet, to his credit be it said, he did not hesitate for a moment. He turned to the musketeers and cried:

'Gentlemen, I think there's some mistake. Monsieur Athos said there were only three of us. I make it four.'

At this the whole nine of them rushed at each other furiously. But they were all skilled swordsmen and kept their heads.

Athos, being the senior of the musketeers, chose his man – Cahusac, one of the Cardinal's favourites. Porthos had Bicarat to deal with, and Aramis found himself alone against two of the guards. As for d'Artagnan, he was face to face with the great Jussac himself.

Our young Gascon's heart was pounding in his chest; not from fright – he had no trace of that, thank God – but from his strong wish to distinguish himself. He fought like a demon, encircling his opponent ten times and more and constantly changing his stance and ground. Jussac was what was known in those days as a glutton for fighting, and was an old hand at the game. Nevertheless he had his work cut out to defend himself against an enemy of such extraordinary speed who kept bounding about and overriding the orthodox rules of the game, attacking from all sides at once and also showing quite a keen sense of self-preservation. At last he began to lose patience. The struggle was going on much too long. He was furious at being held at bay by someone whom he had dismissed as a mere child. He got ruffled and began to make mistakes. D'Artagnan in default of practice had plenty of theory, and attacked with redoubled energy. Jussac now made his longest lunge with the intention of polishing his enemy off once and for all. But d'Artagnan parried quickly and before Jussac could recover his balance glided in like a snake under his guard and drove his sword right through his body. Jussac collapsed in a heap on the ground.

The young man now turned and surveyed the battlefield, taking in the situation at a glance.

Aramis had already killed one of his opponents but was being hard pressed by the other. However he was in good fettle and could obviously hold out for a little longer.

Porthos and Bicarat had lunged together and both had hit. Porthos had been struck in the arm and Bicarat in the thigh. But both wounds were slight and had only whetted the combatants' appetite for more.

Athos had been wounded again by Cahusac and was looking paler than ever. D'Artagnan responded at once; he rushed at Cahusac shouting:

'Turn and face me, guardsman, or I'll run you through the back.'

Cahusac turned and faced d'Artagnan. This flank attack came only just in time. Athos now sank on one knee; his courage alone had kept him on his feet till then.

'Don't kill him, young fellow, for God's sake,' he called to d'Artagnan. 'I've got an old score to settle with him.

When I'm well again I'll fight him on equal terms. Disable him – disarm him – that's right – well done, Sir, well done!'

Athos shouted this out as he saw Cahusac's sword leave his hand, fly into the air and land about twenty yards away. Both combatants immediately rushed after it, Cahusac to pick it up again, d'Artagnan to prevent him doing so. Our hero, the more agile of the two, reached it first and planted his foot on it.

Cahusac now started running towards the guardsman whom Aramis had killed, meaning to take his sword and carry on the fight with d'Artagnan. But he found his way barred by Athos, who had meanwhile recovered his breath and decided to return to the fray himself rather than allow d'Artagnan to polish off his own enemy for him. Realizing that it would be discourteous to rob his friend of the right to kill his man d'Artagnan stood aside and soon had the satisfaction of seeing Cahusac fall to the ground with a sword-thrust in the throat.

At that very moment Aramis was planting his foot firmly on the recumbent figure of his second opponent and was forcing him at sword-point to admit defeat.

Only Porthos and Bicarat were still fighting. Porthos, playing the fool, was keeping up a running fire of chatter as he fought, asking the time and even voicing his congratulations on a happy event in Bicarat's family. But he was not achieving much by these tactics; his enemy was a man of iron to whom a fight was a grim affair which could only be settled by the death of one party or the other.

But it could not go on for ever. A police patrol might come on the scene at any moment and arrest all the combatants in a body, wounded and unwounded Royalists and Cardinalists alike. Athos, Aramis and d'Artagnan surrounded Bicarat and called on him to surrender. Bicarat was now one against four, and had a thigh wound into the bargain. He was, however, still game to carry on.

But Jussac, who had in the meanwhile recovered slightly and was now leaning on one elbow, called out to him to surrender.

'That settles it then,' answered Bicarat. 'An order's an order: you're my senior so I must obey!'

With this he made a quick leap backwards, split his sword across his knee in order not to have to surrender it, threw the pieces over the convent wall and stood with his arms crossed, whistling a jaunty Cardinalist air.

Gallantry is always respected, even in an enemy. The musketeers saluted Bicarat with their swords and then returned them to their scabbards. D'Artagnan followed their example; then, assisted by Bicarat, the only guardsman who was still on his feet, he lifted up Jussac, Cahusac and Aramis' wounded opponent, carried them over to the convent porch and left them there. The fifth guardsman, we remember, was dead. The musketeers then rang the convent bell and made off at once towards Monsieur de Tréville's house, carrying four enemy swords out of five, mad with joy at their sensational victory. They walked along arm in arm, taking up the whole width of the street, and called on every musketeer they met to join them until a regular triumphal procession was formed.

D'Artagnan was walking arm in arm with Athos and Porthos. He was exultant. As they reached the door of Monsieur de Tréville's house he said to his new friends: 'I may not be a musketeer yet, but at least I've been privileged to fight in your ranks.'

This incident made the four young men as inseparable as the Three Musketeers had been before. What is more, when de Tréville explained the episode to the King, His Majesty gave d'Artagnan forty pistoles (with which he immediately hired a servant, Planchet) and ordered Monsieur des Essarts to enrol d'Artagnan as an ensign in his company of guards.

6

A COURT INTRIGUE

It was unfortunate but inevitable that Louis XIII's forty pistoles should, like everything else in this world, come to an end, and that our four friends should be reduced to living on practically nothing. Athos had been the first to pool his own little fortune for the common good. Then it had been Porthos' turn; he had done one of his periodic disappearing tricks and had returned with enough money to keep the four of them going for another fortnight. Then Aramis had taken on the job of financing the party; he had set himself to the task with a good grace, and had managed to find a few pistoles to carry on with. Nobody quite knew where they came from, and his own explanation that they were the proceeds of the sale of some books on theology was taken with a grain of salt.

When these additional supplies were also used up, our four friends went and appealed to Monsieur de Tréville. He made them a small advance on their pay, but this sum could not go very far to support three musketeers who were already pretty heavily in debt and one guardsman who had never had any money at all.

Realizing that they would soon be completely on the rocks they made one last effort and collected eight or ten pistoles which Porthos gambled with. But luck was against him: he lost everything he started with plus an extra twenty-five pistoles for which he had to write out an IOU.

Now the four young men could no longer be described as hard up – they were literally destitute. They walked up and down the streets followed by their lackeys, ravenous and with their tongues hanging out, visiting all their fellow musketeers in turn to get as many free meals as possible. In their prosperous days, prompted by Aramis, they had had the sense to sow meals right and left, and now that they were themselves in need they were able to reap a rich harvest.

Athos got four invitations, and each time he took his friends and their lackeys along with him. Porthos was asked out six times, Aramis eight, and each time the same procession of men and lackeys followed behind their leaders to get their share of the feasts.

D'Artagnan, unfortunately, knew no one in the capital, and the best he could provide was one high tea in the house of a priest, a Gascon like himself, and one dinner with a cornet in the guards. He took his motley army to visit the priest, and they ate the poor man out of house and home. They then visited the cornet, who rose nobly to the occasion. But, as Planchet remarked, however hard you try, you can't stuff down more than a certain amount at a time.

Here were four men, devoted to each other, sharing their luck together, ready to run any risk and dare any danger in the common cause. D'Artagnan sat in his room racking his brains to find some use for this great driving-force. He never doubted for a moment that, if properly directed, like Archimedes' lever, it could overturn the world. While he was thus ruminating there came a sudden gentle knock on his door. D'Artagnan woke up Planchet and told him to go and see who was there.

Planchet went and opened the door and found a man standing outside, a rather drab-looking little man who looked like a tradesman. Planchet showed him in to his master and would have gladly stayed on and listened to the conversation. But the man gave d'Artagnan to understand that he wished to speak to him alone; evidently his business was important and confidential. So d'Artagnan dismissed Planchet and bade his visitor be seated.

There was a moment's silence while the two men sat and sized each other up. D'Artagnan then said:

'Well, Sir, and what can I do for you?'

'Monsieur d'Artagnan,' said the stranger; 'I've heard you spoken of as a young man of great courage, and, believing as I do that the description's accurate, I've decided to let you into a secret.'

'Good, let's hear it,' said d'Artagnan, who felt instinctively that he was on to a good thing.

The stranger paused again a moment and continued:

'I've a wife, Sir, who's maid of the wardrobe to the Queen and who's both intelligent and good-looking.'

'Well?' said d'Artagnan.

'Well,' continued the little man, 'my wife was kidnapped yesterday morning, just as she was leaving her workroom at the Louvre.'

'Who kidnapped her?'

'I don't know for certain, Sir,' answered the stranger, 'but I have my suspicions.'

'And whom do you suspect?'

'A man who has long been pestering her with his attentions.'

'That's bad, that's bad,' said d'Artagnan.

'But if you ask me my opinion,' went on the little man, 'I should say this kidnapping business has something political behind it, and isn't a mere love-affair.'

'Something political,' echoed d'Artagnan. 'I see.'

He suddenly knitted his brows and looked pensive.

'And who's the man you suspect?' he asked.

'I don't know if I should tell you, Sir.'

'Listen,' said d'Artagnan, 'I'd like to point out here and now that I'm not forcing you to tell me anything. You came of your own free will to see me. You told me you had a secret to confide in me. So do exactly as you please. You needn't stay if you don't want to.'

'No, Sir, no. You look to me an honest enough young fellow, and I'll take you into my confidence. I repeat, I don't think my wife's kidnapping concerns any love-affair of her own, but I think it concerns someone else's love-affairs, someone much more important.'

'Not Madame de Bois-Tracy, by any chance?' asked d'Artagnan.

He wanted to show this little bourgeois that he was quite up-to-date in the latest Court scandals.

'More important still, Sir.'

'Madame d'Aiguillon perhaps?'

'More important still.'

'Madame de Chevreuse?'

'More important – much more important.'

'Not the . . . ?' D'Artagnan stopped.

'Yes, Sir,' answered the little man in a low, quavering voice. He now seemed absolutely panic-stricken.

'Her love-affair with whom?'

'Well, Sir, I don't see who else it could be but the Duke of . . .'

'The Duke of . . .'

'Yes, Sir,' answered the little man, lowering his voice even more.

'But how can *you* know all about this?'

'How can I know, you ask? How can I know?' said the little man in a shrill, pained voice.

'Yes. Come on, speak out. I don't want any half-confidences.'

'My wife told me herself, Sir.'

'And who did she get it from?'

'From Monsieur de Laporte. I told you she was Monsieur de Laporte's ward, didn't I? Monsieur de Laporte's the Queen's confidential agent. He saw to it that my wife was given a special post near Her Majesty, so that the poor Queen could have someone at hand she could trust. She has enemies all round her; she's lost the King's confidence; the Cardinal sets spies to watch her and she has no loyal friend at all.'

'Ah!' cried d'Artagnan. 'Now I'm beginning to see daylight.'

'My wife came to see me four days ago,' went on the little man. 'One of the conditions she imposed before taking on her new post was that she should be allowed to come and visit me twice a week. I'm lucky enough, Sir, to have a wife who's devoted to me. So, as I was saying, my wife came and confided to me that the Queen's at present in a great state of alarm.'

'Oh!'

'Yes. I gather His Eminence is pursuing and persecuting her more than ever.'

'Go on, Sir, go on . . .'

'She thinks they've written to the Duke of Buckingham in her name.'

'What? They've used the Queen's name?'

'Yes. To get the Duke to come to Paris, and once they've got him there, to set some sort of trap for him.'

'Good Lord! But how exactly is your wife concerned in all this, may I ask?'

'They know how devoted she is to the Queen, and they're trying either to separate her from her mistress, to bully her into giving away the Queen's secrets or to bribe her to act as a spy for them.'

'Yes, that's probably what they are doing,' answered d'Artagnan. 'But what about the man who kidnapped her? D'you know him?'

'I've told you already – I think I know him.'

'What's his name?'

'I don't know his name. All I do know is that he's the Cardinal's agent, his private spy.'

'But have you actually seen him?'

'Yes, my wife pointed him out to me one day.'

'Can you describe him? Is there anything special about him, something one could recognize him by?'

'Oh yes, he's quite unmistakable. He's a very distinguished-looking gentleman, dark-haired and sallow-skinned, with shrewd black eyes and a scar on his cheek.'

'A scar on his cheek!' cried d'Artagnan. 'Shrewd black eyes, dark-haired, sallow-skinned and distinguished-looking! That's my friend from Meung.'

'Your friend, you say?'

'Yes, yes. But that's neither here nor there. Oh yes, on second thoughts, it does simplify things a bit. If your man and mine are the same I shall be able to kill two birds with one stone, so to speak. Otherwise, it's not important. But how can we get hold of this fellow?'

'I haven't an idea.'

'You don't know where he lives, I suppose?'

'No. I was taking my wife back to the Louvre one day, and he came out just as she was going in. That's the only time I've set eyes on him.'

'That's awkward,' muttered d'Artagnan to himself. 'It's all so very vague. Who told you about your wife having been kidnapped?'

'Monsieur de Laporte.'

'Didn't he give you any details about it?'

'He didn't know any.'

'And you've had no information from other sources?'

'Yes. Actually I've had a . . .'

'A what?'

'Oh dear! I do hope I'm not being rash . . .'

'Now don't start that all over again. If you don't mind my saying so, I think you've gone a little too far to back out now.'

'In that case I won't back out, by God,' cried the little man, swearing to give himself courage. 'Besides, as sure as my name's Bonacieux . . .'

'Bonacieux, you say?' broke in d'Artagnan.

'Yes, Sir.'

'Sorry to interrupt, but the name sounds familiar.'

'Very likely, Sir. You see I'm your landlord.'

'Oh! So you're my landlord,' said d'Artagnan, half rising in his chair and bowing to his guest.

'Yes, Sir. And if I may point out, you've been under my roof for three months now, and you haven't yet paid me my rent. I imagined you were quite taken up with your grand duties and so didn't press you. But I hoped you in return would appreciate my restraint.'

'I do, Monsieur Bonacieux, I do,' said d'Artagnan. 'And as I said before, if I can be of use to you in any way . . .'

'You can indeed, Sir. And as I was about to remark, as sure as my name's Bonacieux, I feel I can trust you.'

'Good. Now get on and finish your story.'

The little man took a scroll of paper out of his pocket and gave it to d'Artagnan to read.

'A letter,' said the young man.

'A letter I got this morning.'

D'Artagnan opened it. The daylight was beginning to fade, so he went to the window to read it. The little man followed him. D'Artagnan read:

Don't try to find your wife! She will be returned to you when we've finished with her. If you make any attempt to find her it will be all up with you.

'Well, that's straight enough,' went on d'Artagnan. 'But it's only a threat after all.'

'Yes, but it terrifies me all the same. You see I'm no fighting man, and I'm frightened of the Bastille.'

'I'm not so keen on the Bastille myself, come to that,' said d'Artagnan. 'If it was merely a question of a fight I wouldn't object.'

'Oh, Sir! And I'd been thinking all the time this was just the job for you! I'd seen you constantly in the company of musketeers, Monsieur de Tréville's musketeers, who I knew were hostile to the Cardinal. I thought you and they'd be twice as ready to do our poor Queen a service when you realized you'd be annoying the Cardinal.'

'Possibly.'

'And I thought also that since you owed three months' rent . . .'

'Yes, yes, you've already suggested that reason, and I thought it excellent.'

'And I'd also made up my mind to charge you no more rent so long as you honoured me by remaining my tenant.'

'Marvellous!'

'Lastly I'd decided that if by chance you were in need of money, which of course wasn't likely, I'd make you a present of fifty pistoles.'

'Marvellous! So you're a man of means, Monsieur Bonacieux?'

'I'm comfortably off, Sir. That's the best way to describe it. I've managed to scrape together enough to bring me in about two or three thousand crowns a year. I made most of it in the drapery business . . .' The little man paused. 'Oh, but good gracious me!' he continued, giving a sudden start of surprise and staring goggle-eyed at some object in the street below.

'What's the matter?' said d'Artagnan, looking to where the little man was pointing.

'It's the fellow himself!' cried he and the little man in one breath. They had both recognized the stranger at the same moment.

'Ye Gods!' cried d'Artagnan. 'This time he won't escape me.'

And, drawing his sword from his scabbard, he rushed headlong out of the room.

On the staircase he ran into Athos and Porthos, who were coming to pay him a visit. They both stood

aside, and d'Artagnan rushed past them like a whirl-
wind.

'Hi, there, what's the hurry?' cried the two musketeers.

'The man from Meung,' shouted d'Artagnan and ran
off.

D'Artagnan had often told his friends about his adventure at Meung, and about the beautiful lady in the coach
with whom the stranger had parleyed outside the inn.
Athos' explanation of the incident was that d'Artagnan
had lost his letter in the scuffle. No gentleman answering
to his description of the stranger would have been capable of such a mean act as stealing a letter. Porthos had
summed up the whole thing as a love intrigue between a
lady and gentleman who had arranged an assignation at
the inn and whose plans had been upset by the arrival of
d'Artagnan and his yellow horse. Aramis had maintained that things of that sort were mysteries which were
better left unsolved.

So now Athos and Porthos realized at once what
d'Artagnan was after and left him to pursue his enemy.
They thought he was bound to return soon, whether he
found the stranger and dealt with him on the spot or
whether he lost sight of him in the crowd. So they went
on up the stairs.

When they entered his room they found it empty. The
landlord, fearing the consequences of the encounter
between the stranger and the young man, had acted in
accordance with the description he had given of himself
to his tenant and taken to his heels.

7

D'ARTAGNAN TAKES COMMAND

As Athos and Porthos had foreseen, d'Artagnan returned home after half an hour. He had lost his man a second time; the fellow had disappeared as though by magic.

In the meantime Aramis had joined his two friends, and when d'Artagnan returned he found all of them assembled in his room.

'Well, and what happened?' they cried as d'Artagnan entered. 'Did you catch him? Have you killed him?'

'That fellow must be the Devil himself!' cried our hero. 'He vanished like a cloud, like a ghost.'

'D'you believe in ghosts?' asked Athos of Porthos.

'Me? I only believe what I see, and as I've never seen a ghost I don't believe in them.'

'In any case,' said d'Artagnan, 'whatever this fellow is, man or demon, illusion or reality, he's my evil genius. He came on the scene just as I was on to a really good thing, gentlemen, something which promised to bring in a hundred pistoles, perhaps more. I caught sight of him and rushed out at the critical moment.'

'What's that? A hundred pistoles? Did we hear you say a hundred pistoles?' cried Porthos and Aramis simultaneously. Athos as usual said nothing and merely gave d'Artagnan a quick look.

D'Artagnan repeated word for word his conversation with his landlord, explaining that the man who had kidnapped Monsieur Bonacieux's wife was the very man with whom he had had the quarrel at the Jolly Miller inn.

'Did the draper, your landlord, actually tell you, d'Artagnan, that the Queen suspected that Buckingham had been lured here on false pretences?' asked Athos.

'He said she was afraid of it.'

'Wait a moment!' broke in Aramis. 'Something's just occurred to me. What you said just now reminded me of something.'

'What?' asked Porthos.

'Let me think a moment. I'm trying to remember.'

'And now I'm sure,' continued d'Artagnan, 'that this woman's kidnapping is in some way connected with these Court intrigues, perhaps even with the Duke of Buckingham's presence in Paris.'

'Our young Gascon certainly has a nose for drama,' said Porthos, laughing good-humouredly, but not at all convinced.

'Gentlemen,' broke in Aramis at this point. 'Listen to this.'

'Let's listen to Aramis,' said the other three in chorus.

'Yesterday I happened to be visiting a friend of mine, a distinguished theologian, who gives me private scripture lessons,' Aramis began.

Athos smiled.

'This theologian friend of mine has a niece,' went on Aramis.

'Oh, he's got a niece, has he?' interrupted Porthos.

'A most respectable woman,' said Aramis.

At this remark the three others burst out laughing.

'Stop laughing or I shan't go on with my story,' said Aramis.

'Quiet, everyone!' cried Athos, holding up his hand in a gesture of mock severity.

Porthos and d'Artagnan controlled themselves.

'Very well then, I'll go on,' said Aramis. 'This niece sometimes comes to visit her uncle. She happened to call last night while I was there and when she left I naturally escorted her to her carriage.'

'So the theologian's niece has a carriage, has she?' interrupted Porthos, who could never restrain his tongue. 'How very convenient! What a nice friend to have!'

'Gentlemen, please!' protested d'Artagnan. He was beginning to see that Aramis' story, disjointed as it was, might provide some valuable clue. 'This is a serious matter, so let's try and stick to the point. Go on, Aramis.'

'As I was escorting this lady to her carriage, a tall, dark, distinguished-looking man, something after the style of your friend from Meung . . .'

'Possibly the same fellow,' interrupted d'Artagnan.

'Possibly. Well, anyway, this fellow advanced towards me, followed by five or six other men who kept about ten yards behind him. He stopped in front of me, bowed low and said: "My Lord Duke and you, Madame," turning to the lady . . .'

'The theologian's niece?' interrupted Porthos.

'Shut up, Porthos,' said Athos. 'You're becoming a bore.'

'"Please get into this carriage," said the man. "Come quietly, and don't try to resist."'

'He mistook you for Buckingham?' cried d'Artagnan.

'I imagine so,' said Aramis.

'And the lady?' cried Porthos.

'He mistook her for the Queen, I suppose,' said d'Artagnan.

'Exactly,' said Aramis.

'No flies on our young Gascon!' exclaimed Athos, looking at d'Artagnan with a glint of admiration in his eyes.

'It's true you're the same height and build as the Duke,' said Porthos. 'And yet I'd have thought your musketeer's uniform . . .'

'I was wearing a long cloak,' said Aramis.

'What? In July?' cried Porthos. 'Does the theologian make you visit him incognito?'

'I can see your clothes might have disguised you,' said Athos. 'But what about your face?'

'I was wearing a big hat,' said Aramis.

'Good Lord!' cried Porthos. 'Do you always put on fancy dress to go to your scripture lessons?'

'Gentlemen, gentlemen!' cried d'Artagnan. 'Don't let's waste time on jokes! Let's get down to solving the mystery. The draper's wife seems to be the key to the problem, so I suggest we split up and go in search of her.'

'I can't believe a draper's wife can be all that important,' said Porthos superciliously.

'She's de Laporte's ward and he's the Queen's confidential agent. I've already told you that, gentlemen. Besides, the Queen's probably done it on purpose. She probably thought it safer to confide in some insignificant person. Important people are always more suspect in affairs of this kind, and the Cardinal's spies are everywhere.'

'You may be right,' conceded Porthos. 'But I suggest that before we do anything we call on the draper himself and drive a hard bargain with him.'

'I don't think there's any need for that,' said d'Artagnan. 'If he doesn't pay us I think we'll find plenty of others who will.'

At this moment there was a noise of hurried footsteps on the stairs. The door was suddenly flung open, and the draper himself came bursting into the room where the four young men were sitting in council.

'Gentlemen,' he cried, 'for pity's sake save me! Four policemen have come to arrest me.'

Porthos and Aramis sprang to their feet.

'Wait a moment,' cried d'Artagnan.

Porthos and Aramis had already half drawn their swords, but d'Artagnan signed to them to resheathe them.

'We've got to be cautious from now on,' he said. 'Don't let's do anything in a hurry.'

'Surely we're not going to allow . . .'

'Leave this to d'Artagnan,' broke in Athos. 'As I said, he's the clever one of us and I'm going to take my orders from him in future. Carry on with your plan, d'Artagnan, and count on me to back you.'

At this moment the four police appeared at the door of the sitting-room. When they saw the four armed musketeers they hesitated on the threshold.

'Come in, gentlemen!' said d'Artagnan. 'This is my room. Come in and make yourselves at home. We're all loyal servants of the King and the Cardinal.'

'In that case, gentlemen,' said the sergeant in charge, 'you won't object to our carrying out our orders at once.'

'Of course not, gentlemen. On the contrary, we're here to support law and order.'

'What the Hell does he think he's doing?' muttered Porthos under his breath.

'You're a nitwit,' whispered Athos. 'Shut up.'

'But you promised . . .' stammered the draper, aghast at d'Artagnan's attitude.

'We can only save you if we're free ourselves,' whispered d'Artagnan to him aside. 'If we tried to defend you they'd send more police and arrest us all.'

'But I thought . . .'

'Come on, gentlemen!' said d'Artagnan, raising his voice. 'We've got no interest in this man. I've never set eyes on him till today, and that was only because he came to ask me for the rent I owed him. Isn't that true, Monsieur Bonacieux?'

'Yes, quite true. But this gentleman hasn't told you . . .'

'For God's sake, be quiet!' whispered d'Artagnan to him aside. 'Don't say a word or you'll ruin us all and you won't help yourself either.'

Then, raising his voice again:

'Come on, gentlemen, take this man off,' he cried.

Upon which he took the wretched draper by the elbow and whisked him into the arms of the police, shouting at him:

'You're a rascal, old fellow. How dare you come and ask money from me, a musketeer! Away with him, gentlemen! To prison with him, and keep him under lock and key as long as you like, with my compliments. That'll teach him to have better manners in future.'

When the police squad finally took their leave and the musketeers were alone again Porthos turned to d'Artagnan.

'What a foul thing to do!' he cried. 'We four musketeers stand and watch an unfortunate man being arrested, without lifting a finger!'

D'Artagnan did not even bother to explain or excuse his conduct to Porthos. Addressing Athos and Aramis he said:

'And now, gentlemen, it's one for all and all for one. That's our motto, and I think we should stick to it.'

'Here, steady on, gentlemen!' protested Porthos.

Athos and Aramis turned on him.

'Put out your hand and swear,' they shouted in chorus.

Porthos had no choice but to yield. He held out his hand but went on muttering angrily to himself. The four friends now repeated in unison the catch-phrase coined by d'Artagnan:

'All for one and one for all!'

'Excellent!' cried d'Artagnan.

Then he continued, taking command instinctively as though he had never done anything but give orders all his life:

'Now, gentlemen, we'd all better return to our quarters. And from now on beware! We've declared war on the great Cardinal himself!'

8
MADAME BONACIEUX

When the police arrest someone who is suspected of a crime, they keep this arrest secret. They post four or five men in ambush in the hall of his house; these men open the door to all callers, close it at once behind them and arrest them. In this way they get all the regular frequenters of the house under lock and key within four or five days of the original arrest. This is what is known as a mouse-trap.

After arresting Monsieur Bonacieux the police proceeded to make his house in the Rue des Fossoyeurs into a mouse-trap. Everyone who came in was seized and cross-examined by the Cardinal's agents. We remember that as well as the main door the house had a side door and passage which led to d'Artagnan's rooms on the first floor, so his callers came and went unmolested.

While Athos, Porthos, and Aramis had been out on the prowl, d'Artagnan had ensconced himself in his room, which he had converted into an observation post. From his windows he could see all the callers at the front door and knew in this way who had fallen into the trap. Besides this he had dislodged one or two of the flagstones of the floor of his room and had scraped away the woodwork underneath until there was only one thin strip of board between him and the room below, where the police inquiries were taking place. By putting his ear to this hole in the floor he could hear everything that was said by the police agents and the prisoners.

The cross-examinations always began with a demand for particulars of the lives and occupations of the accused and ended with the following three questions:

'Has Madame Bonacieux ever given you anything to hand to her husband or to anybody else?'

'Has Monsieur Bonacieux ever given you anything to hand to his wife or to anybody else?'

'Has either of them ever let you into any secret?'

D'Artagnan argued that the police would not cross-examine the prisoners in that way if they knew anything. But what were they trying to find out? Probably whether the Duke of Buckingham was actually in Paris and whether he had had or was about to have a secret meeting with the Queen.

It was now the evening of the day following the unfortunate Monsieur Bonacieux's arrest. Nine o'clock had just struck. Athos had that moment left d'Artagnan to answer the roll-call at Monsieur de Tréville's house, and Planchet was about to prepare his master's bed for the night. Suddenly there was a knock on the street door. It was quickly opened from inside and closed again. Some fresh mouse had just fallen into the trap.

D'Artagnan lay down flat on his stomach, put his ear to the hole in the floor and listened.

Soon he heard screams coming from below; then half-stifled moans. This time there was no cross-questioning.

'Ye Gods!' muttered d'Artagnan. 'I don't mind betting it's a woman they've got hold of. They're trying to search her and she's resisting. They're using violence, the brutes!'

And it was all our hero could do not to cast caution to the winds and start thumping on the floor in protest.

'But I tell you I'm the mistress of this house!' cried the

unfortunate woman. 'I tell you I'm Madame Bonacieux. I work for the Queen.'

'Madame Bonacieux!' muttered d'Artagnan. 'By Jove, I'm in luck! I've found what the whole town's looking for.'

'You're the very woman we've been wanting,' said the officers of the law.

The woman's voice sounded more and more strained. Then there was a great crash which made the walls of the house shake. Madame Bonacieux was struggling as hard as any woman can struggle against four men.

'Please, gentlemen, please!' she cried. Then followed a few inarticulate sounds and then silence.

'They're gagging her! They're going to take her off with them!' cried d'Artagnan, springing up from the floor like a jack-in-the-box. 'My sword! Good! It's here! Planchet!'

'Sir?'

'Run and fetch Athos, Porthos and Aramis. One of them's bound to be at home – perhaps all of them. Tell them to come along at once, armed. Oh, I remember now. Athos is with Monsieur de Tréville.'

'But where are you going, Sir?'

'I'm going to jump down from the window,' cried d'Artagnan. 'It's quicker that way. You put back the flagstones, sweep the floor, go out by the side door and do as I told you.'

'Oh, Sir! You'll kill yourself!' cried Planchet.

'Nonsense,' said d'Artagnan.

Then, hanging on by his hands to the window-sill, he proceeded to let himself down from the first floor on to the street without even grazing his fingers.

Then he went and knocked on the front door of the house, muttering:

'I'll let myself be caught in the police trap like the others. But if they try and get their claws into this mouse . . . well, they'll get something they didn't bargain for.'

At the sound of the knocking the noise inside the house died down. D'Artagnan heard footsteps approach. The door was flung open and our hero rushed into Monsieur Bonacieux's room with drawn sword. The door of the room swung to sharply behind him; a spring had obviously been attached to it.

D'Artagnan did not have a hard fight, for only one of the police-officers was armed and he had only put up a show of fighting. The three others had tried to fell the young man with chairs, stools and chinaware, but the Gascon had given them a scratch or two with his sword which had effectively subdued them. After ten minutes' combat the whole bunch had scuttled off, and d'Artagnan had remained victorious on the battlefield.

The neighbours had opened their windows and watched the affray with the indifference common to Parisians of that date, who were accustomed to constant street brawls and riots. When they saw the four men in black leave the house they closed their windows again; their instincts told them that the trouble was over for the time being.

D'Artagnan was now alone in the room with Madame Bonacieux and turned to look at her. The wretched woman had collapsed into an armchair and was almost unconscious. D'Artagnan ran his eye over her quickly. She was a charming young woman of about twenty-five, dark-haired, blue-eyed, with a slightly tip-tilted nose, dazzling white teeth and a clear, fair complexion. In those respects she was every bit the equal of any lady of rank, but there the resemblance ended. Her hands were white but coarse, and her feet also betrayed her humbler position in life. Fortunately d'Artagnan was not yet concerned with these minor details of his protégée's appearance.

He was kneeling down beside the lady and trying to revive her when he suddenly noticed on the floor at her feet a handkerchief made of the finest cambric. His inquisitive nature prompted him to pick it up and examine it. In one of the corners he saw a monogram; it was the same monogram that he had seen on Aramis' handkerchief, and he remembered how his interference on that occasion had nearly involved him in a duel to the death.

Ever since then he had had a wholesome respect for handkerchiefs with monograms on them. So he gently slipped this handkerchief back into the pocket of Madame Bonacieux's dress.

At that moment Madame Bonacieux regained consciousness. She opened her eyes, gave a terrified glance round the room and saw to her relief that she was alone with her rescuer. She at once smiled and held out her hands to him. Madame Bonacieux had the most engaging smile in the world.

'Oh, Sir,' she said, 'is it you who saved my life? Thank you, thank you for what you've done.'

'I only did what any other man would have done in my place, so you don't owe me any thanks at all.'

'I do, indeed, Sir, and I hope to be able to prove to you that I'm not ungrateful. But what on earth were those men after? I thought at first they were housebreakers. And why isn't my husband here?'

'Those men weren't housebreakers, Madame Bonacieux,' answered d'Artagnan gravely, 'but they were equally dangerous in quite another way. They were the Cardinal's agents and I can easily explain why your husband isn't here. The police came yesterday to arrest him and took him off to the Bastille.'

'My husband in the Bastille?' cried Madame Bonacieux. 'Oh, how terrible! What could they want with him? What crime has he committed? He's as innocent as the day!'

'Your husband has committed no crime, Madame

Bonacieux,' answered d'Artagnan, 'apart from being your husband, which I should have said was a privilege but which apparently has its disadvantages.'

'But, Sir, do you mean to say you know . . . ?'

'I know you've been kidnapped, Madame Bonacieux.'

'Oh, you know that, do you? And d'you know who kidnapped me? If so, for Heaven's sake tell me.'

'A man of about forty-five, with black hair, a sallow skin, and a scar on his left cheek.'

'That's right. But who is he?'

'Ah, that I don't know.'

'And did my husband know I'd been kidnapped?'

'Yes. The man himself wrote him a letter telling him about it.'

'And has my husband any theory as to why I was kidnapped?' asked Madame Bonacieux, blushing slightly.

'I think he suspected some political motive.'

'I suspected that myself from the first, and now I know it. So it never occurred to my dear, worthy husband that there might be some other reason for my disappearance . . .'

'Far from it, Madame Bonacieux. He was too confident in your good sense and in your attachment to him to suppose that for a moment.'

Another faint flicker of a smile passed across Madame Bonacieux's face.

'But how did you manage to escape?' went on d'Artagnan.

'They left me alone for a while. I'd already discovered the reason for my kidnapping, so I made a rope by knotting my bedsheets together and let myself down from my prison window. Then I came running here, hoping to find my husband.'

'To get him to protect you?'

'Oh, no! The poor fellow's quite incapable of that. But

he could have been of use to us in another way, so I wanted to let him know.'

'Let him know what?'

'Ah, that I can't tell you. It's not my secret.'

'No,' said d'Artagnan. 'Besides, though this may sound rather a cowardly thing for a soldier to say, we've got to be careful. This room's not a healthy place to sit and exchange confidences in. The four men I drove out just now are bound to return with reinforcements. If they find us here we're lost. I did send my servant to bring three of my friends along, but he may not have found them.'

'You're quite right,' said Madame Bonacieux, frightened once more. 'We mustn't stay here. We must get away at once.'

As she spoke she slipped her arm under d'Artagnan's arm and tried to drag him out of the room.

'But where can we go?' asked d'Artagnan. 'What safe place is there?'

'Let's first get well away from here and then we can think it over.'

And without even troubling to shut the front door the young couple ran quickly out of the house, down the Rue des Fossoyeurs, from there into the Rue des Fosses-Monsieur-le-Prince and on as far as the Place Saint Sulpice.

'And now what are we going to do?' asked d'Artagnan. 'Where do you want me to take you?'

'I don't honestly know where to go. What I'd meant to do was to get my husband to find out from Monsieur de Laporte what had been happening at the Louvre in my absence and whether it was safe for me to go back there.'

'Why shouldn't I go and see Monsieur de Laporte?'

'Because they know Monsieur Bonacieux at the Louvre and would have let him in. But they don't know you, and they'd only shut the gate in your face. It's unfortunate, but there it is.'

'Oh, come now! There must be some porter at one of the gates of the Louvre who's devoted to you and who'd open it to me if you gave me some password . . .'

Madame Bonacieux looked searchingly at the young man.

'And suppose I did give you the password, would you forget it again the moment you'd used it?'

'On my word of honour!' said d'Artagnan, with an unmistakable note of sincerity in his voice.

'Very well, I believe you. You look to me like a man one can trust. Besides, if you help us you'll more than likely be rewarded.'

'I'll always serve the King and help the Queen, not for any reward but because it's my duty,' said d'Artagnan. 'So use me as you would a friend.'

'And where will you hide me in the meanwhile?'

'Is there no house you can go to until Monsieur de Laporte sends for you?'

'No. There's no one I can trust.'

'We're only about a hundred yards from Athos' lodgings. You might go and wait there.'

'Who's Athos?'

'One of my friends.'

'Very well. Let's go to your friend's lodgings. Where are they?'

'In the Rue Férou, about a hundred yards away.'

'Come on then.'

And the two of them set off again. Athos was out, as d'Artagnan had said. The landlady handed over the key of his room without question, as d'Artagnan was such a regular visitor to the house. The two callers went upstairs and d'Artagnan showed Madame Bonacieux into Athos' room.

'Make yourself at home in here,' he said. 'Lock the door from the inside and don't open it unless you hear three knocks like this . . .' And he knocked three times;

two loud knocks in quick succession, then a pause and a third gentle knock.

'Good. I'll remember that,' said Madame Bonacieux. 'And now it's my turn to give you instructions.'

'Carry on,' said d'Artagnan.

'Go to the Rue de l'Échelle entrance to the Louvre and ask for Germain.'

'Right. And then?'

'He'll ask you what you want and you must answer these three words: "Tours and Brussels". Then he'll do anything for you.'

'What shall I ask him to do?'

'Tell him to fetch Monsieur de Laporte, the Queen's Gentleman-in-Waiting, and when Monsieur de Laporte comes send him to me.'

'Very well. But when and how shall I see you again?'

'Do you want very much to see me again?'

'Yes.'

'Well, leave that part to me, and don't worry.'

'May I count on your promise?'

'Yes.'

D'Artagnan bowed to Madame Bonacieux, giving her such a look of love that the heart of any woman less preoccupied with her own affairs than the little draper's wife would have melted at once. When he was on his way downstairs he heard the door being shut behind him and the key being turned twice in the lock.

Everything went off as Madame Bonacieux had prophesied. When d'Artagnan gave the password Germain bowed and asked his instructions. Ten minutes later Monsieur de Laporte was in the porter's lodge. D'Artagnan told him the whole story in a few words and gave him the address of the house where Madame Bonacieux was hidden. Laporte asked him to repeat it twice for safety's sake, and then started off towards the house at a great rate.

D'Artagnan took a very circuitous route home and appeared to be lost in thought. Our hero, usually so alert and observant, this time actually lost his way and wandered along unfamiliar streets, seeming not to care very much where he was, looking up at the stars and alternately sighing and smiling to himself. What was the cause of this sudden transformation in the young man's character, and what was he thinking of so deeply?

He was thinking of Madame Bonacieux. For a musketeer apprentice the young woman was almost an ideal object of affection. She was pretty, mysterious and initiated into many Court secrets, which made her additionally glamorous in the eyes of a socially ambitious young man from the provinces. She appeared to be not unresponsive to admiration, and this is always encouraging to a novice in the art of love. Moreover d'Artagnan had rescued her from the clutches of those fiends who had wanted to search and use violence on her, and this had established a bond between them, a bond made doubly strong by the fact that the incident which had been the cause of it could not be confided to anyone. Thus the stage was admirably set for a romantic attachment, and it was almost inevitable that the regard which d'Artagnan and Madame Bonacieux at present felt for each other should soon ripen into some more tender sentiment.

Eventually, d'Artagnan found himself in the district where Aramis lived and it occurred to him that he ought to visit his friend and explain why he had sent Planchet to him with that peremptory summons. If Aramis had been at home when Planchet called he had obviously gone off to the police-trap in the Rue des Fossoyeurs, and having found no one there except perhaps his two companions, must have been puzzled – indeed, they must all have been puzzled – about the reason for the summons. D'Artagnan felt that he owed them an explanation for having disturbed them.

D'Artagnan had just passed the Rue Cassette and could already see his friend's house ahead of him, surrounded by sycamore trees and covered almost entirely by clematis, when he noticed a ghost-like figure coming out of the Rue Servandoni. This ghost-like figure was wrapped in a cloak, and d'Artagnan at first thought it was a man. But after a while he realized from its size that it must be a woman. Moreover the woman was apparently uncertain of her way; she kept looking up to take her bearings, stopping, turning back and walking on again. D'Artagnan's interest was aroused.

'Shall I go up and offer to help her?' thought he. 'She's young; one can tell that by her walk: she may be pretty, too. How exciting! But on second thoughts no woman's likely to be out in the street at this time of night unless she's going to meet her lover, in which case it would be more tactful to leave her alone. Damnation!'

Meanwhile the young woman was coming nearer and nearer, counting the houses and windows as she walked. D'Artagnan thought she must soon find the house she wanted; there were only three houses in that part of the street and two windows overlooking the street itself; one belonged to a detached villa opposite the house occupied by Aramis, the other was Aramis' own window.

'Ye Gods!' thought the young man, remembering Aramis and the theologian's niece. 'Might this lovely daughter of the night be calling on our friend? It looks astonishingly like it. This time, Aramis old boy, I really am going to discover something about you.'

The woman came closer and closer. There was now no

doubt that she was young; her light step betrayed
her and at that moment she coughed, a clear, fresh
cough. D'Artagnan thought this cough was probably a
signal.

Either this signal had been answered, or the young
night wanderer had suddenly identified the house, for
she now stepped boldly up to Aramis' window and
rapped three times on the shutter.

'That's Aramis' window all right!' muttered
d'Artagnan to himself. 'Ha, ha, you old hypocrite! So
much for your theology, my boy!'

The knocks on the shutter were immediately
answered. The casement window was opened from
inside and a light shone through the cracks in the shutter.

'Oh!' thought the eavesdropper. 'So the lady was
expected! Now the shutter will be opened and she'll
climb in through the window. Very neat.'

But to d'Artagnan's amazement the shutter remained
closed. Moreover the light which had flickered for a
moment inside the house disappeared and everything
was now in darkness again.

D'Artagnan felt certain that something more was
bound to happen, so he remained where he was,
straining his eyes and ears in order to miss nothing.

He was right; a few seconds later someone inside the
house gave two sharp knocks.

The young woman in the street knocked once in reply
and the shutter was half opened from inside.

Needless to say d'Artagnan stood watching and
listening with the greatest interest.

The young man now observed the lady pull something
white out of her pocket and quickly unfold it – a handkerchief. She then held up one corner of it to the person
inside the house.

D'Artagnan was at once reminded of the handkerchief
which he had found at Madame Bonacieux's feet, which

in its turn had reminded him of the one he had found at Aramis' feet.

What could be the meaning of this handkerchief?

In his present position d'Artagnan could not see Aramis' face. (He was, of course, convinced that it could be no one but Aramis who was having this tryst with the lady.) Curiosity now prevailed over caution and, seeing that the attention of the two conspirators was closely fixed on the handkerchief, the young man darted like lightning out of his hiding-place and squeezed up against the wall at a spot from which he could see clearly inside the room.

What he saw surprised him so much that he almost cried out. It was not Aramis inside the room after all; it was a woman. Unfortunately he could not see her face but only her clothes.

At that moment the woman inside the house pulled a second handkerchief out of her pocket and the two women exchanged handkerchiefs. Then another short conversation ensued, after which the shutter was closed again. The woman outside the window turned and walked down the street, passing within a few feet of d'Artagnan. She drew the hood of her cloak over her head, but not in time to prevent d'Artagnan catching a glimpse of her face. He saw to his amazement that it was Madame Bonacieux.

The idea that it might be Madame Bonacieux had already flashed across the young man's mind when he saw her producing the handkerchief from her pocket. But he had dismissed it as absurd. Was it likely that after summoning Monsieur de Laporte to escort her safely back to the Louvre Madame Bonacieux would then go out and tramp the streets alone at night, and run the risk of being kidnapped a second time?

Now he had seen her with his own eyes. He guessed at once that only something very important could have tempted her out. And what, he argued, is the most important thing to a woman of twenty-five? Love, of course.

But was it for her own sake or for someone else's sake that she was thus endangering her life? The young man pondered this question deeply. The demon of jealousy gnawed at his heart as though he were already Madame Bonacieux's accepted lover.

He realized that it would be quite easy to find out where she was going simply by following her. And this he proceeded to do as though by instinct.

But when Madame Bonacieux saw the young man emerging from the wall like a statue stepping off its pedestal and when she heard the noise of his footsteps behind her she cried out and started running down the street like a hunted hare.

D'Artagnan set off in pursuit of her. It did not take him long to overtake her, handicapped as she was by her long cloak. She had darted down an alley, and he caught up with her after about a hundred yards. The unfortunate creature was exhausted, not by her exertions but by sheer terror, and when d'Artagnan laid his hand on her shoulder she fell on one knee and cried out in a strangled voice:

'Kill me if you must. I'll tell you nothing.'

D'Artagnan put his arm round her waist and lifted her up. Then he realized from the dead weight of her body that she was on the point of fainting, so to reassure her he told her of his love for her. But this did not reassure her at all: men who swear undying love sometimes have the worst intentions in the world. In this case, however, the voice was everything. Madame Bonacieux recognized it at once; she opened her eyes, saw d'Artagnan and gave a cry of relief.

'Oh, it's you!' she said. 'God be praised!'

'Yes,' said d'Artagnan. 'And God has sent me to protect you.'

'Was that why you were following me, in order to protect me?' cried Madame Bonacieux, smiling mischievously. Now that she knew that her pursuer was a friend her fears vanished and the flirtatious side of her nature reasserted itself.

'No,' said d'Artagnan, 'I admit that was not the reason. My meeting you tonight was a mere chance. I saw a woman knocking on my friend's window.'

'Your friend's window?' interrupted Madame Bonacieux.

'Yes. Aramis is one of my best friends.'

'Aramis? Who's Aramis?'

'Oh, come now! You're not going to tell me you don't know Aramis.'

'Know him? I've never even heard of him!'

'You mean this is the first time you've ever been to that house?'

'Certainly.'

'And you didn't know there was a young man living there?'

'No.'

'So it wasn't him you were looking for?'

'Of course not. You saw yourself who I was talking to: a woman.'

'Who was the woman?'

'I can't tell you that; I should be giving someone else away.'

'Dearest Madame Bonacieux, you're a most charming person, but if I may say so, you're extremely mysterious too.'

'Does that make me less attractive?'

'No, more. You're altogether adorable.'

'Give me your arm then.'

'With pleasure, dear Madame Bonacieux. And now what?'

'Now you can take me where I want to go.'

'Where's that?'

'You'll see when we get there.'

'Shall I have to wait for you there?'

'No.'

'Are you going home alone, then?'

'Perhaps. Perhaps not.'

'I see. You may have someone with you. Will it be a man or a woman?'

'I don't know yet.'

'I'll find out, all right.'

'How?'

'I'll wait and watch you come out.'

'Oh, in that case good-bye!'

'What d'you mean?'

'I don't need you. I can manage quite well alone.'

'But you wanted . . .'

'I wanted to be helped by a gentleman, not dogged by a spy.'

'That's putting it a bit strongly.'

'Well, how would you describe people who follow others unasked?'

'I'd say they were a bit inquisitive, perhaps.'

'That's putting it much too mildly.'

'Very well, Madame Bonacieux. I see I shall have to obey you in everything.'

D'Artagnan offered his arm to Madame Bonacieux. Half-laughing, half-trembling she put her arm through his and together they walked to the far end of the Rue de la Harpe. Here she seemed to hesitate, as she had done in the Rue du Vaugirard. She examined several doors and at last seemed to recognize one from certain marks on it. Turning to d'Artagnan she said:

'And now, Sir, I've got some private business in this house. Many, many thanks for coming with me and protecting me. Now please remember your promise and go.'

'You won't be frightened coming back by yourself?'

'Apart from thieves, there's nothing to be frightened of.'

'Well, are they nothing?'

'They can't take anything from me. I've got nothing worth taking.'

'What about that embroidered handkerchief with the monogram on it?'

'Be quiet, be quiet, will you!' cried the young woman in terror. 'You'll ruin us all, you miserable man!'

'Ah, I thought so! You're not nearly so safe as you pretend to be. You get frightened at the mere mention of a handkerchief! And you admit that if anyone heard us talking about it, we'd be lost. Dearest Madame Bonacieux,' cried d'Artagnan, seizing her hand impulsively, and giving her an adoring look, 'be more generous. Take me into your confidence. Look at me! Can't you see how I love you, how I long to share the secrets of your heart?'

'Yes,' said Madame Bonacieux, 'and I reply that I'd gladly share my secrets with you, but other people's secrets, no.'

'I think I've already got a clue to your secret,' went on d'Artagnan. 'Only three months ago I nearly fought a duel with Aramis over a handkerchief very like the one you showed the woman in that house. I don't mind betting it had the same initials on it.'

'Please don't try and probe into things,' said the young woman. 'You only upset me.'

'But do listen, Madame Bonacieux. You're very clever and you must realize that if you were arrested with that handkerchief on you you'd be badly compromised.'

'Not at all. It's got my initials on it. C. B.: Constance Bonacieux.'

'Or Camille de Bois-Tracy.'

'Be quiet, will you, you terrible man!' cried the young

woman, again terrified. 'But I see my safety doesn't mean much to you, or you'd be more careful. So I can only advise you to be careful for your own sake.'

'For my sake?'

'Yes. You could be sent to prison, beheaded even, merely for having known me.'

'In that case I'll never leave you from now on.'

'Sir, I implore you to go,' said the young woman, clasping her hands and looking at d'Artagnan in an agony of entreaty. 'In the name of Heaven, go! I appeal to your honour as a soldier and a gentleman! Listen, there's twelve o'clock striking. That's the hour they're expecting me.'

'Don't worry! I'm off,' said d'Artagnan. 'I trust you. I want to get full credit for my devotion, even though it may be foolish. Good-bye Madame Bonacieux, good-bye.'

And the young man gave his adored one a final look of love and then turned and walked off down the street. He had only gone a few steps when he heard her give three gentle knocks on the door of the house. On reaching the corner of the street he turned and looked back; the door had already opened and closed again and Madame Bonacieux had disappeared.

D'Artagnan walked straight on. He had given his word that he would not spy on Madame Bonacieux, and he meant to keep to it, even though she might be in the most deadly peril. He was sad to think that she did not need his help, but this was a grief he would have to bear.

'Poor Athos,' he muttered to himself. 'He'll either have gone to sleep waiting for me or he'll have returned home, in which case he'll discover there's been a woman in his rooms. A woman in the great Athos' rooms! And he so grand and aloof! What next! But, come to think of it, there was one in Aramis' room too. The whole business is very mysterious, and I wish to God I knew how it would turn out.'

'It'll turn out badly, Sir, mark my words,' said a voice which the young man recognized as Planchet's. He had been so occupied with his thoughts that he had forgotten his surroundings. Now he was surprised to find himself standing in front of his own doorstep and disconcerted to think that he had been expressing his thoughts aloud.

'What d'you mean, idiot?' he said to Planchet. 'Why should it turn out badly? What's been happening?'

'All sorts of terrible things, Sir!'

'What things?'

'In the first place Monsieur Athos has been arrested.'

'Arrested? Athos arrested? What on earth for?'

'They found him in your rooms. They mistook him for you.'

'Who arrested him?'

'The police. The four men in black whom you turned out came back with them.'

'But why didn't Athos say who he was? Why didn't he just say he knew nothing about it?'

'Monsieur Athos was too clever for that. In fact he let himself be arrested on purpose. As they were taking him off he whispered to me: "It's better your master should be free at this moment than I. He knows everything and I know nothing. They'll think they've got him safely under arrest and that'll give him time to act. I'll go on pretending to be d'Artagnan for three days; after that I'll tell them who I am and they'll have to release me."'

'Good old Athos! Well done! That's just like him. And what did the police do with him?'

'Five of them took him off, I don't know where; either to the Bastille or to the For-l'Evêque. Two stayed behind with the men in black; they made a thorough search of the room and removed all the papers. The last two stood on guard at the door while the others were ransacking the room, and finally the whole lot packed up, leaving the house empty and all the doors and windows open.'

'And what about Porthos and Aramis?'

'They never came. I didn't find them.'

'But I presume you left my message for them, so they may turn up at any moment.'

'Yes, Sir.'

'Good. And don't you stir from here. If they come, tell them the news and ask them to meet me at the Pomme-de-Pin tavern. It would be dangerous to meet here; the house is probably being watched. I'm going off now to see Monsieur de Tréville and tell him the news; I'll join them after that.'

'Very good, Sir,' said Planchet.

'You'll stay here, won't you? You won't get frightened by yourself?' asked d'Artagnan.

'Don't worry, Sir,' said Planchet. 'I'll do anything to prove my loyalty to you.'

'Good lad,' said d'Artagnan.

He now made his way to the Rue du Vieux Colombier as fast as his legs would carry him, tired as they were after all the running he had done that day.

Monsieur de Tréville was not at home; his company of musketeers had been summoned to the Louvre to do guard duty and he had gone with them.

D'Artagnan was determined at all costs to see Monsieur de Tréville and report what had happened. So he decided to try and get into the Louvre, hoping that his guardsman's uniform would serve as a passport. He made his way along the Rue des Petits-Augustins with the intention of crossing the river by the Pont Neuf. He thought for a moment of crossing by the ferry, but then remembered that he had no money to pay the fare. When he reached the corner of the Rue Guénégaud he noticed two people, a man and a woman, coming out of the Rue Dauphiné. His attention was at once arrested for there was something familiar about them. The woman had the figure and walk of Madame Bonacieux and the man was exactly the build of Aramis. Moreover the man was wearing musketeer's uniform. The woman had pulled the hood of her cloak over her head and the man was holding his handkerchief in front of his face; It was obvious that they did not wish to be recognized.

The pair started to walk across the bridge. That was the way d'Artagnan happened to be going, so he followed them at a discreet distance. As he walked along he became more and more obsessed by the idea that the woman was Madame Bonacieux and the man Aramis. And as he watched him he felt the pangs of jealousy gnawing at his heart.

He had been doubly betrayed, by his friend and by the woman whom he already loved like a mistress. Madame Bonacieux had sworn by all she held most dear that she did not know Aramis, and here she was half an hour later walking arm in arm with him!

The young man and woman noticed that they were being followed and quickened their pace. D'Artagnan started running, got ahead of them and turned back to meet them as they reached La Samaritaine, where a street lamp shone, lighting up all that part of the bridge. He stopped in front of them and barred their way.

'What do you want, Sir?' asked the musketeer, retreating a step. He spoke with a foreign accent, and d'Artagnan at once realized that he had been mistaken in at least one half of his suppositions.

'So you're not Aramis!' he cried.

'No, Sir, I'm not Aramis. I see you've been mistaking me for somebody else. That explains and I suppose excuses your extraordinary behaviour. So we'll say no more about it. And now please let us pass.'

'Just a moment, Sir. I may not be concerned with you but I am concerned with this lady here.'

'This lady? You don't know her!'

'On the contrary! I know her very well.'

'Oh, Sir!' cried Madame Bonacieux, highly indignant. 'You gave me your word as a soldier and a gentleman! I thought I could trust you!'

D'Artagnan suddenly felt ashamed.

'Well, ma'am, you did promise . . .' he stammered.

'Come, ma'am, take my arm and let's get on,' said the stranger.

D'Artagnan was by now utterly bewildered. He stood motionless in the middle of the road, still barring the way to Madame Bonacieux and the musketeer.

The musketeer now stepped forward angrily and tried to push d'Artagnan aside with his arm. This insult brought our hero to his senses. He leapt back and drew his sword, at which the stranger quickly drew his, and the two naked blades gleamed in the moonlight.

'Stop, stop, Your Grace, this is lunacy!' cried Madame Bonacieux, throwing herself between the two men and grasping the two naked blades, one in each hand.

'Your Grace?' echoed d'Artagnan in amazement. 'Did you say Your Grace?'

Madame Bonacieux, in her excitement, had let slip a vital clue. The truth suddenly dawned on d'Artagnan and he cursed himself for his folly in not having realized it earlier.

'I ask your pardon, Sir!' he said. 'Is it possible you're . . . ?'

'The Duke of Buckingham,' whispered Madame Bonacieux. 'And now we shall all be ruined if . . .'

'Your Grace! Madame Bonacieux!' cried d'Artagnan. 'I ask you both to forgive me. The fact is, Sir, I'm in love, and I was jealous. You know what it is to be in love, Sir. Please forgive me, and tell me how I can best serve Your Grace.'

'You're a good fellow,' said Buckingham, holding out his hand to d'Artagnan, who took it respectfully. 'You say you'd like to do me a service, so I'll take you at your word. Follow us to the Louvre, keeping about ten yards behind us all the way. If you see anyone spying on us, kill him.'

D'Artagnan was thrilled to have the chance of serving the great and famous Duke of Buckingham, Charles I's trusted minister. He unsheathed his sword and slipped the naked blade under his arm, waited until the Duke and Madame Bonacieux had got ten yards ahead and then followed them, prepared to obey the Duke's instructions to the letter. Fortunately there was no occasion for the young hired assassin to commit any act of violence to prove his devotion. Madame Bonacieux and her handsome escort in musketeer's uniform reached the Louvre in safety and were admitted by the Échelle Gate without question.

For the Duke of Buckingham, the risk was worth taking. He loved Anne of Austria, the Queen of France, with all his heart, and knew that only her position prevented her returning his love. He was well aware that the letter had been sent by the Cardinal to trap him, but he had to see her just once before returning to England. He was prepared even to bring England into alliance with the anti-Royalist Protestants of La Rochelle, so that as the English ambassador he might openly come to Paris and have a chance of seeing her. In appreciation of his devotion, the Queen gave him a little rosewood box, which contained twelve diamond tags, a recent gift to her from the King. Then he was gone.

When d'Artagnan had seen them safely inside the palace he went straight off to the Pomme-de-Pin tavern, where he found Porthos and Aramis waiting for him. He did not bother to explain the reason for his earlier summons, but merely told them that, having at first thought he would need their help, he had later decided he could manage the business better alone, and that they could return home.

10

THE MAN OF MEUNG

Meanwhile, Monsieur Bonacieux had been taken off to the Bastille and interrogated. The magistrate, acting on the orders of the Cardinal, suspected him of knowing all about his wife's affairs and getting d'Artagnan to help his wife escape; he thought he would surprise the little draper into confession, by confronting him with d'Artagnan. However, this only confused matters since, of course, it was Athos who was brought in. The next day the terrified draper, convinced he was being taken away for execution, was escorted from prison, taken by coach to the Rue des Bons-Enfants and led, half-fainting, to an upstairs room.

He found himself in a large office, the walls of which were curiously adorned with an assortment of weapons. The room was stuffy as there was a fire burning in the grate, although it was not yet October. In the middle of the room was a square table, covered with books and papers, over which was spread a huge map of the town of La Rochelle.

In front of the fireplace stood a man of medium build but of commanding presence. He had shrewd eyes, a high forehead, and a thin, drawn face, and he wore a small beard which made his face look even longer than it was. He was not more than thirty-six or thirty-seven years old, and yet his moustache and beard were already greying. He carried no sword and yet he looked every inch a soldier, and his buff boots had dust on them, which showed that he had quite recently been in the saddle.

This man was Armand Jean Duplessis, Cardinal Richelieu.

The little draper remained standing near the wall, thoroughly cowed, while the stranger by the mantelpiece fixed his penetrating gaze on him, as though he would read his very thoughts.

'Is this the man Bonacieux?' he asked after a moment's silence.

'Yes, Monseigneur,' replied the officer who had brought Bonacieux.

'Good. Just hand me his papers and go.'

The officer took the papers off the table, handed them to the stranger by the mantelpiece, bowed low and left the room.

Bonacieux recognized the papers as the forms which the magistrate at the Bastille had filled in in answer to his questions. Every now and then the stranger by the fireplace would look up from these papers and fix his eyes on Bonacieux; so fierce was his gaze that the wretched man felt his knees quake beneath him.

The Cardinal took about ten minutes to read the files and ten seconds to examine his prisoner and was then apparently satisfied.

'That man's no conspirator,' he said to himself. 'He hasn't the wit for it. However, I'll question him first to make sure.'

'Monsieur Bonacieux, the charge against you's high treason,' he said, speaking slowly and sternly.

'So they told me, Monseigneur,' cried Bonacieux, addressing his examiner by the title used by the officer. 'But I swear I knew nothing about it.'

The Cardinal smiled inwardly at this.

'You plotted with your wife, with Madame de Chevreuse, and with His Grace the Duke of Buckingham.'

'I certainly heard my wife mention those names,' answered the draper.

'In what connection?'

'She said that Cardinal Richelieu had lured the Duke of Buckingham to Paris in order to expose him and the Queen with him.'

'Oh, she said that, did she?' cried the Cardinal furiously.

'Yes, Monseigneur. But I told her she shouldn't say such things, that the Cardinal wouldn't stoop so low as that . . .'

'Hold your tongue, Sir. You're a fool,' interrupted the Cardinal.

'That's just what my wife said, Monseigneur.'

'D'you know who kidnapped your wife?'

'No, Monseigneur.'

'But I understand you suspect somebody.'

'I did, Monseigneur. And I confided my suspicions to the magistrate. But what I said only seemed to annoy him, so I don't suspect anyone now.'

'Your wife's escaped. Did you know that?'

'No, Monseigneur. I only heard about it when I was in prison, and then only because the magistrate was good enough to tell me. A most kind and considerate man, the magistrate, if I may say so, Sir.'

At this the Cardinal again smiled to himself.

'So you don't know where your wife went after she escaped?'

'I haven't a notion, Monseigneur. I can only suppose that she returned to the Louvre.'

'She hadn't returned at one o'clock this morning.'

'Oh dear, oh dear! Where can she have got to?'

'We'll find out, never fear. The Cardinal finds out everything sooner or later. He knows everything.'

'In that case, Monseigneur, d'you think the Cardinal will consent to tell me where my wife is?'

'He may. But first of all you must tell us everything you know about your wife's connection with Madame de Chevreuse.'

'I know nothing about it, Sir. I've never seen Madame de Chevreuse.'

'When you went to fetch your wife from the Louvre did you always go straight home with her?'

'No, hardly ever. She always had a call or two to make at drapers' shops with orders for the Queen.'

'How many of these drapers' shops were there?'

'Two, sir.'

'Where were they?'

'One was in the Rue de Vaugirard; the other in the Rue de la Harpe.'

'D'you know the numbers?'

'Yes. 25 Rue de Vaugirard and 75 Rue de la Harpe.'

'Excellent,' said the Cardinal.

He now rang a little silver bell which stood on the table in front of him, and the officer came in.

The Cardinal spoke to him aside.

'Go and find Rochefort,' he said. 'If he's already back bring him in here at once.'

'Count de Rochefort's here,' answered the officer, 'and wants to see Your Eminence urgently.'

'Bring him in, then, and hurry,' said the Cardinal sharply.

The officer left the room with the alacrity which distinguished all the Cardinal's servants.

'His Eminence!' muttered Bonacieux under his breath, looking thoroughly scared. 'So it's the Cardinal himself!'

In a minute or two the door opened again and a new visitor was ushered in.

'That's the man!' cried Bonacieux.

'What man?' asked the Cardinal.

'The man who kidnapped my wife.'

The Cardinal rang the bell a second time, and again the officer came in.

'Put the prisoner Bonacieux in charge again,' said the Cardinal, 'and keep him here until I send for him.'

'No, Monseigneur, no! That's not the man after all,' cried Bonacieux in terror. 'I was wrong. The man who kidnapped my wife was quite different – nothing like this gentleman at all. This gentleman's a good, honest gentleman – anybody could tell that . . .'

'Take this idiot away,' cried the Cardinal.

The officer took Bonacieux by the arm, led him back into the ante-room and handed him over to two guards.

The new arrival watched impatiently until the rat-like figure of Bonacieux had left the room. The moment the door closed he turned to the Cardinal and said sharply:

'They've been seeing each other.'

'Who?' asked the Cardinal.

'She and he.'

'The Queen and the Duke?' cried Richelieu.

'Yes.'

'Where?'

'At the Louvre.'

'You're sure of that?'

'Positive.'

'Who told you?'

'Madame de Lannoy, who's absolutely trustworthy.'

'Well, that's that! We've been outwitted. Now we must get our revenge.'

'I needn't tell you, Monseigneur, that you can count on my loyal support in everything.'

'How was the meeting arranged?'

'Just after midnight, when the Queen was in her bedroom with her ladies-in-waiting, a messenger came in with a handkerchief. Apparently one of the Queen's maids had given it to him to give to Her Majesty.'

'Well?'

'When the Queen saw the handkerchief she was terribly upset and went deathly pale.'

'Go on!'

'She got up and in a stifled voice said to her ladies, "Wait for me please, I'll be back in ten minutes." She then left the room.'

'How long did the Queen stay away?'

'Three quarters of an hour.'

'And did she return to her room after that?'

'Yes, but only to fetch a little rosewood box with her initials on it. She then went out again.'

'And when she returned later did she bring the rosewood box back with her?'

'No.'

'Does Madame de Lannoy know what was in the box?'

'Yes. The diamond tags which the King gave the Queen for her birthday.'

'And you say she returned without the box?'

'Yes.'

'Does Madame de Lannoy think she gave the box to Buckingham?'

'She's convinced of it.'

'What makes her so sure?'

'In her capacity as Mistress of the Robes she spent the next day searching for the box, pretended to be greatly concerned about its loss and finally mentioned the matter to the Queen.'

'And what did the Queen do?'

'She looked extremely embarrassed and invented

some story about having broken one of the tags the previous day and having sent the box to her jeweller to have the tag repaired.'

'We must call on the jeweller and find out if the story's true.'

'I've done that already, Your Eminence.'

'Oh, and what did the man say?'

'He knew nothing whatever about it.'

'Excellent. The game's not lost yet, Rochefort, not by any means. In fact what's happened may turn out to be all for the best.'

'I'm confident Your Eminence's genius will . . .'

'Make good my agent's blunders, eh?'

'That's just what I was going to say, Sir, if you'd allowed me to finish my sentence.'

'And now another thing. D'you know where the Duchesse de Chevreuse and the Duke of Buckingham have been hiding all this time?'

'No, Monseigneur. My men haven't been able to get any definite information about that.'

'I know where they've been hiding.'

'You, Excellency?'

'Yes. At any rate I've a pretty shrewd idea. One of them was at No. 25 Rue de Vaugirard, the other at No. 75 Rue de la Harpe.'

'D'you wish me to arrest them both?'

'It's too late. They'll have left by now.'

'It would be as well to find out for certain.'

'Very well. Take ten men of my company and search both houses.'

'I'll go now, Sir.'

And Rochefort turned and left the room.

The Cardinal stood alone in silence for a moment. Then he rang the bell for the third time, and the same officer came in again.

'Bring back the prisoner,' said the Cardinal.

Monsieur Bonacieux was led in once more and at a sign from the Cardinal the officer left the room.

'You've been lying to me, Sir,' said the Cardinal sternly.

'I?' cried Bonacieux. 'Lie to Your Eminence? Never!'

'Those addresses in the Rue de la Harpe and the Rue de Vaugirard where your wife used to call weren't drapers' shops at all.'

'What were they then, in Heaven's name?'

'They were the headquarters of enemy agents. Madame de Chevreuse was hiding in one of them and the Duke of Buckingham in the other.'

'Oh yes, Your Eminence,' cried Bonacieux, recollecting everything in a flash. 'You're perfectly right. I remember often saying to my wife that it was a queer district for drapers' shops, and wondering why there were no signboards outside. My wife used always to laugh at me. Oh, Monseigneur,' he continued, suddenly throwing himself at His Eminence's feet, 'you are indeed the Cardinal, the great Cardinal, the world-famed man of genius.'

To have won the admiration of a drab little fellow like Bonacieux could not be counted as a great triumph, and yet the Cardinal was flattered for a moment. Then almost immediately his eyes lit up as though an idea had suddenly struck him. He looked down at the prostrate figure of the draper, held out his hand to him and said affably:

'Get up, my friend. You're a good, honest fellow and I like you.'

'The Cardinal's taken my hand,' cried Bonacieux in a positive frenzy of joy. 'I've touched the great man's hand. The Cardinal's called me his friend.'

He was shouting at the top of his voice, as though haranguing an invisible crowd.

'Yes, my friend, yes,' said the Cardinal, in the 'bene-volent father' tone which he liked to adopt on certain occasions and which deceived only those who did not know him well. 'And I'm afraid you've been sadly misjudged and most unfairly treated, so some compensation's owing to you. Take this purse of 300 pistoles. And please forgive me the wrong I've done you.'

Bonacieux was quite overwhelmed. He was frightened at first to take the purse, suspecting that the Cardinal was playing a joke on him.

'I forgive you, Your Excellency?' he cried. 'But that's absurd! You had a perfect right to arrest me; you've a perfect right to torture me, to have me hanged if you wish. You're Lord and Master and it's not for a humble citizen like myself to criticize or blame. You ask me to forgive you, Sir? The very idea!'

'Monsieur Bonacieux, you're very good, and I appreciate your generosity. I take it then that you'll accept this purse and leave with not too bad an impression of me?'

'I'm more than content, Your Excellency.'

'Well good-bye for the time being. I hope we shall meet again before long.'

'Whenever and as often as Your Eminence pleases. I'm entirely at your service.'

'Don't worry. I think we shall be seeing quite a lot of each other. I find you a most interesting companion.'

'Oh, Sir!'

'Good-bye for the present, then, Monsieur Bonacieux.'

And the Cardinal nodded genially to his guest. Bonacieux bowed to the ground and walked backwards out of the room. When he was in the ante-room he shouted at the top of his voice:

'Long live His Excellency. Long live His Eminence. Long live the great Cardinal.'

The Cardinal, alone in his study, smiled when he heard this somewhat naïve display of enthusiasm on the part of the worthy draper. Then as his guest's cries died away in the distance, he said to himself:

'Good, I've got another staunch supporter in that man, fool though he is. He'd give his life for me.'

Then he turned to the map of La Rochelle which was spread out on his desk and stood staring at it, deep in thought.

He was still deeply immersed in his strategical imaginings when the doors opened again and Rochefort came in. The Cardinal looked up at once from his desk.

'Well?' he said.

He stared at Rochefort so sharply that it was obvious he attached great importance to the result of his mission.

'Well, Sir,' answered Rochefort, 'I've discovered that a young woman of about twenty-eight and a man of thirty-five to forty did stay at each of the two houses mentioned by Your Excellency, the woman five days, the man four. But the woman left last night and the man this morning.'

'They were the Duke and Madame de Chevreuse!' cried the Cardinal. Then he looked at the clock and said:

'The Duchess'll have reached Tours by now and the Duke'll be in Boulogne. We shall have to catch up with them in London.'

'What do you suggest as the next move, Sir?'

'The whole thing must be kept absolutely dark. The Queen must suspect nothing. She must never know we know her secret. She must think we're trying to investigate some political plot. Bear that in mind. And now I've thought of something. I want you to fetch Séguier, the Keeper of the Seals.'

'What about the other fellow? What did Your Eminence get out of him?'

'Who?'

'The fellow who was here just now, Bonacieux.'

'I've got as much as anyone can hope to get from anyone else in this world. I've got him to act as a spy against his own wife.'

Count Rochefort gave the Cardinal a look of awe and admiration.

'Once again I bow to your genius, Sir,' he said.

Then he turned and left the room.

Alone once more the Cardinal sat down at his desk and wrote a letter which he sealed with his own private seal. Then he rang the bell for the fourth time.

'Send Vitray to me,' he said, 'and tell him to put on travelling clothes.'

A few minutes later Vitray was standing before the Cardinal, booted and spurred.

'Vitray, you're to set off post-haste for London. You must make the journey in one stretch, and not stop anywhere. The moment you reach London go to Milady with this letter. Here's a bill for 200 pistoles; my treasurer will cash it for you. There'll be another bill for you for the same amount if you succeed in your mission and get back within six days.'

The messenger took the letter and the treasury bill and went out.

This is what was written in the letter:

Milady,
When the Duke of Buckingham next attends a ball go to it. He will be wearing twelve diamond tags on his doublet. You must manage somehow to get near him and to cut off two.

Let me know the moment the studs are in your possession.

11
Soldiers and Magistrates

On the day following these events Athos had not returned home, so Porthos and d'Artagnan reported his disappearance to Monsieur de Tréville. Meanwhile Aramis had asked for five days' leave, and had gone to Rouen on the plea that he had some family business to settle.

Monsieur de Tréville was like a father to his soldiers. The least of them, provided he wore the musketeers' uniform, could be as certain of his support and protection as any member of his family. So directly he learnt of Athos' arrest he called at the Office of Criminal Investigations and asked to see the officer in charge of the Croix-Rouge district. Inquiries were made and it was eventually discovered that Athos had been provisionally detained in the For-l'Evêque prison.

Meanwhile Athos had been put through a cross-examination similar to that imposed on Bonacieux, and had then been driven off to see the Cardinal. But unfortunately the Cardinal was at that moment with the King at the Louvre.

At precisely the same hour Monsieur de Tréville also called to see the King. After leaving the Office of Criminal Investigations he had called on the Governor of the For-l'Evêque prison but had not been able to get Athos released. So he now went off to plead his case with the highest authority. In his capacity as Captain of the Musketeers he had a right of audience with the King at any hour of the day.

Everyone knows how prejudiced the King was against the Queen, and how these prejudices were cleverly played upon by the Cardinal, who feared women far

more than men in matters of intrigue. One of the King's
main causes of complaint was the Queen's friendship
with Madame de Chevreuse. The two women caused
him more anxiety than the Spanish wars, the strained
relations with England and the country's financial dif-
ficulties combined. The King was convinced that
Madame de Chevreuse helped the Queen not only in her
political intrigues but, what was far more galling to him,
in her love-affairs.

When the Cardinal told the King that Madame de
Chevreuse, whom everyone supposed was living in
permanent exile in Tours, had in fact spent five days in
Paris and had managed to keep her whereabouts secret
from his police, His Majesty flew into a violent rage.

Having thus successfully kindled the King's wrath the
Cardinal kept the flame alight by recounting in detail
Madame de Chevreuse's subsequent activities in the
capital. He described how she had got in touch with the
Queen through her secret agents, how he, the Cardinal,
had been on the point of unravelling the more obscure
threads of the plot and of arresting the little seamstress,
the Queen's intermediary with Madame de Chevreuse,
with all the proofs of her guilt on her, when an obscure
musketeer had interfered with the course of the law by
making an armed assault on four police officers who were
carrying out their duty of examining criminal witnesses
and collecting evidence of the plot for His Majesty's
personal perusal. When the King heard this his anger
knew no bounds. He got up and strode across the room
to the door which led to the Queen's apartments, meaning to go straight to Her Majesty and accuse her to her
face of intriguing against him and of being privy to a plot
which defied his authority.

But at that moment Monsieur de Tréville came in. His
mood contrasted strangely with the King's mood, for he
was calm and perfectly controlled. Seeing the Cardinal

there and observing the King's agitation he realized at once what had happened.

'So it's you, Sir, is it?' said the King, his voice trembling with rage. 'You've come to see me! Yes. And high time too! What about these damned musketeers of yours now? I've been hearing some fine stories, I can tell you. Monstrous behaviour! Kindly explain at once!'

There was no beating about the bush this time, for when the King was really roused he always gave vent to his feelings.

Monsieur de Tréville replied coldly:

'And I, Sir, have been hearing some fine stories about your police force, for which I'd also like an explanation from the proper quarter.'

'I beg your pardon, Sir?' said the King haughtily.

'I have the honour to inform Your Majesty,' continued Monsieur de Tréville in the same tone, 'that a party of State police and detectives took it into their heads to break into a house, arrest one of my musketeers, drag him through the streets and throw him into the For-l'Evêque dungeon, on an order which they refused to show even to me, his Commanding Officer. This musketeer is, I may say, a man of the highest character, with a most distinguished record, and is known personally to Your Majesty. His name's Athos. Monsieur Athos had gone to call on one of his friends, a young recruit from Béarn in des Essarts' company of Your Majesty's Guards, and finding him out had sat down in his room to wait for him. He had only been there a few seconds when a mixed party of police and detectives laid siege to the house, forced several doors . . .'

Here the Cardinal made a sign to the King to show that this was part of the investigation to which he had previously referred.

'We know all about that,' said the King. 'Those gentlemen were acting in my interests.'

'So I'm to believe, Sir,' retorted de Tréville, 'that it was in your interests that they arrested one of my musketeers on no charge at all, put him in the hands of two guards like a common thief and paraded him up and down the streets in front of a yelling mob, a gallant soldier who's shed his blood in Your Majesty's service ten times and more and has no thought but to serve his King.'

'H'm!' said the monarch, slightly shaken by this. 'Did all that really happen?'

Here the Cardinal broke in:

'Monsieur de Tréville doesn't mention the fact that his innocent musketeer, his gallant subordinate, had an hour previous to his arrest attacked and wounded four police officers who were carrying out an important secret inquiry by my special order.'

'I defy Your Eminence to prove that,' cried de Tréville sharply. His bluff address, typical of a soldier, was in striking contrast to the Cardinal's studied suavity. 'I'd like to point out that one hour previous to his arrest Monsieur Athos was honouring me with his company in my house. He had previously dined with me and stayed on afterwards to talk to Monsieur de la Trémouille and Monsieur de Chalus, who were my other guests that night.'

The King glanced quickly at the Cardinal as though asking for support.

'An official report's proof positive in law,' said the Cardinal in answer to the King's mute appeal. 'The injured parties have drawn up their report – here it is, Sir.'

'I should have thought a soldier's word of honour counted above a mere police report,' said de Tréville haughtily.

The Cardinal began to feel that he was losing ground.

'How d'you explain the fact that Monsieur Athos was

found and arrested in that house in the Rue des Fossoyeurs?' he asked.

'Surely there's no law forbidding friends to call on each other, or musketeers to associate with men of Monsieur des Essarts' company!'

'Yes, if the house where they meet's being watched by the police.'

'That house *was* being watched, Tréville,' said the King. 'Perhaps you didn't know that?'

'As a matter of fact I didn't, Sir,' answered de Tréville. 'And I don't know which part of the house is being watched, but I'm sure it's not the part where young d'Artagnan lives. For I assure you, Sir, as he's told me himself, he's a loyal and devoted servant to Your Majesty and a staunch supporter of His Eminence.'

'Wasn't it d'Artagnan who wounded Jussac in that unfortunate affray near the Carmelite Convent the other day?' asked the King.

As he spoke he cast a sly look at the Cardinal, who flushed an angry red.

'Yes, Sir. Your Majesty has a good memory.'

'Well, and what are we to conclude from all this?' asked the King.

'It's for Your Majesty to decide, not me,' said the Cardinal. 'I myself would be prepared to swear to the guilt of the accused.'

'And I deny it absolutely,' cried de Tréville. 'But you have your judges and your Courts of Law, Sir, and the matter had better be referred to them.'

'I agree, I agree,' said the King. 'We'll leave it for the law to decide.'

'And yet it's sad to think that in this year of grace no man, however virtuous, should be safe from arrest and persecution,' said de Tréville. 'And speaking as a soldier, I can assure you that the army will feel insulted to a man that one of its members should have been forcibly detained by the police on a false charge, and cross-examined about some sordid political crime of which he knew nothing.'

This was a very challenging remark and Monsieur de Tréville made it with the deliberate intention of provoking the Cardinal. He wanted an explosion, because explosions cause fire, and fires light up the surrounding landscape.

'Political crime?' echoed the King. 'What do you know about political crimes, may I ask? All this fuss about one miserable musketeer! By God, I'll have ten of them arrested at once, a hundred of them, the whole damned company if it comes to that, and let one soul in France dare question my action!'

At this de Tréville changed his tone. The expression on his face was stern and his voice hard and cold as he said:

'Sir, I must beg you to command either that my musketeer be returned to me at once or that he be fairly tried in a Court of Law.'

'Listen, Tréville,' said the King. 'Do you swear on the memory of my father that young Athos was in your house while the assault was going on and that he took no part in it?'

'I swear it by your father, Sir, and by you, who are what I love and respect most in the world.'

Here the Cardinal broke in:

'Remember, Sir, if you let the prisoner go without a cross-examination we shall never discover the truth.'

'Athos will always be at hand,' said de Tréville. 'I guarantee that. He won't desert, and he can be summoned at any time to answer questions.'

'No, I'm sure he won't desert,' said the King. 'And as Tréville says, we can get hold of him whenever we want him. Besides,' he added in an aside to the Cardinal, giving him an almost imploring look, 'let's be lenient in this case; it's good policy.'

Louis XIII's idea of good policy made Richelieu smile.

'You've only to say the word for the prisoner's release, Sir,' he replied. 'You have the right of pardon.'

'The right of pardon's only used when the party concerned's guilty,' put in de Tréville, who was determined to make his point clear. 'My musketeer's innocent, Sir, so if you release him you'll only be enforcing the law. You won't be exercising your special right.'

'And he's in the For-l'Evêque prison, you say?'

'Yes, Sir, in solitary confinement in a cell, like a common criminal.'

'Oh damnation take it!' muttered the King. 'What am I to do?'

'Sign the order for the prisoner's release, Sir,' said the Cardinal. 'I think it'll be better that way. Like you I consider Monsieur de Tréville's guarantee a sufficient safeguard.'

De Tréville acknowledged the compliment with a bow. He was delighted at his success and a little frightened too. Why had the Cardinal suddenly decided to climb down? He would have been happier if his enemy had shown more stubbornness.

The King signed an order of release and handed it to Tréville. As the captain was leaving the room the Cardinal smiled and waved to him in a most friendly manner.

'He'll have his knife into me from now on,' thought de Tréville as he left the palace. 'It's impossible to have the last word with a man like that. But I must hurry now. The King may change his mind at any moment and at least I've achieved something. It's more difficult to get a man back into prison once he's escaped than to keep him there when you've got him.'

So Monsieur de Tréville called immediately at the For-l'Evêque prison and carried off Athos in triumph. He then went home and sent for d'Artagnan.

'You only escaped by the skin of your teeth, my lad,' he said. 'This is what you get for wounding Jussac.'

Monsieur de Tréville was perfectly justified in his mistrust of the Cardinal and quite correct in supposing that there was further trouble brewing in that quarter. For hardly had the good captain closed the door of the King's study behind him than His Eminence turned to His Majesty and said:

'And now that we're alone, Sir, let's have done with trivialities and talk seriously. I have to inform Your Majesty that the Duke of Buckingham arrived in Paris five days ago and left again early this morning.'

12

THE KEEPER OF THE SEALS

It is almost impossible to describe the effect produced on Louis XIII by the Cardinal's words. First he flushed scarlet, then he went very pale, and the Cardinal saw at a glance that with one stroke he had regained all the territory he had lost.

'Buckingham in Paris?' cried the King. 'And what was he doing here?'

'Probably plotting with your enemies, the Huguenots and the Spaniards.'

'No. I'll swear he wasn't doing that. He was most likely plotting with Madame de Chevreuse, Madame de Longueville, and the Condés to dishonour me privately.'

'Oh no, Sir! That's a terrible suggestion and quite absurd. The Queen's much too sensible to do anything so rash. Besides, she's devoted to Your Majesty.'

'Women are weak, my dear Cardinal,' said the King. 'And as for her attachment to me, well, I've got my own views as to that.'

'Even so, Sir, I stick to my view that the Duke of Buckingham came to Paris for political reasons,' said the Cardinal.

'And I say he came for personal reasons, Cardinal. And, by God, if the Queen's guilty, she'll be made to pay for it.'

'I hate to let such an idea enter my mind for one moment,' said the Cardinal. 'And yet when you talk like that, Sir, you half persuade me there may be something in what you say. I remember now something Madame de Lannoy said to me when I cross-questioned her as you suggested. She said that last night the Queen had stayed up very late, that this morning she cried a lot, and that she spent the whole of today at her desk writing.'

'That proves it! She was obviously writing to him. Cardinal, I must get hold of the Queen's correspondence at once. And in any case I've decided once and for all to put a stop to all these petty political intrigues and secret love-affairs. The Queen has a certain de Laporte in her employ . . .'

'Yes, and I must confess I think he's the chief agent in this particular plot,' said the Cardinal.

'So you agree that the Queen's being unfaithful to me?' asked the King.

'I've already told Your Majesty what I think. I think the Queen's plotting against Your Majesty politically but not privately.'

'And I say she's plotting against me in both ways. I say she doesn't love me; she loves that unscrupulous rogue, Buckingham. Why on earth didn't you arrest him while he was in Paris?'

'Arrest the Duke of Buckingham! Charles I's Prime Minister! I couldn't possibly do that! Just think of the scandal! And if your suspicions turned out to be justified, which of course I still don't believe, what a mortifying position you'd be in, Sir!'

'But at least you had him watched all the time he was in Paris?' asked the king.

'Yes, Sir.'

'Where did he stay?'

'At No. 75 Rue de la Harpe.'

'And you're sure the Queen and he didn't meet?'

'I think the Queen's too wise to stoop to such folly.'

'But we know they've been corresponding; it was to him the Queen was writing when she spent all the time at her desk. Cardinal, I must have the Queen's letters.'

'But, Sir . . .'

'I want those letters, Cardinal. I'll do anything to get hold of them.'

'I can think of only one way of getting them.'

'What's that?'

'To get Séguier, the Keeper of the Seals, to do it. It's quite within his province.'

'Good. Send for him at once.'

'He should be at my house at this moment, Sir. I asked him to call on me just now, and when I went out I left a message telling him to wait for me.'

'Send for him at once, I say,' shouted the King, banging the table with his fist.

'Very good, Sir. Only . . .'

'Only what?'

'The Queen may refuse to allow it.'

'Refuse to obey my orders?'

'Yes, unless she knows for certain that they are your orders.'

Whereupon the King opened the door which led from his study to the Queen's apartments. He rudely ignored the ladies, walked straight up to the Queen and said in a voice harsh with anger:

'The Keeper of the Seals will shortly be paying you a visit, Ma'am. I've asked him to do something for me, and I wish you to know he's acting under my orders.'

The unhappy Queen turned pale and said:

'What can the Keeper of the Seals do for you that you couldn't do for yourself, Sir?'

The King turned on his heels without answering and at that very moment the Captain of the Guard came in to announce Monsieur de Séguier's arrival. As he entered the Queen's room the King left by another door.

De Séguier came in blushing and with a sheepish smile on his face.

The Queen was still standing when the Keeper of the Seals came in, but when she saw him she at once sat down again and signed to her ladies to do likewise. Then she turned to the intruder and said very haughtily:

'What's the explanation of this visit, Sir, and why have you presumed to come into my private apartments?'

'I've come in the King's name, Ma'am, and with all due respect for Your Majesty, to make a thorough search through your papers.'

'I beg your pardon, Sir? You've come to search my papers? How dare you, Sir! That's a downright insult!'

'Forgive me, Ma'am. I'm only acting for the King in this. And hasn't he prepared you for my visit? Didn't I see His Majesty leave the room as I came in?'

'Very well, Sir, proceed with your search. It appears I'm a common criminal now, and am to be treated as such.'

The Keeper of the Seals went through all the bureaux as a matter of form, although he knew only too well that the important letter of which he was in search would not have been put away in an odd drawer.

Having completed his search of the room and found nothing, Séguier now had to bring his mission to its logical end, in other words, to search the Queen herself.

So he approached Her Majesty with mincing steps, and in a shamefaced, hesitant manner said:

'And now, Ma'am, I still have my principal task to perform. You'll remember I was told to make a thorough search.'

'What do you mean, Sir?' asked the Queen.

Séguier did not know whether she was pretending not to understand or whether he had not made his intention clear.

'His Majesty's convinced you wrote a letter yesterday, and he knows it hasn't yet been given to the courier. That letter's not in any of your tables and yet it must be somewhere in this room.'

'Would you presume to touch your Queen, Sir?' asked Anne of Austria, drawing herself up to her full height and staring at the Keeper of the Seals, her eyes ablaze with hatred.

'I'm a loyal subject of the King, Ma'am, and everything he tells me to do, I do.'

'Very well, I admit it,' said the Queen. 'I see the Cardinal's spies have served him well. I did write a letter today and I've still got it. It's here!'

And the Queen laid her lovely hand on her breast.

'In that case please give it to me, Ma'am,' said Séguier.

'I shall give it no one but the King,' answered Anne.

'If the King had wanted you to give it to him, Ma'am, he'd have asked you for it himself,' replied the Keeper of the Seals. 'He said you were to give it to me and if you don't . . .'

'Well?'

'His Majesty told me to take it from you by force.'

'What do you mean?'

'I mean I've got instructions to search Your Majesty herself for that letter.'

'I won't allow it. I'd sooner die!' cried the Queen, the

hot blood of Imperial Spain and Austria mounting to her temples.

Séguier bowed low, but stood his ground. It was obvious he meant to carry out his orders to the letter. And now he advanced slowly towards the Queen, one step, two steps, like an executioner bearing down on the prisoner in the condemned cell.

Anne of Austria backed away in horror. Her face was deathly pale and she was trembling so much that she had to rest her left arm against a table to support herself. With her right hand she took the letter out of her dress and handed it to the Keeper of the Seals.

'Here's your letter, Sir!' she cried, her voice harsh with rage. 'Take it and remove your odious presence from my sight.'

The Keeper of the Seals went straight to the King with the letter. The King took it with a shaking hand, looked for an address on the envelope, found none, went very white, slowly opened the letter and began to read. When he saw that it was to the King of Spain he gave a deep sigh of relief and read on rapidly.

The letter was entirely concerned with the organization of a large-scale plot against the Cardinal. The Queen proposed that her brother and the Emperor, who were irritated by Richelieu's never-ceasing attempts to humiliate Austria, should threaten joint hostilities against France, and make the Cardinal's dismissal a condition of peace. There was no mention of love in the whole letter.

The King was delighted. He inquired for the Cardinal and when they told him His Eminence was waiting in his study he at once went off and joined him.

'My dear Cardinal,' he said, 'I see you were right all the time, and I was wrong. The plot was entirely political, and there's not one word of love in the whole letter. It's entirely concerned with you. Look, read it.'

The Cardinal took the letter and read it twice through from beginning to end with the closest attention. Then he said:

'The Queen's hostile to me, Sir, but not to you. To you she's a devoted, obedient, and loyal wife. So let me beg Your Majesty not to be too harsh with her.'

'Let her come and make it up with me then.'

'No, Sir. Remember you were in the wrong this time, as you suspected her of something she hadn't done. In this case I think you should go and make it up with her.'

'I'd never do that!' cried the King.

'I wish you would, Sir!'

'In any case how can I make it up with her?'

'By doing something you know will please her.'

'What, for instance?'

'Give a ball. You know how the Queen loves dancing. I guarantee she'll forget her grievances very soon if you do that.'

'Cardinal, you know how I hate balls!'

'Then the Queen will be doubly grateful to you, knowing you're making a sacrifice for her sake. Besides it'll be an excuse for her to wear the magnificent diamond tags you gave her for her last birthday. It'll be the first time she's worn them.'

'Very well, Cardinal, we'll see,' said the King.

He was delighted to have discovered the Queen guilty of a crime which he considered of little importance and innocent of a fault which meant a great deal to him, and was quite prepared to patch up their quarrel.

At that moment the clock struck eleven. The Cardinal got up, and after repeating his request to the King to make peace with the Queen, bowed and begged leave to retire.

After Séguier's visit Anne of Austria had been expecting some stern rebuke from the King. She was not a little surprised, therefore, to find him making overtures of peace to her on the day following the seizure of the letter. She at first refused to respond, for her woman's pride and queenly dignity had been cruelly insulted. But in the end her ladies-in-waiting persuaded her that it would be better policy for her to suppress her resentment and agree to forget the whole matter. Louis took advantage of her change of mood to tell her of his intention to give a ball in the near future.

A ball was such a rare event in the poor Queen's life that when she heard this news the last trace of vexation left her, as the Cardinal had prophesied, and she appeared radiant. She asked what day the ball would be held, and the King replied that that would have to be settled with the Cardinal. And from then on he kept pestering His Eminence to fix a date, and His Eminence kept putting him off with excuses.

Ten days passed in this way.

A week after Séguier's visit to the Queen and the Cardinal's interview with the King His Eminence received a letter with a London postmark on it, which contained these few lines:

I have got them. But I can't leave London as I have no money. Send me pistoles and I'll be in Paris in four or five days.

On the day on which this letter arrived the King put his usual question to the Cardinal:

'Have you fixed a date for the ball yet?'

Richelieu started to count on his fingers and muttered to himself:

'She says she'll be here four or five days after getting the money. It'll take the messenger four or five days to reach her; that makes ten days. Allow another two for contrary winds and tides and the dangers of the road; that makes twelve.'

'Well, Cardinal, have you finished your calculations?' asked the King.

'Yes, Sir,' replied His Eminence. 'Today's 20 September. The City Councillors are giving a ball on 3 October. That'll do admirably. You and Her Majesty can go to their ball and then it won't look as though you were giving way to her.'

He paused. Then he added:

'Oh, and by the way, Sir, don't forget to remind Her Majesty just before the ball that you'd like to see how she looks in the diamond tags you gave her.'

13

THE LOVER AND THE HUSBAND

When the King told the Queen to wear her diamond tags at the ball, the Queen guessed that the Cardinal was behind this petty insistence, and realized that all was lost unless she could get a message to Buckingham. She herself was closely watched, as was Laporte, but she entrusted a letter to loyal Madame Bonacieux, who assured her that she would find someone to go to London. She was thinking of her husband, but when she went home she found him changed: a Cardinalist and no longer entirely at her bidding. Indeed, she only just stopped herself from saying too much. She pretended that the visit to London was merely to purchase some trinkets for the Queen, but her husband's suspicions were aroused, and he went off to report to Rochefort.

Then d'Artagnan, who had been listening from upstairs, knocked on her door. When she had let him in, the young man first made sure that no one was eavesdropping, and then turned to her and said:

'Well, Madame Bonacieux, you seem to have chosen a pretty poor specimen of a man for a husband.'

'Oh, so you overheard our conversation?' replied Madame Bonacieux, looking at d'Artagnan anxiously.

'From beginning to end.'

'How on earth?'

'Just as I overheard your other conversation with the Cardinal's agents. By a little secret method of my own.'

'And what did you make of it?'

'Quite a lot. Firstly that your husband's a fool, which is a good thing. Secondly that you're in trouble yourself, which pleased me, because now I can offer to help you, and Heaven knows I'd go through fire and water for you. Lastly that the Queen wants a brave, intelligent and reliable man to go to London on a mission. I think I can claim to have at least two of those qualities, and here I am at your service.'

Madame Bonacieux did not at first answer, but her heart leapt for joy and a fresh look of hope shone in her eyes. At last she said:

'If I did decide to trust you with this mission what guarantee could you give?'

'My love for you. Come on, tell me what I've got to do!'

Madame Bonacieux still wavered. She gave the young man a long, searching look as though to read into his soul. He looked so frank and eager and there was such a pleading note in his voice that she felt irresistibly drawn towards trusting him. Moreover she was in a situation in which half-measures were ruled out. She must dare all to win all. The Queen's interests would be jeopardized as much by over-suspiciousness as by over-credulity. But, truth to tell, what weighed with her most in her present state of doubt were her personal feelings for the young man, which were instinctive. On a sudden impulse she decided to speak.

She told the young man her deadly secret, the first part of which he already knew through his chance encounter with the Duke of Buckingham and his guide on the Pont Neuf. Then she handed him the Queen's letter. The fact of their sharing this secret and that she had entrusted the all-important letter to his care was their mutual declaration of love.

D'Artagnan's pride and joy knew no bounds. The precious secret and letter were now his and the woman he loved trusted and loved him. He had a sense of double possession which uplifted him and gave him the strength of ten.

'I'll leave now,' he cried. 'This very moment!'

'Oh, you're kind!' cried Madame Bonacieux. 'You can be sure the Queen won't forget what you're doing for her.'

'If you mean she'll reward me, I say I've already had my reward. I love you and you've allowed me to tell you so. That's more than I ever dared hope for.'

Madame Bonacieux gave a sudden start.

'Hush!' she whispered.

'What is it?'

'I heard voices in the street. Listen! That's my husband. Don't you hear?'

'Yes. I recognize his voice,' whispered the young man.

Upon which he ran to the door and bolted it.

'He mustn't come in till I've gone,' he said. 'When I've gone go down and open the door for him.'

'But I don't want him to find me here either.'

'Well, then, you must come up to my room.'

'Oh dear,' cried Madame Bonacieux. 'I'm so frightened!'

As she spoke her eyes filled with tears. D'Artagnan noticed her tears and was moved. He knelt in front of her.

'Dearest Madame Bonacieux, I promise you you'll be quite safe with me,' he cried.

'Very well, Monsieur d'Artagnan, I trust you,' she replied. 'Let's go.'

D'Artagnan very quietly drew back the bolt of the door and the two glided out of the room like shadows, down into the hall and up the stairs which led to d'Artagnan's room. The young man barricaded the door with sofas and chairs, and the two crept to the window and peered out into the street through a chink in the shutter. Immediately below them they saw Monsieur Bonacieux talking to a man wrapped in a heavy cloak.

When d'Artagnan saw the man in the cloak he gave a start, half drew his sword, and rushed to the door. It was the man from Meung.

'What on earth are you doing?' cried Madame Bonacieux. 'Have you gone mad? D'you want to ruin us all?'

'I've sworn to kill that man! Don't you understand?'

'Your life's no longer yours to risk as you like,' cried she. 'You're pledged to someone else now and you should only think of your mission. In the Queen's name I order you not to leave this room.'

'Any orders in your own name?'

'In my own name I order you not to risk your life unnecessarily. But listen,' she added, lowering her voice. 'I think I heard them say something about me just then.'

D'Artagnan went back to the window and listened. Monsieur Bonacieux had meanwhile gone into the sitting room, and, finding it empty, had rejoined his companion in the street.

'She's not there,' he was saying. 'She's obviously gone back to the Louvre.'

'You're sure you didn't make her suspicious by leaving her so suddenly?'

'Quite sure,' replied Monsieur Bonacieux, complacently. 'She's too stupid to notice a thing like that.'

'Is the young guardsman at home?'

'I don't think so. Look! His shutters are closed and there's no light shining through the chinks.'

'All the same we'd better make sure.'

'How?'

'By going and knocking on his door.'

'I'll ask his servant.'

'Yes. Do that, please.'

Bonacieux went back into the house, this time through the side door in the alley. He walked up the stairs which led to d'Artagnan's landing and knocked on his door.

There was no reply. Porthos happened that day to have arranged a tryst with a lady of rank and had borrowed Planchet for the evening to make an impression. And, needless to say, d'Artagnan and his companion did not respond to the gentle rap-tapping of Monsieur Bonacieux's knuckles on the door. They stood motionless like two statues, waiting in agonized suspense for what seemed hours, until at last they heard his footsteps retreating down the passage.

The little draper went out again into the street.

'There's no one there,' he said.

'Never mind,' said the man in the cloak. 'We'd better go into your sitting-room in any case. We're less likely to be overheard in there than out here in the street.'

'What a nuisance!' whispered Madame Bonacieux. 'Now we shall miss the rest of the conversation.'

'On the contrary,' replied d'Artagnan, 'we shall hear even better now.'

He proceeded to take up four or five already loosened flagstones from the floor of the room. He then spread a mat on the floor, knelt down on it and leaned over the hole, signing to Madame Bonacieux to do the same.

'You're sure there's no one in the house?' said the stranger.

'Positive,' replied Monsieur Bonacieux.

'And you think your wife . . .'

'Has gone back to the Louvre.'

'You're certain she talked to no one but you?'

'Quite.'

'That's a very important point, as I hope you realize.'

'So the information I brought was really of some value?'

'Of great value, Monsieur Bonacieux. I can promise you that.'

'So the Cardinal will be pleased with me?'

'He's bound to be.'

'Long live His Eminence!'

'You're sure your wife didn't mention anybody by name when you were talking?'

'No.'

'Not Madame de Chevreuse, the Duke of Buckingham or Madame de Vernet?'

'No. All she said was that she wanted to send me on a mission to London on behalf of someone very high up.'

'Vile beast!' hissed Madame Bonacieux from her vantage-post in the room above.

'Hush!' said d'Artagnan. He took her hand and she allowed him to hold it.

'Never mind,' went on the stranger. 'But you were foolish to let such a chance slip. You should have agreed to go; she'd have then given you the letter and you could have given it to us. You'd have helped to defeat a dangerous plot, and you yourself would have . . .'

'What?'

'Well, you'd have benefited considerably. The Cardinal was prepared to honour your name.'

'Did he tell you that?'

'Yes. He wanted to give you a token of his esteem.'

'Don't worry,' replied Bonacieux. 'My wife thinks the world of me, and it's not too late to put things right.'

'Silly old fool!' hissed Madame Bonacieux.

'Hush!' said d'Artagnan again, squeezing her hand hard.

'How do you mean?' asked the man in the cloak.

'I'll go at once to the Louvre, ask for Madame Bonacieux, tell her that after thinking things over I've decided to go, get her to give me the letter and take it straight to the Cardinal.'

'Good. Hurry and do that. I'll go now and return in an hour or so to find out how you got on.'

With these words the stranger turned and left the room.

'Now that he's gone you must hurry and be off yourself,' said Madame Bonacieux. 'I don't need to tell you to be brave, but I'd like to remind you again that your life's no longer yours to risk as you like, now that you've pledged it to the Queen.'

'To the Queen and to you!' cried d'Artagnan. 'But don't worry, I fully realize how serious this thing is. I'll put the Queen's interests first and the memory of you will help me to success.'

Madame Bonacieux made no reply. But she flushed deeply and in so doing betrayed her true feelings for the young knight-errant. She gave him the purse of 300 pistoles which the Cardinal had given to her husband and which she had discovered hidden in a cupboard. A few minutes later d'Artagnan himself left the house, also wrapped in a heavy cloak, under which could be seen the stiff, menacing outline of a long rapier. He carried the Queen's letter in the pocket of his doublet.

D'Artagnan's first move was to ask Monsieur de Tréville to persuade des Essarts to let him have a fortnight's leave. De Tréville did better than that: without wishing to hear the details of d'Artagnan's mission, and knowing only that it involved the honour of the Queen and that the Cardinal would try to stop it succeeding, he granted the Three Musketeers leave as well, so that they could accompany d'Artagnan.

At two o'clock in the morning our four adventurers left Paris by the Saint-Denis gate. They rode through the night like shadows, swift and silent. They were all brave men, but the darkness had a sobering effect on their spirits, and they imagined ambushes behind every clump of trees along the road.

The lackeys followed behind their masters, armed to the teeth.

The party arrived safely in Chantilly at eight that morning. Here the four friends decided to breakfast. They dismounted at an inn with a painted sign depicting St Martin sharing his cloak with a beggar. The servants were told not to unsaddle the horses and to be ready to leave again at a moment's notice.

The four men went into the communal dining-room and sat down to have their breakfast. A gentleman who had just arrived by the Dampmartin road was breakfasting at the same table. He bowed to the four friends, made some polite remarks about the weather and then drank to their healths. They responded and the atmosphere seemed friendly enough.

But just as Mousqueton, Porthos' servant, came in to say that the horses were ready and they were all preparing to leave, the stranger turned to Porthos and proposed the health of the Cardinal. Porthos agreed and then in his turn proposed the King's health. The stranger cried out that he knew no King but His Eminence. Porthos called him a drunken sot, at which he at once drew his sword.

'That was a damned silly thing to do,' said Athos. 'However, it can't be helped. You can't back out now. Polish the fellow off quickly and come on after us.'

The three others then mounted again and rode off at the gallop, while Porthos squared up to his enemy and began threatening to carve him in pieces with every thrust known to the duellist.

'There's one of us gone already,' said Athos after they had ridden on a little way.

'Why d'you suppose that fellow fixed on Porthos rather than on any of us three?' asked Aramis.

'Porthos talks so loud he probably thought he was in command of the party,' said d'Artagnan.

'I always said our Gascon was a bright lad,' said Athos. And the three of them galloped on.

They made a halt of two hours at Beauvais to give the horses a rest and also to wait for Porthos. When the two hours were up and Porthos had not appeared they continued their journey.

A mile or so beyond Beauvais they reached a narrow stretch of road with an embankment on either side. Here they came face to face with a party of eight men who were apparently engaged on some kind of road work. The road was not paved here and the men were digging holes in it and appeared to be trying to make the way passable by clearing away the mud and slush. Aramis noticed the quagmire ahead, feared for his boots and began cursing the men roundly for their clumsy work. Athos tried to restrain him but it was too late. The workmen now hurled insults at the riders and actually succeeded in provoking

the imperturbable Athos, who spurred his horse at one of
them to get him to stand aside. At this the whole gang
retreated into the ditch at the side of the road, reappearing a moment later with eight loaded muskets which they
had concealed there and which they now proceeded to
discharge point blank at the party of riders. Aramis got
a bullet through the shoulder and Mousqueton one
through the buttock. Aramis kept his seat on his horse
but Mousqueton fell off; his wound was not serious,
but being unable to see it, he thought it was worse than
it was and fell off from fright rather than pain.

'It's an ambush,' said d'Artagnan. 'Don't fire! Let's get
on quick.'

Wounded as he was, Aramis managed to cling on to
his horse's mane and to ride on with the others.
Mousqueton's horse cantered along behind them
riderless.

'We've now got a spare horse to use as a remount,'
remarked Athos.

'I'd rather have a spare hat,' said d'Artagnan. 'Those
devils shot mine off. Thank God I wasn't carrying the
precious letter in it.'

'When poor old Porthos gets there they'll murder him,'
said Aramis.

'If Porthos were on his feet he'd have caught us up
before now,' said Athos. 'I'm rather afraid that drunk-
ard turned out to be sober enough when it came to
fighting.'

The little cavalcade galloped on for another two hours,
although by now the horses had been ridden almost to
death.

The travellers had struck across country, hoping to
avoid any further unpleasant encounters. But when they
reached Crèvecœur Aramis declared that he could go no
further. In fact only the grim courage which lay behind
his rather foppish appearance and affected ways had

kept him going until then. He had gone whiter and whiter in the face and the two others had had to support him on his horse. Now they helped him to dismount in front of an inn, left with him his servant Bazin, whom they could well do without in an adventure like this, and rode on, hoping to reach Amiens before nightfall.

The party was now reduced to two masters and two servants, Grimaud and Planchet.

'I won't be had like that again in a hurry,' cried Athos. 'Nothing on God's earth'll make me utter another word or lift a finger between here and Amiens. Damn those swine!'

'Don't let's waste our breath swearing,' answered d'Artagnan. 'Let's just ride on, that is if the horses don't collapse under us.'

The four dug their spurs into their horses' flanks and urged them on. They reached Amiens at midnight and dismounted at the Golden Lily inn.

The innkeeper looked a thoroughly honest fellow. He received his guests holding a lighted candle in one hand and his nightcap in the other, explaining that he had been roused from sleep by the knocking on the door. He wanted to put the two new arrivals in two charming rooms, one at one end of the inn and the other at the other. This offer they refused. The innkeeper then declared that he had no other rooms worthy of two such grand guests, at which the latter replied that they would sleep in the dining-room on mattresses. The innkeeper tried to dissuade them, but they insisted, so he finally had to yield.

Athos and d'Artagnan arranged their beds on the floor and then proceeded to barricade the dining-room door from the inside. Suddenly they heard the window shutters being violently rattled by someone in the courtyard. They called out to inquire who was there and two familiar voices answered them, the voices of their two servants,

Planchet and Grimaud. Athos immediately unfastened the shutters and parleyed with them in the dark.

'Grimaud can perfectly well manage the horses by himself,' said Planchet. 'If you agree, Sir, I'll come and lie down across the door of your room, so that no one can get in during the night without disturbing me. That ought to make things quite safe for you two gentlemen.'

'What do you propose to sleep on?' asked d'Artagnan.

'On this,' said Planchet, holding up a bundle of straw.

'Yes, I think you'd better do that,' said d'Artagnan. 'I don't like our host at all. He's too obsequious for my taste.'

'And for mine!' said Athos.

Planchet climbed in through the window and lay down across the door, while Grimaud went off to spend the night in the stables, promising to come round with the four horses punctually at five o'clock next morning.

The night passed fairly quietly. The only disturbance occurred at two in the morning, when someone tried to open the door. But Planchet woke with a start and cried out, 'Who's there?' At which the intruder mumbled some apology and shuffled off.

At four o'clock they heard a great hullabaloo in the stables. Grimaud had tried to waken the stable boys and they had turned on him and were beating him. Athos and d'Artagnan opened the windows and saw the wretched fellow lying unconscious in the courtyard with head wounds. They had belaboured him out of his senses with the handles of their pitchforks.

Planchet went round to the courtyard and tried to saddle the horses himself. But he found them still quite unfit for work. Only Mousqueton's horse, which had been riderless for the last five or six hours of their journey, was in a fit state to travel, but by some extraordinary accident the veterinary surgeon, who had apparently been summoned to bleed the innkeeper's horse, had bled Mousqueton's horse instead.

Athos and d'Artagnan now began to be alarmed. These disasters following one upon another might have been coincidental, but they might also be the work of some hostile organization. Planchet was sent to inquire from the innkeeper whether there were any horses for sale in the neighbourhood, while his master and Athos went out. At the main door of the inn Planchet noticed two saddled and bridled horses, fresh and obviously ready for the road. They exactly fitted the bill. Planchet inquired about them and was told that they belonged to two gentlemen who had spent the night at the inn and were at that moment settling their account in the host's private room.

Athos now went himself to pay his bill, leaving d'Artagnan and Planchet standing at the main door of the inn. One of the inn servants took Athos down a long passage, at the far end of which was the host's room. Athos entered the room unsuspecting.

He found the innkeeper alone, seated behind his desk, one of the drawers of which was half-open. Athos handed him two crowns in settlement of the account. The host took them and examined them closely, turning them over in his hand and clinking them on a piece of metal on his desk. Suddenly he sprang to his feet, cried out that the money was false and that he would have Athos and his companion arrested as coiners.

'You rogue, you!' cried Athos, advancing on him menacingly. 'Just you try and arrest me! I'll slit your throat for you.'

But the host ducked down, snatched two pistols out of the half-open drawer of his desk, levelled them at Athos and called out for help.

Instantly four men armed to the teeth rushed into the

room through two side doors and threw themselves on Athos.

Athos called out at the top of his voice:

'They've got me! Get away quick, d'Artagnan. Ride like the devil!'

And he raised his pistol and fired two shots into the air.

D'Artagnan and Planchet heard his cry and the two shots, and the same idea occurred to them both. They swiftly untethered the two saddled and bridled horses which were standing at the main gate, mounted them, dug their spurs into their flanks and galloped off.

'Did you see what happened to Athos?' d'Artagnan asked Planchet, as they reached the outskirts of the town.

'Well, Sir,' answered Planchet, 'I saw him run two of the blighters through and he seemed to be defending himself very well against the other three, though it was difficult to see through the glass of the door.'

'Good old Athos!' said d'Artagnan. 'It's rotten having to leave him like that. However we've probably got something equally nasty waiting for us ahead. So let's get on, Planchet.'

The two rode on without slackening speed and reached St Omer in a single stretch. Here they gave their horses a rest, but stayed beside them the whole time for safety's sake, eating a scrap meal standing in the crowded street; after their experience at Amiens they thought it unwise to let the animals out of their sight. They then remounted and continued their journey.

When they were within a hundred yards of the gates of Calais d'Artagnan's horse collapsed and remained lying in the road with blood oozing from its nose and even from its eyes. Nothing d'Artagnan or Planchet could do would get it on its feet again. Planchet's horse was still on its feet but it, too, refused to move. The riders had no choice but to leave both horses on the high road and to run the rest of the way to the harbour. As they approached Planchet noticed a gentleman and his valet passing through the harbour gate about fifty yards ahead of them – apparently also travelling to England – and pointed them out to his master. The gentleman was evidently in a great hurry; his boots were covered in dust and he was talking excitedly to the captain of a ship which was about to set sail. D'Artagnan approached to within a few feet of him and stood behind him saying nothing, trying to overhear his conversation and also to make it appear that he was travelling with him.

'I'd have liked to take you across, Sir,' the captain was saying, 'but an order came through this morning forbidding anyone to embark on any ship without a permit from the Cardinal.'

'I've got one,' said the stranger, pulling a paper out of his pocket. 'Here it is.'

'You must have it stamped and signed by the Governor of the Port,' said the captain. 'Then I'll take you on board.'

'Where does the Governor live?'

'About a mile outside the town. You can see the house from here, that tiled roof underneath the hill.'

'Right,' said the stranger, 'I'll go at once.' And he and his servant started off on foot towards the house.

D'Artagnan and Planchet turned and followed them, keeping about a hundred yards behind them.

When they reached the outskirts of the town d'Artagnan quickened his pace and overtook the stranger as he was entering a wood.

'Sir,' he said, 'you seem in a great hurry.'

'I am in a great hurry,' answered the stranger.

'I'm sorry about that, Sir,' went on d'Artagnan, 'because I'm also in a hurry and I wanted to ask a favour of you.'

'What's that?'

'To allow me to pass ahead of you.'

'Impossible, Sir,' said the stranger. 'I've travelled 180 miles in forty-four hours, and I've got to be in London by noon tomorrow.'

'I've covered the same distance in forty hours,' answered d'Artagnan, 'and I've got to be in London by ten tomorrow.'

'I'm sorry. I can't do it,' replied the stranger. 'I arrived in Calais first and I intend to leave first.'

'I regret too, Sir. I know I arrived second but I also intend to leave first.'

'Are you on a mission?'

'No, I'm travelling on my own.'

'Then I see no excuse for your offensiveness,' said the gentleman.

'I've got a very good excuse if you only knew.'

'What's that?'

'I want your travel permit. I haven't got one and I must have one.'

'Are you mad?'

'Not at all. I simply want your travel permit.'

'Let me pass at once!'

'No, Sir,' said d'Artagnan.

And he stood barring the stranger's way.

'In that case, Sir, I shall have to blow your brains out. Hi, there, Lubin, my pistols!'

'Planchet,' said d'Artagnan, 'you deal with the servant and I'll deal with the master.'

Planchet sprang at Lubin and, being young and hefty, bore him down, laid him flat on his back, straddled him and gripped him by the throat. He then called out to d'Artagnan:

'My job's done, Sir. Now do yours.'

When the stranger saw his servant overpowered he drew his sword and bore down on d'Artagnan. But the Gascon proved more than a match for him. In under ten seconds he had given him three thrusts through the body, saying after the first, 'One for Athos', after the second, 'One for Porthos', and after the third, 'One for Aramis.'

The stranger collapsed in a heap on the ground. D'Artagnan, supposing him dead, or at any rate unconscious, came up to him, meaning to take the permit from him. But just as he was putting out his hand to search through his pockets the wounded man, who still had hold of his sword, raised himself on one elbow and stabbed our hero through the chest, crying:

'And one for you!'

'And one more for myself! And a good long one to end with!' cried d'Artagnan in a rage, this time nailing his enemy to the ground with a sword thrust through the belly driven right up to the hilt.

And now the stranger's eyes closed and he lost consciousness.

D'Artagnan searched through his pockets and drew out the travel permit. It was made out in the name of the Comte de Wardes. He then looked down at the young man lying at his feet unconscious, perhaps dead, whom he fully intended to leave to his fate, and began to ponder over the strange destiny which governs men, driving them to kill each other in the service of strangers, who often do not know of their existence.

But he was soon roused from these musings by Lubin, who had recovered from the shock of Planchet's onslaught and was now yelling for help like a maniac.

'As long as I keep my hand round his throat he won't yell,' said Planchet. 'But directly I let go he'll start again.'

He was right. Even with Planchet's fingers squeezing his throat Lubin managed to let out a few howls.

'This ought to fix him,' said d'Artagnan, taking out his handkerchief and gagging him.

'Now let's tie him to a tree,' said Planchet.

This they proceeded to do with great thoroughness.

Then they lifted the prostrate Comte de Wardes and laid him down beside his servant. It was now growing dark and the bodies of the two victims were hidden well inside the wood, so it was unlikely that anyone would discover them before morning.

'And now on to the Governor's house!' cried d'Artagnan.

'But you're wounded, Sir.'

'That's nothing. Let's deal with the more urgent things first. My wound can wait. It's only a scratch.'

The two of them started off, half running, half walking, and before long found themselves at the door of the Governor's house. The servant led them up a wide staircase, opened the door of a large sitting-room and announced:

'The Comte de Wardes.'

'You have a signed permit from the Cardinal?' asked the Governor.

'Yes, Sir,' answered d'Artagnan. 'Here it is.'

'Yes. That's valid all right,' said the Governor.

'I know that,' said d'Artagnan. 'You see I'm on fairly close terms with His Eminence.'

'I gather His Eminence is interested in preventing one particular man from reaching England.'

'Yes, a certain d'Artagnan, a Gascon from Béarn, who left Paris with three friends a day or two ago, bound for London.'

'Do you know him personally?' asked the Governor.

'Very well indeed.'

'Then you could help me a lot by describing him to me.'

'I'll do so with pleasure,' replied d'Artagnan.

And he proceeded to give the Governor a detailed description of the Comte de Wardes.

'Has he got anyone with him?'

'Yes, a valet called Lubin.'

'I'll send a report based on your description to the local

authorities and if they're lucky enough to catch the fellow I'll see to it that he's sent back to Paris under a strong escort.'

'If you do that the Cardinal will be very pleased with you, Sir.'

'Shall you be seeing His Eminence when you return, Comte?'

'I shall indeed.'

'Will you mention my name to him as one of his most loyal supporters?'

'I won't forget you, Sir. Don't worry.'

The Governor was delighted with this promise, and countersigned the travel permit forthwith.

D'Artagnan wasted no time in an exchange of futile compliments. He snatched the permit from the Governor and hurried out of the room. He and Planchet then made their way back by a circuitous route, avoiding the wood and entering the town by a different gate.

The ship was still waiting to start, and the captain was standing on the quay.

'Well,' he said, as d'Artagnan approached.

'Here's my pass countersigned,' said the young man.

'What about the other gentleman?'

'He's not leaving today after all,' said d'Artagnan. 'But I'll pay the two fares.'

'In that case we'll start right away, Sir,' said the captain.

'Excellent,' said our hero.

And he and Planchet jumped into the rowing-boat. Five minutes later they were on board.

They were only just in time. The ship was about a mile out to sea when d'Artagnan, who was looking back to shore, saw a flash of light and heard the report of a gun. It was the signal for the closing of the harbour.

Now d'Artagnan was at last free to attend to his wound; the point of his enemy's sword had struck a rib which had deflected its course, and his shirt had adhered to the open sore and acted as a dressing, so he had lost very little blood.

But he was exhausted from his efforts. They spread out a mattress for him on the deck, and he sank down on it and fell fast asleep.

When dawn broke the ship was still about twelve miles off the English coast. There had been only a light wind and they had made very slow progress.

At ten o'clock the ship dropped anchor in Dover harbour.

At ten-twenty d'Artagnan set foot on foreign soil and cried out:

'England at last!'

But he and Planchet still had to get to London, and the language problem made the last part of the journey difficult too. But at that time in England stage travel was fairly reliable. The two men were soon in the saddle, with an outrider to escort them, and in six hours were at the gates of the capital.

D'Artagnan did not know London. Nor did he know a word of English. But he wrote the Duke of Buckingham's name on a piece of paper and showed it to various people on his route, all of whom knew exactly where the great man lived and directed him on his way. Before long he found himself at the Duke's front door.

The Duke was at Windsor that day, hawking with the King.

D'Artagnan asked to see His Grace's confidential servant. This man, Patrick, always travelled with his master abroad and therefore spoke excellent French. He explained to the man Patrick that he had come from Paris on a matter of life and death and that he must see his master at once.

D'Artagnan's brusque manner and the note of urgency in his voice convinced the servant that his business was really important. He ordered two horses to be saddled at once and declared that he would himself escort the young man to Windsor. As for Planchet, he had had to be lifted off his horse. The poor fellow's limbs were completely cramped and he was speechless with exhaustion. D'Artagnan seemed to be made of iron.

When they arrived at the castle they were told that the King and the Duke were hawking in the marshes about six miles out.

The two men rode off at the gallop and reached the marshes in under half an hour. Soon the servant heard his master's voice in the distance, calling his falcon.

'How shall I announce you to His Grace?' he asked.

'Tell him I'm the young man who insulted him one night on the Pont Neuf, opposite La Samaritaine.'

'Won't he think that rather odd?'

'No. I think it'll make him want to see me.'

The servant put spurs to his horse, approached the Duke and announced d'Artagnan in the manner suggested. Upon this the Duke left his hawking and quickly rode over to greet the messenger from France. He recognized d'Artagnan at a glance and suspected at once that he had come with some sensational news which directly concerned himself. The servant tactfully stood aside to allow Buckingham and the young man to converse in private.

'What have you to tell me, Sir?' said the Duke. 'Has something happened to the Queen?'

For answer d'Artagnan put his hand into the inner pocket of his doublet and pulled out the Queen's letter.

'Read this, Sir,' he said.

'What's this letter? Who's it from?' cried the Duke.

'From Her Majesty, I believe,' answered d'Artagnan.

'From Her Majesty?' echoed Buckingham, going deathly pale.

Buckingham opened the letter and read, one page, two

pages. Suddenly he looked up and there was terror in his eyes.

'Good God!' he cried. 'The position's desperate! Patrick, go and make His Majesty my humblest apologies and tell him I have to leave for London at once on a matter of life and death. Come, Sir,' he added to d'Artagnan, 'let's be off.'

And the Duke and the young man put spurs to their horses and galloped off at breakneck speed in the direction of the capital.

15
THE BALL

The horses went like the wind, and the Duke and his companion were soon at the gates of the capital. When the two riders reached the Duke's house they rode straight into the courtyard. Buckingham dismounted, flung his horse's reins over its neck and strode indoors, leaving the animal unattended. D'Artagnan did the same, but was not happy about it, for he hated to see horses ill managed. At that moment, however, three or four grooms came running from the stables at the far end of the yard to take charge of the mounts, so his mind was set at rest.

The Duke walked so fast that d'Artagnan could scarcely keep pace with him. At last the young man found himself in what looked like a small chapel, the walls of which were hung with beautiful gold-embroidered Persian tapestries, and which was brilliantly lit by rows of candles. At the far end of the room was a sort of altar, surmounted by a blue velvet canopy; in between the altar and the canopy hung a life-size portrait of Anne of Austria, so excellent that d'Artagnan gave a start of surprise; it was as though the Queen herself were present, and he expected the portrait to come down from the wall and speak.

On the altar, immediately below the portrait, was the rosewood box containing the diamond tags.

The Duke gazed in rapt silence at the diamonds he was to see no more. Suddenly he started back and gave a cry.

'What is it, Your Grace?' asked d'Artagnan in alarm. 'Are you ill?'

'Good God, is it possible!' said Buckingham in a hoarse whisper, turning pale as death. 'Yes, two of the tags are missing. There are only ten here. Oh horror!'

'Did you lose them, Your Grace, or d'you think they've been stolen?' asked d'Artagnan.

'They've been stolen,' answered the Duke. 'It's a plot of the Cardinal's. Look, the ribbon they were fixed to has been cut with scissors!'

'Who can have done it and when?' cried d'Artagnan. 'Doesn't Your Grace suspect anyone? If you could think of someone who might have done it the diamonds might be traced. The thief might not yet have got rid of them.'

'Let me think!' cried the Duke. 'Ah, yes, I remember now. I only wore the tags once and that was last week at the King's ball at Windsor. I recollect that Lady de Winter was particularly pleasant to me that night and I was surprised because we'd had a quarrel. I realize now that her attitude was a pretence. She's one of the Cardinal's agents.'

'What? Has he agents abroad as well as in France?' cried d'Artagnan.

'He has agents everywhere,' replied the Duke. 'He's a fiend. But we may defeat him yet. When's this ball to be held in Paris?'

'Next Monday.'

'In five days. That just gives us time,' said the Duke.

The Duke immediately set about arranging that no more ships should leave any English port without his special permit, so that if the diamonds were not already on their way to France, they would not leave England. This would be interpreted as a preliminary to war with France, but the Duke was prepared to go to any lengths to assist his beloved Queen.

Next he ordered his jeweller, who was the most skilled in the land, to make two identical tags to replace the stolen ones, and to make them within two days.

On the second morning after d'Artagnan's arrival in London the two diamond tags were ready. The work was so perfect that Buckingham himself could not distinguish the old from the new; moreover the greatest experts could not have said which were the copies and which the originals.

The Duke immediately summoned d'Artagnan.

'Here are the diamond tags you came for,' he said. 'Take them and bear witness that all that was humanly possible to do I've done.'

'Your Grace, I promise to give an exact report of everything I've seen.'

'Go to the Port of London. Ask for a brig called the *Sund* and give this letter to the captain. He'll sail you into a little French port where there's no chance of anyone looking out for you, and where usually only fishing-boats put in.'

'What port's that, Sir?'

'Saint-Valéry. But wait. There's more to come. When you go ashore at Saint-Valéry look out for a cheap-looking inn without name or signboard. You can't mistake it; there's only one. Call in there and ask to see the landlord.'

'And then?'

'Say the word "Forward" to him. That's the password.

He'll have a saddled horse ready for you and tell you the road you're to take. You'll find three similar remounts at intervals along your route. And now give me your hand, young man. Perhaps we shall soon be meeting on the battlefield. But in the meantime I hope we part friends.'

'Yes, Your Grace, but in the firm hope of soon becoming enemies.'

'Don't worry. I think I can guarantee that.'

'I count on your promise, Sir,' said d'Artagnan.

Upon which he bowed to the Duke, took his leave and went straight down to the port, where he found the brig *Sund* berthed opposite the Tower of London. He handed the Duke's letter to the captain, who took it to the Governor of the port for countersignature and then promptly hoisted sail.

There were fifty other outward-bound ships in the port waiting for permission to weigh anchor. The *Sund* sailed close alongside one of these and d'Artagnan fancied he saw seated in the stern the lady from Meung, with whom the stranger had had a hurried conversation at the inn, the lady of the long, golden ringlets, lustrous blue eyes, and lily-white hands. But the brig was borne swiftly downstream by a strong wind and tide and the other vessel and its occupants were soon out of sight.

At about nine o'clock on the following morning the brig dropped anchor in the little port of Saint-Valéry. D'Artagnan immediately set off in search of the inn. Distant shouts guided him in his quest, and he soon found the inn, where a crowd of sailors had assembled to discuss the latest news, using the likelihood of imminent war with England as an excuse for a little extra celebration.

D'Artagnan elbowed his way through the crowd, approached the landlord and gave the password 'Forward'. The host immediately signed to him to follow him, took him out through a back door and into a stables where he found a horse ready saddled and bridled. The host then asked him if he could oblige him in any other way.

'Tell me what road I'm to take,' said d'Artagnan.

'From here you must make for Blangy and from Blangy for Neuchâtel. When you get to Neuchâtel go to the "Golden Harrow", give the password to the landlord and he'll have another thoroughbred like this waiting for you.'

'Do I owe you anything?' asked d'Artagnan.

'Everything's already been paid for, and handsomely,' said the landlord. 'So good-bye, Sir, and God speed.'

'Amen,' said the young man.

Then he leapt into the saddle and galloped off.

Four hours later he was in Neuchâtel. He obeyed his instructions to the letter. At Neuchâtel, as at Saint-Valéry, he found a saddled horse awaiting him.

'What road do I take from here?' inquired d'Artagnan.

'Take the Rouen road, but branch off to the left before reaching the town. You'll come to the little village of Ecoins, where there's only one inn, the "French Crown". It's a cheap-looking place, but don't be put off by that. Ask there and you'll find another thoroughbred waiting to do the next stretch with you.'

'Same password?'

'Yes.'

'Good-bye, mine host!'

'Good-bye, young gentleman. Anything more I can do for you?'

'Nothing, thanks,' cried d'Artagnan, vaulting into the saddle and galloping off at breakneck speed.

At Ecoins the same performance took place; d'Artagnan found another solicitous host who provided him with another magnificent mount. He galloped off towards Paris at breakneck speed. There was another change of mounts at Pontoise, the last on his journey, and by nine that evening his horse's hoofs were clip-clopping on the cobbles of Monsieur de Tréville's courtyard in the Rue du Vieux Colombier. He had travelled about 180 miles in twelve hours.

When Monsieur de Tréville welcomed the young man he showed nothing of whatever inner excitement he might have been feeling. He may have gripped his protégé's hand a little harder and looked at him a little more searchingly than usual but that was all. He asked him no questions and told him nothing. He merely suggested that as Monsieur des Essarts' company was on special guard at the Louvre that night d'Artagnan had better report for duty at once.

On the day following d'Artagnan's return the whole of Paris was talking about the ball which the City Councillors were giving for the King and Queen.

At six o'clock the guests began to arrive and were all in turn ushered into the great hall and shown to their places on the raised benches.

At nine o'clock the President's wife arrived. She was the most important woman guest at the ball after the Queen, so she was received by the City Councillors and conducted to a box immediately opposite the Queen's box.

At ten o'clock a special light supper for the King was laid in the little hall near the Saint-Jean Church and placed in front of the sideboard on which stood the city plate, which was guarded by four archers.

At midnight the people near the Town Hall heard distant shouts and cheers. The King had started from the Louvre and was being acclaimed by the people lining the route to the Town Hall. All the streets were lit with coloured lanterns.

Now the City Councillors, dressed in their robes and preceded by six police officers carrying torches, went out on to the steps of the hall to greet the King. The Mayor made a short speech of welcome and the King made another in reply, in which he apologized for arriving late and blamed the Cardinal for having detained him with State business until eleven.

Everyone remarked that the King was looking worried and depressed.

Half an hour after the King's appearance fresh shouts and cheers were heard along the route from the palace. This time the crowd was acclaiming the Queen. The City Councillors again went out on the steps to welcome Her Majesty.

As the Queen entered the ballroom everyone remarked that she, too, looked sad and tired. At that very moment the curtains of a small gallery, which had been closed till then, were drawn back and the Cardinal's head appeared in the aperture. He was wearing a Spanish nobleman's plumed hat and looked pale and anxious. His eyes were riveted on the Queen, and suddenly a look of fiendish glee came into his face. Her Majesty was not wearing her diamond tags.

The Queen stood for some time in the ballroom receiving the compliments of the city magnates and their wives.

Suddenly the King appeared with the Cardinal at one of the entrances to the hall. His Eminence was saying something to him in a low voice and His Majesty was very pale. Before anyone had grasped what was happening the King had forced his way through the crowd in the ballroom and was at the Queen's side. He had not changed his dress and the ribbons of his doublet were half untied. Everyone standing near the Queen remained transfixed as His Majesty came up and addressed his consort.

'Why aren't you wearing your diamonds, Ma'am?' he asked in a strained voice. 'I expressly asked you to.'

The Queen noticed the Cardinal standing behind the

King with a diabolical smile on his face. She replied falteringly:

'I was afraid I might be jostled by this crowd, Sir, and that the diamonds might get lost.'

'And you were wrong, Ma'am. When I gave you those tags it was my wish you should wear them. You should have done as I asked.'

By now the King was almost trembling with rage. Everyone was watching the scene with amazement, quite in the dark as to the cause of it.

'I'll have the diamonds fetched from the Louvre at once, if that will please Your Majesty,' said the Queen.

'Do so, Ma'am, and quickly. The ballet starts in an hour.'

The Queen curtsied in token of submission. Then she turned and followed the ladies who were to escort her to her dressing-room.

The King walked off in the other direction and made for his private room.

And now an awkward silence fell on the company and for a few moments no one dared stir. Everyone had noticed that the King and the Queen had had a quarrel, but Their Majesties had spoken so low that those within earshot had retreated a few steps out of respect, not wishing to intrude. So not a word of their conversation had been heard. The violins were playing sweet melodies but no one was listening.

The King was the first to come out of his private room. He and his suite were all dressed in picturesque hunting clothes. It was the style of dress which suited the King best, and turned out as he now was he certainly ranked as the first gentleman in France.

Then the Cardinal appeared, went up to the King and handed him a box. The King opened it and found two diamond tags inside.

'What's the meaning of this?' he asked.

'If the Queen has her diamonds, Sir, which I doubt,'
answered the Cardinal, 'count them, and if you find she
has only ten, ask her if she remembers who stole these
two from her.'

The King looked sharply at the Cardinal as though he
wished to question him further. But at that moment there
was a loud burst of applause in the hall. The Queen had
just appeared in her fancy dress. If the King ranked as the
first gentleman, the Queen certainly ranked as the first
lady in the land.

Her hunting clothes suited her to perfection. She wore
a beaver hat with blue feathers, a long hunting-coat of
pearl-grey velvet fastened with diamond clasps and a
blue satin skirt embroidered with silver. On her left
shoulder she was wearing the diamond tags attached to
her dress by a blue velvet bow which matched her skirt
and the feathers in her hat.

When the King saw the diamonds sparkling in the light
of the two hundred candles he gave a start of joy, while
the Cardinal gave a start of rage. At that distance, however, neither could count the number of tags on the
Queen's shoulder. Her Majesty was certainly wearing the tags, but was she wearing all twelve or only
ten?

At that moment the violins struck up the opening
chords of the ballet. The King offered his arm to the
President's wife, whom he was to partner in the dance,
while his brother offered his arm to the Queen. All the
dancers then took their places on the floor of the hall, and
the ballet began.

The King was dancing opposite the Queen, and every
time he passed close to her he stared hard at the glittering
constellation on her shoulder, in a vain attempt to count
the diamonds. The Cardinal's forehead was bathed in
sweat.

When the dance finally ended the gentlemen led their

partners back to their seats amid the applause of the crowd. The King, however, rudely left his partner, the President's wife, standing alone on the floor of the hall and walked up to the Queen.

'Thank you, Ma'am,' he said, 'for obeying me so promptly. But I understand you've lost two of the tags and I'm returning them to you now.'

So saying he handed the Queen the two tags which the Cardinal had given him.

The Queen pretended to be surprised.

'What, Sir?' she cried. 'You're giving me two more? But that makes fourteen!'

The King now counted the tags on Her Majesty's shoulder and, sure enough, there were twelve! He turned and beckoned to the Cardinal; he was by now furious.

'Well, Cardinal,' he cried, 'what is all this about? Is it a joke or what?'

'No, Sir,' replied the Cardinal. 'The truth is, I wanted to make Her Majesty a present of these two tags. I didn't dare offer them to Her Majesty myself so I thought out this plan for getting her to accept them.'

The Queen replied with a smile which proved that she was not deceived by this ingenious improvisation:

'Your Eminence is too good. And believe me, Sir, I value your present to the full, for I realize that these two tags alone must have cost you as much as the other twelve cost His Majesty.'

Upon which she curtsied to the King and the Cardinal and retired to her private room to change out of her hunting-dress.

The Queen had just retired to her room and d'Artagnan, who was one of the minor guests, was preparing to leave when he felt a light touch on his shoulder. He turned round and saw a young woman in a black velvet mask beckoning to him. The mask was but a poor disguise and d'Artagnan at once recognized the woman as his beloved Constance Bonacieux.

On the previous night d'Artagnan had asked Madame Bonacieux to meet him at the Louvre in the lodge of Germain, the Swiss porter. But the lovers had hardly had time to say a word to each other, for Madame Bonacieux's first thought had been to let her royal mistress know that her messenger had returned and that all was well. So now the young man was only too glad to follow her; both love and curiosity drove him on. Madame Bonacieux led him along empty, winding corridors towards the back of the building. D'Artagnan followed her meekly and in silence until at last they came to a door. Madame Bonacieux opened it, led the young man into a little room which was completely dark, and closed the door behind them. After warning him again not to make a sound she opened a second door hidden by a tapestry, through the folds of which a light shone suddenly, slipped through it and disappeared, leaving the door ajar.

D'Artagnan stood stock still and tried to imagine what this room could be. As his eyes became accustomed to the gloom he saw a ray of light shining through the half-open door. Then he smelt a faint scent, and heard women's voices speaking in low, respectful tones and using the word 'Majesty' from time to time. He realized then that he must be in a room adjoining the Queen's private dressing-room.

The young man hid himself in the darkest corner and waited.

Suddenly, as he stood in the darkness, watching and waiting, an outstretched arm appeared in the opening in the tapestry, an arm superbly white and lovely in outline. D'Artagnan stood for a while transfixed. Then he realized that this was his reward. He rushed forward, fell on his knees, took the fair white hand in his and pressed it to his lips. As he held the Queen's hand he felt something slip from her fingers into his; then she withdrew her hand again and the door was closed. The young man was now in complete darkness. He clenched his hand and realized that what he held was a ring. He slipped it on to his finger and stood waiting, convinced that his little adventure was not yet over. He had been rewarded for his courage and now expected to be rewarded for his love. Moreover the night was yet young, and the ball had only just started. Supper was at three and the St Jean clock had struck the three quarters some little time before.

The sound of the voices in the adjoining room grew gradually fainter, and finally ceased. Then the communicating door opened again and Madame Bonacieux came tiptoeing into the little room where d'Artagnan was imprisoned.

'You, at last!' cried the young man.

'Hush!' said his guide, putting her finger to her lips. 'Don't make a sound and go back the way you came.'

'But when shall I see you again?' cried d'Artagnan.

'You'll find a note in your room when you get home,' said Madame Bonacieux. 'Now go quickly!'

And with these words she opened the door leading into the passage and pushed the young man out of the room.

D'Artagnan obeyed like a child, without a word of protest. And this shows how very deeply in love he was.

16
THE TRYST

D'Artagnan ran all the way home from the City Hall. He found the little side door into his house ajar. He ran up the stairs and gave the special knock on his door which he and his servant had arranged together. He had sent Planchet home two hours previously, and now the faithful fellow was there to greet him.

'Did anyone call with a letter for me?' asked d'Artagnan quickly.

'Nobody called with a letter, Sir,' answered Planchet, 'but one came by itself.'

'What do you mean, idiot?'

'I mean that although I had the key to this place in my pocket all the evening, when I came in I found a letter on the table in your bedroom.'

'Where is the letter?'

'I left it where I found it, Sir. It's not natural for letters to come into people's houses on their own, like that. If the window'd been open or even on the latch I wouldn't say no. But everything was bolted and barred. I should take care, Sir, if I were you. There's something queer about that letter.'

While Planchet had been talking d'Artagnan had rushed into his bedroom and opened the letter. He read as follows:

I have my own and other people's thanks to convey to you. Come to St Cloud at ten o'clock to-night, and wait opposite the summer-house at the corner of Monsieur d'Estrées' house.

C.B.

As he read this letter d'Artagnan felt his heart leap for joy. It was the first love-letter he had ever received and the first tryst that had ever been granted him.

Planchet had seen his master's face change colour as he read.

'Well, Sir,' he said, 'didn't I guess right? Isn't there some evil attached to that letter?'

'No, Planchet, you're wrong,' answered d'Artagnan, 'and to prove how wrong you are here's a crown for you. Go out and drink my health.'

'Thank you, Sir. You're very generous. I'll do that with pleasure. But I say all the same that letters which get into houses by themselves . . .'

'Fall from Heaven, Planchet, from Heaven.'

'So you're happy, Sir?'

'I'm the happiest man alive.'

'In that case, Sir, perhaps you'll allow me to go to bed.'

'Yes, run along.'

'May everything turn out for the best, Sir. But I still say that letters . . .'

And Planchet went off shaking his head and muttering to himself, still uneasy in spite of his master's generosity and the prospect of a good tipple.

D'Artagnan was now alone. He read and reread the letter, pressed it to his lips and kissed it passionately. Although it was near dawn he went to bed, fell fast asleep and dreamed golden dreams.

Later that morning, when he went out, he found Monsieur Bonacieux standing at his front door. His first impulse was to ignore the little draper. But Bonacieux made him such a deep and courteous bow that he felt obliged, as his tenant, not only to return the bow but to go up and speak to him.

Their conversation naturally turned to Bonacieux's imprisonment in the Bastille. The draper discoursed at length on the Bastille, with its bolts, barred windows, air-holes, grilles, and instruments of torture.

D'Artagnan listened with exemplary patience. When the little man at last stopped talking he said:

'And what about Madame Bonacieux? Did you ever discover who kidnapped her? You remember it was the kidnapping that first brought us together.'

'Ah,' said Monsieur Bonacieux, 'you may be sure they took good care not to tell me that, and my wife swears she has no idea who the man was. And now how about you, young Sir?' he continued, rubbing his hands good-humouredly. 'What have you been up to lately? I haven't seen you or your friends for some time, and I can't believe all that dust and mud which Planchet was wiping off your boots yesterday was picked up on the paved roads of Paris.'

'You're quite right, Monsieur Bonacieux. My friends and I've been on a little trip.'

'Did you go far?'

'Oh no. Only about a hundred miles. We escorted Monsieur Athos to Forges, where he went to take the waters. My other two friends stayed on with him there.'

'And you had to return, I suppose?' said Monsieur Bonacieux, putting on a knowing look. 'I don't suppose a handsome young fellow like you gets much time off. The ladies would have something to say if you left Paris for long. Eh, Monsieur d'Artagnan?'

The young man laughed heartily. 'Ha, ha, Monsieur Bonacieux,' he replied. 'I see one can't hide much from you. You're quite right, the ladies would have something to say; one in particular was keen to have me back.'

Monsieur Bonacieux's face darkened slightly at this, but so slightly that d'Artagnan never noticed it.

'Well, don't pretend you've never had a tryst!' said d'Artagnan with a laugh.

'No, I only asked because I wanted to know if you'd be coming back late tonight.'

'Why d'you want to know that, Monsieur Bonacieux? Are you proposing to wait up for me?'

'No. But the fact is, since my arrest and the entry of the

police I get terrified every time I hear the door opening, especially at night. You can't really blame me, Sir. I'm not a fighting man.'

'No. But you don't need to be frightened when I come in, however late it is, one, two, or even three in the morning. You'll know it's me. Even if I don't come home all night you needn't be frightened.'

This time Bonacieux turned so chalky white that even d'Artagnan noticed it. He asked him what was the matter.

'Nothing,' said Bonacieux. 'Since my recent misfortunes I've been liable to sudden fainting attacks; I had one just then, that was all. Don't worry about me. Your only concern should be to try and enjoy yourself.'

'There's no effort needed for that. I am enjoying myself.'

And the young man went off, laughing aloud at the irony of the situation, and imagining that he was the only one who saw the joke.

'Laugh while you may,' muttered Bonacieux ominously at his retreating figure.

But d'Artagnan was already too far away to hear, and even had he heard he was in too merry a mood to pay attention to anyone so unimportant as Monsieur Bonacieux.

He walked off in the direction of Monsieur de Tréville's house; as we know, his previous day's visit to the Rue du Vieux Colombier had been short and not very explanatory.

He found de Tréville in the highest spirits. Both the King and the Queen had been most gracious to him at the ball. The Cardinal, on the other hand, had been most disagreeable, but that had not worried him very much. He had gone home at one o'clock, pleading indisposition. The King and the Queen had stayed at the ball till six in the morning.

'And now,' said de Tréville, lowering his voice and looking round to make sure that they were alone, 'now we've got you to consider, my lad. I gather that Their Majesties' and the Cardinal's sudden change of mood is somehow connected with your return from wherever you've been. You'll have to mind your step from now on.'

'Surely I'm all right if I've got Their Majesties' support.'

'You're not all right, believe me. The Cardinal never forgets an injury till he's had his revenge. And I think in this case the man he's after is a certain young Gascon I know.'

'D'you really think His Eminence knows it was I who went to London?'

'Oh, so you've been to London, have you? Was that where you got that diamond ring you're wearing? Take care, d'Artagnan. It's not healthy to accept presents from enemies.'

'This diamond wasn't given me by an enemy, Sir,' answered d'Artagnan. 'It was a present from the Queen.'

'From the Queen?' echoed Monsieur de Tréville. 'Yes, now I look at it I see it's magnificent – a real crown jewel. I should say it was worth at least 1,000 pistoles. Whom did the Queen send with it?'

'She didn't send anybody. She gave it to me herself.'

'Where?'

'In a room next to her dressing-room in the City Hall.'

'How did she give it to you?'

'She was holding it when she gave me her hand to kiss.'

He then told Monsieur de Tréville exactly what had taken place.

'Oh these women!' cried the old soldier. 'These women with their romantic ideas, their love of mystery and intrigue! That's typical of them. So all you saw was the

Queen's arm, which means that if ever you meet you'll neither of you recognize each other!'

'No, Sir. But I've got this diamond and . . .'

'May I give you a piece of advice, my lad?' broke in de Tréville.

'Of course, Sir.'

'Go into the first jeweller's shop you pass on your way home and sell him that diamond for whatever price he offers you; however mean he is he can't give you less than 800 pistoles for it. Pistoles have no name and no history, d'Artagnan. But that ring has a history, a terrible history, and could bring disaster to anyone found wearing it.'

'Sell this ring!' cried d'Artagnan. 'The ring given me by my sovereign! Never!'

'Well, at least wear it back to front. Penniless Gascons don't find diamond rings in their mothers' jewel-cases. Everyone knows that.'

'So I'm really in some danger, am I, Sir?'

'A man asleep on a mine with the fuse alight is safe compared with you.'

Monsieur de Tréville spoke so seriously that d'Artagnan began to be alarmed.

'What d'you think I ought to do, Sir?' he asked.

'You must keep your eyes skinned and never be caught napping. The Cardinal has a long memory and enormous power. Take my word for it, he'll play some dirty trick on you all right.'

'What'll he do, for Heaven's sake?'

'He might do anything. He's got the devil's whole armoury at his disposal. The least bad thing that can happen to you is that you'll be arrested.'

'Would they dare arrest someone in the King's service?'

'They didn't worry much about Athos, did they? Take the word of a man who's had thirty years' experience of

Court life, and don't lull yourself into a state of false security. Go to the other extreme and see potential enemies everywhere. Don't be led into an argument with anyone, not even a child. If anyone attacks you give way and don't feel ashamed about it. When you're crossing a bridge feel the planks to see there's not a loose one; when you walk under a scaffolding look up first to see that no one's holding a stone ready to throw down on your head; if you come home late get your servant to dog your footsteps, and arm him, that is, of course, if you can trust him. Don't confide in anyone, friends or relations, not even in your mistress, in fact least of all in her.'

D'Artagnan blushed at this.

'Why least of all in her?' he asked.

'Because mistresses are the Cardinal's favourite weapons of attack.'

D'Artagnan thought at once of his assignation that night with Madame Bonacieux. But he was fond enough of his pretty landlady not to let Monsieur de Tréville's bad opinion of women in general shake his confidence in her.

'By the way, that reminds me,' went on de Tréville, 'what's become of your three friends?'

'I was just going to ask you, Sir, if you'd had any news of them.'

'I? No, I've heard nothing.'

'Well, Sir, I had to leave them all in turn on the journey. I left Porthos at Chantilly with a duel on his hands, Aramis at Crèvecœur with a bullet in the shoulder and Athos at Amiens held up by a party of rogues on a trumped-up charge of coinage.'

'You see!' cried de Tréville. 'What did I tell you? And how did you get through?'

'Only by the skin of my teeth, I confess, Sir. I got a sword-thrust through the chest from the Comte de Wardes and left him half dead on a road near Calais.'

'De Wardes! There you are! Another of the Cardinal's agents; Rochefort's cousin. Listen, my lad, I've just thought of something. The Cardinal will be pretty well combing Paris for you for the next few days, so why not go quietly off to Picardy and look up your three friends? Damn it, that's the least you can do in return for what they've done for you.'

'That's a good idea, Sir. I'll go tomorrow.'

'Why not tonight?'

'Tonight I've got an appointment in Paris, which I simply must keep.'

'Shall I see you again before you leave?'

'I shouldn't think so, Sir, unless I hear any fresh news in the meanwhile.'

'In that case, good-bye and good luck to you.'

'Thank you, Sir.'

And the young man took leave of Monsieur de Tréville with a feeling of intense gratitude to him for his unfailing loyalty and support.

He now called at the lodgings of all his three friends in turn. None of them had returned, nor had any of their lackeys, and no one had had word of them. D'Artagnan would not have hesitated to call on their mistresses to get news of them, but unfortunately he did not know either Porthos' or Aramis' mistresses, and as for Athos he had no mistress.

At nine o'clock that evening, d'Artagnan left Paris, rode through the Bois de Boulogne and towards St Cloud. When he reached the town he avoided the main street and turned instead up a side street which led to the back of the Castle and then swung down a narrow lane which led straight to the summer-house where Madame Bonacieux had arranged to meet him. It was in a completely deserted neighbourhood. One side of the lane was bordered by a high wall, at a corner of which stood the summer-house, the other side by a hedge, behind which stood a tumble-down hut, fronted by a small garden.

The young man had kept his tryst. He had had no instructions about giving a signal so went and stood opposite the summer-house and waited.

It was a still night and not a sound was to be heard. Paris might have been a thousand miles away. D'Artagnan peered cautiously into the darkness to make sure that no one was lurking there and then leaned back against the hedge. Beyond the hedge, the garden, and the hut lay the vast expanse of sleeping Paris, now cloaked by a thick mist, a yawning gulf in which a few pinpoints of light still glittered, sinister sparks rising from that inferno.

But for d'Artagnan at this moment every prospect charmed, every thought cheered, and every cloud was silver-lined. The hour of his tryst was at hand.

Indeed at that very moment the belfry bell of St Cloud struck the magic hour of ten in its slow, booming tone. To an ordinary ear there would have been something un-canny in the clanging of that bronze clapper in the darkness. But not to d'Artagnan. His heart sang in har-mony with the tolling of the bell which was to him as an angel's trump proclaiming the opening of Heaven's gates. He was standing with his eyes fixed on the little summer-house in the recess of the wall. All the windows of the house were shuttered except one on the first floor, through which a soft light shone, shedding a silvery gleam on a little cluster of lime-trees whose branches reached out beyond the high park wall. Behind that window, in that softly lit room, his beloved Madame Bonacieux was obviously waiting for him.

And now the St Cloud clock struck ten thirty.

This time d'Artagnan felt a sudden shiver go through him which he could not account for. Was it merely the cold night air striking through his clothes and had he mistaken a physical sensation for a pang of fear?

He now began to think that he must have misread the letter, and that the appointment was for eleven. He went and stood under the window in a ray of light and took the letter out of his pocket. No, there was no mistake; the appointment was for ten o'clock.

Eleven o'clock struck.

D'Artagnan was now convinced that Madame Bonacieux had had an accident. He clapped his hands three times loudly, which is the acknowledged signal of lovers. But no sound came in reply, not even an echo.

His next thought was a sobering one; perhaps Madame Bonacieux had grown tired of waiting for him and had fallen asleep. He went up to the wall and tried to grip hold of it to climb up it. But it had been freshly plastered and he only succeeded in tearing his hands.

At that moment he noticed the branches of the trees shining silver in the lamplight, and saw that one of them jutted out over the road. He decided to climb the tree and sit on the branch, from where he hoped to get a good view into the summer-house.

The tree proved easy to climb: in a few seconds he was comfortably perched on the branch, gazing through the glass panes of the window into the interior of the room.

What he saw made him start and tremble. The soft light which looked so peaceful from outside shone not on an orderly and cosy room but on a scene of incredible confusion. One of the panes of the window had been smashed; the door at the back of the room had been broken down and was hanging lopsided on its hinges; a table which had obviously been laid for supper was lying on its side and broken decanters and crushed fruit were strewn all over the floor. Everything pointed to the fact that the room had been the scene of a desperate struggle.

The young man now clambered down the tree and proceeded to examine the ground under the summer-house for further traces of violence. His heart was pounding in his chest and beads of sweat stood on his forehead.

A little gleam of light still shone out into the tranquil darkness. D'Artagnan now noticed something which had at first escaped his attention because his eyes had been riveted on the summer-house. The ground under the window was trampled down in places and had large potholes in it. Moreover there were footprints and horses' hoof-prints on it, and two deep carriage-wheel ruts which d'Artagnan traced for a certain distance along the road from Paris; these stopped and made an about turn in front of the summer-house.

Pursuing his researches d'Artagnan eventually discovered a woman's torn glove lying close under the wall. It was mudstained in patches, but d'Artagnan could tell that it was new and there was a faint scent on it which seemed familiar. It was the sort of glove that lovers steal from their mistresses as keepsakes.

The little lane was as deserted as before and the lamp in the window still shed its gentle light over the scene. Its rays lit up the hut at the bottom of the garden opposite the summer-house. That hut looked dead and desolate enough, but it must have been a silent witness of the drama. And perhaps not such a silent witness after all, thought d'Artagnan. Perhaps it could be made to speak.

With this thought in mind the young man leapt over the hedge and walked up to the hut. As he approached, a dog which was fastened to a chain at the door started barking furiously.

In a moment or two he saw the old worm-eaten shutter to the right of the door swing slowly back on its hinges. It opened only a few inches and was then pushed quickly to again; not, however, before d'Artagnan had caught a glimpse of an old man's head reflected in the dim light of an oil lamp which was burning inside the room. The old man had obviously seen d'Artagnan's shoulder-belt, sword-hilt, and pistol butts and had been frightened.

'In Heaven's name listen,' called out d'Artagnan. 'I'd arranged to meet a friend here, but my friend hasn't arrived. I'm very worried about it. Has there been some trouble in the neighbourhood? Have you seen or heard anything? Speak! Answer me.'

The shutter swung back again slowly on its hinges and the old man's head and shoulders appeared in the opening; he was very pale and seemed panic-stricken.

'Don't question me, Sir, please,' said the old man. 'If I told you what I'd seen no good would come of it.'

'So you have seen something!' cried d'Artagnan. 'Then for God's sake say what it was. I swear on my honour to repeat nothing.'

To reinforce his request d'Artagnan threw a pistole to the old man.

It was obvious from the young man's face and voice that he was genuinely distressed and the old peasant was reassured and decided to trust him. He signed to him to come closer and began talking in a low monologue.

'At about nine o'clock this evening,' he said, 'I heard a noise on the road outside. I went up to my door to find out what was happening and saw three men in my garden. I'm poor and therefore not afraid of thieves, so I opened the door and asked the men what they wanted. A carriage-and-four and three saddled horses were drawn up under the trees. The three saddled horses obviously belonged to the three men who were booted and spurred.'

'"Well, my good Sirs," I said to them, "what can I do for you?"

'"Have you a ladder you can lend us, old man?" said the spokesman of the party.

'"Yes, Sir," I answered; "the one I use for picking fruit."

'"Give it to us, and go back indoors," said the man. "And here's a crown for your pains. I may warn you you're going to see something quite out of the usual very soon. I know it's no good telling you not to look or listen, but remember if you repeat a word of what you see and hear you're a dead man."

'So saying the gentleman threw me a crown and all three went off with the ladder.

'I shut the garden gate behind them and pretended to go back into the cottage. But I went out again at once by the back door and, keeping in the shelter of the trees, managed to creep forward as far as yonder clump of elders; standing in the shadow there I could see everything without being seen.

'The three men had managed to draw the carriage up right opposite the summer-house without making a sound. Now a short, stout, shabby-looking man with grey hair stepped out and began climbing slowly up the ladder. When he got to the level of the first-floor window he took a quick look inside the room, crept stealthily down the ladder again and said to the others in a low voice:

'"It's she!"

'At this the man who'd spoken to me walked up to the door of the summer-house, opened it with a key which he took out of his pocket and went in, closing the door behind him. His two followers, acting like soldiers rehearsed in a drill, then began climbing up the ladder. The little grey-haired man remained standing at the carriage door, while the coachman held the carriage horses and a groom the saddled mounts.

'Suddenly I heard screams coming from the summer-house and a woman rushed to the window, flung it open and seemed to be preparing to throw herself out. But when she saw the two men on the ladder she fell back into the room and the two men climbed in through the window after her.

'I saw nothing more after that, but I heard the noise of furniture being thrown about the room. The woman kept screaming and shouting for help. But then her cries were stifled and the three men reappeared at the window carrying her in their arms. Two of them then came down the ladder with her and lifted her into the carriage and the little grey-haired man stepped in after her. The man who'd remained inside the house now closed the window and came out a moment later by the door. He looked into the carriage to make sure the woman was inside; then he joined his two companions who were waiting with their horses and all three swung together into the saddle. The groom jumped on to the box beside the coachman, the carriage drove off at breakneck speed escorted by the three riders, and that was the end. Since then I've seen no one and heard nothing.'

D'Artagnan was stunned by this terrible news and remained speechless, while the demons of fury and jealousy raged in his heart. The look of dumb despair on his face impressed the old man much more than any tears or wild outbursts could have done.

'Don't despair, Sir,' he said. 'They didn't kill the young lady, and that's the most important thing after all.'

'Can you tell me anything about the ringleader of this damnable plot?' asked the young man.

'No, Sir, I don't know him.'

'But you say he spoke to you. You must have seen what he looked like.'

'Oh yes, Sir. He was tall, a lean man, dark-skinned, with a black moustache, dark eyes, and with the dress and manners of a gentleman.'

'That's the fellow all right!' cried d'Artagnan. 'Him

again. It's always him! He's my evil genius, I swear. And what about the other man?'

'Which man?'

'The little man with grey hair?'

'Oh him? He's no gentleman, I can promise you. For one thing he wasn't carrying a sword, and the others ordered him about like a nobody.'

'Some servant, I suppose,' said d'Artagnan. 'Oh, poor woman, poor woman! What have they done with her?'

'You promised you'd repeat nothing, Sir,' the old man reminded him.

'Don't worry,' answered d'Artagnan. 'I won't. On my honour as a gentleman.'

D'Artagnan walked off in the direction of the ferry, utterly sick at heart. His mind was numbed with horror and he could still hardly believe that the woman was really Madame Bonacieux. He tried to persuade himself that it was all a dream and that tomorrow he would call at the house and find her there as usual. Then he felt convinced that she was the victim; that she had been having a love-affair with another man and that this other man had abducted her in a fit of jealousy. He was distracted with grief and despair.

'If only I had my friends with me I might have some hope of finding her,' he muttered to himself. 'But they're all prisoners themselves.'

17

ATHOS' WIFE

D'Artagnan stopped at Monsieur de Tréville's house on his way home. He had decided this time to tell him everything as he badly needed his advice. Moreover he knew that Monsieur de Tréville saw the Queen practically every day, and he hoped he might persuade Her Majesty to make inquiries about the unfortunate woman who was obviously paying the price of her loyalty to her mistress.

Monsieur de Tréville listened closely to the young man's story, which proved that he saw more in the kidnapping of Madame Bonacieux than a mere love intrigue. When d'Artagnan had finished his account de Tréville said:

'That sounds to me very much like the Cardinal's work.'

'But what can we do?' asked d'Artagnan.

'Absolutely nothing at present. The best thing you can do is to leave Paris, and that quickly. I'll see the Queen and tell her all the details of the kidnapping which she probably knows nothing about. That'll give her something to go by when she starts making inquiries. I may possibly have some good news for you when you get back. At any rate I'll do all I can.'

D'Artagnan knew that Monsieur de Tréville was not one to make rash promises, and that one could always reckon on his achieving more than he said. And as he now took leave of his officer his heart was full of gratitude for his past acts of kindness and for his pledge of support for the future. De Tréville was also greatly attached to his brave and enterprising subordinate; he bade him an affectionate farewell, and wished him the best of luck.

D'Artagnan decided to follow Monsieur de Tréville's advice and leave the capital without delay. He walked straight back to his lodgings to give Planchet his marching orders. As he approached the house he saw Monsieur Bonacieux dressed in morning clothes standing at his front door.

Monsieur Bonacieux hailed him as heartily as he had done the day before.

'Well, young man,' he said. 'We're having one or two nights out, I see. D'you realize it's seven o'clock? You seem to be turning normal behaviour upside down, and coming in at an hour when most people go out.'

'Of course you don't need to transgress in that way, do you, Monsieur Bonacieux?' retorted the young man. 'You've got your happiness at home, haven't you?'

Bonacieux turned as white as a sheet and tried to force a smile.

'You're a great one for jokes, young man, a great one indeed,' he replied. 'But where on earth can you have been last night?' he continued, staring at d'Artagnan's boots. 'It must have been pretty heavy going in the lanes.'

D'Artagnan looked down at his boots and saw that they were covered in mud. But at the same time he happened to glance at the little draper's shoes and stockings and noticed that they were just as soiled as his boots; moreover the pattern of the stains was exactly similar. They might both have been dipped in the same mud-pit.

Suddenly an idea flashed across d'Artagnan's mind. The short, squat man with greying hair, described by the cottager as wearing shabby clothes and being treated with contempt by the ringleaders of the plot! Could it be – yes of course it was – Bonacieux himself! He had played a leading part in the abduction of his own wife.

The young man felt a sudden wild impulse to spring at the draper's throat and strangle him. But caution forbade this and with a great effort he restrained himself. Nevertheless his change of expression and the sudden light of anger in his eyes had been so noticeable that Bonacieux was frightened and shrank back. But he was standing close to his own front door, which was shut, so he could not retreat very far.

'Monsieur Bonacieux,' said d'Artagnan, 'before you start chaffing me you'd better take a look at your own shoes and stockings; they seem to be in much the same state as my boots. Don't tell me you've been having nights out too! At your age and with a young and pretty wife like you've got! Shame on you, Monsieur Bonacieux!'

'No such thing, no such thing, Sir,' answered Bonacieux. 'If you want to know where I've been, I've been to St Mandé to make inquiries about a servant whom I urgently need. The roads were very bad and that's where I picked up all this mud. I haven't had time to get it cleaned off yet.'

That Bonacieux should mention St Mandé as his destination was further evidence in support of d'Artagnan's suspicions. He had obviously chosen it because its position on the map was diametrically opposed to that of St Cloud.

The probability of Bonacieux having collaborated in the plot gave d'Artagnan his first ray of hope. If the draper knew where his wife was it would be possible, in an emergency, to force his secret out of him by physical violence. But first he must try and turn the probability of his guilt into a certainty.

'May I presume on your kindness, Monsieur Bonacieux?' he asked. 'Lack of sleep makes one hoarse and I'm feeling very thirsty at the moment, so with your leave I'll go into your room and help myself to a glass of water. I think we can regard that as a tenant's privilege.'

And before Monsieur Bonacieux could reply

d'Artagnan pushed past him into the house, walked into his bedroom and took a quick look at his bed. It had not been slept in. So Bonacieux had been out all night and could only have returned an hour or two before. He had obviously gone with his wife to where they had taken her, or at any rate part of the way.

'Thank you, Monsieur Bonacieux,' said d'Artagnan, emptying his glass. 'That's all I wanted from you. Now I'm going up to my own room to get Planchet to clean my boots for me. When he's finished I'll send him down to do your shoes for you.'

So saying he walked round to the side door and entered the house. The little draper stared after him, quite taken aback by this extraordinary farewell and feeling that he had got the worst of this duel of wits.

D'Artagnan found Planchet standing at the top of the stairs. The fellow was all of a fluster.

'Oh, Sir,' he cried, 'there's no end to our troubles. I thought you were never coming back.'

'What's happened now?'

'You've had a visitor, Sir. You'll never guess who it was, not if you try till Kingdom come.'

'Well, who was it and when did he come?'

'About half an hour ago, when you were with Monsieur de Tréville.'

'And who was it? Come on, Planchet, tell me!'

'Monsieur de Cavois.'

'Monsieur de Cavois? The captain of the Cardinal's Guards?'

'Yes, Sir. In person.'

'Did he come to arrest me?'

'I suspected so. I didn't like those fawning ways of his. Not one bit I didn't.'

'Oh, he fawned, did he?'

'Well, Sir, he was most affable. Let's put it that way. He said he'd called on His Eminence's instructions to escort you to the Palais Royal; that His Eminence was most anxious to meet you as he'd heard such excellent accounts of you.'

'And what did you say?'

'I said I was afraid you wouldn't be able to go, as you were not at home.'

'What did he say to that?'

'He told me to tell you not to fail to call on him some time today. Then he added in a whisper: "Tell your master His Eminence has a very high opinion of him and that his whole future may depend on this interview."'

'That little dodge was a bit transparent,' said d'Artagnan with a smile. 'Don't you agree, Planchet? Not up to the Cardinal's usual standard of wiliness.'

'I saw through the dodge all right, Sir. I answered the gentleman that I knew you'd be disappointed to have missed his visit when you heard about it on your return. He then asked where you'd gone and when, and I said you'd gone off last night to Troyes in Champagne.'

'Planchet, you're a marvel,' said d'Artagnan. 'You couldn't have done better.'

'I knew that if it turned out you did want to see Monsieur de Cavois I could always take back what I'd said about your having gone away. I'd have been the liar, not you. And I'm not a gentleman, so no one thinks the worse of me for telling lies.'

'Don't worry, Planchet. As it happens you won't have lied. We're leaving Paris in half an hour.'

'That's the best news I've heard yet, Sir,' said Planchet. 'And may I ask where we're going?'

'In the opposite direction to where you said I'd gone, of course. Incidentally, aren't you keen to find out what's happened to your pals Grimaud, Mousqueton and Bazin? I know I'm very keen to get news of Athos, Porthos and Aramis.'

'Yes indeed, Sir,' said Planchet. 'And I'm ready to

leave the moment you say. The air of the provinces would be better for us at present than the air of Paris. I'm sure of that.'

'Good,' said d'Artagnan. 'Pack our bags then, and let's be off. I'll leave the house ahead of you; I'll take nothing in my hand so that no one will suspect. You follow on with the luggage and join me at Guards' Headquarters.'

D'Artagnan left the house first, as arranged. On his way to Headquarters he called once more at his three friends' lodgings to make sure they had not returned. No news had been received of any of them. A letter had arrived for Aramis in a scented envelope addressed in an elegant hand, and that was all. D'Artagnan took charge of this letter. Ten minutes later he and Planchet met in the Guards' stables, and each proceeded to saddle his own horse to save time.

Then they were off. The two travellers reached Chantilly without mishap and found Porthos laid up in the inn. He had been badly wounded in the sword fight, but his pride was just as hurt, and he was pretending he had merely sprained a knee. Mousqueton had recovered and was attending to his master. Porthos was too ill to travel so d'Artagnan left him there and went on to Crèvecœur to see about Aramis. He too was alive, but not quite in a fit state for travelling. He had been convinced that his wound was a sign from Heaven that he should renounce his worldly ways and return to his neglected theological studies. However, the sight of d'Artagnan rekindled his love of adventure, and the letter d'Artagnan brought, which was postmarked 'Tours', also made Aramis realize that he was not yet ready to forsake the world completely.

The next morning d'Artagnan and Planchet took their leave of Aramis, promising to return soon, and followed the road to Amiens. They had left Athos there surrounded by enemies and had little hope of finding him

alive. At about eleven in the morning they sighted
Amiens and at eleven-thirty pulled up at the gate of the
ill-fated inn.

D'Artagnan had often meditated taking revenge on
the treacherous landlord. He had got some satisfaction
merely from imagining the scene, and had rehearsed it so
often in his mind that now, on entering the inn, he acted
as though by instinct; he pulled his hat well down over
his eyes, gripped his sword-hilt in his left hand, and with
his right cracked his riding-whip imperiously.

The landlord came forward to greet him.

'Do you recognize me?' asked d'Artagnan.

The landlord was dazzled by his guest's brilliant
turn-out.

'I haven't that honour, Sir,' he replied, bowing low.

'You mean to say you don't know me?' repeated
d'Artagnan. 'In that case I must refresh your memory.
What have you done with the gentleman you had the
cheek to detain here a fortnight ago on a charge of
passing bad money?'

As he spoke he looked the landlord sternly in the eye.
The landlord turned pale.

'Oh, don't mention that unfortunate episode, Your
Honour,' he said in whining, cringing tones. 'God knows
I've had to pay dearly for that blunder. What a time I've
had!'

'I repeat, what have you done with the gentleman?'

'Pray be seated, Sir, and be good enough to listen to my
story.'

D'Artagnan was white with fury. He sat down, as stern
and silent as a judge, while Planchet stood behind his
chair, eyeing the landlord with the utmost scorn.

'I'll tell you exactly what happened, Sir,' went on the
host nervously. 'I recognize you now. It was you who
rode off while I was having that unfortunate scene with
the other gentleman, your friend.'

'Yes, it was. So you see unless you tell the truth you can expect no mercy from me.'

'No, Sir. And if you'll kindly listen I'll tell you the whole sad tale.'

'I'm listening.'

'I'd been warned by the local authorities that a party of notorious coiners were going to put up at my inn, and that they'd all be wearing Guards' or Musketeers' uniforms. I'd been given a full description of all you gentlemen, your horses and your servants.'

D'Artagnan realized at once from what source this description had come.

The landlord continued:

'I'd been given six extra men by the authorities to help me arrest this party of coiners.'

'For the third time, mine host, I ask you: what's become of the gentleman? Where is he? Is he alive? Is he dead?'

'Patience, Your Honour,' went on the host. 'We're just coming to that. Well, you know yourself what happened next. And if I may say so, Sir,' he added, with a sudden crafty look on his face which was not lost on d'Artagnan, 'your own hurried departure made me think that what I'd been told about you might be true. At any rate the other gentleman, your friend, fought like a demon. His servant had unfortunately annoyed the men sent to me from headquarters, who were disguised as grooms . . .'

'You miserable blackguard!' cried d'Artagnan. 'You were all in the plot together! I've a good mind to slaughter the whole lot of you here and now.'

'No, Sir. We were not all in the plot together, as you'll soon see. The gentleman, your friend (forgive me for not giving him his proper title, which, alas, I don't know), put two of my men out of action with the two shots from his pistols and kept the rest of us at bay with his sword, retreating all the time, and, what's more, maiming another of my men with the point and knocking me senseless with the flat end of it.'

'Curse you, landlord! Will you never come to the point?' cried d'Artagnan. 'Athos! What happened to Athos?'

'He retreated in the direction of the cellar, Your Honour. The door happened to be open and he darted in like a flash, banging the door to behind him. Then he started to barricade himself in. Knowing that he couldn't escape from there, my men left him alone.'

'But where is he now?' cried d'Artagnan. 'For God's sake tell me where Athos is now.'

'He's in the cellar, Sir.'

'What, you rogue? You've kept him in the cellar all this time?'

'We keep him! Good Heavens no! What an idea! Don't you realize what he's doing in there, Sir? If you could make him come out I'd be grateful to you all my life.'

'So he's in there now, is he? I shall find him there, shall I?'

'Yes, Sir. He insisted on staying there. He only opened his barricade once, to let his servant in. Every day we've had to hand down bread to him through the skylight on a pitchfork, and meat whenever he asked for it. If it were only bread and meat he wanted it wouldn't be so bad. But there are other things still more to his taste. One day I tried to break in to the cellar with two of my boys, but he flew into a terrible rage and I heard him loading his pistols and his servant priming his musket. We tried to parley with him through the door, but he said he and his servant had forty rounds of ammunition between them and that they'd fire off the whole lot before they'd let any of us in.'

The landlord's look of woe was so comical that d'Artagnan could hardly contain his laughter.

'From that day to this,' the man continued, 'this inn's

been the most miserable place in the world. You see, Sir, all my stores are in the cellar: my bottled and my casked wine, my beer, oil and groceries, my bacon and sausages. We can't get down there at all now; I can't feed my guests and I'm steadily losing custom. If your friend stays in the cellar another week I shall be ruined.'

'And you deserve to be, you rogue! You ought to have known from our looks that we were gentlemen and not coiners. Anyone with any intelligence could have seen that.'

D'Artagnan now lost no time in letting Athos know that it was safe to emerge. Athos was overjoyed to hear a friendly voice and immediately began to demolish his barricade.

A moment later the door split in two and Athos' head appeared in the opening. His face was ashen white as he stood there, trying in a dazed fashion to take stock of his surroundings.

D'Artagnan rushed towards him and hugged him affectionately. His first impulse was to drag his friend out of his dank cave into the daylight, but as he took his arm he noticed that he was staggering.

'Are you wounded?' he asked.

'No, I'm not wounded. I'm dead drunk, and so I deserve to be after my noble efforts of the past few days. Well, landlord, I must have accounted for at least 150 of your bottles on my own.'

'Heaven help me!' cried the landlord. 'If the servant's drunk only half as much as the master, I'm ruined!'

'Grimaud's a servant of the old type,' said Athos. 'He wouldn't presume to drink the same quality wine as I. No, he drank from the barrel; incidentally I rather think he forgot to replace the stopper. Listen! I hear wine flowing now!'

D'Artagnan gave a shout of laughter while the landlord groaned and wrung his hands.

At that moment the figure of Grimaud emerged from the darkness. He had his musket slung over one shoulder and his head was lolling from side to side. He was smeared from head to foot with a greasy fluid, which the host recognized as his best olive oil.

The four in procession, d'Artagnan and Planchet, Athos and Grimaud, now crossed the main hall and were shown into the best room in the inn, where they proceeded to make themselves comfortable, and to call for wine.

'Wine!' cried the host in horrified amazement. 'You've already drunk a hundred pistoles' worth of my best! I'm ruined, lost, destroyed entirely.'

'Nonsense,' said Athos. 'We didn't even drink our fill.'

'And you didn't only drink; you broke all the bottles as well!'

'That was your fault. You shoved me against a case of bottles which collapsed.'

'And all my oil gone!'

'Oil's a sovereign remedy for sword-wounds. It was only natural the wretched Grimaud should dress the wounds you'd given him, and quite fair that he should use your oil to do it with.'

'And all my stock of sausages gone!'

'That cellar's full of rats, you know!'

'You'll have to pay back every penny of damage you've done,' cried the host in a passion.

'You scoundrel, you rogue, you . . . !' shouted Athos.

He tried to get to his feet but fell back at once; he had reached the limit of his capacity. D'Artagnan went to his rescue with his riding-whip raised.

The host shrank back and began to sob.

'This'll teach you to be more civil in future towards the guests whom the good Lord sends to you.'

'The good Lord! The Devil, you mean!'

'Listen, landlord,' said d'Artagnan. 'If you don't stop

pestering us with your ridiculous complaints we'll all four go down into your cellar and make quite sure the damage really is as great as you say it is.'

The host bustled off to carry out his orders.

'And now, my dear d'Artagnan,' said Athos, 'while we're waiting for our wine tell me about the other two. What happened to them?'

D'Artagnan described how he had surprised Porthos in bed with a sprained knee and Aramis at a table with two theologians. In a few moments the host returned with the bottles and a ham which he had fortunately omitted to store in the cellar.

'Well, so much for Porthos and Aramis,' said Athos, filling his and his friend's glasses. 'And what about you? What's been happening to you? There's a sinister look in your eye which I don't like much.'

'If you want to know,' said d'Artagnan, 'I am the most unhappy of the lot of us.'

'You unhappy?' asked Athos. 'What have you got to be unhappy about?'

'I'll tell you another time,' said d'Artagnan.

'Why not now? I know, because you think I'm drunk. Actually I'm never so clear-headed as when I've had a bottle or two. So come on, tell me, I'd like to know.'

D'Artagnan described his experience with Madame Bonacieux in detail. Athos listened with the closest attention. When the young man had finished his tale Athos said:

'A wretched business – an altogether wretched business.'

It was his one and only comment on all love-affairs.

'You always say that, Athos,' said d'Artagnan. 'How can you make a remark like that when you know nothing about it? You've never been in love!'

Athos' lacklustre eyes lit up for a second. But only for a second. They then became dull and lifeless again.

'You're right,' he said quietly. 'I've never been in love.'

'Stony-hearted fellows like you've no right to be hard on poor soft-hearted fools like us,' said d'Artagnan.

'Soft hearts – broken hearts,' muttered Athos.

'What's that you're saying?'

'I'm saying that love's a lottery in which the prize is death. You're very lucky to have lost, d'Artagnan, believe me. And if you're wise you'll take care always to lose.'

'And I thought she loved me!'

'You thought!'

'I know she loved me!'

'So gullible! Every man thinks his mistress loves him and every man's mistress is unfaithful to him.'

'Except yours, Athos, because you've never had one.'

'No,' said Athos after a moment's pause. 'I've never had one. Come on, let's drink.'

'Well, you old Socrates,' said d'Artagnan. 'Teach me your philosophy. Let me drink at the fount of your wisdom. I need to know and be comforted.'

'Comforted in what?'

'In my sorrows.'

'Your sorrows are nothing,' answered Athos. 'I wonder what you'd say if I told you a love story, in return for the one you've told me.'

'Your own love story?'

'Mine or a friend's. It doesn't really matter.'

'Come on, let's hear it, Athos. I'm dying to hear it.'

'Let's drink instead. It's more fun.'

'Let's do both. You can drink and tell me your story at the same time.'

'Yes, I could do that,' answered Athos. 'Drinking and talking go well together.'

'Good. I'm listening,' said d'Artagnan.

Athos sat lost in thought for a moment and d'Artagnan noticed that his thoughts were agitating him; he had reached the stage of drunkenness at which the common run of drinkers collapse and lose consciousness. Athos was like a man in a trance; he was dreaming and yet awake. When he spoke he seemed to be talking as much to himself as to his companion. There was something uncanny about this state of somnambulism.

'You really want to hear the story?' he asked.

'I long to hear it,' said d'Artagnan.

'Very well then, you shall. A friend of mine – a friend of mine, you understand, not I – one of the counts of my native province of Berry fell in love at the age of twenty-five with a young girl of sixteen, as beautiful as the dawn. Child as she was, she was marvellously gifted; she had not a woman's but a poet's mind; she was more than charming – she was enchanting. She lived in a little village with her brother, the local priest. Neither brother nor sister were native to the province; they'd settled there a short while back. No one knew where they came from, but the sister was beautiful and the brother good, so no one bothered to inquire. They were said to be of good birth. My friend was the Seigneur of the district and could have seduced the girl or even ravished her, had he wished; he had sovereign rights and no one would have bothered to protect two strangers from another province. Unfortunately he was an idealist and like a fool went and married the girl!'

'Why a fool if he loved her?' asked d'Artagnan.

'Wait and you'll see,' answered Athos. 'He took her to his home and made her the first lady in the province. And in fairness it must be said she did full justice to her position.'

'Well?' asked d'Artagnan.

Athos lowered his voice and began talking very fast.

'One day she was out hunting with her husband and had a fall,' he said. 'Her horse threw her heavily and she lost consciousness. The man rushed to help her and seeing that her tight riding-habit was stifling her slit it open with a knife as she lay on the ground and exposed her shoulder.'

Athos paused; then he suddenly gave a shout of laughter.

'Guess what she had on her shoulder, d'Artagnan!' he said.

'I can't guess. Tell me,' replied the young man.

'A fleur-de-lis,' said Athos. 'She was branded!'

And he tilted up his glass and drained the contents at one draught.

'How horrible!' cried d'Artagnan. 'What a horrible story!'

'The truth, my dear fellow. The angel was a fiend, the innocent child a thief; she'd stolen the Communion plate from a church.'

'What did your friend do?'

'He was sovereign ruler in his province, with rights of criminal and civil justice. He stripped his wife of the rest of her clothes, tied her hands behind her back and hanged her to a tree.'

'Good God, Athos! You mean he murdered her?' cried d'Artagnan.

'Yes,' replied Athos.

He was as pale as death.

'But look,' he went on, 'my glass is empty. That won't do at all.'

And he seized the last remaining bottle, lifted it to his mouth and drained the contents as though it were a glass.

Then he leaned over the table and buried his head in his arms. D'Artagnan sat facing him, speechless with horror.

After a moment's silence Athos looked up and continued:

'That cured me for ever of women, of enchanting

creatures lovely as the dawn and with the souls of poets. God grant you the same experience!'

At last he had admitted his identity as the hero of the tale.

'So the woman died?' stammered d'Artagnan.

'Of course. But come on, reach me your glass. What, no more wine? Well then, bring the ham, landlord! And hurry!'

D'Artagnan was still horror-struck and hardly dared speak. At last he asked timidly:

'But what happened to her brother?'

'Her brother?' echoed Athos.

'Yes, the priest.'

'Oh, I sent for him to have him hanged too. But he'd stolen a march on me; he'd left his parish the previous night.'

'Did you ever discover who he really was?'

'Yes, he was the creature's first lover and her accomplice. A worthy fellow who'd posed as a priest in order to marry his mistress off and ensure her and himself a livelihood. I trust he's also been hanged by now.'

D'Artagnan could only mutter to himself:

'How horrible!'

'Have some of this ham, it's delicious,' said Athos calmly, carving a slice and laying it on his friend's plate. 'If only there'd been four more hams like this in the cellar I'd have polished off fifty more bottles of wine!'

D'Artagnan felt he could bear no more. The conversation was driving him mad. It was his turn to bury his head in his arms and pretend to go to sleep. Athos observed him pityingly and muttered to himself:

'The youth of today certainly can't drink. That fellow's one of the best. And just look at him!'

18

IN SEARCH OF EQUIPMENT

The next morning, Athos pretended that the story had been dreamed up by him in his drunken state. D'Artagnan, who greatly respected his friend, said nothing. Soon they set out for Paris, picking up Aramis and Porthos on the way. The four friends were together again!

When they arrived back in Paris d'Artagnan found a letter from Monsieur de Tréville telling him that the King had decided to open the campaign against La Rochelle on 1 May (this was a coast-town whose Protestant population was in constant revolt against the Catholic King), and that he must start buying his equipment at once. Though he had only parted from his friends half an hour before he ran off at once to find them again. He discovered them all in Athos' rooms; they all looked worried, and d'Artagnan suspected at once that they had had some fairly serious news.

It turned out that they had all received letters from Monsieur de Tréville telling them about the campaign and ordering them to buy their equipment. All three looked despondent; they knew that Monsieur de Tréville was very strict in matters of discipline and the problem of how to buy equipment for the campaign with their little stock of money seemed insoluble.

'How much d'you think this equipment will cost?' asked d'Artagnan.

'At least 1,500 livres each,' said Aramis. 'And we can't raise more than a hundred each at the most.'

'I think we ought to try and manage on 1,000 apiece,' said d'Artagnan.

'And how d'you think we're going to get that much?' asked Porthos. Then his face suddenly brightened.

'I've got an idea,' he said.

'You're lucky,' said Athos. 'I haven't the faintest shadow of one. As for d'Artagnan I think he's mad. A 1,000 livres indeed! I tell you all here and now I'm not spending a sou less on my outfit than 2,000 livres.'

'Four times 2,000 is 8,000,' remarked Aramis. 'So to get properly turned out we need 8,000 livres. Quite a tidy sum!'

D'Artagnan was undoubtedly the most harassed of the four friends, although as an ordinary guardsman his campaign equipment presented far less of a problem than that of the musketeers, who formed the King's personal bodyguard. The young Béarn recruit was thrifty almost to the point of avarice, but strangely enough, he was vain too. The question of how to cut a good figure in the campaign worried him a lot, and he was also concerned about Madame Bonacieux. The efforts he had made on her behalf had so far led to nothing. Monsieur de Tréville had mentioned the matter to the Queen, who had promised to make inquiries. But d'Artagnan had regarded this promise as a mere formality, which would probably lead nowhere.

Athos would not leave his room; he was determined to make no effort at all to find equipment.

'We've got another fortnight,' he said to his friends. 'If I haven't found anything by then, or rather if nothing has found me by then, I can see only one way out. My religion forbids suicide, so I shall pick a quarrel either with five of the best of His Eminence's Guards or with eight Englishmen and go on fighting till one of them kills me, which is pretty well bound to happen with those odds against me. Then the world will say I died in the King's service, and I shall have done my fighting without needing to get equipment.'

Porthos kept pacing up and down the room, with his hands behind his back, nodding his head solemnly and muttering to himself:

'I must think out my plan; I must get on with my plan.'

Aramis sat looking worried and saying nothing.

From this short summary we can see that an atmosphere of gloom reigned over the little community.

Porthos was the first to hit on a plan, so he was the first to act. He was not a man who readily admitted defeat. One day d'Artagnan noticed him wending his way towards the Saint-Leu church, and curiosity prompted him to follow him. He noticed him curl his moustache and stroke out his beard before entering the church and presumed from this that he was on an errand of conquest. D'Artagnan followed him into the church, but took care to keep out of his sight, so that Porthos should not know that he was being watched.

The big man walked up the aisle and stood beside a pillar near the chancel. D'Artagnan followed him and leant against the other side of the pillar, still hidden from his friend's sight.

A sermon was being preached that day, so the church was full. Porthos, who had a roving eye, was soon busy ogling all the female members of the congregation.

D'Artagnan soon noticed a woman seated in a pew nearby, a woman in the early autumn of life, slightly parched and wrinkled of skin, but a dignified enough figure in her black hat and dress. Porthos cast a quick look or two at this woman out of the corner of his eye and then started ogling the other ladies of the congregation in earnest.

The lady in black, for her part, let her gaze rest for a second on the handsome Porthos, upon which he, as though in answer to a signal, started fluttering his eyelashes wildly down the aisle. This manoeuvre obviously irritated the lady in the black hat, for she now began biting her lip and fidgeting uneasily in her seat.

Seeing this Porthos once more curled his moustache, and began casting sheep's eyes at a beautiful lady seated near the choir. Besides being beautiful this lady was obviously someone of rank, for in the pew behind her sat a little Negro boy who carried the cushion upon which she knelt to pray and a maid who carried the embroidered bag which contained her prayer-book.

The lady in black followed every dart and roll of Porthos' eyes and noticed his gaze rest at last on the lady with the velvet cushion, the maid, and the Negro page. Porthos played his cards cunningly; he now ogled the beauty so shamelessly that the lady in black became frantic.

The beautiful lady with the velvet cushion was the cynosure of all eyes. But she impressed three people in particular; the lady in black, who saw in her a formidable rival; Porthos, who thought her ten times more attractive than the lady in black; and lastly d'Artagnan, who recognized her as the woman of Meung whom his evil genius, the man with the scar, had addressed as Milady.

The young man was determined not to let the lady out of his sight. Meanwhile he continued to watch Porthos' little comedy with considerable amusement. He deduced that the lady in black must be a former mistress of Porthos', a rich attorney's wife whom Porthos had once mentioned.

When the sermon was over the attorney's wife stepped up to the stoup of holy water. Porthos also walked up to it, reached it just before she did and dipped not one finger but his whole hand into the water. The attorney's wife imagined that he was paying her this attention and gave him a sweet smile. But the next moment she was cruelly undeceived. When she was only three feet from him he turned away and gazed fixedly at the other lady who was at that very moment approaching with her maid and her black page. Porthos waited until she was quite close and then lifted his dripping hand from the stoup. The lady laid her slender fingers on Porthos' broad hand, smiled her thanks, crossed herself, and left the church.

This was more than the attorney's wife could bear. She was by now convinced that Porthos and her rival had a secret understanding. Had she been a lady of rank she would have fainted. But she was only an attorney's wife, so was content to hiss furiously at the musketeer:

'Well, Monsieur Porthos! Aren't you going to offer me some holy water too?'

At the sound of her voice Porthos pretended to start with surprise.

'Well, well, Ma'am!' he said. 'Fancy seeing you! And how's Monsieur Coquenard, your husband? As mean as ever? Where can my eyes have been that I never noticed you during the whole of that two-hour sermon?'

'I was only a few feet away from you, Sir,' said the attorney's wife. 'You didn't notice me for the simple reason that you had eyes only for that beautiful lady you gave the holy water to.'

Porthos pretended to be embarrassed.

'Oh, so you noticed, did you . . . ?'

'I'd have had to be blind not to notice.'

'Yes,' said Porthos coolly. 'The lady's a friend of mine, a duchess. She has a very jealous husband who tries to stop her seeing me. It's been very difficult to arrange meetings with her, and today she came all the way to this church in this God-forsaken district on purpose to meet me.'

'Monsieur Porthos,' answered the attorney's wife, 'will you be good enough to take a stroll with me? I want to talk to you.'

'With pleasure, Ma'am,' said Porthos. And he smiled

to himself like a gambler gloating at the thought of a trick he is about to play on an unsuspecting opponent.

At that moment d'Artagnan came out from behind the pillar and walked down the aisle in pursuit of Milady. As he passed Porthos and the attorney's wife he stole a quick look at his friend, noticed the gleam of triumph in his eye and thought cynically:

'That's one of us set up for the campaign, at any rate!'

D'Artagnan followed Milady unknown to herself; he watched her get into her carriage and heard her tell the coachman to drive to Saint-Germain. He found Planchet and ordered him to fetch their horses. Then they mounted and set off in pursuit.

They were riding along an empty street, keeping a sharp lookout for any trace of the beautiful English-woman, when he suddenly noticed a man standing in the porch of a house by the roadside. The man's face seemed to d'Artagnan vaguely familiar, but Planchet recognized him first.

'D'you see that fellow standing there star-gazing, Sir?' he asked.

'Yes, who is he?'

'You ought to remember him, Sir,' replied Planchet. 'That's Lubin, the servant of the Comte de Wardes, the gentleman you had the duel with a month ago in the wood near Calais.'

'By Jove, so it is!' cried d'Artagnan. 'I recognize him now. D'you think he's recognized you?'

'Well, Sir, I spent such a lively quarter of an hour with him that I don't suppose he's kept a very clear picture of me in his head.'

'Go and talk to him, then,' said d'Artagnan, 'and find out whether his master's dead.'

Planchet dismounted and walked boldly up to Lubin. As he had foreseen the man did not recognize him and the two started chatting together quite amicably.

Meanwhile d'Artagnan led the two horses up a side-road and round the back of a neighbouring house, and approached the first house under cover of a hazel hedge, drawing close enough to overhear the conversation of the two servants.

A few minutes later d'Artagnan heard the noise of carriage wheels, and the next moment a coach, Milady's coach, drew up in front of the house only a few yards away from him.

Yes, there was no mistake, Milady herself was seated inside!

D'Artagnan crouched down against his horse's neck and from that position could see without being seen.

Milady leaned her charming head out of the coach window and called out an order to her maid. The maid, a pretty, lively young girl of twenty, jumped down from her seat on the footboard of the coach and walked over to the terrace where Planchet and Lubin had been standing. D'Artagnan watched her from his vantage-point behind the hedge.

It so happened that Lubin had meanwhile been summoned indoors on an errand, and Planchet was now standing on the terrace alone, anxiously looking to right and left for traces of his master. The maid came up to him and, mistaking him for Lubin, handed him a letter.

'For your master,' she said.

'For my master?' replied the astonished Planchet.

'Yes,' replied the maid. 'As you see, the letter's marked "urgent", so please deliver it at once.'

So saying she turned and walked quickly over to her mistress. The coach had meanwhile been backed round and was now facing the direction from which it had come. The young girl stepped lightly on to the footboard and the coach immediately drove off.

Planchet turned the letter over in his hand, puzzled how to act. Then, trained as he was in unquestioning obedience he ran down the terrace steps, turned up the side-road, and after about twenty yards came face to face with d'Artagnan, who had seen everything and was on his way to join him.

'For you, Sir,' said Planchet, handing him the letter.

'For me?' asked d'Artagnan. 'Are you sure?'

'Positive, Sir. The maid said "For your master". You're my only master, so the letter must be for you, mustn't it?'

D'Artagnan opened the letter and read as follows:

Someone who is deeply interested in you wishes to know when you will be well enough to take a walk in the forest.

A footman in black and red livery will await your reply tomorrow at the Field of the Cloth of Gold inn.

'This is really too much!' muttered d'Artagnan. 'Milady and I seem to have a common interest in the Comte de Wardes' health. Well, Planchet, and how is the good Count? I gather he's not dead after all.'

'No, Sir. He's progressing as well as a man can hope to progress after receiving four sword-thrusts in the body – that was what you gave the poor gentleman, Sir. But he's still very weak, having lost nearly all his blood. As I thought, Sir, Lubin hadn't recognized me and actually gave me a graphic account of our meeting with him and his master.'

'Excellent, Planchet. You're the king and prince of lackeys. Now hop on your horse again and let's see if we can overtake that coach.'

It did not take them long; after a five minutes' ride they turned a corner and saw the coach drawn up in front of them on the wrong side of the road. A well-dressed man on horseback was parleying with Milady through the coach door. Their conversation was so lively that d'Artagnan was able to approach to within a few feet of the other side of the coach, unobserved by all save the pretty maid.

Milady and the man on horseback were talking in English, so d'Artagnan could not understand what they were saying. But from the tone of her voice he gathered that the beautiful Englishwoman was in a rage. She brought the conversation to a close with a gesture which betrayed her state of mind; she rapped the stranger's knuckles very violently with her fan, shattering it. At this the stranger merely roared with laughter, which seemed to incense Milady still more.

D'Artagnan thought this an excellent moment to intervene. He rode up to the off-side door of the coach, took off his hat, bowed and said:

'Can I be of service to you, Madame? This gentleman's apparently been annoying you and with your permission I'll teach him a lesson in manners.'

Milady had turned at the sound of d'Artagnan's voice and now stared at him in surprise. In answer to his little speech she said in excellent French:

'At any other time I'd have been glad of your support, Sir, but this gentleman happens to be my brother.'

'Then please accept my apologies, Ma'am,' replied d'Artagnan. 'If I'd known that I wouldn't have interfered.'

'What does this young idiot think he's doing?' cried the stranger on the horse, lowering his head to the level of the carriage door. 'Why doesn't he go away and mind his own business?'

'Idiot yourself!' said d'Artagnan, bending down and addressing him through the body of the coach. 'And I'm not going away to please you, Sir!'

The man on horseback now said a few words to his sister in English.

'I addressed you in French, Sir,' said d'Artagnan. 'So be good enough to answer me in that language. You're this lady's brother, I know, but you're not mine, for which I thank God.'

If Milady had been timid, like most women, she would have interfered at this point and tried to prevent the quarrel becoming serious. But she did the very opposite. She leaned back against the cushions of her seat and called out calmly to the coachman:

'Drive back to the house!'

The pretty maid threw a quick, anxious glance at d'Artagnan, whose good looks had apparently attracted her. Then the coach drove off, hiding him from her sight and leaving the two men face to face on the empty road.

The stranger was preparing to canter off after the coach when d'Artagnan rode up to him, seized his horse by the bridle and held him back.

'I haven't got a sword, Sir, as you can see for yourself,' said the Englishman. 'You're surely not going to start blustering against an unarmed man.'

'I expect you've got a sword at home, Sir. If you haven't I've got two and I'll gladly play you for one.'

'No need for that, Sir,' answered the Englishman. 'I've got all the swords I'm ever likely to want.'

'Good,' said d'Artagnan. 'Then pick your longest and come and show it to me this evening.'

'Where?'

'Behind the Luxembourg. An ideal spot for two people who've got something urgent to discuss.'

'Right. I'll be there.'

'State your time, Sir.'

'Six o'clock.'

'Oh, and by the way, I dare say you've a friend or two in Paris.'

'I know three who'd be delighted to take my side in this dispute.'

'Marvellous! I've got three dying to take my side.'

'And now, Sir, your name, please,' said the Englishman.

'D'Artagnan, Squire of Gascony, attached to des
Essarts' company, King's Guards. And yours, Sir?'

'Lord de Winter.'

'Your servant, my Lord!' said d'Artagnan. 'Six o'clock
then, behind the Luxembourg!'

And putting spurs to his horse he galloped off in the
direction of the capital.

As was his habit on an occasion like this he called at
once on Athos. He found him lying stretched out on a
large sofa, waiting, as he said, for his campaign equipment to come and find him. The young man related word
for word all that had happened, but did not mention
Milady's letter to the Comte de Wardes.

Athos was enchanted with the news, for his one wish
had been to fight an Englishman. The two lackeys were
immediately sent off to fetch Porthos and Aramis, who
arrived posthaste and were at once told the story.

Porthos was overjoyed at the prospect of the duel. He
drew his sword and started making imaginary passes at
the wall, lunging and feinting and capering about like a
dancer. Aramis calmly retired into Athos' little writing-
room to finish writing a poem, begging his friends not to
disturb him until the very moment when swords were to
be drawn.

Athos signed to Grimaud to bring in another bottle of
Spanish wine.

As for d'Artagnan, he sat down to work out a little
private scheme of his own. From the smiles which from
time to time crossed his face as he sat brooding it was
clear that he was picturing some amusing intrigue which
might result from his machinations.

19

ENGLISH AND FRENCH

At the time appointed the four friends and their four
servants arrived at the site agreed upon for the duel, an
enclosed piece of meadow-land which was used as a
pasturage for goats. Athos gave the goatherd some
money to remove his goats elsewhere for the time being.
The four lackeys were then posted as sentries at each of
the four gates into the enclosure. In a few moments
another silent party of four entered the enclosure and
joined the musketeers. As was customary in England
before duelling they gave their names and waited for
their opponents to do the same. All four Englishmen
were members of distinguished families, and were therefore both astonished and dismayed to hear their opponents announce themselves as Athos, Porthos and
Aramis.

'And after that,' said Lord de Winter, 'we're none the
wiser as to who you really are. I'm sorry, but we can't
fight men with names like those. They're mythical
shepherds' names.'

'Of course you realize they're assumed names, Sir?'
said Athos.

'Yes. And that's why we must insist all the more that
you tell us your real names,' replied the Englishman.
'Gentlemen only fight with their equals.'

'True, Sir,' said Athos.

Upon which he took aside the Englishman whom he
was to fight and whispered his name to him.

Porthos and Aramis did the same with their two
opponents.

'Are you satisfied?' said Athos to his foe. 'D'you

consider me your equal and qualified to cross swords with you?'

'Yes, Sir,' said the Englishman, bowing.

'Good,' said Athos. 'And now may I say something to you in return?'

'Pray do,' answered the Englishman.

'You'd have been wiser not to force me to tell you my real name.'

'Why?'

'Because I'm supposed to be dead and have good reasons for not wanting anyone to know I'm alive. So I shall be forced to kill you to make sure my secret never leaves your lips.'

The Englishman stared at Athos in amazement. Could he be talking seriously? Athos was, in fact, perfectly serious.

'Well, gentlemen,' he said, addressing the whole company, 'are we ready?'

'Yes,' replied the two opposing parties in one voice.

'On guard then,' said Athos.

Immediately eight sword blades gleamed in the rays of the setting sun and a fierce battle began. These eight men were fighting in a double cause, for their own personal honour and for the honour of their country.

Athos was the first to kill his man. He struck him only once, but the thrust was mortal and he collapsed with a wound through the heart. Porthos, the next to score, sent his man sprawling on the grass with a thigh wound. The Englishman surrendered and handed over his sword, upon which Porthos picked him up in his arms and carried him to his coach. Aramis, pressing hard, forced his man to give ground about fifty feet and finally to surrender. D'Artagnan, fighting Lord de Winter, played an entirely defensive game; he waited for the Englishman to tire and then disarmed him with a clever feint.

Lord de Winter, defenceless, retreated a few steps out

of d'Artagnan's reach. But his foot caught in a stone and he tripped and fell on his back. D'Artagnan was on him in a trice; he put his sword point to his throat and cried:

'You're in my power now, Sir. I could kill you if I liked, but I'll spare you for the sake of your sister, whom I love.'

D'Artagnan was triumphant. Everything had turned out as he had planned. The scene which had caused him to smile as he had pictured it was exactly realized.

Lord de Winter was delighted to find his enemy so tractable. He embraced him with many expressions of gratitude and paid compliments to each of his three friends. So much for him. Porthos' opponent was already ensconced in his carriage and Aramis' foe had taken to his heels. So there was now only the dead man to consider. Porthos and Aramis undressed him to make sure that his wound was fatal. In doing so they discovered a heavy purse attached to his belt.

D'Artagnan untied it and handed it to Lord de Winter.

'What d'you expect me to do with that?' asked the latter.

'Return it to his family, Sir,' said d'Artagnan.

'His family won't worry about a trifle like that,' said Lord de Winter. 'They'll be coming into an income of £15,000. Keep that purse for your servants.'

Then, turning to d'Artagnan, he continued:

'And now, my young friend, if you'll allow me to call you that, I shall be delighted to present you tonight to my sister, Clarice de Winter. I'd like her to know you too, for her own sake, and as she has some influence at Court she might be able to put in a good word for you.'

D'Artagnan flushed with pleasure, bowed and accepted the invitation with thanks.

Meanwhile Athos had approached the young man. He waited till Lord de Winter had stopped talking; then, taking the purse from his friend's hand, he whispered to him:

'Let's give this purse not to our servants but to the English servants.'

And he threw the purse to the coachman, crying:

'For you and your fellows.'

This act of generosity, coming from a man so poor as Athos, impressed even Porthos. The musketeer's action was later quoted everywhere by Lord de Winter as an example of French liberality and delighted everyone except Masters Grimaud, Mousqueton, Planchet and Bazin.

Before leaving the scene of the duel Lord de Winter gave d'Artagnan his sister's address in the Place Royale, the most fashionable district of Paris. He also promised to call for the young man at Athos' lodgings, drive him to the house and present him to his sister personally.

The knowledge that he was to meet Milady greatly excited the young man, for he remembered how a strange Fate had already caused their ways to cross. He was convinced that she was an agent of the Cardinal and yet some peculiar instinct, of which he himself was only half aware, seemed to drive him towards her, though his better judgement told him he was acting rashly.

His only fear was that she might remember their two previous meetings, at Meung and at the Port of London. For she would then know that he was a friend and protégé of Monsieur de Tréville and therefore Royalist to the core. He would then lose all his advantage in the battle of wits with her, for from the start she would know as much about him as he about her and they would be fighting on equal terms.

After leaving the Luxembourg he went straight home and changed into his smartest clothes. He then called on Athos and, as was his habit of late, confided everything to him. Athos listened closely to his story, shook his head disapprovingly and recommended caution.

'I can't understand you,' he said. 'You've only just

parted from one woman whom you describe as good, charming, and altogether perfect, and here you are running after another.'

D'Artagnan felt the justice of this rebuke.

'I love Madame Bonacieux with my heart, and Milady with my head,' he explained. 'My only object in meeting her is to find out exactly what position she holds at Court.'

'From what you say I should have thought it was obvious what she was,' said Athos. 'She's an agent of the Cardinal, a dangerous woman who'll entrap you and get your head chopped off.'

'You're a gloomy devil, Athos.'

'My dear fellow, I'm suspicious of women. I can't help it. I've had bitter experiences with them. I'm particularly suspicious of fair women. I think you said Milady was fair.'

'She's got the fairest hair I ever saw!'

'Oh, my poor d'Artagnan!' said Athos.

'I promise you I only want to find out about her. When I've done that I'll stop seeing her.'

'Very well. Good luck to you in your quest,' replied Athos calmly.

Lord de Winter arrived at the hour arranged. Athos, forewarned, retired discreetly into the back room and the Englishman found d'Artagnan alone. It was already eight o'clock so the two men left the house at once, got into the Englishman's carriage and drove off to the Place Royale.

Lady de Winter received d'Artagnan graciously. Her house was furnished in the greatest luxury. The threat of war had already driven most English people out of France, but Milady was still busy altering her house to her taste, which proved that she was exempt from the general measure expelling British subjects from the country.

Lord de Winter, introducing d'Artagnan to his sister, said:

'Here's a young man who had my life in his hands and spared me. We were enemies on two counts; we'd had a personal quarrel and also had our countries' honour to defend. And yet he spared me. So if you've a spark of affection for me, Clarice, I'm sure you won't refuse to thank him.'

Milady frowned and her face darkened ever so slightly. Then she smiled a queer smile. That smile made d'Artagnan feel very uncomfortable. Her brother, however, noticed nothing; he had turned his back and was playing with Her Ladyship's pet monkey, which had clawed at his doublet.

'I'm indeed glad to see you, Sir,' said Milady in a voice of singular sweetness, which contrasted strangely with the expression of annoyance which d'Artagnan had noticed on her face. 'I shall always be grateful to you for what you did today.'

The Englishman now turned to her again and described the meeting in the enclosure in detail. Milady listened with the greatest attention and pretended to be delighted by the story. But it was obvious from the way she kept flushing and tapping the floor with her foot beneath her dress that she was inwardly furious.

Lord de Winter, however, noticed nothing. When he had finished his tale he walked across the room, filled two glasses from a decanter of Spanish wine on a table and invited d'Artagnan to drink with him. D'Artagnan knew that the English regarded a refusal to drink as a mortal insult. So he went over and joined his host. But at the same time he kept his attention fixed on Milady, watching her reflection in the mirror. When she thought herself unobserved an amazing change came over her. Her face was distorted by an expression of almost murderous rage and she bit savagely at her handkerchief.

At that moment the pretty maid whom d'Artagnan had noticed on the footboard of the coach came in and said something in English to Lord de Winter. The latter at once asked d'Artagnan to excuse him on the grounds of an appointment and suggested that his sister entertain his young guest in his absence.

D'Artagnan shook hands with Lord de Winter and then returned to his hostess. Milady's face, which was extraordinarily mobile in expression and seemed to reflect her every changing mood, was now gracious and smiling; there were, however, a few drops of blood on her handkerchief from her torn lips.

The conversation now took a light, easy turn. Milady seemed to have entirely recovered her spirits. She told d'Artagnan that Lord de Winter was her brother-in-law and not her brother; that she had married the younger son of the de Winter family who had died, leaving her a widow with one child. If Lord de Winter did not marry, this child would inherit the name and the family fortune.

D'Artagnan learned a little of what he wanted to know from Milady's talk. But he had an uneasy feeling that it was a screen, a camouflage, put up to hide something else. At present he could not see beyond the screen.

After half an hour's talk he was convinced of one thing, that Milady was a Frenchwoman; she spoke the purest and most polished French imaginable.

At last the time came for him to take his leave. He bade Milady farewell and left the room the happiest of men.

At the head of the stairs he came face to face with the pretty maid. She brushed his arm lightly as he passed, blushed modestly, and asked his pardon so prettily that it was at once granted.

D'Artagnan called again next day and Milady gave him an even kindlier welcome. Lord de Winter did not appear this time and Milady entertained her young guest alone. She seemed to take a great interest in him, asked him what province he came from, who his friends were, and whether he had ever considered entering the Cardinal's service.

D'Artagnan was, we know, quite shrewd for a man of his years, and at this point he remembered his earlier suspicions of Milady. He immediately embarked on a long eulogy of the Cardinal and declared that he would certainly have joined His Eminence's Guards and not the King's Guards if he had known Monsieur de Cavois and not Monsieur de Tréville.

Once or twice in the course of the conversation Milady bit her lip with annoyance; she had hoped to be able to lead the young man on, but began to realize that he was no fool.

D'Artagnan took his leave at the same hour as before. On the stairs he again came face to face with Kitty, the pretty maid. This time she shot him a shy, admiring glance which spoke volumes. But the young man was so preoccupied with the mistress that he never gave the maid a thought.

He returned next day and the day after. Each time Milady gave him a warmer welcome, and each time, whether by accident or design, he came face to face with the pretty maid, either in the ante-room, in the passage, or on the stairs. But he continued to ignore her.

D'Artagnan was growing daily more enamoured of
Milady. His conscience, Athos' words of wisdom, happy
recollections of Madame Bonacieux, none of these things
had succeeded in deterring him from his pursuit of the
beautiful Englishwoman and he continued to visit her
and pay her compliments. He was confident enough
to believe that sooner or later she would yield to his
courtship.

One day he arrived at her house holding his head high
and treading on air as usual. In the porch he ran into the
pretty maid Kitty. This time she did not merely give him
her customary fond look; she actually took him by the
hand.

'Good,' thought d'Artagnan. 'She's got some special
message for me from her mistress, some note proposing a
tryst which the lady daren't suggest to my face.'

And he gave the pretty maid one of his most engaging
smiles.

'May I say something to you, Sir?' stammered the
unfortunate Kitty.

'Of course, child! What is it?'

'I can't say it here, Sir. It would take too long. Besides
it's a private matter.'

'Where can we go then?'

'I could take you somewhere if you'd be good enough
to follow me, Sir,' said Kitty timidly.

'With pleasure, my dear.'

'Come then, Sir.'

She still had hold of his hand and now turned and led
him up a narrow spiral staircase. They climbed about

twenty steps and came to a little door which Kitty opened.

'Come in here, Sir,' she said. 'We can talk in here and we won't be disturbed.'

'What room's this?' asked d'Artagnan.

'It's my room, Sir. And that door there leads into my mistress's room. But she never goes to bed before midnight so there's no danger of her overhearing us.'

D'Artagnan looked round him. It was a charming little room, clean and pleasantly furnished. But, as may be supposed, what interested him most in the room was the door which led into the room beyond.

Kitty guessed what was in his mind and sighed.

'You're very fond of my mistress, Sir, aren't you?' she asked.

'Fonder than I can say, Kitty. I'm madly in love with her.'

Kitty sighed again.

'I'm very sorry about that, Sir,' she said.

'Why on earth?'

'Well, Sir, my mistress doesn't love you at all.'

'Doesn't she, by Jove?' said d'Artagnan. 'And did she tell you to tell me so?'

'Oh, no, Sir! I made up my mind to tell you myself, for your own advantage.'

'Thank you, Kitty,' replied d'Artagnan. 'Thank you for your intentions, which I'm sure are good; not for your message, which is not so good!'

'So you don't believe me?'

'It's always difficult to believe things like that. One's pride revolts, if nothing else.'

'Won't you really believe me?'

'Not unless you give me some proof.'

'Well, what do you think of this?' asked Kitty.

And she pulled a letter out of her bodice, folded but unaddressed.

'For me?' cried d'Artagnan.

He snatched the letter from her hand and, before Kitty could stop him, opened it and started to read.

'Oh, Sir, what are you doing?' she cried.

'Well, don't you want me to read a note that's addressed to me?' asked the young man.

He read as follows:

You never answered my first note. Are you ill or have you forgotten how you smiled at me at Madame de Guise's ball? Now's your chance, Comte. Don't miss it.

D'Artagnan went white. He was hurt, not, as he supposed, in his affections, but in his pride.

'This note's not for me at all!' he cried.

'No, it's for someone else. I tried to tell you but you wouldn't listen.'

'Who is it for?'

'The Comte de Wardes.'

D'Artagnan at once recalled the scene on the terrace at Saint-Germain, which confirmed what Kitty had just said.

'Poor Monsieur d'Artagnan,' said Kitty, taking the young man's hand in hers and pressing it fondly.

'So you're sorry for me, are you, my dear?' said d'Artagnan.

'Very sorry indeed. You see I know what it is to be in love.'

'You know?' asked d'Artagnan. He looked at Kitty for the first time with some interest.

'Yes, unfortunately.'

'Well, then, instead of being sorry for me you'd better help me get my revenge on your mistress.'

'What revenge do you want?'

'I want to make her fall in love with me; I want to do down my rival.'

'I'll never help you to do that, Sir,' said Kitty firmly.

'Why not?' asked d'Artagnan.

'For two reasons. Firstly because my mistress'll never love you.'

'What makes you think that?'

'You've done her a mortal injury.'

'I? Do her an injury? But that's nonsense! Why, ever since I first met her I've been at her feet like a slave. What on earth do you mean?'

'I can't explain except to the man who can read my heart.'

D'Artagnan again eyed Kitty with interest. He saw that she had a freshness and charm for which many princesses would have exchanged their wealth and rank.

'I'll read your heart, Kitty,' said the young man. 'So don't let that prevent you talking. There!'

And he kissed her, at which the poor girl blushed a cherry red.

'Oh no,' she cried. 'You don't love me; it's my mistress you love; you told me so only a moment ago.'

'Does that prevent your telling me your second reason for refusing to help me?'

'My second reason, Sir,' said Kitty, gaining courage as she looked into the young man's eyes, 'is that in love it's everyone for himself.'

Only then did d'Artagnan remember Kitty's languishing glances, those apparently accidental encounters in the ante-room, on the stairs or in the passage, how she had brushed his sleeve with her hand and the stifled sighs she had uttered. He had noticed nothing of all this at the time, so obsessed was he with thoughts of her mistress. Who in quest of an eagle takes note of a thrush?

But now our Gascon saw in a flash all the advantages to be gained from Kitty's attachment to himself, which she had so naïvely confessed. It would now be possible, he thought, to intercept letters addressed to the Comte de

Wardes, to get political news at first hand, to enter the house at any hour of the day or night by the side staircase leading to Kitty's room, which adjoined that of her mistress. The unscrupulous and ambitious young man was already planning to sacrifice the humble servant to the great lady.

'Well,' he said, in answer to her protest that it was not her he loved but her mistress. 'Shall I give you a proof of the love you seem to doubt?'

'What love?' asked the young girl.

'The love I'm prepared to feel for you.'

'How can you prove that?'

'Suppose this evening I were to spend with you the time I usually spend with your mistress?'

'Oh, that would be wonderful!' cried Kitty, clapping her hands.

'Very well, my dear,' said d'Artagnan, settling himself down in an armchair. 'Come here and let me tell you you're quite the prettiest girl I ever saw.'

And he continued in this vein so long and so adroitly that the unfortunate Kitty, who was already half-way to being persuaded, ended by believing him. And yet, to d'Artagnan's surprise, she put up a quite stubborn resistance before yielding to him.

Time spent in attacks and defences of this nature passes swiftly. Midnight struck and almost at once the bell rang from Milady's bedroom.

'Good Heavens!' cried Kitty. 'That's my mistress ringing for me! You must leave the house at once. Hurry!'

D'Artagnan got up and seized his hat as though preparing to leave. Then, instead of going to the door, he went over to a big cupboard in the corner of the room, opened it, stepped in, locked the door from the inside, and hid himself among Milady's dresses and night-dresses.

'What on earth are you doing?' cried Kitty.

There was no reply from inside the cupboard.

'Well,' cried Milady angrily from the next room, 'are you asleep, Kitty? Why don't you answer when I ring?'

D'Artagnan heard the communicating door being thrown open.

'I'm just coming, Milady!' cried Kitty, running forward to meet her mistress.

The two women went back into the bedroom, leaving the communicating door open, so that d'Artagnan could hear every word that was said in Milady's bedroom. Milady continued to scold Kitty for a while. Then she calmed down, and while Kitty was undressing her turned the conversation on to himself, d'Artagnan.

'Well,' she said. 'I didn't see my Gascon friend this evening.'

'Didn't he call tonight?' asked Kitty. 'Has he lost interest before getting his way with you?'

'Oh no,' said Milady. 'He hasn't lost interest. He must have been kept back by Monsieur de Tréville or Monsieur des Essarts. I'm experienced in these things, Kitty, and I know I've got that young man.'

'What will you do with him, Milady?'

'Just you wait and see, Kitty! I've a score to settle with him which he knows nothing about. He nearly made me lose my position with His Eminence. I'll make him pay dearly for that.'

'I thought you loved him, Milady!'

'Love him? I hate him! Why, the fool had Lord de Winter's life in his hands and spared him, thereby losing me an income of 300,000 livres.'

'Yes, of course,' said Kitty. 'Your son was His Lordship's sole heir and you'd have had control of his fortune until he came of age.'

D'Artagnan, listening from inside the cupboard, felt his blood freeze in his veins. What horror was this he heard? This creature whom he had idolized, whom he had thought as good as she was fair, was actually cursing him, in a voice unrecognizably harsh and strident, for his failure to kill a man for whom she had previously professed deep affection.

'I'd have revenged myself on him before now,' continued Milady. 'But for some reason the Cardinal asked me to deal gently with him.'

'Yes, Milady. You've been gentle with him, but you weren't so gentle with that woman he was so fond of.'

'You mean the draper's wife from the Rue des Fossoyeurs! Oh, he's forgotten her ages ago! That's not much of a revenge.'

D'Artagnan broke out into a cold sweat. Was this woman a complete monster? He strained his ears to hear more, but Milady had now finished her toilet for the night.

'That'll do, Kitty,' she said. 'You can go to bed now. And first thing tomorrow take the letter I gave you and try to get an answer from the person concerned.'

'You mean Monsieur de Wardes?'

'Of course.'

'You may be unkind to poor Monsieur d'Artagnan, Milady, but you're certainly not unkind to Monsieur de Wardes.'

'Don't be impertinent, Kitty. Leave the room, please.'

D'Artagnan heard the door being closed again. Then he heard a noise of bolts being drawn, and a key being turned very gently in the lock. Milady was shutting herself in on one side of the door and Kitty was making assurance doubly sure on the other.

Now d'Artagnan opened the cupboard and stepped out.

'Good Heavens, what's the matter?' whispered Kitty. 'You're as white as a sheet!'

'What a vile creature!' muttered d'Artagnan.

'Hush!' said Kitty. 'Go away at once. The partition

wall's very thin and Milady can hear everything that goes on in this room.'

'That's just why I'm not going.'

'What d'you mean?' asked Kitty, blushing.

'At least . . . not just yet.'

And he pulled Kitty towards him. It was hopeless to resist now, for resisting meant making a noise, so Kitty yielded.

The love-making of d'Artagnan and Kitty was to a great extent inspired by their common wish to be revenged on Milady. And d'Artagnan had good reason to agree with the old adage that revenge is a joy not scorned by the Gods. And had he had more heart and less pride and ambition he would have been content with this one triumph. But he was no saint. It can be said to his credit, however, that the first use he made of his influence over Kitty was to try and discover the whereabouts of Madame Bonacieux.

The poor girl swore on the Bible that she knew nothing, and that her mistress only let her in to half her secrets. All she could be sure of was that the draper's wife was not dead. And Milady's remark about d'Artagnan having undermined her influence with the Cardinal had completely baffled her.

But on that point d'Artagnan was better informed than she. He had caught sight of Milady on a ship anchored in the Port of London at the moment when he himself was leaving England, so he guessed that she had been referring to the affair of the diamond tags. But from what he had overheard he concluded that the main reason for her hatred of him was that he had not killed her brother-in-law.

D'Artagnan called on Her Ladyship again next day and found her in a very bad temper. He guessed that the reason for this was that she had had no answer from the Comte de Wardes.

However, as the evening wore on Her Ladyship calmed down and listened graciously to d'Artagnan's compliments. She even allowed him to kiss her hand.

The young man took leave of her, not knowing what to make of her behaviour. But, as we know, he was not easily flummoxed, and while paying court to Milady he was also hatching a little plot of his own. He found Kitty waiting for him at the door, and again went up to her room to hear what news she had for him. She told him she had been severely scolded and accused of carelessness in handling the letter. Milady had been upset by the Comte de Wardes' silence and had ordered Kitty to come to her next morning at nine o'clock for fresh orders. D'Artagnan suggested that she call at his lodgings afterwards to pass on her orders to him, and the poor child, in her foolish infatuation for the young guardsman, agreed to do so.

At eleven o'clock next day Kitty called on d'Artagnan, bringing another note in Milady's handwriting. This time she did not even try to prevent him reading it; she just let him have his way. She was his slave now, ready to obey him in everything.

D'Artagnan opened this second letter which was also unaddressed and unsigned and read as follows:

This is my third letter to you telling you I love you. Take care I don't write a fourth telling you I hate you.

If you repent of your behaviour the girl who brings this will tell you how you can make amends.

D'Artagnan changed colour several times as he read. Kitty kept her eyes fixed on him while he was reading.

'So you still love her!' she said.

'No, Kitty,' he replied. 'I don't love her, but I mean to have my revenge on her.'

Kitty sighed. D'Artagnan took up a pen and wrote:

Lady de Winter,

Until now I was in doubt whether your first two notes were really intended for me, so unworthy did I feel of such an honour.

But today I am compelled to believe in your goodness, for I both read in your letter and hear from your maid's lips that I have the incredible good fortune to have won your love.

I shall come at eleven this evening to make amends. To let one more day pass would be unpardonable.

Your humble servant, the man blessed above all others.

de Wardes

His plan was quite simple. He would enter Milady's bedroom through her maid's room and take her by surprise. He would compromise her, terrify her with threats of a scandal and force her to confess to the kidnapping of Madame Bonacieux and to disclose her whereabouts. He foresaw that if he played his cards well he might even obtain her release.

'Here, Kitty,' he said, putting the sealed note into her hand, 'give this letter to Milady; it's Monsieur de Wardes' reply.'

Kitty went as pale as death, for she suspected what the note contained.

'Listen, my dear,' said d'Artagnan. 'You must realize that you're now in this plot as much as I and that it's too late to back out. Milady may discover that you gave her first note to my servant instead of to de Wardes' servant and that I, and not de Wardes, opened the two others. If she finds that out she'll sack you, and you know her well enough to realize that she won't be content with a small revenge like that.'

'Oh dear!' sighed Kitty. 'And who am I doing all this for, d'you suppose?'

'For me, Kitty. I know that,' replied the young man. 'And I'm very grateful to you.'

'You might at least tell me what you've written in the note.'

'Milady will tell you.'

'I see you don't love me and I'm very unhappy.'

To such accusations from a woman there is only one reply. D'Artagnan replied in such a way that Kitty's illusions were completely restored. She cried a good deal before consenting to deliver his note to Milady. But at last she agreed, and that was all d'Artagnan wanted. To please her he promised that he would leave her mistress early that night and come to her.

That promise succeeded in banishing Kitty's last doubts.

21
ALL CATS ARE
GREY AT NIGHT

No sooner had Kitty gone than d'Artagnan set off for Athos' lodgings. Since Athos had vowed that he would not cross his threshold until money for his equipment had turned up, the four friends regularly met there. Shortly after d'Artagnan arrived, Aramis burst in with the news that his 'publisher' (in fact Madame de Chevreuse) had forwarded him enough money to buy his equipment. So now both he and Porthos were set up.

The evening, so eagerly awaited by d'Artagnan, arrived at last.

As usual d'Artagnan called at nine o'clock at Milady's house. He found her in excellent spirits, and more gracious than he had ever known her. He rightly attributed Her Ladyship's good humour to the fact that she had at last received an answer from the Comte de Wardes.

When Kitty came in with the sherbet her mistress smiled kindly at her, but the poor girl was so distressed to see d'Artagnan sitting there that Milady's smiles were wasted on her.

D'Artagnan looked at both women and was forced to admit that nature had made a mistake when she created them. She had given the mistress a cunning, scheming mind and the maid an affectionate and loyal heart.

At ten o'clock Milady began to show signs of restlessness. D'Artagnan guessed the reason for this. She kept looking at the clock, fidgeting uneasily in her chair and smiling at d'Artagnan in a manner which seemed to say: 'I'm sure you're very nice, but you'd be even nicer if you went away.'

So d'Artagnan got up and took his leave, and Milady gave him her hand to kiss. She pressed his hand gently, this time, as d'Artagnan guessed, not from coquetry, but from gratitude to him for leaving her.

'She loves him desperately,' he thought.

Then he went out. This time Kitty was not waiting for him either in the ante-room, in the passage, or at the front door. So the young man had to find his way alone up the staircase and into Kitty's little room.

He found the poor girl sitting with her face buried in her hands, crying. She did not look up when he came in, so he went over to her and took her hand. At this she burst into loud sobs.

As d'Artagnan had foreseen Milady had been overjoyed to receive the note which she took to be from the Comte de Wardes; in her excitement she had confided everything to Kitty and had then given her a well-filled purse as a reward for her success in obtaining an answer. Kitty had thrown the purse into a corner of her room, where it now lay unfastened, disgorging a few coins on to the carpet.

D'Artagnan, suddenly conscience-struck, begged the

wretched girl to stop crying. At the sound of his voice she
at last looked up, clasped her hands in front of her and sat
gazing at him, not daring to say a word. Unimpression-
able though he was, the young man was moved by the
look of dumb misery on her face. But he was too set on
carrying out his plan to allow sentiment to intervene at
the last moment.

Kitty saw that it was hopeless to try and restrain him.
His mind was made up. All he would do was to reassure
her in regard to his motives which, he declared, were
merely to take revenge on Milady for having given him
false hopes and to find out the whereabouts of Madame
Bonacieux; he hoped to achieve his second aim by using
his one and only weapon against Milady, her fear of
scandal. Fate seemed bent on furthering his designs, for
that night Milady, anxious no doubt to hide her blushes
from her lover, had taken it into her head to have all the
lights put out in her room and in her maid's room.
Monsieur de Wardes was to leave before daybreak, and
he and she were to spend all the hours of their tryst in
total darkness. This would enable d'Artagnan to slip into
her room without her recognizing him.

In a few moments d'Artagnan and Kitty heard Milady
coming upstairs. The young man immediately hid himself in the cupboard as he had done before. Hardly had he
closed the cupboard door when Milady's bell rang. Kitty
went into her mistress' room, shutting the door behind
her. But the dividing wall was so thin that d'Artagnan
could hear almost all that was said in the room beyond.
Milady seemed to be in the seventh heaven of joy. She
made Kitty describe to her every detail of her interview
with the alleged Comte de Wardes; she asked if he had
been glad to get her letter, if he had answered it at once,
how he had looked when writing his reply and whether
he had seemed very much in love. Kitty answered all
these questions in a strained, stilted manner, trying to

make her voice sound natural. But Milady noticed nothing unusual either in her face or voice, so absorbed was she in her own fantasies.

As the hour of her appointment with the Comte de Wardes approached Milady reminded Kitty to put all the lights out; she then told her to return to her room and to show Monsieur de Wardes in as soon as he arrived.

Kitty did not have to wait long. When d'Artagnan, peeping through the keyhole in the cupboard door, saw that everything was in darkness he stepped out of his hiding-place just as Kitty was closing the door into her mistress' bedroom.

'What's that noise?' called out Milady.

'It's I, de Wardes!' answered d'Artagnan in a low voice.

'Oh dear!' thought Kitty. 'He can't even wait till eleven, the time he fixed himself.'

'Well?' said Milady, her voice trembling with excitement. 'Why doesn't he come in?'

Then she called:

'Comte, Comte, you know I'm expecting you!'

At this summons d'Artagnan pushed Kitty gently aside and strode into Milady's bedroom.

No pain is so great as that endured by a man who listens to endearments from his mistress which he knows are intended for another. D'Artagnan now found himself in a distressing situation which he had not foreseen; he was smitten with jealousy and suffered almost as much as poor Kitty, who was weeping in the next room.

Milady was cooing in her softest voice, holding d'Artagnan's hand in hers.

'Oh Comte,' she said, 'the look of love in your eyes and the charming things you said each time we met made me so happy! I, too, love you. Send me some token to prove your devotion and I'll give you this ring so that you won't forget me.'

She took a sapphire and diamond ring off her finger

and slipped it on d'Artagnan's. The young man's first impulse was to return it to her, but Milady stopped him.

'No, keep it out of love for me,' she said.

Then she added in a voice suddenly strained:

'And by keeping it you'll be helping me in another way which I can't explain now.'

'This woman's a real mystery,' thought d'Artagnan.

At that moment a sudden impulse seized him to confide everything to her, to tell her who he was and confess his true motives in visiting her. But she interrupted him as he was about to speak.

'My poor angel,' she said. 'How near you were to being killed by that frightful Gascon.'

That frightful Gascon! Himself! D'Artagnan winced.

'Are your wounds still hurting you?' asked Milady.

The young man found this question difficult to answer. He replied lamely:

'Yes, a little.'

'I'll avenge you, I'll avenge you. Never fear!' hissed Milady in a voice which made the young man shiver. He thought to himself:

'No. This would not be a good moment to confess.'

It took him quite a time to recover from this little dialogue. All his ideas of revenge had vanished. This woman had an astonishing power over him. He was drawn to and repelled by her at the same time, and was perturbed to find himself swayed by two such conflicting emotions. The passion she roused in him was uncanny and somehow evil.

Now the clock struck one and the lovers had to part. When d'Artagnan bade Milady farewell he felt nothing but strong regret at having to leave her. And as they kissed for the last time they arranged another meeting for the following week. Poor Kitty had hoped to be able to say a few words to d'Artagnan as he passed through her room. But Milady insisted on leading him through the dark room herself and out on to the landing.

Early next morning d'Artagnan paid a call on Athos. He had become involved in such a fantastic intrigue that he felt he must ask his friend's advice. He told him everything.

Athos frowned several times as he listened to the story. 'This Milady seems to be an inhuman monster,' he said. 'But even so you were wrong to play that trick on her. You've only succeeded in making an enemy for life.'

As Athos talked he kept staring at the sapphire and diamond ring on d'Artagnan's finger. The young man had put it on instead of the Queen's ring, which he had carefully locked away in a box.

'Are you looking at my ring?' he asked, proud to be able to show off such a handsome present to his friend.

'Yes,' replied Athos. 'It reminds me of a sapphire which used to belong to my family.'

'It's beautiful, isn't it?' said d'Artagnan.

'Magnificent,' said Athos. 'I didn't know there was another stone like that anywhere in the world. Have you bartered your diamond for it, or what?'

'No,' said d'Artagnan. 'It's a present from my beautiful Englishwoman. Incidentally I think she's French; I've never asked her, but I'm somehow convinced she was born in France.'

'Milady gave you that ring?' cried Athos.

His voice was suddenly strained and he was obviously struggling to hide some emotion.

'Yes, last night.'

'Let me have a look at it.'

D'Artagnan slipped the ring off his finger and handed it to his friend.

Athos examined it closely and turned pale. Then he tried it on the fourth finger of his right hand. It fitted perfectly. D'Artagnan was surprised to see a look of rage suddenly cross his face. Then he seemed to regain his self-control.

'It couldn't possibly be the same,' he said, speaking half to himself and half to d'Artagnan. 'How on earth could Lady de Winter have got hold of that ring? And yet it's difficult to believe there are two sapphires so exactly alike.'

'Have you seen that ring before?' asked d'Artagnan.

'I thought I had. But I suppose I must be wrong.'

He returned the ring to d'Artagnan but still kept his eyes fixed on it. After a moment's silence he said again:

'D'Artagnan, be a good fellow and turn that ring round so that the stone's underneath. It brings back such bitter memories that I couldn't go on talking to you seeing it glittering on your finger. And I think you said you wanted my advice. No, on second thoughts, show it to me again. The sapphire I'm thinking of had one of its facets slightly scratched from an accident.'

D'Artagnan again slipped the ring off his finger and handed it to the older man, who examined it closely and then gave a start.

'Look, d'Artagnan!' he exclaimed. 'Curious coincidence, isn't it?'

And he pointed to a scratch on the sapphire exactly as he had described it.

'But who gave you the ring?' asked d'Artagnan.

'My mother left it to me, and my father gave it to her. As I told you, it's an heirloom which should never have been allowed to go out of the family.'

'And you . . . sold it?' suggested d'Artagnan.

'No,' said Athos with a strange look on his face. 'I gave it away during . . . an hour of perfect happiness, just as it was given to you.'

Athos' words set d'Artagnan thinking in his turn. His thoughts centred round Milady, who seemed to him more than ever a creature of mystery, with dark and as yet unfathomed secrets in her soul. He took the ring back from his friend, but instead of slipping it on his finger put it in his pocket.

'Listen, d'Artagnan,' said Athos, taking his friend's hand. 'You know I'm fond of you. I'm as fond of you as though you were my son. Well, here's my advice to you; give this woman up. I don't know her, but some instinct warns me she's dangerous and that there's something evil about her.'

'I think you're right,' answered d'Artagnan. 'Very well, I'll give her up. I won't deny she even frightens me.'

'Will you have the strength of mind to do that?'

'Yes, I'll do it at once,' replied d'Artagnan.

'I really think you're wise, my dear boy,' said the older man, grasping the younger's hand affectionately. 'Thank God this woman's only just come into your life, and God grant she may not have left some curse on it already.'

Whereupon he nodded to his friend to show that he would now like to be left alone with his thoughts.

When d'Artagnan arrived home he found Kitty waiting for him. A month's illness could not have ravaged the poor girl's looks more than her one hour of jealous suffering. She had come with a message from her mistress for the Comte de Wardes. Milady was mad with joy, crazed with love, and had sent to inquire when the Comte would pay her a second visit. And now poor, ill-used Kitty stood and waited for d'Artagnan's reply.

Athos had a great influence over his young friend. His advice, the promptings of d'Artagnan's own instincts, the recollection of Madame Bonacieux, which never left him for long, and the knowledge that he had saved his pride and had his revenge, combined to decide the Gascon to part finally with Milady. In reply to her message through Kitty he therefore wrote as follows:

Lady de Winter,

Do not force me at present to give you a definite date for our next meeting. Since my recovery I have had so many engagements of a similar nature that I have had to make a sort of time-table.

I will have the honour to inform you when your turn comes.

Respectfully,

de Wardes

D'Artagnan had handed his letter to Kitty without sealing it. The girl read it through but at first could make neither head nor tail of it. When she finally grasped its meaning she went half mad with joy. She could scarcely believe the good news and would not be satisfied until d'Artagnan had repeated word for word what he had written.

Knowing her mistress' violent temper Kitty realized the risk she ran in handing her this letter. But this did not prevent her from returning to the Place Royale as fast as her legs would carry her. Even the best-natured women are indifferent to the sufferings of their rivals in love.

Milady opened the letter with a joy as intense as Kitty felt in handing it to her. But when she read the first words she went livid. She crumpled the letter in her hand and then faced Kitty, her eyes flashing fire.

'What's the meaning of this letter?' she asked.

'It's in answer to yours, Milady,' replied Kitty, trembling from head to foot.

'Impossible,' said Milady. 'No gentleman would write a woman a letter like that.'

Then she suddenly cried out:

'Good God! Could he have seen . . . ?'

She stopped. Her teeth were chattering, her face ashen pale. She now turned and tried to walk over to the window to get air, but could only raise her arms; her legs gave way under her and she collapsed into an armchair.

Kitty thought she had had an attack of some sort and

rushed up to her to unlace her bodice. But Milady shrank back at her touch and glared at her.

'What d'you want?' she cried. 'Why did you take hold of me like that?'

Kitty was appalled by the expression of mingled rage and fear on her mistress' face.

'I thought you'd fainted, Milady,' she said, 'and I wanted to do something to help you.'

'You thought I'd fainted?' cried Milady. 'What d'you take me for? A silly, weak woman? No. When I'm insulted I don't faint. I strike back. D'you hear? I say I strike back. Now go!'

And with an imperious gesture she waved Kitty out of the room.

22
PLANS FOR REVENGE

That evening Milady gave orders that d'Artagnan was to be shown in to her the very moment he called. But that night for the first time he did not appear.

The next day Kitty called a second time on the young man and told him exactly what had happened the previous night. D'Artagnan smiled grimly at the description of Milady's furious outburst; that was his revenge.

That evening Milady was more impatient even than before. She repeated her orders to her household to show d'Artagnan in when he arrived. But once more she waited for him in vain.

The following day Kitty called again on d'Artagnan,

but this time, instead of being gay and lively as on the two previous occasions, she was in despair. When d'Artagnan inquired the reason for her gloom she took a letter from her pocket and handed it to him without a word. It was addressed in Milady's handwriting, and this time not to the Comte de Wardes but to Monsieur d'Artagnan.

The young man opened the letter and read as follows:

Dear Monsieur d'Artagnan,

You are unkind to neglect your friends like this, especially now that you are soon going away.

My brother-in-law and I were expecting you yesterday and the day before, but you never came.

I hope it will not be the same again this evening?

Your ever grateful friend,

Clarice de Winter

'That's just what I expected,' said d'Artagnan. 'As the Comte de Wardes' stock falls mine rises.'

'Are you going?' asked Kitty.

The young man had every intention of going but had to justify himself to himself for breaking the promise he had made to Athos. In answer to Kitty's question and to still the voice of his conscience he said:

'It would be most unwise to ignore such a pointed invitation. If I didn't go this evening Milady would wonder why I'd suddenly broken my habit of visiting her. She'd suspect something, and a woman like her might do anything to revenge herself for a slight.'

'Oh dear,' sighed Kitty. 'You always manage to put things so that everything you want to do seems right. But you're bound to start making up to her again, and if this time you succeed with her under your own name it'll be ten times worse than before.'

The poor girl had instinctively guessed what was likely to happen. D'Artagnan comforted her as best he could and assured her that he would remain impervious to Milady's charms. He then sent her back to her mistress with a message that he would be delighted to call on her that evening. (He did not dare write lest Milady's experienced eye should recognize his handwriting.)

As the clock struck nine d'Artagnan arrived at the house in the Place Royale. The servants on duty in the ante-room had apparently been warned that he was coming, for when he appeared one of them ran at once to announce his arrival before he even had time to inquire whether Her Ladyship was at home.

'Show him in,' said Milady quickly and so loudly that d'Artagnan heard her in the ante-room.

'I'm not in to anyone else,' she added. 'You understand? To no one else.'

The servant went out and ushered in the young man. As d'Artagnan entered the drawing-room he took a quick look at Milady and noticed that she was pale and that her eyes were tired, either from weeping or from lack of sleep. The light had purposely been dimmed, but even so, traces of her sufferings of the past two days were visible on her face.

D'Artagnan began paying court to her as usual. She braced herself to respond to his compliments, but the effort was obviously painful, and never had such haggard looks belied so sweet a smile.

Milady laid herself out to delight the young man with her charm and to dazzle him with her wit. And the fire of anger which burned within her added sparkle to her eyes and colour to her cheeks. D'Artagnan felt himself falling under her spell again. Then Milady smiled and the young man knew that he would risk damnation for that smile. He even began to feel remorse for having tricked her.

From generalities the conversation gradually changed to matters more intimate and personal. Milady asked d'Artagnan if he was in love. D'Artagnan sighed deeply, laid his hand on his heart and replied:

'That was a cruel question, Lady de Winter. You know that since I first met you I've lived for you and because of you alone.'

Milady smiled a strange smile.

'So you love me?' she said.

'Do I need to tell you? You must have noticed.'

'Yes,' she replied. 'But as you know, proud hearts are hardest won.'

'I enjoy a hard fight. I only shy off if a thing's impossible.'

'Nothing's impossible to true love,' said Milady.

'Nothing, Lady de Winter?'

'Nothing.'

'Ye gods,' thought d'Artagnan. 'The tables are turning. Is the fickle creature preparing to fall in love with me? Is she going to give me another sapphire like the one she gave me as de Wardes?'

'You say you love me, Monsieur d'Artagnan,' went on Milady. 'What would you do to prove it?'

'Anything!' cried d'Artagnan, fully aware that in committing himself thus he was not risking much.

'Then come closer and let's talk,' said Milady, inviting d'Artagnan to bring his chair up to her armchair.

'Well, Lady de Winter?' asked the young man.

Milady paused for a moment, as though in doubt. Suddenly she seemed to make up her mind and said:

'I have an enemy, Monsieur d'Artagnan.'

D'Artagnan pretended to be surprised.

'You, Lady de Winter?' he cried. 'How could anyone hate you, good and charming as you are?'

'A mortal enemy.'

'Incredible!'

'A man who's insulted me so cruelly that it's open war between us. Can I count on you as an ally in this?'

D'Artagnan realized in a flash what she was leading up to.

'You can, Lady de Winter,' he said. 'My life's yours.'

'Very well,' said Milady. 'Since you're so ready to prove your love . . .'

She paused.

'Well?' prompted d'Artagnan.

'Well, never again talk of impossibilities.'

'Oh, you make me so happy!' cried d'Artagnan, falling on his knees before her and covering her hands with kisses.

Then he looked up at her.

'I'm ready,' he said.

'So you know what I want you to do, dear Monsieur d'Artagnan?' said Milady.

'I could read your thoughts merely by gazing at you.'

'And you'll risk your life to avenge my honour?'

'Just say the word.'

'And what shall I do for you in return? I know men; I know they always expect some reward.'

'I only ask you to let me love you,' replied d'Artagnan.

And he drew her gently to him.

Milady struck while the iron was hot.

'My enemy's name is . . .' she began.

'De Wardes, I know it,' said d'Artagnan.

Milady started and drew back.

'How did you know that?' she asked, seizing his hands and staring at him as though she would read his thoughts.

D'Artagnan realized that in the excitement of the moment he had blundered.

'Tell me how you knew!' insisted Milady.

'How I knew?'

'Yes.'

'Because yesterday, in front of a crowd of people,

myself included, de Wardes produced a ring which he
said was a present from you.'

'The fiend!'

As may be imagined Milady's words cut d'Artagnan to
the quick.

'Well?' she continued.

'Well, I'll slay this fiend for you!' cried the young man
melodramatically.

'Thank you, brave friend! And when will you do it?'

The young man now said gravely:

'Let's make it tomorrow. Tomorrow either you'll be
avenged or I shall be dead.'

'I shall be avenged but you won't be dead,' said
Milady. 'He's a coward.'

'Yes, but Fortune's fickle. She favours a man one day
and spurns him the next.'

At that moment they heard footsteps on the stairs.

'Quiet!' whispered Milady. 'I hear my brother. You'd
better not meet him tonight.'

She rang the bell and Kitty appeared.

'Go out this way,' said Milady to d'Artagnan, opening
a hidden door in the tapestry. 'And come back at eleven.
Kitty will let you in.'

When the poor girl heard this she thought she would
faint.

'Now then, Kitty,' said Milady sharply. 'Don't stand
there gaping! Hurry up and show Monsieur d'Artagnan
out, and show him in again at eleven. Do you hear?'

After leaving Milady, d'Artagnan went straight out of
the house, ignoring Kitty's entreaties that he should wait
in her room until the hour of his appointment with her
mistress. He did this firstly in order to avoid the maid's
reproaches, and secondly, because he wanted time to
think things over and if possible fathom what was in
Milady's mind.

The fact which stood out most clearly in the affair was

that he, d'Artagnan, loved her madly, while she did not love him at all. A moment's calm thought told him that his wisest course would be to return home and write a long letter to Milady, explaining that he and de Wardes were the same; that he could only kill de Wardes by committing suicide and that the real de Wardes was innocent of any crime against her.

Unfortunately the young man was himself spurred on by a fierce longing for revenge. He wanted to possess this woman under his own name, and as the nature of his revenge promised to be very sweet he was reluctant to give up his plan.

He walked about a dozen times round the Place Royale, looking up every now and then at the light in Milady's drawing-room windows, which shone dim through the blinds. She was obviously not so keen to keep her tryst that night as on the first occasion.

At last the light disappeared and with it d'Artagnan's last doubts. He remembered every detail of the first night he had spent with Milady and ran back to the house and up the stairs to Kitty's bedroom, his heart pounding with excitement, his senses on fire.

The little maid was standing at the door as pale as death, trembling in every limb. She tried to bar the young man's way. But Milady had been listening closely and had heard him arrive; she now opened the communicating door and called:

'Come in!'

Kitty, left alone on the far side, flung herself against the door in a frenzy. She felt all the pangs of jealousy, rage, and hurt pride, and at that moment had an overwhelming impulse to expose the whole intrigue. But then she realized that if she confessed her complicity in the plot she would not only be ruined herself but would lose d'Artagnan for ever. She decided that rather than lose him she would submit to this final indignity.

D'Artagnan had meanwhile realized his heart's desire. His mistress no longer loved him under the name of a hated rival; it seemed she now loved him as himself. Some still, small voice did indeed whisper to him that he was only an instrument of vengeance for her, that in caressing him she was merely coaxing him for her own purposes. But pride and his insane passion silenced that voice, stifled that whisper.

We cannot say how long that night seemed to Milady. To d'Artagnan barely two hours seemed to have passed when dawn began to filter through the cracks in the blinds and gradually spread through the room. Seeing that the young man was preparing to go, Milady again reminded him of his promise to avenge her.

'Yes, I'll do it,' said d'Artagnan. 'But I'd like first to be certain of one thing.'

'What?'

'That you love me.'

'I should have thought I'd given you proof enough of that,' she replied. 'And now it's for you to prove your love for me.'

'Yes. And I'll do so,' replied d'Artagnan. 'But if you love me as you say you do, aren't you at all concerned for my safety?'

'Why? What danger is there?'

'I might be seriously wounded, killed even.'

'Not with your courage and good swordsmanship.'

'Wouldn't you prefer some other revenge which would save my having to fight a duel?'

Milady looked at the young man in silence. In the first faint rays of dawn her eyes shone with a sinister light.

'I really believe you're fighting shy of it,' she said at length.

'No,' he replied. 'But I confess I'm sorry for poor de Wardes now you no longer love him. I feel that to have lost your love is punishment enough in itself.'

'Who said I ever loved him?' asked Milady.

'Well, at least I can fairly say now that you love someone else. And I repeat, I'm sorry for de Wardes.'

'Why?'

'Because I happen to know . . .'

'What?'

'That as far as you're concerned he's not nearly so guilty as you think.'

'Not guilty?' cried Milady uneasily. 'What d'you mean? Please explain yourself.'

And she looked at d'Artagnan, who was still holding her in his arms, with eyes in which now shone a truly hostile light. D'Artagnan decided to end this ridiculous farce at once.

'I'm a man of honour,' he said, 'and now that I know you love me . . . for you do love me, dear heart, don't you?'

'Yes, yes, go on.'

'Well, to know that makes me so happy that I want to confess something to you.'

'Confess something?'

'Yes. You know how much I love you, and if I've wronged you through excess of love will you forgive me?'

'Perhaps. But what have you to confess?'

Milady's voice was hard and she was now deathly pale.

'You had an assignation with de Wardes last Thursday in this very room, didn't you?'

'Certainly not!'

Milady spoke so emphatically and showed so little concern that had d'Artagnan not known the truth he would have doubted. Instead he smiled a sickly smile and said:

'Don't lie, dear heart, it's no use.'

'What d'you mean? Explain yourself. You frighten me!'

'Don't be frightened. You've done me no wrong and I've already forgiven you.'

'Well, go on!' cried Milady.

'De Wardes hasn't been boasting at all.'

'What d'you mean? You told me yourself he was flaunting my ring about.'

'I've got that ring, dear heart. You see it was I who was here on Thursday night . . . not de Wardes!'

The rash young fellow expected nothing more from his mistress than surprise and mortification, a petulant storm which would resolve itself in tears. But he was very much mistaken and was soon to discover his mistake.

Milady started up wild and pale. She forced d'Artagnan away with all her strength and sprang out of bed.

It was now almost daylight.

D'Artagnan caught hold of her flimsy crêpe-de-Chine nightdress and held her back, meaning to coax her into forgiving him. As she tried to jerk herself free the cambric of the dress tore, leaving her beautiful white shoulders bare. And on her left shoulder d'Artagnan saw to his horror the fleur-de-lis, the mark of the criminal. Milady was branded!

The young man let go of her nightdress and lay there motionless, paralysed with fear.

'God in Heaven!' he whispered.

Milady saw the look of horror on his face and guessed the cause of it. He had obviously seen everything; he now knew her secret, which no other living soul knew.

She turned on him. She was no longer an angry woman; she was a wounded animal at bay.

'Fiend!' she shrieked. 'You've played a vile trick on me and you know my secret! You shall die!'

She ran over to her dressing-table, half naked as she was, and with trembling hands opened a marquetry jewel-case, took out a little gold-hilted dagger with a

thin, pointed blade and with one bound was back at
d'Artagnan's side.

Brave as he was the young man flinched and shrank
back at the sight of her. Her face was transformed. The
pupils of her eyes were horribly dilated, her cheeks
deathly pale, her teeth bared in a snarl. He backed away
from her as far as the alcove, eyeing her warily like a wild
beast, and when his hand, damp with sweat, accidentally
touched his sword he clutched hold of it and drew it from
its scabbard.

But Milady showed no alarm at the sight of the sword.
She came nearer and nearer to the young man to strike
him with the dagger and stopped only when she felt the
point of his sword against her breast.

She now tried to catch hold of the naked blade with her
hands. But d'Artagnan managed to keep it from her
grasp and to hold her at bay by pointing it first at her eyes
and then at her throat. As he did so he slid gradually
down to the bottom of the bed; his plan was to get as close
as possible to Kitty's door, through which he hoped to
escape.

Meanwhile Milady made frenzied attempts to get near
him and strike him, uttering low growls of baffled rage.
So fierce was her onslaught that d'Artagnan began to feel
he was duelling with a man and took courage again.

'All right, my beauty,' he kept saying. 'That'll do,
that'll do. Calm down or by God I'll carve another fleur-
de-lis on your other shoulder!'

'Fiend of Hell! Fiend of Hell!' shrieked Milady.

D'Artagnan's one thought was to get to the door and
out of the room, so he kept on the defensive. And now
Kitty, startled by the noise as Milady turned the room
upside down in her efforts to reach d'Artagnan, burst
open the door and looked in. D'Artagnan had by careful
manoeuvring at last succeeded in approaching to within
three feet of this door. Now with one bound he was in

Kitty's room; quick as lightning he slammed the door behind him and held it closed, while Kitty drew the bolts across.

With a man's strength Milady now tried to break down the door. Finding this impossible, she stabbed the door panel over and over again with her dagger. Some of her blows drove the point right through the woodwork and each time she struck she cursed aloud.

When the bolts were drawn safely across d'Artagnan whispered to Kitty:

'Get me out of the house, quick. I must leave before she calms down, or she'll set her household at me.'

'But you can't go out like that,' said Kitty. 'You're stark naked!'

Only then did d'Artagnan notice his condition.

'Well, bring me some clothes, quick! Anything! Only hurry! If I don't get out I shall be killed.'

Kitty understood this as well as he. In a twinkling she had rigged him out in a flowered dress, a large bonnet and a tippet, and put slippers on his bare feet. The two of them then rushed headlong out of the room and down the stairs to the street door.

They were only just in time. Milady had by now rung her bell and wakened all the household. As the night porter was unbolting the door on Kitty's order Milady leaned from her bedroom window, also half-naked, and screamed:

'Don't let him out!'

And as the young man fled down the street she stood watching him, shaking her fist in impotent rage and hurling curses at his retreating figure. No sooner had he vanished from her sight than she fell down on the floor of her room in a dead faint.

D'Artagnan ran non-stop to Athos' rooms, and woke his friend up. Athos' first reaction was to laugh at d'Artagnan's ludicrous appearance.

'Don't laugh, Athos, for God's sake,' said d'Artagnan. 'I can assure you there's nothing to laugh at.'

He said this so seriously and with such a look of genuine terror on his face that Athos was startled. He seized his friend's hands and said:

'You're not wounded, are you? You look very pale.'

'No, I'm not wounded. But I've just had a horrible experience. Are you alone, Athos?'

'Who d'you expect to find here at this hour of the night?'

'That's all right then.'

And the young man rushed into Athos' bedroom. Athos closed the door behind him and bolted it to make sure that no one would disturb them. Then he said:

'What is it, for Heaven's sake? Is the King dead? Have you killed the Cardinal? You look scared stiff. What's happened? Tell me! You've frightened me now.'

D'Artagnan quickly threw off his clothes and stood only in his shirt.

'Prepare to hear a really horrifying story,' he said.

'Right. But first put on this dressing-gown,' said the musketeer.

D'Artagnan shuffled into the dressing-gown and stood with it half on and half off. He was too upset to pay attention to details of dress.

'Well?' asked Athos.

D'Artagnan lowered his voice.

'Well,' he said. 'Milady's branded with a fleur-de-lis on her shoulder.'

Athos drew in his breath sharply and started back as though he had been shot.

'Listen,' went on his friend. 'Are you quite sure the other one's dead?'

'The other one?' murmured Athos in a voice so faint that d'Artagnan could hardly hear him.

'Yes. The one you told me about that day at Amiens.'

Athos groaned and buried his head in his hands.

'This woman's about twenty-eight.'

'Fair?'

'Yes.'

'With very light blue eyes, black eyebrows and eyelashes?'

'Yes.'

'Tall and beautifully made?'

'Yes.'

'The fleur-de-lis is small, reddish-brown and rather indistinct as though some sort of ointment was put on it to hide it?'

'Yes.'

'And yet you say this woman's English?'

'They call her Milady, but she might be French all the same. Lord de Winter's only her brother-in-law.'

'I must see her, d'Artagnan.'

'I should keep well out of her way, Athos. You tried to kill her once and she'll want to punish you for that. She's revengeful.'

'She wouldn't dare report me; she'd only be giving herself away.'

'She's capable of anything. Have you seen her in a rage?'

'No,' said Athos.

'She's the devil incarnate. Oh, Athos, I'm afraid I've made a terrible enemy in that woman – an enemy for both of us.'

D'Artagnan then described the scene in Milady's bedroom and her attempts to murder him.

'You're right,' said Athos. 'Our lives aren't worth a moment's purchase now. Luckily we're leaving Paris the day after tomorrow; we'll probably be going to La Rochelle and once we're on the march . . .'

'If she sees and remembers you she'll never rest till she's got even with you, Athos. So steer clear of her and let her vent her rage on me.'

'I wouldn't much care if she did kill me,' said Athos. 'I don't think this world's such a very wonderful place.'

'There's some mystery behind it all, Athos. I'm sure that woman's the Cardinal's spy.'

'In that case take care on your own account. Either the Cardinal admires you very much for the London episode, or he hates you like Hell for it. There's nothing he can openly get you for and yet he must vent his rage somehow. So take care. If you go out late at night don't go alone; don't eat or drink anything you're not sure of. Be on your guard all the time in fact.'

'Thank God we've only got two more days to get through. After that we'll be with the army and then we'll only have men to fear.'

'From now on I renounce my vows of seclusion,' said Athos. 'I propose to go about with you everywhere. The first thing you must do now is get back to the Rue des Fossoyeurs and I'm coming with you.'

'It's not far, I know,' said d'Artagnan. 'But I can't go in your dressing-gown all the same.'

'No, you can't,' said Athos.

He rang a little bell on the table and Grimaud came in. Athos signed to him to go to d'Artagnan's lodgings and bring back his clothes; Grimaud clicked his heels, bowed, and went off without a word.

'D'you realize we're worse off now than we were before as far as equipment goes?' said Athos. 'You've left your uniform in Milady's house and I don't suppose she'll be in any hurry to return it. Luckily you've still got your sapphire.'

'The sapphire's yours, Athos. Didn't you tell me it was a family heirloom?'

'Yes. My father bought it for 2,000 crowns; it was one of his wedding presents to my mother. It's magnificent. My mother gave it to me, and I, like a fool, instead of treasuring it, gave it to that fiend.'

'Well, here it is. Take it. I expect you're longing to have it back.'

'I take that ring! After that fiend's had it? Never! That ring's defiled now.'

'Sell it or pawn it, then. They're bound to advance you 1,000 crowns on it. That'll fix you for the time being; directly you get hold of some ready cash, redeem it. It'll be undefiled again then because it'll have passed through the hands of the money-lenders.'

Athos laughed.

'You're a good fellow, d'Artagnan,' he said. 'Your wit's a tonic. Very well, we'll pawn the ring. But on one condition.'

'What's that?'

'That we share the proceeds – take 500 crowns each.'

'I wouldn't dream of it, Athos. I don't need a quarter of that. I'm only a guardsman, remember. Besides I've got a ring of my own.'

'Yes, but I think you value yours even more than I value mine.'

'True. You see that ring could be used to save our skins as well as our pockets. It's a gold mine and a talisman too.'

'I don't know what you mean, but I'll take your word for it. But as regards my ring, either you consent to take half the proceeds or I throw it into the Seine.'

'Very well then. I agree,' said d'Artagnan.

At that moment Grimaud came in followed by Planchet; the latter, concerned for his master's safety, had insisted on bringing the clothes himself.

D'Artagnan and Athos now dressed. The two masters and the two servants then set off for the Rue des Fossoyeurs.

Monsieur Bonacieux was standing at his front door; he winked slyly at d'Artagnan and said:

'Hurry up, Sir, hurry up. A beautiful young lady's called to see you, and women don't like to be kept waiting, you know.'

'It must be Kitty!' cried d'Artagnan.

And he rushed down the alley, in at the door, and up the stairs.

On the landing outside his room he did, indeed, find Kitty. She was standing hunched up against his door; her face was pale and she was trembling. When she caught sight of him she cried out:

'You promised to protect me; you promised to protect me from her! Don't forget it's you who got me into trouble.'

'I hadn't forgotten you,' said d'Artagnan. 'Don't worry. What happened after I left?'

'I don't know,' answered Kitty. 'She went on shouting and yelling and all the men came running up. She was mad with rage. She hurled every insult under the sun at you. Then I realized that she might remember how you always went into her room through my room and might suspect me of being in league with you. So I took what little money I had and a few things and fled.'

'Poor child! But what d'you think I can do for you? I'm leaving Paris the day after tomorrow, you know.'

'Surely you can think of something, Sir. Get me out of Paris, out of France if possible.'

'You don't expect me to take you to the siege of La Rochelle, do you?' asked d'Artagnan.

'No. But you could find me a place in the provinces somewhere, with some relation or friend of yours; in your own province, for instance.'

'Alas, the ladies of my province don't have maids. But I think I can do something for you all the same. Planchet, run and fetch Aramis; tell him to come at once; say we need his help urgently.'

'I'd live anywhere provided I was well hidden and no one knew where I was,' said Kitty.

'Now that we're going to part, Kitty,' said d'Artagnan, 'and that you won't be jealous of me any more . . .'

'Oh, Sir, near or far, I shall love you always,' said Kitty.

'Is there such a thing as constancy in this world?' muttered Athos under his breath.

'And I'll always love you, Kitty,' replied d'Artagnan. 'But now I'm going to ask you a question which concerns me vitally. D'you remember ever hearing your mistress mention a young woman being kidnapped one night?'

'Let me think a moment! Oh Sir! You don't still love that woman?'

'No. One of my friends is in love with her. This fellow here, Athos.'

'Me!' cried Athos in horror.

'Yes, you,' repeated d'Artagnan, nudging his friend in the ribs. 'You know how interested we all are in that unfortunate Madame Bonacieux. Besides, Kitty won't repeat anything, will you, Kitty? D'you realize she's the wife of that revolting ape you met on the doorstep of this house?'

'Good Heavens!' cried Kitty. 'That reminds me. I knew there was something on my mind. I do hope that man didn't recognize me.'

'Recognize you? Why? Have you met him before?'

'He came twice to see Milady.'

'Oh, he did, did he? When exactly?'

'About a fortnight or three weeks ago.'

'I see.'

'And then again last night.'

'Last night?'

'Yes, only a moment or two before you arrived.'

'My dear Athos, we're caught up in a web of spies! D'you think he did recognize you, Kitty?'

'I pulled my bonnet well down over my eyes, but it may have been too late.'

'Go down and see if he's still on his doorstep, Athos. He's less suspicious of you than he is of me.'

Athos went down and came up again at once.

'He's gone,' he said, 'and the house is closed.'

'He's obviously gone to report that all the doves are safely in the dovecote,' said d'Artagnan.

'Well, the doves must spread their wings and fly,' said Athos. 'All of them. We'll leave only Planchet here to watch what happens.'

'What about Aramis?' asked d'Artagnan. 'Remember we sent Planchet to fetch him.'

'So we did!' said Athos. 'Well, we'll have to wait for him.'

At that moment Aramis came in. They told him the whole story and asked him to help them find a place for Kitty with one of his grand friends.

Aramis thought for a moment. Then he said, blushing:

'Would I really be doing you a good turn if I did that, d'Artagnan?'

'I'd be grateful to you all my life.'

'Very well then. I'll do what I can. Oddly enough Madame de Bois-Tracy asked me to look out for a lady's maid for a friend of hers who lives in the country. If you can vouch for this girl's character, d'Artagnan . . .'

'Oh, Sir,' interrupted Kitty, 'I'd do anything for any-one who'd give me a chance to leave Paris.'

'Right, that's settled then,' said Aramis.

He sat down at a table and wrote a short note, sealed it with his signet ring and handed it to Kitty.

'And now, my dear,' said d'Artagnan, 'you know it's no healthier for us here than it is for you. So let's say good-bye quickly and hope to meet again in better times.'

'Wherever and whenever that may be,' said Kitty, 'you'll find me just as much in love with you as I am today.'

'H'm,' muttered Athos to himself again.

D'Artagnan escorted Kitty to the top of the stairs. A few minutes later the three young men separated, arranging to meet again at four o'clock at Athos' lodg-ings, and leaving Planchet to watch the house. Aramis returned home and Athos and d'Artagnan went off to pawn the sapphire. As the Gascon had foreseen they had no difficulty in getting 300 pistoles for it.

So active were Athos and d'Artagnan and so know-ledgeable in military matters that it took them a bare three hours to buy their two complete outfits for the campaign.

24
A VISION

At the appointed hour the four friends met in Athos' rooms. Their concern about equipment had completely vanished and they were now all in the highest spirits. They were talking and laughing together when suddenly

Planchet came in, bringing two letters addressed to d'Artagnan. One was a small letter neatly folded lengthways and sealed with a green seal bearing the mark of a dove carrying an olive branch. The other was a large, square envelope adorned with the impressive crest and coat-of-arms of His Eminence, the Cardinal Duc de Richelieu.

When d'Artagnan saw the little note his face lit up, for he recognized the handwriting. He had only seen that handwriting once before, but he had kept the memory of it in his heart. He seized the note, broke the seal and read as follows:

> *Could you manage to be somewhere on the Chaillot road next Wednesday evening between six and eight? I shall be driving along that road at that time, so look carefully into every passing coach. If you see me don't appear to recognize me. If you do you'll be endangering your own and your friends' lives. I myself am running a great risk in doing this but can't resist the temptation of getting a moment's glimpse of you.*

No signature.

'It's a trap,' said Athos. 'Don't go, d'Artagnan.'

'I think I recognize the handwriting,' said d'Artagnan.

'It might be a forgery,' said Athos. 'Just now the Chaillot road's quite deserted at that hour.'

'I suggest we all go,' said d'Artagnan. 'Good God! They can't eat all of us, four lackeys, four horses, arms and all! They'd get a belly ache.'

'Yes,' agreed Porthos. 'Let's risk it. We've got to try out our arms in any case.'

'It ought to be quite good fun,' added Aramis in his slow drawl.

'Very well,' said Athos, 'I'll come with you.'

'Gentlemen,' said d'Artagnan, 'it's already half-past four and if we start now we'll only just get to the Chaillot road by six.'

'And if we start too late no one'll see us,' added

Porthos, 'and that would be a pity. Let's go and get ready, gentlemen.'

'How about that second letter, d'Artagnan?' said Athos. 'The one in the large envelope. You've forgotten all about that in your excitement over the first. And to judge from the seal I should say it was well worth opening.'

'Right,' said d'Artagnan, 'let's see what His Eminence wants with me.'

He unsealed the letter and read as follows:

> *Monsieur d'Artagnan, des Essarts' Company, King's Guards, is commanded to be present at the Palais Cardinal this evening at eight o'clock.*
>
> *La Houdinière,*
> *Captain of the Guards*

'Ye Gods,' said Athos. 'That's another exciting invitation, but in a different way.'

'I shall accept both,' said d'Artagnan. 'One's for seven and the other for eight. I can fit both in easily.'

'I wouldn't go if I were you,' Aramis advised him. 'A man can't honourably refuse a tryst with a lady, but he's quite justified in refusing one with His Eminence, especially if he knows he hasn't been asked for his charm.'

'I agree with Aramis,' said Porthos.

'Remember, gentlemen,' said d'Artagnan, 'I had one invitation from His Eminence before, through Monsieur de Cavois. That was the day after Constance was kidnapped. I ignored that and I've never seen Constance since. This time I'm going, whatever happens.'

'If you've made up your mind to go, go,' said Athos.

'But the Bastille!' objected Aramis.

'Oh, you'll get me out of that all right,' said d'Artagnan.

'Yes, we'd do that all right,' said Aramis and Porthos

airily, as though rescuing a man from a strongly guarded fortress were the easiest thing in the world. 'The only snag is that we're due to leave Paris the day after tomorrow and might not be able to manage it before then.'

'We can do better than that,' said Athos. 'We can stop him getting in at all. We can stay with him all the evening. I suggest one of us waits with three musketeers at each of the three entrances to the palace, four men at each entrance. If we see any suspicious-looking carriage with closed doors drive out we'll attack it. It's a long time since we had a set-to with the Cardinal's Guards, and Monsieur de Tréville must think we're dead.'

'Athos, you're a born strategist,' cried Aramis. 'What d'you think of the plan, gentlemen?'

'Admirable!' shouted the other two.

'Well, I'll go off now to headquarters and tell the other fellows to be ready at eight o'clock,' said Porthos. 'We'll all meet in front of the Palais Cardinal; you three had better go and get the horses saddled.'

The little quartet made a fine show trotting through the streets towards the quay, Athos astride a horse for which he was indebted to his wife, Aramis a horse presented to him by his mistress, Porthos one provided by the attorney's wife, and d'Artagnan one supplied by Dame Fortune, the best mistress of all.

The four servants rode along in procession behind their masters.

Near the Louvre the four friends ran into Monsieur de Tréville, who was returning from St Germain. He stopped them to compliment them on their fine turn-out, and this picturesque encounter brought a crowd of about a hundred idlers running to the spot.

D'Artagnan took advantage of this chance meeting to tell Monsieur de Tréville about the letter with the large red seal and the ducal crest and coat-of-arms. Needless to

say, he did not mention the other letter. Monsieur de
Tréville approved the young man's decision and assured
him that if he did not put in an appearance the following
morning he would find him and rescue him, wherever he
was.

At that moment the Samaritaine clock struck six. The
four friends excused themselves on the grounds of an
appointment, took leave of Monsieur de Tréville and
galloped off towards the Chaillot road. When they
reached it twilight was setting in and carriages were
passing to and fro. D'Artagnan took up his position at
the roadside, while his friends waited under the trees
a few yards behind him. The young man scrutinized
all the carriages closely but at first saw no familiar
face.

After about a quarter of an hour, just as the daylight
was fading entirely, d'Artagnan noticed a carriage
approaching at a great rate along the Sèvres road. He had
a presentiment that this carriage contained the person
who had arranged the tryst with him and felt a thrill of
excitement. The next moment the carriage swept past
and he saw a woman look out of the window and hold
two fingers to her lips, either to enjoin silence or to send a
kiss. At the sight of her the young man gave a shout of
joy, for he had recognized Madame Bonacieux. Then the
carriage swept on and he was left with only the memory
of what he had seen, a fleeting vision, a phantom.

D'Artagnan's three friends now rode up and joined
him. All three declared that they had also seen a woman's
head at the carriage window, but of the three only Athos
knew Madame Bonacieux. Athos agreed that it was she,
but, being less preoccupied than d'Artagnan with her
pretty face, had noticed a man's head behind hers in the
carriage.

'If there was a man there,' said d'Artagnan, 'he was
obviously taking her from one prison to another. Oh

God, what are they doing with my poor Constance, and shall I ever see her again?'.

At that moment the clock struck seven-thirty. The carriage had been twenty minutes late arriving. D'Artagnan's friends reminded him of his second engagement for that evening, but also pointed out that he could still get out of it if he wanted to.

But d'Artagnan was by nature both obstinate and inquisitive. He had made up his mind to go to the Palais Cardinal and find out why His Eminence wanted to see him. And nothing his friends said could alter his decision.

So all four set off and soon reached the Rue St Honoré and the Place du Palais Cardinal. Here they found awaiting them the twelve musketeers whom Porthos had recruited for the evening. They were now told the reason for the summons and what they were expected to do. All the musketeers knew d'Artagnan and knew that he was destined to join their ranks one day, so they agreed unanimously to stand by him that night. It was an escapade which particularly appealed to them, for it might lead to a scrap with the Cardinal's Guards, which they always enjoyed. Athos split them into three parties, put himself in command of one, Aramis of another and Porthos of another, and posted each party under cover opposite each of the entrances to the palace.

The young man walked up the great staircase and into the ante-chamber in some trepidation. He handed his invitation card to the page on duty, who showed him into a smaller ante-room and then disappeared into the private apartments. About half a dozen of the Cardinal's Guards were waiting in this ante-room. They at once recognized d'Artagnan as the man who had wounded Jussac and exchanged meaning glances, which d'Artagnan regarded as ominous. But he was not easily intimidated, as we know. He summoned up his native pride, faced up to them squarely and stared them straight in the eye, showing no sign of fear.

At last the page returned and signed d'Artagnan to follow him. He led him along a passage, across a large drawing-room and into a library in which a man was seated at a table writing. The page announced him and then retired without a word. D'Artagnan stood and observed the man seated at the table. He thought at first that he was a lawyer going through some briefs. But then he noticed that he was writing, or rather correcting, lines of unequal length and scanning them by tapping his fingers on the table. He then realized that the man was a poet.

After a few moments the poet closed his manuscript and looked up. D'Artagnan recognized the Cardinal.

25
THE CARDINAL

Richelieu rested his elbow on his manuscript and his head in his hand and stared at d'Artagnan for a moment in silence. No one had a keener gaze than the Cardinal and under his scrutiny the young man felt his heart sink. But outwardly he seemed perfectly at ease as he stood there, holding his plumed hat in his hand, respectfully awaiting His Eminence's pleasure.

'Are you one of the d'Artagnans of Béarn, Sir?' said the Cardinal at last.

'Yes, Your Eminence.'

'You're the young man who left home seven or eight months ago to seek your fortune in Paris?'

'Yes, Monseigneur.'

'You travelled through Meung, where you had trouble of some kind. I can't remember now what it was exactly, but I know something happened.'

'I'll tell you exactly what happened if you like, Sir.'

'Don't trouble,' said the Cardinal with a smile which seemed to say that he knew the story as well as the young man himself.

'You had a letter of introduction to Monsieur de Tréville, did you not?'

'Yes, Monseigneur, but during that unfortunate episode at Meung . . .'

'Your letter of introduction was lost,' said the Cardinal. 'I know that. But Monsieur de Tréville's a good judge of character and enlisted you in the company of Monsieur des Essarts, his brother-in-law, so that you could join his own company of musketeers later.'

'Your Eminence knows my story inside out.'

'Since then a great deal has happened to you. You went for a stroll one day behind the Carmelite Convent when it would have been better if you'd stayed at home. Then you made an expedition with your friends to Forges to take the waters. Your friends stopped half-way but you went on. I know all about that – you had special business in England.'

D'Artagnan was completely taken aback. He stammered out:

'I was going . . .'

'You were going to hunt at Windsor, or somewhere,' broke in the Cardinal. 'But that's your affair. I know about it merely because it's my business to know everything. On your return you had an interview with a certain lady of high position. And by the way, I'm delighted to see you've kept the present she gave you!'

D'Artagnan put his hand quickly over the Queen's ring and turned it round on his finger. But it was too late.

'Two days later, if you remember, you had a visit from Monsieur de Cavois,' went on the Cardinal. 'He brought you an invitation from me, which you ignored. That was foolish of you.'

'Your Eminence, I thought you were displeased with me.'

'Why should you have thought that?' went on the Cardinal. 'You'd shown unusual courage and resource in carrying out your Sovereign's orders. Was that a reason for being displeased with you? I wasn't at all displeased. I admired you. I punish people when they disobey orders, not when they obey them . . . too well, as you did. In proof of this let me remind you of what happened the night before I sent you that invitation which you ignored.'

D'Artagnan remembered that that had been the night of Madame Bonacieux's kidnapping. He felt a sudden chill of fear, for this in turn recalled to his mind the incident on the Chaillot road of only half an hour ago. The Cardinal's words seemed to hint that his beloved Constance was still in the hands of her enemies.

The Cardinal went on:

'I hadn't heard from you for some time, so I wanted to find out what you were up to. Besides you've some cause to be grateful to me; you've been treated very leniently so far; you must have noticed that.'

D'Artagnan bowed.

'Your Eminence is too good,' he murmured.

The Cardinal continued:

'I've been lenient with you partly because I felt you deserved it and partly because I've thought of a possible career for you.'

D'Artagnan gave a start of surprise.

'That was what I wanted to discuss with you the day I sent you that invitation which you ignored. Fortunately nothing's been lost by the delay, and we can discuss it today instead. Sit down there opposite me, Monsieur d'Artagnan. We don't need to be too formal.'

The young man was so amazed that he stood staring at the Cardinal without moving, and the latter had to repeat his invitation to him to sit down.

'Listen,' continued the Cardinal. 'What would you say to the offer of an ensignship in my Guards and a captaincy after the campaign?'

'Monseigneur . . .!'

'Well?'

D'Artagnan looked embarrassed.

'Monseigneur!' he repeated.

'Why are you hesitating?' cried the Cardinal.

D'Artagnan replied:

'I'm in His Majesty's Guards, Monseigneur, and I'm very happy there.'

'Are you suggesting that my Guards aren't His Majesty's Guards? Remember, whatever French regiment you belong to you're in His Majesty's service.'

'That wasn't what I meant, Sir.'

'Oh, I see. You want an excuse for accepting. Is that it? Well, you've a very good excuse. Desire for promotion, the coming campaign, the chances I'm offering you – that's your excuse to the world. And your excuse to yourself is that you need protection. For let me tell you frankly, Monsieur d'Artagnan, I've had some very serious complaints about you from certain quarters. You don't devote all your days and nights exclusively to your duties as you should.'

D'Artagnan flushed. The Cardinal laid his hand on a file of papers on the table.

'I actually have a whole dossier about you here,' he said. 'But I wanted to have a word with you before reading it. You've got plenty of energy and if you'd direct it into the right channels you might make your fortune. At present you're only doing yourself harm.'

D'Artagnan replied:

'It's very good of you to take this interest in me, Sir. I don't deserve it, I know, and I'm all the more grateful to you for your kindness. But I think you said I might speak frankly . . .'

He paused.

'Go on,' said the Cardinal. 'Say what's on your mind.'

'Only this, Sir. For some strange reason all my friends seem to be either musketeers or King's Guards and all my enemies your men, Sir. If I accepted your offer I wouldn't be welcome in your ranks and all my friends would say I'd behaved badly.'

The Cardinal smiled scornfully.

'Are you so proud as to think my offer's not good enough?' he asked.

'No, Sir, I never thought that. You're being far too generous to me and I don't think I've done nearly enough to deserve your attention. The campaign's just starting, Sir. I shall be serving under your command, and if I have the good luck to distinguish myself in some way I shall feel more worthy of your interest in me. Perhaps one day I'll be in a position to offer you my services. At present I might be accused of selling myself.'

The Cardinal was irritated. At the same time he admired the young man for his integrity. He replied:

'So you refuse to join me, Sir. Very well. I can't decide for you. You're free to choose whom you want as your friends and whom you want as enemies.'

'Monseigneur, I beg you not to look on me as an enemy!' cried d'Artagnan. 'I've been honest with you, Sir. I can't expect to enjoy your favour, I know. But at least bear me no malice!'

'Young man,' replied Richelieu. 'If we meet again after the war's over and I can ever repeat the offer I made you today you may be sure I shall do so.'

This last speech alarmed d'Artagnan more than any

open menace would have done. It was a warning. The Cardinal was obviously hinting to him that some imminent danger threatened him. He was about to reply, but the Cardinal dismissed him with an imperious gesture.

D'Artagnan bowed and turned to leave the room. But as he reached the door he was seized with sudden panic and was on the point of yielding. Then he saw in his mind's eye Athos' stern, accusing face. If he made a pact with the Cardinal his friend would disown him and turn his back on him. This thought strengthened him in his resolve to stand firm.

He walked down the same staircase and out by the same door. At the entrance he found Athos and his four musketeers; they had had a long wait and had begun to grow anxious. D'Artagnan reassured them with a word and sent Planchet off to tell the other two parties of musketeers that they could now disperse, as his master had come out of the Palais Cardinal unscathed.

When the four were back in Athos' rooms Aramis and Porthos inquired the reason for the interview. D'Artagnan merely told them that Richelieu had summoned him to offer him an ensign's commission in his Guards and that he had refused.

'You were quite right!' cried Porthos and Aramis in one breath.

Athos frowned and said nothing. But when he was alone with d'Artagnan he said:

'You did the only thing you could do. But perhaps you were unwise.'

D'Artagnan was silent. He was too depressed to speak. For Athos' words strengthened his own conviction that some calamity was in store for him.

That night a select few of the Guards and the Musketeers had a joint farewell supper. They would be meeting again when it pleased God and if it pleased God. As can be imagined the evening was wildly hilarious, for one can only drive out care of that kind with extreme frivolity.

On the following morning as reveille sounded on the bugles the friends took leave of each other. The Musketeers ran to report at Monsieur de Tréville's house and the Guards at Monsieur des Essarts' headquarters. The two captains then rode with their companies to the Louvre where the King was to review them.

After the review the Guards marched off alone, for the Musketeers were due to leave only when the King left. Porthos took advantage of these few hours of grace to ride in solitary state down the Rue aux Ours to show off his equipment.

Aramis meanwhile was writing a long letter. To whom? No one knew. The document was to be given to Kitty, who was due to leave for Tours that evening, and who was waiting for it in the next room.

Athos spent the few intervening hours at home, sipping the remains of his store of Spanish wine.

Meanwhile d'Artagnan was riding out of Paris with his company of Guards. When his troop reached the Faubourg St Antoine the young man turned round and sent a challenging salute to the Bastille, from whose clutches he had so far escaped. He was so busy looking at the fortress that he failed to observe at a crossroads a woman mounted on a bay horse, who was watching him closely. The woman was Milady, and she was pointing the young man out to two sinister-looking men. The latter immediately approached the troop of riders to take a close look at him, and then glanced back at Milady, who nodded to confirm that he was the man. Having made sure that her orders were fully understood Milady spurred her horse to a canter and rode off. The two men now turned and followed the company of guards on foot. At the end of the Faubourg St Antoine they mounted two horses which were waiting for them in the

charge of an unliveried groom, and rode along in rear of
the soldiers, following them through the gates of the
capital and out into the country.

26
THE SIEGE OF LA ROCHELLE

La Rochelle was the last Protestant stronghold in France,
and its harbour was the last French door open to
England. But apart from motives of statesmanship, the
Cardinal never forgot that it was Buckingham who
supported the Rochellese. Richelieu, in undertaking the
siege, was concerned not only with ridding France of an
enemy but also with taking personal revenge on a rival.
And he was determined that this revenge should be
glorious and dazzling, worthy of a man who had the
resources of a vast kingdom to back him. He knew that by
fighting England he was fighting Buckingham; that if he
triumphed over England he would triumph over
Buckingham; in short, that in humiliating England he
would be humiliating Buckingham in the eyes of the
Queen, with whom Richelieu had once been in love
himself.

Monsieur des Essarts' company of Guards was billeted
in the Minimes. D'Artagnan's main ambition in life was,
as we know, to be transferred to Monsieur de Tréville's
Musketeers. He had therefore not attempted to make
friends with his fellow guardsmen and now found himself isolated and a prey to his own thoughts. These
thoughts were by no means cheerful. Almost immediately on his arrival in Paris a year ago he had got involved

in affairs of State and had consequently been frustrated both in his love-affairs and in his ambitions. As far as his love-affairs went, the only woman he really cared for was Madame Bonacieux, and Madame Bonacieux had disappeared and he had lost all trace of her. As for his ambitions, he had succeeded, young as he was, in making an enemy of the Cardinal, a man feared by all the greatest in the land, the King included. This man could have easily crushed him and yet for some reason had not done so. D'Artagnan was shrewd enough to augur good things from the Cardinal's behaviour to him and to see a ray of hope in this direction. He had also made another enemy, one less to be feared, perhaps, than the Cardinal, but by no means to be despised. This enemy was Milady.

To set against all this he had won the Queen's favour. But at that time the Queen's favour was usually more of a curse than a blessing, and those who enjoyed it nearly always found themselves victims of persecution. D'Artagnan's most practical acquisition in the past year was the Queen's diamond, which was worth between five and six thousand livres. But the young man was far-sighted enough to see that if he wished to make his way in the world his best course was to keep and not sell the diamond, so that he could prove his identity to the Queen later. And until then the ring was as valueless as the pebbles under his feet. While brooding thus, d'Artagnan happened to be walking along a pretty little path which led from the camp to a neighbouring village. So immersed was he in his thoughts that he strayed farther than he had intended. Night was already falling when he suddenly noticed, in the last rays of the setting sun, the glint of a musket barrel behind a hedge. D'Artagnan had a quick eye and quick wits. He realized that the musket had not got there by itself and that the man who carried it, whoever he was, had certainly not hidden behind the hedge with any friendly intention. So he decided to take to his heels. But then he noticed, on the other side of the road, the end of another musket barrel gleaming behind a rock. It was obviously an ambush. The young man glanced back at the first musket and saw to his alarm that it was now pointing in his direction. Quick as lightning he threw himself to the ground and at the same moment heard the shot being fired and the bullet whistling over his head. There was no time to lose. He sprang to his feet again and now the bullet from the other musket scattered the pebbles at the exact spot where his head had been when he had been prostrate. D'Artagnan, like all sensible men, believed that there was no virtue in courage for its own sake, in standing firm against superior odds. Besides, it was not a question of courage now; he had fallen into a trap. He muttered to himself:

'The third shot'll get me.'

And he started running like the wind in the direction of the camp. But the man who had fired the first shot had meanwhile reloaded his musket and now sent a second shot, this time so well aimed that the bullet pierced d'Artagnan's hat and sent it flying in the air. D'Artagnan had no other hat, so he retrieved it and then ran on. In a few minutes he was back at the camp, breathless and dead white in the face. He retired to his billet without saying a word to anyone, sat down and started to think hard.

There were three possible explanations for this attack. The first and most likely was that it was a piece of sniping-work by the defenders of La Rochelle. His Majesty's Guards were fair prizes; they were picked soldiers and sometimes had well-filled purses in their pockets. D'Artagnan examined the bullet-hole in his hat. It had not been made by a musket bullet but by a bullet from an arquebus. The sniping was therefore not the work of soldiers as the bullet was not of regulation army calibre.

Could it have been a memento from the Cardinal? This was the second possible explanation, but d'Artagnan dismissed it as unlikely. The Cardinal rarely adopted underhand methods in dealing with those powerless to defend themselves. Thirdly, the attack might have been an act of revenge on the part of Milady. This was much more likely. D'Artagnan tried to recall the faces and dress of the two assassins, but he had been too busy running away from them to notice much. He began to feel depressed and moaned aloud: 'Athos, Porthos, Aramis! Where are you? Why aren't you here to support me?'

That night he hardly slept at all. He kept starting up in bed, imagining that he saw a man standing over him with a knife. However the next day dawned and found him without a scratch. But he suspected that more trouble was in store for him. He spent all that day in his billet; the weather was bad and he welcomed this as an excuse to remain under cover.

Two days after the attempt on the young man's life, the defenders of La Rochelle recaptured a bastion which the Royalist army had previously held. Monsieur des Essarts chose d'Artagnan to lead a reconnaissance party. D'Artagnan called for four volunteers.

Two of his fellow guardsmen immediately stepped out of the ranks and two soldiers from another regiment joined them. The party had to discover whether the Rochellese had evacuated the bastion or whether they had left a garrison there. To do this it had to get within fairly close range of the bastion. D'Artagnan and his men marched off along the trench, the two guardsmen marching in line with him and the two soldiers in rear. Advancing under cover of the trench they got to within about forty yards of the bastion. There they halted. D'Artagnan looked round and saw to his surprise that the two soldiers had disappeared. He thought that they had probably panicked and he and the two guardsmen continued to advance. They reached the bend of the counterscarp and found themselves within twenty yards of the bastion. They could see no one and the bastion appeared to be unoccupied. D'Artagnan and his men were deliberating whether to advance further when suddenly a cloud of smoke belched from the stone tower and a dozen bullets whistled round the heads of the three men. They now had the information they wanted; the bastion was occupied. They had done their job and now turned and ran back to the trench. Just as they reached it and were preparing to take cover a single shot rang out and one of the guards collapsed with a bullet through the chest. The other was untouched and continued his flight down the trench. D'Artagnan, not wishing to abandon his fellow guardsman, bent down to lift him up and help him back to the camp. But at that moment two shots rang out and the wounded guardsman again fell back, this time with a bullet through the head; the other bullet whizzed past d'Artagnan's ear and flattened itself against the rock behind him. The young man whipped round, for he realized that these shots could not have come from the bastion, which was masked by the angle of the trench. He suddenly recollected the two soldiers who had deserted earlier and then thought of the two assassins who had attacked him two days before. This time he was determined to discover the truth. He had a sudden inspiration and collapsed over his friend's body, pretending to be dead. In a moment he saw two heads peering cautiously over the top of an abandoned earthwork about twenty yards away. He recognized them as the two soldiers who had deserted. His suspicions were justified; the two men had volunteered with the object of killing him, hoping that his death would be attributed to enemy bullets. Now, fearing that their victim might be merely wounded and might later report them, they were coming up to him to finish him off. Luckily they had been deceived by d'Artagnan's trick and, imagining him to be seriously wounded, had not bothered to reload their guns. D'Artagnan in falling had been careful not to leave go of his sword, and when the two men were about ten feet away he sprang up suddenly and rushed at them. The assassins realized that if they fled back to the camp without having killed him he would report them, and that their only hope now was to go over to the enemy. One of them took his musket by the barrel and, using it like a club, aimed a fearful blow at d'Artagnan, which the young man managed to dodge. The bandit then rushed past him in the direction of the bastion. The Rochellese in the bastion thought he was attacking them and opened fire on him. A bullet struck him through the shoulder and he collapsed. Meanwhile d'Artagnan was at grips with the second soldier, attacking him with his sword. It was a short struggle, for the rogue had only his empty arquebus to defend himself with. In a few moments the young man succeeded in wounding his enemy in the thigh; he fell down and d'Artagnan was on him like a flash, pressing the point of his sword against his throat.

'Don't kill me, Sir, don't kill me!' cried the bandit. 'Spare me and I'll confess everything!'

'Why should I spare you? What can you confess that could interest me?'

'If you value your life at all you'll do well to listen to me.'

'You blackguard!' cried d'Artagnan. 'Well confess then. Who employed you to murder me?'

'A woman I don't know; a woman they call Milady.'

'If you don't know her, how d'you know what they call her?'

'The other fellow knows her and used to call her that. He was the one who had the dealings with her – not me. He actually has a letter from her in his pocket, which I'm sure would interest you, Sir.'

'How do you happen to be mixed up in the plot?'

'He suggested I should join him and we should do the job together.'

'And how much did the lady offer you for this . . . job?'

'A hundred louis.'

D'Artagnan laughed.

'I see she rates me pretty high,' he said. 'A hundred louis' no mean sum for a couple of rogues like you. I can well understand you're taking on the job for that much and I'll spare you. But on one condition.'

'What, Sir?' asked the soldier anxiously. His sly mind could not take such magnanimity at its face value and he suspected some trick.

'That you go back and retrieve the letter from the other fellow's pocket.'

'But that's just another way of getting me killed, Sir,' cried the bandit. 'How can I get that letter with the enemy in the bastion firing at me almost point blank?'

'You'll jolly well have to; if you don't I swear I'll kill you myself.'

'No, Sir, no!' cried the bandit. 'Spare me for the sake of the lady you love! You probably think the lady's dead, Sir. But I can tell you she's not.'

As he spoke the bandit fell on his knees, abject and grovelling. He had to support himself on one arm for his strength was giving out with the loss of blood from his wound.

'How d'you know about this lady?' asked d'Artagnan. 'And how d'you know I thought she was dead?'

'It's all written in that letter the other fellow has in his pocket, Sir.'

'All the more reason why I must have that letter,' said d'Artagnan. 'So hurry up and get it. If you don't, much as I dislike the thought of staining my sword again with the blood of a rogue like you . . . I swear I'll . . .'

The young man accompanied his words with such a

fierce look that the bandit sprang up. Sheer fright seemed to have brought life back to his limbs.

'All right, Sir, all right!' he cried. 'I'll go!'

D'Artagnan took the man's arquebus from him, stood behind him and forced him forward, prodding him in the back with the point of his sword. As the unfortunate man walked along he left a trail of blood behind him. Pale and sweating with fear at the thought of the almost certain death which awaited him, he was a piteous spectacle as he tried to slink along under cover towards his friend who lay prostrate about twenty yards away. D'Artagnan watched him for a while with scorn. Then he took pity on him.

'All right,' he said. 'Stay where you are. I'll go. And I'll show you the difference between a brave man and a coward.'

And he proceeded to stalk up to the second soldier, treading warily, watching the enemy's every movement and taking advantage of every possible piece of cover. Having reached the man he had two courses open to him: either to search him on the spot or to carry him back, making a shield of his body, and search him in the trench. D'Artagnan chose the second course. He had just lifted the man on to his back when the enemy opened fire. D'Artagnan felt the man's body jolt against his shoulder, heard him scream and give a final shudder of agony. The man had achieved the very opposite of what he had intended; he had shielded his victim and instead of killing him had saved his life. D'Artagnan jumped back into the trench and threw the corpse down beside the wounded man, who was almost as pale as his dead comrade. And now he proceeded to search the rogue's pockets. A leather wallet, a purse containing a sum of money which was evidently part of the fee paid by Milady for the crime, a dice-box and some dice composed the man's entire stock of this world's goods. D'Artagnan threw the dice and the box over the side of the trench, flung the purse to the wounded man and quickly opened the wallet.

Buried among a lot of other papers he found the following letter, the letter he had risked his life to recover:

You let the woman escape and she's now in safety in a convent. That was a bad slip. Don't fail with the man. If you do I shall see that you pay dearly for the hundred louis you got from me.

No signature. But the letter was obviously from Milady. D'Artagnan put it carefully in his pocket for future use as evidence of her guilt. He was now sheltered from the enemy's fire by the angle of the trench, so he proceeded to question the wounded man. The latter confessed that he and his friend had been hired to kidnap a young woman who was due to leave Paris on a certain day by the La Villette gate, but that they had stopped to have a drink in an inn and had missed the carriage by ten minutes.

'What were you told to do with the woman?' asked d'Artagnan anxiously.

'To take her to a house in the Place Royale,' answered the man.

'To Milady's own home; I thought so,' muttered d'Artagnan.

He was suddenly appalled to think how vindictively this woman was pursuing him and his friends, and how well versed she must be in State affairs to have discovered everything. No doubt the Cardinal had told her a great deal. On the other hand he was overjoyed to know that the Queen had at last found out where Madame Bonacieux was imprisoned and that Her Majesty herself had taken her out of that prison. The letter he had received from Constance and his glimpse of her on the Chaillot road were now explained to him. Now, as Athos had foreseen, it would be possible to find her again;

convents were easily stormed. This thought rejoiced his heart and made him feel more friendly to the world in general. He turned to the wounded man, who was anxiously watching the changing expressions on his face, and, holding out his hand to him, said:

'Come on. I'm not going to leave you like this. Lean your weight on me and let's get back to the camp.'

The man was amazed at this magnanimity.

'Very well,' he said. 'But I suppose you're taking me back just to have me hanged.'

'No,' said d'Artagnan. 'You can trust me. I've decided to spare you once and for all.'

The wounded man fell on his knees again and abjectly kissed his rescuer's feet. But d'Artagnan now wanted to get away from the enemy as quickly as possible, so he cut short his expressions of gratitude. The guardsman who had run back to the camp after the enemy's first volley had reported the death of his four companions. So when the young man reappeared safe and sound he was greeted with cheers and many expressions of goodwill.

D'Artagnan accounted for the bandit's sword wound as a wound inflicted in a sortie by the enemy. He reported the other soldier's death and the whole expedition in detail. His story impressed everyone and rumours of it spread like wildfire through the camp. Monsieur, the King's brother, sent him his personal congratulations. And besides the honour and glory which accrued to him through this act of gallantry the young man had the inner joy of an increased sense of security. Of his two enemies one was now dead and the other his friend for life.

But he was not destined to remain long in this comfortable state of mind. And the fact that his fears were so easily lulled proved one thing – that he did not yet know Milady very well.

D'Artagnan's fears were a trifle eased and his dread of Milady's wrath diminished as the days and weeks passed. Only one thing now grieved him – that he had received no news of his friends. But one morning early in November he got a letter which elated him. The letter was postmarked 'Villeroy' and ran as follows:

Monsieur d'Artagnan,

Your friends, Monsieur Athos, Monsieur Porthos and Monsieur Aramis recently spent a very good evening at my hotel and became very lively. They created such a disturbance that the provost-marshal of the Castle, who is a strict disciplinarian, sentenced them to several days' detention. Before their arrest, however, the gentlemen ordered me to send you twelve bottles of my Anjou wine which they found very much to their taste. They wish you to drink to their health in their favourite wine. I am therefore sending you the wine and remain

   Your most respectful and obedient servant,

   Godeau,
   Innkeeper to their Honours
   His Majesty's Musketeers

'Marvellous!' cried d'Artagnan. 'They think of me when they're enjoying themselves just as I think of them when I'm bored. I'll drink their healths with all my heart, but not alone.'

And the young man ran off to invite two of the guards with whom he was on more intimate terms than the rest to join him in sampling the excellent Anjou wine which had just arrived from Villeroy. One of the two guards was on duty that night and the other the following night. So the party was arranged for midday two days ahead.

On returning to his billet d'Artagnan had the wine sent to be stored in the Guards' messroom. At nine in the morning of the day for which the lunch party was fixed he sent Planchet off to make preparations. Planchet was proud to be promoted to the position of butler and, in order to make the party a success, hired as waiters the servant of one of his master's guests, Fourneau by name, and Brisemont, the assassin. The latter, whose life d'Artagnan had spared, being attached to no company, had become d'Artagnan's or rather Planchet's personal servant.

At the appointed hour the two guests arrived. The three men sat down and the dishes were placed on the table. Planchet served the meal, Fourneau uncorked the bottles, and Brisemont decanted the wine. Everyone noticed that the wine was curiously cloudy, but attributed this to the effects of the journey. The first bottle was so very cloudy that Brisemont poured the dregs into a special glass which d'Artagnan said he might drink himself as he was still rather weak from his wound. The guests had just finished their soup and were lifting their glasses to sip the wine when salvoes were fired from the guns of Fort Louis and Fort Neuf. The three guardsmen, taking this to be a warning of a surprise attack by the English or by the Rochellese, seized their swords and rushed out to report at their posts. But they soon discovered the real reason for the gunfire. They heard loud cries of 'Long live the King', 'Long live the Cardinal', and the drums beating through the whole camp. The King, in his impatience to reach the scene of action, had done two days' marches in one and had at that moment arrived with all his household at the head of an army of 10,000 men. His Musketeers formed his bodyguard. D'Artagnan, drawn up in line with his company to honour the King's arrival, signed to his three friends in greeting as they marched past and after the parade was over ran to welcome them.

'You couldn't have arrived at a better time!' he cried.

He then introduced them to the two guardsmen who had been his guests and added:

'The food won't have had time to get cold yet, will it, gentlemen?'

'Ho, ho!' said Porthos. 'So you were having a party!'

'I hope there are no women at your party,' said Aramis.

'Is there any drinkable wine in your pot-house?' asked Athos.

'Well, there's your wine, you know,' replied d'Artagnan.

'Our wine?' queried Athos, astonished.

'Yes. The wine you sent me.'

'We never sent you any wine!'

'You remember! The light Anjou stuff. Twelve bottles of it.'

'So you've ordered some Anjou, have you?' said Porthos. 'That's very extravagant of you!'

'No. I mean the stuff you sent me.'

'We sent you!' cried the three musketeers.

'Did you send any wine, Aramis?' asked Athos.

'No.'

'Did you, Porthos?'

'No.'

'Did you, Athos?'

'No.'

'Well, if you didn't, your innkeeper did,' said d'Artagnan.

'Our innkeeper?'

'Yes, your innkeeper, Godeau. The innkeeper to their Worships the Musketeers.'

'Well,' said Porthos, 'let's sample it, wherever it comes from. It mightn't be too bad.'

'No,' said Athos. 'Don't let's drink any wine without knowing its origin.'

'You're right, Athos,' said d'Artagnan. 'Did none of you order wine from the innkeeper, Godeau?'

'Definitely not. Did he tell you we had?'

'Here's his letter,' said d'Artagnan, showing the note to his friends.

'That's not his writing,' cried Athos. 'I remember his writing. I settled all our accounts with him before we left.'

'That letter's a forgery,' said Porthos. 'We were never given detention.'

Aramis said reproachfully:

'D'Artagnan, can you imagine us *creating a disturbance*!'

D'Artagnan suddenly went very white and began to tremble.

'Look here, what's all this about?' said Athos sharply. 'D'Artagnan, why are you looking like that?'

'Listen, all of you!' said d'Artagnan. 'Something frightful's just occurred to me. D'you think this could be another of that woman's tricks? We must get back to the inn at once. Come on, hurry!'

Now Athos also went white. And all six men, the four friends and the two guardsmen, turned and ran hell for leather back to the inn.

The first thing d'Artagnan saw as he entered the dining room was Brisemont lying full length on the floor, writhing in ghastly convulsions. Planchet and Fourneau were standing over him, trying to help him. But it was obvious that nothing could be done for him. He was dying and his face was distorted with pain. When he saw d'Artagnan he cried out:

'What a vile trick! You pretend to spare my life and then poison me!'

'I!' cried d'Artagnan. 'I poison you! You fool! You don't know what you're saying!'

'It was you who gave me that wine,' said Brisemont. 'You made me drink it. You were getting your revenge. It was a vile trick!'

'You mustn't think that, Brisemont!' said d'Artagnan. 'It's not true. I swear . . .'

'But the Lord is there! The Lord will punish you. Oh God, make him suffer one day what I'm suffering now!'

D'Artagnan knelt down beside the dying man.

'By all that's holy I swear I didn't know the wine was poisoned,' he said. 'I was going to drink it myself.'

'I don't believe you,' said the soldier.

Then he had another attack of convulsions and died.

'How horrible!' muttered Athos.

Porthos now proceeded to smash all the remaining bottles of wine and Aramis sent one of the men off to fetch a priest.

'Oh, my dear friends!' cried d'Artagnan. 'That's the second time you saved my life! And you've saved the lives of these fellows as well.'

Then he added, addressing the guardsmen:

'Gentlemen, I beg you to keep this affair a dead secret. Some well-known people may be involved in it, and if you spread the story round it might be very unpleasant for us.'

The two guardsmen agreed and tactfully went off, leaving the four friends alone.

The latter first made sure that there were no eavesdroppers about and then shot quick looks at each other, which showed that they were all alive to the seriousness of the situation.

'We'd better get out of this room first,' said Athos. 'Dead men are poor company.'

'Planchet,' said d'Artagnan, 'look after that unfortunate devil and see he's buried in consecrated ground. It's true he was a crook but he'd repented of his crime.'

The four friends went out, leaving Planchet and Fourneau to see that Brisemont received a decent burial. The innkeeper showed them into another room and served them with boiled eggs, and water which Athos drew from the well himself. Porthos and Aramis were told the whole story of Milady and her villainy in a few words. Then d'Artagnan said to Athos:

'So you see it's war to the death.'

'Listen,' said Athos. 'Try and get in touch with her and have the whole thing out. Face her with the alternative "war or peace". You give your word of honour to say and do nothing against her on condition she swears to do nothing against you. If she refuses, threaten to go to the Chancellor, to the King, to the Public Executioner; say you'll rouse the Court against her, proclaim her branded and start criminal proceedings against her, and that if she's acquitted you'll take the law into your own hands, chase her to some lonely spot and destroy her like a mad dog.'

'I rather like that idea,' said d'Artagnan. 'But how can I get in touch with her?'

'We'll find some way in time,' replied Athos. 'We'll have to wait, that's all.'

'Yes, but can we afford to wait with all these murderers and poisoners about?'

Then he added in an undertone:

'But what about her?'

'Who?' asked Athos.

'Constance.'

'Madame Bonacieux! Of course, I'd forgotten!' said Athos. 'Poor fellow, I'd forgotten you were in love with her.'

Here Aramis broke in.

'Didn't you read in the letter you found in the dead man's pocket that she was in a convent? Convents are very pleasant places, I'd have you know. I'm going into retirement myself directly the siege of La Rochelle's over.'

'Yes, Aramis,' said Athos. 'We all know how you long to hide away from the world and its wickedness.'

'I'm only a musketeer for the time being,' said Aramis primly.

Athos whispered to d'Artagnan:

'I gather he hasn't heard from his mistress for some time. But don't refer to it; we know how these moods take him.'

'I think I see an easy way out,' said Porthos.

'What's that?'

'She's in a convent, you say? Well, as soon as the siege is over we'll rescue her.'

'We've first got to find out which convent she's in.'

'True,' said Porthos.

'Listen,' said Aramis. 'I've had an idea. Didn't you say the Queen had found this convent for her?'

'Yes. I'm almost sure it was the Queen.'

'In that case I'll find out,' said Aramis.

'You, Aramis?' cried the three friends. 'How?'

Aramis coloured slightly. 'Through the Queen's almoner,' he said. 'I'm on fairly close terms with him.'

The other three agreed to accept Aramis' proposal. They had now finished their frugal meal, so they parted, arranging to meet again that evening. D'Artagnan returned to the Minimes and the three musketeers went off to the King's Headquarters to settle themselves in their new billets.

27
THE RED DOVECOTE INN

The Musketeers, who formed the King's bodyguard, were not much used in the conduct of the siege itself. They were not under strict discipline and could lead a fairly free life. Athos, Porthos and Aramis were even more fortunate than their fellows in this respect, for they were personal friends of Monsieur de Tréville and could get special permits from him to remain out of camp after dark. One evening, when d'Artagnan was on duty in the trenches and had been unable to accompany his three friends, the latter had ridden out to an inn on the Jarrie road called the Red Dovecote, which Athos had discovered two days before. Shortly before midnight they left the inn and were riding back to the camp on their battle chargers, dressed in their service cloaks and with their hands on their pistol butts, when suddenly, about a mile from the village of Boisnau, they thought they heard the sound of horses' hoofs coming towards them. All three immediately reined in, closed ranks and waited in the middle of the road.

At that moment the moon came out from behind a cloud, and a few seconds later two riders appeared round a bend in the road. When they caught sight of the three friends they too reined in and seemed in doubt whether to advance or retreat.

The strangers' hesitation roused the musketeers' suspicions. Athos rode forward a few yards and called out in a loud voice:

'Who goes there?'

At which one of the men called back:

'Who are you?'

'That's no answer,' replied Athos. 'Who goes there, I said! Answer at once or we charge.'

At this the stranger called back:

'I shouldn't do that if I were you, gentlemen!'

His voice rang out sharp and clear; it was obviously the voice of a man used to command.

'It must be some senior officer going his rounds,' said Athos to his friends. 'What shall we do?'

'Who are you?' repeated the stranger who had spoken last. 'Answer at once or you'll regret it later.'

The man's voice convinced Athos that he was within his rights in thus challenging them.

'King's Musketeers,' he replied.

'What company?'

'De Tréville.'

'Advance in formation and account for your presence here at this hour of the night.'

The three friends rode forward. They were by now rather crestfallen, for they were convinced that their challenger was someone of high rank. Athos, with the tacit consent of Porthos and Aramis, acted as spokesman of the party.

The stranger who had spoken had halted a few yards ahead of his companion. Athos signed to Porthos and Aramis to remain behind and rode forward.

'My apologies, Sir,' he said. 'We didn't know who we were talking to. I hope you noticed we were keeping a sharp lookout.'

The officer was holding his cloak over the lower part of his face.

'Your name?' he asked.

Athos suddenly began to feel irritated at his insistence.

'And what about you, Sir?' he asked. 'I think you might show me your warrant or give me some proof of your right to cross-question me.'

The officer now let his cloak fall and revealed his face.

'Your name!' he repeated.

Athos stared at him, stupefied.

'The Cardinal!' he cried.

'Your name?' repeated His Eminence for the third time.

'Athos,' said the musketeer.

The Cardinal turned and beckoned to his groom.

'I want these three musketeers to come with us,' he said to him aside. 'I don't want it known that I've left camp, and if they come with us they won't be able to report having seen me.'

'Monseigneur, we're gentlemen,' said Athos. 'You can trust us to keep a secret. We won't mention having seen you if you ask us not to.'

The Cardinal was annoyed to have been overheard. He frowned and replied:

'You've got sharp ears, Monsieur Athos. But please don't take offence. I'm not asking you to follow me because I mistrust you but because I need your support. Your two friends are, I presume, Monsieur Porthos and Monsieur Aramis.'

'Yes, Your Eminence.'

Porthos and Aramis now rode forward, hats in hand.

'I know you, gentlemen,' said the Cardinal. 'I know you and I know that you're not too well-disposed towards me, which I regret. But I also know you're brave and can be trusted. Monsieur Athos, if you'll honour me by accompanying me, you and your two friends, I'll have an escort which the King himself would envy.'

The three musketeers bowed so low that their heads touched their horses' necks.

'I think you're wise to take us with you, Sir,' said Athos. 'We've met some proper ruffians tonight; in fact we had a bit of an argument with four of them at the Red Dovecote inn.'

The Cardinal frowned.

'An argument?' he said. 'Why? You know I don't like brawling.'

Athos replied:

'Speaking for myself, Sir, I didn't draw my sword at all. I took my fellow round the waist and threw him out of the window. Apparently he broke his thigh in falling.'

'H'm!' said the Cardinal. 'And what about you, Monsieur Porthos?'

'I knew duelling was illegal, Monseigneur, so I took up a bench and dealt my fellow a blow which I believe broke his shoulder.'

'I see,' said the Cardinal. 'And you, Monsieur Aramis?'

'Me, Monseigneur? Well, I'm peaceful by nature, and I don't like fighting. Besides, you may not know, Sir, but

I'm on the point of taking Orders. So I was trying to smooth things over when one of the rogues thrust me through the arm when I wasn't looking. That maddened me and I simply had to draw my sword. He lunged at me again, but this time I think he must have spitted himself on my sword. I know he fell down and I think I saw them carrying him out with his two companions.'

'Good God!' said the Cardinal. 'Three men put out of action in a tavern brawl! That's a bit drastic, isn't it? And how did it all start?'

'Those rogues were drunk,' said Athos. 'They knew a woman had arrived that evening at the inn and wanted to force open her door.'

'Force open her door?' said the Cardinal. 'What for?'

'Presumably to take advantage of her, Sir,' said Athos. 'They were drunk, as I told you.'

The Cardinal frowned again.

'And what about the woman?' he asked. 'Was she young and good-looking?'

'We didn't see her, Sir,' replied Athos.

'Oh, you didn't see her!' said the Cardinal sharply. 'Excellent. And you were quite right to defend her. As it happens I'm on my way to the Red Dovecote now, so I'll soon find out if you've been telling the truth.'

Athos replied coldly.

'We wouldn't lie to you, Sir, not to save our lives. We're gentlemen.'

'That's why I don't doubt your story, Monsieur Athos. Not for a moment,' said the Cardinal.

Then, to change the conversation, he added: 'Was the woman alone?'

'No, Sir,' said Athos. 'She had a man with her in her room. That's what I couldn't understand. He never came out. He must have heard the row going on. I suppose he was a coward.'

'Well, gentlemen,' said His Eminence. 'Thank you for

telling me about this affair. I now know all I want to know. So let's be off.'

The little party soon arrived at the inn, which at this hour of the night was quite deserted. When they were about ten yards away the Cardinal signed to his groom and to the three musketeers to halt, rode forward alone and rapped three times sharply on the door. A saddled horse was tethered to the wall. In answer to the Cardinal's knock a man in a cloak immediately came out and had a hurried conversation with him. He then mounted the horse and rode off at the gallop in the direction of Surgères, which was also the direction of Paris. The Cardinal then turned to his escort and beckoned them on.

'I see you've told me the truth about what happened this evening, gentlemen,' he said. 'Our meeting has in fact been most opportune, and I'll see it turns out to your advantage. Now follow me please.'

The Cardinal and the three musketeers dismounted; the Cardinal threw his horse's reins to his groom, while the three musketeers tethered their horses to the wall. His Eminence then entered the inn, followed by his escort.

The innkeeper received him in the hall. He had no suspicion of the Cardinal's true identity and took him for an officer who had an assignation with a lady.

'Have you a room on the ground floor with a good fire where these gentlemen can wait for me?' asked the Cardinal.

The innkeeper opened the door of a large room in which he had recently replaced a worn-out stove with a large and excellent fireplace.

'The gentlemen can have this room,' he said.

'Good,' said the Cardinal. 'Kindly wait for me in there, gentlemen. I shan't keep you more than half an hour.'

The three friends now realized that in trouncing the

drunkards at the inn earlier that evening they had done a bigger thing than they supposed. They had rescued someone who was very high in favour with the Cardinal. Who was this someone? They were all agog to know. But they realized that they could never solve this problem by thought, so Porthos called the innkeeper and asked for dice. He and Aramis then sat down at a table and started to play. Athos paced up and down the room, lost in thought. As he paced up and down he kept passing the broken stove pipe belonging to the stove which had been removed, the bottom end of which hung half-way down from the ceiling, while the top end protruded into the first-floor room. Each time he passed the pipe he heard a subdued murmur of voices from above. His curiosity was aroused and he finally stopped in front of the pipe, put his ear to the opening and tried to hear what the voices were saying.

What he heard was apparently of the greatest interest, for he suddenly signed to his two companions to keep quiet and went on listening intently.

It was the Cardinal speaking.

'This is a matter of vital importance, Milady,' he said. 'So let's get it settled at once. Sit down.'

'Milady!' muttered Athos.

A woman's voice now spoke. At the sound of it the musketeer started and turned pale.

'Tell me what I'm to do, Monseigneur,' replied Milady.

'A brig with an English crew and a captain in my pay is waiting for you at the mouth of the Charente, by Fort la Pointe. It's to set sail tomorrow morning.'

'So I'm to go on board tonight?'

'At once. That is, when I've given you your instructions. There are two men waiting outside this inn to escort you to the coast. I shall leave the inn ahead of you. You'll wait on half an hour and then leave yourself.'

'Very well, Monseigneur. And now tell me what

mission you're sending me on. My one wish is to succeed in it and to continue to enjoy Your Eminence's favour. So please explain very carefully what I'm to do, so that I make no mistake.'

Athos signed to his two companions to lock the door of the room from the inside and to come and put their ears to the pipe so that they could all listen together. Porthos and Aramis liked comfort so they brought their chairs with them and an extra chair for Athos. All three then sat down with their ears to the mouth of the pipe.

'You're to go to London again,' said the Cardinal. 'When you get there you're to see Buckingham.'

'I'd like to remind Your Eminence that Buckingham mistrusts me since the affair of the diamond tags,' said Milady. 'He suspects me of having stolen them.'

'This time I'm not sending you to England as a spy but as an official agent of France,' said the Cardinal. 'In that capacity you must approach Buckingham frankly and openly.'

'Frankly and openly,' echoed Milady in a tone of infinite guile.

'Yes, frankly and openly,' said the Cardinal. 'All this has to be done in the open.'

'I understand, Your Eminence,' replied Milady. 'Please go on.'

'Tell Buckingham from me that my spies have told me all about his plans of campaign, and that if he makes a move, I will expose the Queen. I know about his secret meetings with her, and I have a letter proving that she is plotting with the enemies of France.'

'But suppose the Duke decides to ignore these threats and to go on with his plans against France? What then?'

Richelieu replied bitterly:

'The Duke's madly, besottedly in love. Like the Paladins of old he embarked on this war merely to get a smile from his mistress. When he sees that the war may bring dishonour to her, may even lead to her imprisonment, he'll be relúctant to go on with it.'

But Milady was not yet satisfied. She wished to be able to judge for herself how far her mission was likely to succeed. So once more she said:

'But suppose he does decide to go on?'

'That's not likely,' said the Cardinal.

'But if he does . . .'

His Eminence paused. Then he answered:

'In every age and in every country, particularly in countries divided in religion, you'll find fanatics who long for martyrs' crowns. And now I come to think of it, the Puritans in England hate the Duke of Buckingham; their preachers denounce him as anti-Christ.'

'Well?' asked Milady.

The Cardinal shrugged his shoulders.

'Well,' he said casually, 'the first thing would be to discover a young, handsome, intelligent woman who wanted revenge on Buckingham. Some such person might be found. The Duke's a man of many loves; his romantic nature has won him hearts enough, and his infidelities have made many hate him.'

'It shouldn't be difficult to find the woman,' said Milady calmly.

'Well, a woman like that might in turn inspire a fanatic to assassinate Buckingham. That woman would save France.'

'Yes, but she'd be an accomplice in the crime.'

'That's perfectly fair,' said Richelieu. 'Well, what would you like me to do?'

'I'd like you to give me an order ratifying in advance everything I might feel compelled to do in the interests of France.'

'But the first step would be to find a woman such as I described just now, who wanted to take revenge on the Duke.'

'She's found,' said Milady calmly.

'Then one would have to find the abject fanatic who'd serve as the instrument of God's justice.'

'He'll be found.'

'Very well,' said the Cardinal. 'Find him first and then come to me and I'll give you the order.'

'Your Eminence is right,' said Milady, 'and I was wrong to see in this mission more than it really is, which is to let the Duke know what weapons Your Eminence holds against the Queen. That's right, Your Eminence, is it not? That's all you wish me to do.'

'That's all, Milady,' the Cardinal replied coldly. Then he added:

'When you've talked to the Duke return to this country at once, go to Béthune, to the Carmelite Convent there, and await further orders. I'll tell the Abbess she's to take you in.'

Milady pretended not to notice the Cardinal's sudden change of manner and replied:

'Very well, Monseigneur. And now that I have Your Eminence's instructions for dealing with your enemies, will you allow me to say a few words about mine?'

'Have you enemies?' asked Richelieu.

'Yes, Monseigneur – enemies against whom you owe me your support, for I acquired them by acting for you.'

'Who are they?' asked the Cardinal.

'First of all there's a little schemer called Madame Bonacieux.'

'She's in the Nantes prison.'

'She was,' replied Milady. 'But the Queen got an order from the King to have her removed to a convent.'

'To a convent?' said the Cardinal.

'Yes.'

'Which?'

'I don't know. That was kept secret.'

'Don't worry. I'll find out.'

'And will you tell me?'

'Yes, if you wish it,' replied the Cardinal.

'Thank you, Sir,' said Milady. 'Then I've got another enemy more formidable than Madame Bonacieux.'

'Who's that?'

'Her lover.'

'What's his name?'

Milady burst out angrily:

'You know him well enough, Sir. He's our evil genius, yours and mine. The man who helped the King's Musketeers to defeat Your Eminence's Guards in a brawl, the man who wounded your agent de Wardes and who thwarted us in the affair of the diamond tags. Your Eminence, this man has sworn to kill me; he knows it was I who had his mistress kidnapped.'

'We'll have to have proofs of his dealings with Buckingham,' said the Cardinal.

'Proofs!' cried Milady. 'I'll get a dozen at least.'

'In that case it's the easiest thing in the world,' said the Cardinal. 'Get me those proofs and I'll send him to the Bastille.'

'Thank you, Monseigneur. And after that?'

'There's no "after that" for people in the Bastille,' said the Cardinal grimly. 'Good God!' he continued. 'If I could crush my enemy as easily as I can crush yours, and if you asked for protection only against people like that . . .'

'Monseigneur,' broke in Milady, 'man for man, life for life, give me your enemy and I'll give you mine.'

'I don't know what you mean,' said the Cardinal, 'and I don't even want to know. But I'll gladly do you a favour and I'll certainly give you a free hand to deal with someone so subordinate as d'Artagnan, the more so since from what you say the fellow's a libertine, a duellist and a traitor to France.'

'A bad character, Monseigneur, a thoroughly bad character.'

'Give me a pen and paper,' said the Cardinal.

'Here, Monseigneur.'

There was a moment's silence while the Cardinal wrote out the order. Athos, listening below, had not missed one word of the conversation. He now took his two friends by the arm and led them over to the far corner of the room.

'Why didn't you leave us to hear the end?' asked Porthos.

'Sh!' whispered Athos. 'We've heard all we need to hear. You two go on listening if you want to; I must leave this place at once.'

'Leave the inn?' exclaimed Porthos. 'And suppose the Cardinal asks for you? What shall we say?'

'Don't wait for him to ask. Directly he comes down tell him I went on ahead to reconnoitre, because I heard the innkeeper say something which made me think there was trouble on the road. I'll fix it with the Cardinal's groom. What happens after that's my affair; leave it to me.'

'Don't do anything rash, Athos,' said Aramis.

'Don't worry,' said Athos. 'I can take care of myself.'

Porthos and Aramis went back to the stove pipe. Athos left the inn, sauntered coolly over to his horse, which was standing with his friends' horses by the door, untethered it, whispered to the groom that he was going on ahead to act as advance-guard for the return journey, made a show of adjusting the flints of his pistols, unsheathed his sword and galloped off alone in the direction of the camp.

Almost immediately after Athos' departure the Cardinal came down; he looked into the room in which he had left the musketeers and found Porthos and Aramis deeply engrossed in a game of dice. He glanced quickly round and noticed that one of his escort was missing.

'Where's Monsieur Athos?' he asked.

'Your Eminence, he went on ahead to reconnoitre. The innkeeper said something which made him suspect the road was unsafe.'

'And what have you been doing, Monsieur Porthos?'

'I've been busy winning five pistoles from Aramis,' replied Porthos.

'Are you ready to come back with me now?'

'Yes, Sir.'

'Well, come quickly then, gentlemen. It's getting late.'

The groom was at the door, holding His Eminence's horse by the bridle. A little further off stood a group of two men and three horses, barely visible in the darkness. These two men were Milady's escort, who were to take her to Fort la Pointe and see her safely on board. The Cardinal questioned the groom about Athos and the man confirmed Porthos' story that he had gone on ahead to spy out the land. The Cardinal nodded his approval and started off along the road to the camp, making the musketeers and the groom follow ten yards behind him as before.

Athos meanwhile had galloped a hundred yards or so down the road. When he was out of sight of the inn he plunged into the dense undergrowth at the side of the road, made a complete about turn and rode half-way back to the inn under cover of the trees. Here he halted, still under cover, and waited for the Cardinal and his escort to pass down the highway. Then he galloped back to the inn, dismounted and knocked on the door. The innkeeper recognized him at once. Athos said:

'My officer sent me back with a message for the lady on the first floor, something he meant to tell her and forgot.'

'Go up, Sir,' said the host. 'The lady's still there.'

Athos went up the stairs, treading as lightly as he could. When he reached the landing he saw through the half-open door Milady tying on her hat. He walked quickly across the landing, pushed open the door and walked straight into the room, closing the door behind him. Then he stood stock still, facing Milady, with his cloak wound round him and his plumed hat pressed well down over his eyes. When Milady saw this silent figure by the door she was frightened.

'Who are you? What do you want?' she cried.

Athos muttered to himself:

'Yes, it's her.'

Then he let his cloak fall open, took off his hat and walked up to her.

'Do you recognize me?' he asked.

Milady looked at him for a moment in silence. Suddenly she flinched and shrank back as though she had seen a ghost.

'Good,' said Athos. 'I see you do recognize me.'

Milady went deathly pale and retreated before him until she was standing with her back pressed against the wall.

'Comte de la Fère!' she muttered.

'Yes,' replied Athos. 'Comte de la Fère, returned from the past on a matter of vital importance. So, as the Cardinal said just now, let's get it settled at once. Sit down!'

Milady, struck dumb with terror, sat down without a word. Athos sat down facing her.

'You're a fiend,' he said, 'an evil spirit sent into this world to torture men. Your power's great, I know, but with God's help men have conquered worse demons than you. You've already come into my life once. I thought I'd crushed you then. But either I was wrong or Hell's resurrected you.'

Athos' words brought horrifying recollections to Milady's mind. She groaned and buried her head in her hands.

'You thought I was dead, didn't you?' he continued. 'And I thought you were dead. I took the name of Athos to hide the identity of the Comte de la Fère, just as you took the name of Lady de Winter to hide the identity of Anne de Breuil. Wasn't that the name you went by when your worthy brother married us?'

Milady broke in in a low voice:

'For God's sake tell me why you've come here tonight and what you want.'

In reply Athos pulled out a pistol, stretched out his hand until the muzzle was almost touching her forehead, and in a coldly determined voice said:

'Lady de Winter, hand over at once the order the Cardinal signed for you, or by God I'll blow your brains out.'

Had it been anyone but Athos Milady might have doubted his carrying out his threat. But she knew Athos.

And yet she made no move.

'I'll give you one second to decide,' he said.

Milady saw from the contraction of his face muscles that he was about to pull the trigger. She quickly put her hand to her bodice, pulled out a scroll of paper and handed it to him.

'Here, take it,' she said. 'And curse you to all eternity.'

Athos took it. He then replaced the pistol in his belt and, to make sure that what he held was really the Cardinal's order, took the paper to the lamp, unrolled it and read it.

Athos now drew his cloak round him and put on his hat. Then, looking at Milady with loathing, he said:

'Now I've drawn your viper's fangs. Strike if you can!'

With that he turned and left the room.

Outside in the courtyard he met the two mounted men and the spare horse which they were holding on a leading rein.

'Gentlemen,' he said, 'my officer's orders to you are, as you know, to escort this lady at once to Fort la Pointe and not to leave her until you've seen her safely on board.'

This order tallied with the order the men had already received, so they nodded assent.

Now Athos sprang into the saddle and galloped off. But instead of following the high road towards the camp he branched off across country, urging his horse forward at a great rate and reining in from time to time to listen. At last he heard the sound of horses' hoofs on the road a short way in rear. Convinced that they were the horses of the Cardinal and his escort, he pushed forward again a short distance, then halted and gave his own horse a good rubbing down with heather and leaves. Then he turned sharp right, rode out of the wood and placed himself in the middle of the road, a little ahead of the oncoming party of riders and facing them. The camp was now only about a hundred yards away. Directly he caught sight of the Cardinal and his escort he called out:

'Who goes there?'

'That must be Athos,' said the Cardinal.

'Yes, Monseigneur,' shouted the musketeer. 'It's Athos!'

'I'm most grateful to you for your help, Monsieur Athos,' said the Cardinal. 'Well, here we are, gentlemen, at last.'

Then he rode off.

When the Cardinal was out of earshot Porthos and Aramis turned to Athos and said:

'She got the order out of him.'

'I know,' said Athos calmly. 'And I got it out of her. In fact I've got it on me now.'

The three friends rode back in silence to their billets, only speaking to give the password to the sentry. But they sent Mousqueton to tell Planchet to beg his master to call on them the moment he came off duty.

28

THE BASTION OF ST GERVAIS

When d'Artagnan received his friends' message he came round at once to their billets.

'Well, gentlemen,' he said, 'let's hope you've got something really worthwhile to say, otherwise I shan't forgive you for disturbing me. I was enjoying a well-earned rest after a night spent capturing and dismantling a bastion. You can thank your lucky stars you weren't there, all of you. God, the heat!'

'Where we were it was none too cold either, I can tell you,' said Porthos with a smug smile.

'Quiet! Not so loud!' said Athos, waking out of his reverie.

D'Artagnan was quick to notice the frown on his friend's face.

'H'm!' he said. 'I see you really have got some news for me.'

Athos said:

'Aramis, didn't you dine the night before last at the Parpaillot inn?'

'Yes.'

'What was it like there?'

'They gave me a very nasty and expensive meal. It was their bad day and they only had meat.'

'That wasn't what I meant, Aramis,' said Athos. 'I meant were you left to yourself or did people keep disturbing you?'

'I was left pretty well to myself,' said Aramis. 'Yes, Athos, I see what you're driving at. I think we'd be pretty safe at the Parpaillot.'

'Well, let's go there,' said Athos. 'Here the walls are like paper.'

The little party soon arrived at the Parpaillot inn. It was now seven o'clock in the morning and dawn was just breaking. The four friends ordered breakfast and went into a room where the host assured them they would not be disturbed.

Unfortunately they had chosen a bad hour for a conference. Reveille had just sounded. Everyone was shaking off the night's sleep and had come to drink a tot of brandy at the inn to drive away the effects of the early morning damp. Dragoons, Swiss mercenaries, foot-guards, musketeers, and life-guards kept passing in and out, much to the satisfaction of the landlord and much to the annoyance of the four friends, who gave very surly replies to their fellow-customers' jovial greetings.

'We shall find ourselves involved in an argument if we don't take care,' said Athos, 'and we want to avoid that at all costs. D'Artagnan, describe your night to us, and we'll describe ours later.'

A life-guard was standing by, sipping a glass of brandy. He broke in at this point.

'Yes, you were up the line last night, you guards,' he said. 'I gather you had a bit of trouble with the Rochellese.'

'Didn't you capture a bastion?' asked a Swiss guard, who was drinking rum out of a beer glass.

'Yes,' replied d'Artagnan, nodding to the Swiss. 'We had that pleasure. As you may have heard, we also had the pleasure of stuffing a barrel of gunpowder under one of the corners of the bastion, setting light to it and making a pretty breach in the wall. The bastion was fairly old so the rest of it was badly shaken as well.'

A dragoon was also standing by; he held impaled on his sabre a goose, which he was taking to the fire to roast, using his sabre as a spit.

'Which bastion was it?' he asked.

'The St Gervais bastion,' replied d'Artagnan. 'The

Rochellese were occupying it and worrying our pioneers in the trenches.'

'Quite a lively affair, wasn't it?'

'Yes, we lost five men and the Rochellese eight or ten.'

'They'll probably send their pioneers this morning to repair the bastion,' said the life-guard, Monsieur de Busigny.

'Probably,' said d'Artagnan.

Athos broke in: 'I'll make a bet with you, gentlemen!'

'Good, a bet!' said the Swiss guard.

The dragoon laid his sabre like a spit across the two large iron dogs which supported the fire.

'Wait!' he said. 'I want to be in on this bet.'

'Yes,' said the life-guard. 'I want to be in on it too.'

'Well, Monsieur de Busigny,' said Athos. 'I bet you that I and my three friends here, Porthos, Aramis and d'Artagnan, will breakfast in the St Gervais bastion and that we'll hold it for an hour, no more and no less, against all opposition from the enemy.'

Porthos and Aramis threw each other quick looks. They had both grasped at once what lay behind this apparently frivolous proposal. But d'Artagnan bent over Athos and whispered:

'What's the idea? Are you trying to get us all killed?'

Athos whispered back:

'We're much more likely to be killed if we don't go.'

Porthos leant back in his chair and twirled his moustache.

'Well, gentlemen,' he said, 'how's that for a bet?'

'I'll take that bet,' cried de Busigny. 'What are the stakes?'

'There are four of you and four of us,' said Athos. 'What d'you say to a slap-up dinner for eight to be paid for by the losers?'

'Excellent!' said de Busigny.

'Excellent,' said the dragoon.

'That goes with me too,' said the Swiss.

The fourth man, who had been a silent witness of the scene, nodded to show that he, too, agreed to the terms.

At that moment the innkeeper called out:

'Your breakfast's ready, gentlemen!'

'Bring it in then,' said Athos.

The innkeeper obeyed.

Athos now summoned Grimaud to wrap up the food in napkins and pack it in the basket. He packed up the food, placed the bottles of wine on top and lifted the basket with its contents on to his shoulder. At this the innkeeper tried to protest.

'Where are you proposing to eat my breakfast, gentlemen?' he asked.

'That's no concern of yours provided we pay for it!' replied Athos.

And with a flourish he drew two pistoles from his pocket and threw them on the table.

Now the four young men bade the astonished onlookers good morning and set off for the St Gervais bastion. Grimaud followed them, carrying the basket; the poor fellow was quite in the dark as to their objective.

'Why didn't we have breakfast at the Parpaillot?' asked d'Artagnan.

'Because we've some very important things to discuss, and we couldn't have talked in that inn with those nosy devils pestering us all the time,' replied Athos.

He added, pointing to the bastion: 'There's no fear of them following us in there!'

D'Artagnan, reckless as he was at times, had a strain of common sense deep down in him.

'Couldn't we have found some secluded spot on the dunes near the sea?' he asked.

'The four of us in close conclave would have attracted attention at once. The Cardinal's spies would have told him about us in no time.'

'I think we might at least have brought our muskets,' objected Porthos.

'Friend Porthos, you're a fool. Why bring unnecessary lumber?'

'I don't see how a good regulation musket with twelve rounds and a powder flask can be called lumber. Most useful for keeping the enemy at bay, I should have said.'

'Didn't you hear what d'Artagnan told us?' asked Athos.

'No. What?'

'He told us that in last night's skirmish five of our fellows were killed and about eight or ten Rochellese.'

'Well, what about it?'

'They didn't have time to strip them, remember. They were too busy doing other things.'

'Well?'

'We shall find their muskets, their ammunition, and their powder flasks on them. We'll have more than we need in the way of arms, fifteen muskets and a hundred rounds at least between the four of us instead of only four muskets and twelve rounds.'

'Athos, you're a genius!' cried Aramis.

When they reached the bastion the four friends turned round. Over 300 men of all arms had gathered at the gates of the camp, and they could just discern de Busigny, the dragoon, the Swiss mercenary and their companion forming a little group by themselves.

Athos took off his hat, stuck it on the end of his sword and waved it above his head. At this all the watchers in the camp raised a mighty cheer, of which the four friends heard a faint echo.

As Athos had prophesied there were about a dozen dead men lying in the bastion, five French and seven Rochellese.

'Gentlemen,' he said, 'while Grimaud's laying the breakfast let's start collecting the guns and the cartridges.

We can talk at the same time. We're quite safe,' he added, pointing to the dead men, 'these gentlemen aren't listening.'

'Why not throw them down into the moat all the same?' remarked Porthos. 'Of course we must search their pockets first.'

'Yes,' said Aramis. 'But that's Grimaud's job.'

'Very well,' said d'Artagnan, 'let Grimaud search them and then throw them over the wall.'

'Let him search them, yes,' said Athos, 'but he mustn't throw them over the wall; they may be of use to us.'

'What possible use could they be?' asked Porthos. 'Don't talk nonsense, Athos.'

'Just you wait and see, my lad,' continued Athos. 'How many guns are there, gentlemen?'

'Twelve,' replied Aramis.

'How many rounds?'

'A hundred.'

'That's plenty. Load the guns.'

The four musketeers set to work. Just as they had finished loading the last gun Grimaud announced that breakfast was ready. Athos now signed to him to go and stand in a kind of watch-turret at one end of the bastion and act as sentry. To break the monotony of his task Athos allowed him to take a loaf of bread, two cutlets and a bottle of wine with him.

'And now let's start eating,' said Athos.

The four friends sat down on the ground with their legs crossed like Turks or tailors.

'Look here, Athos,' said d'Artagnan. 'There's not the faintest chance of anyone hearing us now, so I insist that you tell me your secret at once.'

'Here it is in five words: I saw Milady last night.'

D'Artagnan was just lifting his glass to his lips, but when he heard this his hand began to tremble so much that he had to put it down.

'What!' he cried. 'You saw your . . . ?'

Athos silenced him with a gesture.

'Remember these gentlemen don't know as much about my private life as you do,' he said. 'I repeat, I've seen Milady.'

'Where on earth?' asked d'Artagnan.

'Only about a couple of miles from here, at the Red Dovecote inn.'

'Oh, in that case I'm finished!' said d'Artagnan.

'No, not quite yet,' replied Athos. 'She's not staying here. In fact she must have left the country by now.'

D'Artagnan gave a deep groan of relief.

'Who is this Milady, for God's sake?' cried Porthos.

Athos sipped his glass of sparkling wine and replied:

'A charming woman who was very kind to our friend d'Artagnan, who, to reward her, played some low trick on her for which she tried to revenge herself a month ago by hiring two thugs to shoot him, a week ago by poisoning him, and only yesterday by asking the Cardinal for his head.'

D'Artagnan went white.

'What?' he cried. 'She asked the Cardinal for my head?'

'Yes,' said Porthos. 'I can vouch for that. I heard her with my own ears.'

'So did I,' said Aramis.

D'Artagnan hid his face in his hands.

At that moment Grimaud reported a party of about twenty of the enemy advancing towards the bastion.

'How far away are they?' asked Athos.

'About 500 yards.'

'Good. We've got time to finish this chicken and drink a bottle of wine.'

Soon they saw the enemy platoon; it was advancing along a tributary trench which connected the bastion to the town.

'Ye Gods,' said Athos. 'Just look at them! Did we really

need to get up for rabble like that armed with picks and shovels? I bet if Grimaud'd shaken his fists at them they'd have gone away.'

'I doubt that,' said d'Artagnan. 'They look determined enough to me. And they're not only pioneers – they've got four soldiers and a sergeant with them, armed with muskets.'

'They haven't seen us yet,' said Athos. 'Wait till they see us.'

'I must confess I don't like the idea of firing on a lot of untrained civilians,' said Aramis.

'I agree with Aramis,' said Athos. 'I'm going to give them a chance to go away.'

Whereupon he sprang into the breach in the wall, holding his gun in one hand and his hat in the other, and began addressing the oncoming party.

'Gentlemen,' he called, 'I and a few friends are breakfasting in this bastion. As I'm sure you'll agree, nothing's so odious as to be interrupted in the middle of a meal. So if you must occupy this bastion, please either wait till we've finished or go home and come back later. That is, unless you'd consider changing sides, leaving the rebels and joining us in a toast to His Majesty.'

The enemy platoon, astounded at this remarkable harangue, had halted about thirty yards from the bastion.

'Look out, Athos!' broke in d'Artagnan. 'They're taking aim at you. Can't you see?'

At that very moment four shots rang out and the bullets spattered against the wall of the bastion all round Athos. But none touched him. Almost simultaneously four answering shots rang out. And these were better aimed; three soldiers of the attacking party fell dead and one pioneer was wounded.

Athos, who was still standing in the breach, called out: 'Grimaud, another musket!'

Grimaud quickly handed him one. Meanwhile the other three defenders of the bastion had reloaded and now fired a second volley. This time the sergeant and two pioneers fell dead and the rest of the party took to flight.

'Come on, gentlemen; a sally!' cried Athos.

The four friends sprang out of the bastion, ran to where the dead men were lying and collected the four soldiers' muskets and the sergeant's pike. They decided not to pursue the retreating party and returned to the bastion bearing the trophies of their victory.

'Reload the muskets, Grimaud,' said Athos. 'Good, now we're ready for the enemy's next move. And now, gentlemen, let's continue our conversation. Where were we?'

'You were telling how Milady'd left France after asking the Cardinal for my head,' said d'Artagnan.

'Yes, I remember,' replied Athos.

'Where was she going?' asked d'Artagnan anxiously.

'To England.'

'What for?'

'To get Buckingham assassinated. She was either going to do it herself or get someone else to do it for her.'

D'Artagnan cried out:

'But that's monstrous!'

'Oh, I can't worry very much about that,' replied Athos.

Then, turning to Grimaud:

'When you've finished reloading,' he said, 'take our sergeant's pike, tie one of these napkins to it and plant it on top of the bastion, to show the rebels we're loyal soldiers of the King.'

Grimaud obeyed in silence and a moment later the white flag was floating over the bastion. Its appearance was hailed with shouts and cheers from the onlookers in the camp. By now half the besieging army was collected at the gates.

D'Artagnan protested:

'D'you really mean you don't care if Buckingham's killed? He's our friend, surely.'

'Very well,' said Athos, 'we'll return to Buckingham later, if you like. But as you can imagine, d'Artagnan, what concerned me most at the time was to get back from that woman what she'd got from the Cardinal. And that amounted to nothing less than a full warrant to get you put out of the way, and perhaps the rest of us as well.'

'Is this woman a vampire from the lower regions or what?' asked Porthos.

Then, almost in the same breath he said, handing his plate to Aramis, who was carving the chicken:

'Cut me off a thigh like a good chap.'

'And that warrant?' asked d'Artagnan. 'Has she still got it?'

'No. I took it away from her,' said Athos. 'I can't pretend I didn't have the devil's own job getting it.'

D'Artagnan said with tears in his eyes:

'My dear fellow, that must be the fourth time you've saved my life!'

'So that was why you left us!' said Aramis. 'To go back to her.'

'Yes.'

'Have you still got the warrant?' asked d'Artagnan.

'Yes, I've got it on me now,' replied Athos. 'Here, read it!'

And he pulled the precious document out of his pocket. D'Artagnan trembled violently as he unrolled the paper and made no attempt to hide his fear. He read the order aloud:

It is by my order and for the benefit of the State that the bearer of this note has done what he has done.

3 December, 1627   *Richelieu*

'Yes,' said Aramis. 'That's complete absolution.'

As he stared at the order d'Artagnan felt that he was looking at his death sentence.

'We must destroy this at once!' he cried.

'On the contrary,' said Athos. 'We must guard it with our lives. I wouldn't part with that document for a thousand pistoles.'

'What d'you suppose she'll do now?' asked the young man.

Athos shrugged his shoulders:

'She'll probably write to the Cardinal from England to say that a damned musketeer called Athos stole her safe-conduct pass from her. She'll probably advise him at the same time to get rid of his two friends, Porthos and Aramis. The Cardinal'll remember them as the fellows who were always getting in his way. One fine day he'll have d'Artagnan arrested and send us three to keep him company in the Bastille for fear he should get bored there all by himself.'

Porthos protested.

'I think that joke's in rather bad taste,' he said. 'Incidentally I also think this chicken's horribly tough.'

'I wasn't joking,' said Athos. 'She's just as dangerous in England as she is in France.'

'When you had her in that room why in God's name didn't you strangle her, put her head in a bucket or string her up?' cried Porthos. 'Then we'd all be enjoying ourselves instead of worrying our heads off about her. The dead never return.'

'That's what you think, Porthos!' said Athos, throwing a quick, meaning look at d'Artagnan.

There was silence for a moment. Suddenly d'Artagnan exclaimed:

'I've got an idea!'

'Good! What is it?' cried the other three.

At that moment Grimaud called out:

'Enemy approaching!'

The young men scrambled to their feet, picked up their guns and ran to their posts. They saw a small troop of about twenty-five men approaching. This time they were not pioneers but garrison soldiers.

'How about returning to the camp?' said Porthos. 'I think the odds are rather against us this time.'

'Impossible for three reasons,' replied Athos. 'One, we haven't finished breakfast; two, we've still got a lot to discuss; three, there's another ten minutes to go before the hour's up.'

'Well then, let's work out a plan of action,' said Aramis.

'We'd better wait till the enemy's within range and then open fire,' said Athos. 'If they continue to advance we fire again, and go on firing till we run out of ammunition. If what's left of the enemy tries to attack the bastion we wait till they're in the moat and then shove this section of wall down on their heads; as you see, it's quite loose and only holding up by a miracle of balance.'

This is exactly what they did. Then Athos looked at his watch.

'Gentlemen,' he said. 'We've been here an hour now, so strictly speaking we've won our bet. But let's stay on a little longer and win it handsomely. Besides, d'Artagnan hasn't told us his idea yet.'

Upon which he leaned his musket against the wall and calmly sat down in front of the remains of the breakfast.

'My idea?' said d'Artagnan.

'Yes,' said Athos. 'You were just telling us you had an idea.'

'Of course,' said d'Artagnan. 'My idea was to pay a second visit to England, find Buckingham and warn him of this plot against his life.'

'No, d'Artagnan. That you will not do,' said Athos coldly.

'Why not? I did it before!'

'Yes, but we weren't at war then. At that time Buckingham was an ally, not an enemy. What you propose doing's treason.'

D'Artagnan saw that Athos was right and did not persist.

Porthos now broke in.

'I think I've got an idea,' he said.

'Silence for Porthos' idea!' said Aramis.

'I'll ask Monsieur de Tréville for leave on some pretext or other. You'll all have to think out the pretext; I'm bad at that sort of thing. I shall then go and call on Her Ladyship. She doesn't know me so she won't suspect anything. I'll manage somehow to get left alone with her and then strangle her.'

'That's not at all a bad idea,' said Athos.

'Kill a woman!' cried Aramis. 'Not on your life! No, I've got a much better idea than that.'

'Let's hear your idea, Aramis,' said Athos, who had a great respect for the young musketeer's intelligence.

'We must let the Queen know about it.'

'Yes, of course!' cried Porthos and d'Artagnan. 'That's the obvious thing to do!'

'Let the Queen know?' repeated Athos. 'And how d'you suggest we do that? We've got no connections at Court, and we couldn't send anyone to Paris without the whole camp knowing. It's 280 miles from here to Paris. We'd all be in detention before our letter reached Angers.'

'I'd guarantee to get a letter through to Her Majesty,' said Aramis, colouring slightly. 'I know someone in Tours who'd do that for me.'

Athos smiled at this. Aramis noticed him smile and hesitated.

'Well?' asked d'Artagnan. 'And what d'you think of that plan?'

'I don't dismiss it entirely,' said Athos. 'But I'd like to

point out that if Aramis left camp he'd get the rest of us into serious trouble. And if we sent anyone else with the letter two hours after he'd left all the Cardinal's spies would know it by heart and arrest both Aramis and his friend in Tours on the spot.'

'Not to mention the fact that the Queen would protect Buckingham but wouldn't bother her head about any of us,' said Porthos.

'True enough, Porthos,' agreed d'Artagnan.

Athos suddenly raised his hand to command silence.

'What's all that racket going on in the town?' he cried. 'That's a call to arms!'

The four friends listened and heard the ominous rumble of the drums in the distance.

'You wait!' said Athos. 'They'll be sending a whole regiment against us now.'

'You don't propose to hold out against a regiment, do you?' asked Porthos.

'Why not?' asked the musketeer. 'I feel in fine form today and if we'd had the sense to bring another dozen bottles with us I'd take on an army corps!'

'Listen!' said d'Artagnan. 'The drums are getting louder. The enemy's advancing.'

'Let them come,' said Athos. 'It'll take them a good quarter of an hour to get here. That's ample time for us to settle on a plan. If we left now we'd never find anywhere else as good as this to talk in. And if you'll all listen a moment, I think I've hit on the solution of our problem.'

'Well, let's hear it.'

'I must just say a word to Grimaud first,' said Athos.

And he beckoned to his servant to leave his look-out post and come and take his orders. Pointing to the corpses lying in the bastion he said:

'Grimaud, lift up these gentlemen and prop them against the wall. Then put their hats on their heads and their guns in their hands.'

'Oh, bravo,' exclaimed d'Artagnan. 'I see it all now!'

'Do you?' asked Porthos. 'I wish I did!'

'Do you see it, Grimaud?' asked Aramis.

Grimaud nodded. Then he set to work to lift up the corpses.

'That's right, Grimaud,' said Athos. 'Get down to it. That's all we need do as far as the enemy goes. And now for this idea of mine.'

'I wish you'd first explain what you're doing with those dead fellows,' said Porthos.

'You'll soon see.'

'Come on, Athos, we're waiting for the big idea!' cried d'Artagnan and Aramis.

'D'Artagnan, didn't you tell me this Milady of yours, woman, vampire, or whatever she is, had a brother-in-law?'

'Yes. I know him personally. And I don't think there's much love lost between him and his sister-in-law.'

'That's all to the good,' said Athos. 'If he hated her it'd be better still.'

'He's the man for us, then.'

'I do wish you'd tell me what Grimaud's supposed to be doing,' interrupted Porthos.

'Shut up, Porthos!' said Aramis.

'What's this brother-in-law's name?'

'Lord de Winter.'

'Where's he now?'

'He returned to London at the beginning of the war.'

'Well, he's the very fellow we want,' said Athos. 'He's the man we must get in touch with. We must tell him his sister-in-law's on the point of murdering someone, and advise him to keep a close watch on her.'

'I think we'd better warn both the Queen and Lord de Winter,' said Aramis. 'I think that'll do the trick.'

'Yes, but who can we get to take the letters, one to Tours and the other to London?'

'Bazin can take one,' suggested Aramis.

'Yes, and Planchet the other,' suggested d'Artagnan.

'A good idea!' said Porthos. 'We can't leave camp, I know, but there's nothing to prevent our servants leaving.'

'Of course not,' said Aramis. 'We'll write the letters today, at once; then we'll give them both money and send them off.'

'Money?' cried Athos. 'And where's the money coming from?'

The four friends darted quick glances at each other. A moment before they had been cheerful and excited; now they were in despair again.

At this point d'Artagnan suddenly jumped up, shouting:

'Look out, look out! The enemy! I can see little black and red dots moving down there. Did you say something about a regiment, Athos? Lord! It's a whole army corps!'

'Ah yes, there they come!' said Athos. 'Look at them, the dirty dogs, sneaking along without drums or bugles. Trying to surprise us, were they! Hi, there, Grimaud, have you finished the job?'

Grimaud nodded and pointed to a dozen corpses which he had grouped most artistically round the walls, some holding their muskets at the porte, others pointing them at the enemy, and others with drawn swords.

'Well done, Grimaud!' said Athos. 'That's excellent and does credit to your imagination.'

'I still don't understand,' said Porthos. 'Do explain to me, someone . . .'

'Let's get away first,' said d'Artagnan. 'We'll explain later.'

'We must wait till Grimaud's packed up the breakfast things,' said Athos.

'Those little black and red dots are much larger now,'

said Aramis. 'I really think d'Artagnan's right; we'd better get back to camp.'

'Very well,' said Athos. 'I think we're justified in getting out now. Our bet was for an hour and we've held the fort an hour and a half. No one can complain of that. So let's go.'

Grimaud had already started off with the basket and the remains of the food. The four friends followed him. But they had only gone about ten yards when Athos suddenly stopped.

'We've forgotten something, gentlemen,' he said.

'What?' asked Aramis.

'The flag. We can't leave our flag in enemy hands, even though it is only a napkin.'

Whereupon he ran back into the bastion, climbed into the breach and removed the flag.

But the advancing Rochellese were now within range. When they saw the foolhardy young musketeer exposing himself to their bullets they immediately opened fire on him. But Athos seemed to bear a charmed life. The bullets whistled round his head but none touched him. As a final gesture before abandoning the bastion he waved the standard defiantly at the enemy and in greeting to the men in the camp.

At this loud cries came from both sides, from one side cries of anger and from the other of applause. A second enemy volley succeeded the first and three bullets pierced the flag, converting it from a napkin into a proper standard. And now all the watchers in the camp began shouting:

'Come down, come down.'

Athos jumped down from the bastion. His friends were waiting anxiously for him twenty yards away and beckoned him on.

'Hurry, hurry!' cried d'Artagnan. 'We'd better run for it. We've got everything nicely worked out now except the money business, and it'd be silly to get killed at the last moment.'

But Athos refused to be hurried. He walked along at a steady pace and his companions, seeing that argument was useless, set their pace by him. Grimaud had gone on ahead with his basket and was now well out of gunshot. In a moment or two the four friends heard a furious burst of fire behind them.

'What was all that about?' asked Porthos. 'What are they firing at? I didn't hear any bullets and I can't see anyone.'

'They're firing at our corpses,' replied Athos.

At this Porthos cried out:

'Oh, I see now! Athos, you're a genius.'

'Glad you think so!' replied Athos coolly.

When the watchers in the camp saw the four friends returning not at the double but taking their time over it, they burst into loud cheers. The next moment there was another volley of fire from behind and this time the bullets whistled unpleasantly round the friends' ears and sent the pebbles flying round their feet. The Rochellese had just occupied the bastion.

'What an incompetent lot of devils they are!' said Athos. 'How many of them did we pot? Twelve, wasn't it?'

'About that.'

'And how many did we crush with that wall?'

'About ten.'

'In return for which we've none of us got a scratch. But what's that on your hand, d'Artagnan? Blood, isn't it?'

'That's nothing,' said d'Artagnan.

'A bullet?'

'Not even a bullet.'

'What is it then?'

Athos, as we know, loved d'Artagnan as his son and,

stern and sad as he was, sometimes felt a father's concern for him.

'It's a graze,' said d'Artagnan. 'My hand got caught between two stones, the stone of the wall and the stone on my finger. The skin got rubbed off.'

Athos snorted contemptuously:

'That's what comes of wearing diamond rings, my lad,' he said.

'Look here!' said Porthos suddenly. 'We've got a diamond ring. Why are we worrying about money when we've got a perfectly good diamond ring?'

'Good Lord, I never thought of that!' exclaimed Aramis. 'Good old Porthos! You've had a brainwave at last!'

Porthos gave his moustache a proud twirl.

'What's to stop us selling the ring?' he asked.

'But it's the Queen's ring,' objected d'Artagnan.

'All the more reason for using it,' said Athos. 'It'll help the Queen to save her lover Buckingham. What better use could it be put to? And it'll help her to save us, her friends. Quite as it should be. Let's sell the diamond. What does Father Aramis say? We won't ask Porthos; we already know what he thinks.'

Aramis coloured and replied:

'The ring's not a present from his mistress and therefore not a love token. So I think d'Artagnan's justified in selling it.'

D'Artagnan was satisfied.

'Right,' he said, 'we'll sell it then.'

Meanwhile the enemy troops were keeping up their fire. But the friends were now out of range and the Rochellese were only firing to ease their consciences. Athos remarked:

'You came out with that bright idea just in time, Porthos. Here we are back at the camp. And now, gentlemen, not another word about the whole business.

We're already being watched. They're coming out to meet us and I think we're going to be carried back in triumph.'

When the Cardinal heard about the four friends' daring exploit, he remarked:

'Well, I see there's nothing for it; I must have them all on my side!'

That evening the Cardinal himself mentioned the exploit to Monsieur de Tréville. Indeed it would have looked strange had he not, for it was now the talk of the whole camp. Monsieur de Tréville had heard the story from the lips of the men who had been the heroes of it, so he was able to relate it in detail to the Cardinal, not forgetting the napkin incident.

'Get hold of that napkin for me, Monsieur de Tréville,' said the Cardinal, 'and I'll have three gold fleur-de-lis embroidered on it and present it to your company as its camp colours.'

'That wouldn't be fair to the Guards, Your Eminence,' objected de Tréville. 'Young d'Artagnan's not in my company; he's in Monsieur des Essarts' company.'

'Well, you take him on, Sir,' said the Cardinal. 'Those four rogues are so hand-in-glove they ought all to be together.'

Later that evening Monsieur de Tréville announced the good news to the three musketeers and d'Artagnan and invited them all to lunch with him the next day. The latter was in the seventh heaven of joy. As we know, it was the ambition of his life to be a musketeer. His three friends were also delighted.

At ten o'clock that night d'Artagnan went to pay his respects to Monsieur des Essarts and to tell him of his promotion. Monsieur des Essarts was very much attached to d'Artagnan. He knew that this change of corps would mean a new outfit for him, so he suggested giving him a small advance on his pay. D'Artagnan declined the offer but instead asked Monsieur des Essarts to be good enough to have the Queen's diamond valued and sold for him. Des Essarts took the ring and promised to carry out the young man's commission.

At eight o'clock next morning Monsieur des Essarts' valet called at d'Artagnan's quarters and handed him a purse containing 7,000 livres in gold. This was the price of the Queen's diamond.

29
A FAMILY AFFAIR

Athos' inventive genius had found the solution. The campaign against Milady was to be carried on as a family affair. Family affairs were not open to investigation by the Cardinal and his agents; they concerned no one outside the family and could be discussed in front of anyone.

The lunch with Monsieur de Tréville was uproariously gay. After lunch the four friends agreed to meet that evening at Athos' billet and make the final arrangements. D'Artagnan spent the rest of that day parading up and down the camp in his new uniform. That evening, at the time arranged, the four friends met. Aramis agreed to compose the letter to Lord de Winter in England.

'But first tell me the whole story,' he said. 'I gather His Lordship de Winter's sister-in-law's a dangerous woman. I've even got evidence of that through listening to her conversation with the Cardinal.'

'Not so loud,' begged Athos.

'But I don't know the story in full,' said Aramis.

'Nor do I,' said Porthos.

D'Artagnan and Athos stole a quick glance at each other. The latter sat for a moment lost in thought. Then he looked up and nodded at d'Artagnan. D'Artagnan took this to mean that he could speak out.

'Well, this is what you must write,' he said.

'My Lord, your sister-in-law is a wicked woman. She tried to get you killed in order to inherit your fortune. But her marriage with your brother was illegal. She had been married in France before and had been . . .'

D'Artagnan paused and waited for Athos to prompt him.

'Sent away by her husband,' said Athos.

'Because she had been branded,' continued d'Artagnan.

'Branded! Good God!' cried Porthos. 'Branded and tried to get her brother-in-law murdered?'

'Yes.'

'And a bigamist?' asked Aramis.

'Yes.'

'And her husband discovered she had a fleur-de-lis on her shoulder?'

'Yes.'

'Who's actually seen this fleur-de-lis?' asked Aramis.

'D'Artagnan and I, or rather I and d'Artagnan, to keep the chronological order,' said Athos.

'And is this fiend's husband still alive?' asked Aramis.

'Yes.'

'Are you certain of that?'

'Quite.'

There was dead silence for a moment. All four men were moved, each in a different way. Athos was the first to speak.

'D'Artagnan's given us an excellent start,' he said. 'We must write a properly expressed letter, using d'Artagnan's suggestion as a rough draft.'

Aramis took up the pen and, after a moment's thought, wrote eight or ten lines in a neat hand. These he proceeded to read aloud, with slow emphasis, as though he had weighed each word carefully as he wrote.

My Lord, he read:

> The man who is writing this once had the honour of crossing swords with you in a little enclosure in the Rue d'Enfer.
>
> As you were kind enough to give this man frequent proofs of your goodwill he, in return, feels obliged, in token of his goodwill, to send you a word of warning.
>
> You have a close relation who has twice tried to kill you. You believe her to be your rightful heir but she is not. Before marrying in England she was already married in France.
>
> This woman, as I say, has twice tried to kill you. The third time, this time in fact, she might succeed.
>
> Your relation has left La Rochelle for England. Keep a close watch on her; she is engaged in dangerous intrigues. If you wish to know what she is guilty of you can read her past on her left shoulder.

'That's marvellous!' said Athos. 'Aramis, you write like an angel. That letter will put de Winter thoroughly on his guard, that is, if it ever reaches him. And if it falls into the hands of His Eminence himself we shan't be compromised.'

Aramis then took up the pen again, to write just as subtle a letter to warn the Queen of the danger to Buckingham. He thought for a moment and then wrote a few lines which he proceeded also to read aloud to his friends and which ran as follows:

> 'My dear Cousin,

'Oh!' interrupted Athos. 'So she's a relation of yours?'
Aramis began again:

My dear Cousin,

> His Eminence the Cardinal, whom God preserve for the glory of France and the destruction of her enemies, is about to annihilate the heretic rebels of La Rochelle. It is unlikely that the relieving English

fleet will even come within sight of the town. I can almost certainly prophesy that some important event will stop the Duke of Buckingham leaving England.

His Eminence is the greatest statesman the world has ever seen or ever will see. He would snuff out the sun if it stood in his way.

Pass on this good news to your sister, dear cousin.

I dreamed that this accursed Englishman was dead. I can't remember whether he died of a wound or by poison. I'm only certain of one thing – that he was dead. And as you know, my dreams are always right.

So you can count on my returning very soon.

'Magnificent!' cried Athos. 'Aramis, you're the king of letter-writers. Everything in that letter's true and it has an oracular ring about it. The only problem now is how to address it.'

'That's easy,' said Aramis.

He folded up the letter carefully, and wrote on it:

> *To Mademoiselle Marie Michon*
> *Seamstress*
> *Tours*

The three friends looked at each other and laughed. Their curiosity had been defeated.

The friends now summoned Planchet and gave him his instructions. D'Artagnan had already warned him that his services might be needed; he had mentioned first the glory and lastly the dangers attached to the errand.

'I'll carry the letter in the lining of my coat,' said Planchet. 'And if I'm caught I'll swallow it.'

'But then you won't be able to deliver the message,' said d'Artagnan.

'Give me a copy tonight, Sir, and I'll learn it by heart before tomorrow.'

It was arranged that Planchet was to leave at eight o'clock the next morning. This would give him time to memorize the letter first. And he was to be back not later than eight p.m. on the fourteenth day.

The next morning, as Planchet was getting into the

saddle, d'Artagnan, who had a soft spot in his heart for
the Duke of Buckingham, took him aside.

'Listen,' he said. 'When you've delivered the letter to
Lord de Winter give him this message as well: "Warn the
Duke of Buckingham that there's a plot to assassinate
him!" This is a very important message, Planchet. I
haven't even dared tell my friends I'm doing this and I
wouldn't put that message on paper for anything in the
world.'

'Don't worry, Sir,' said Planchet. 'I won't let you
down.'

And he put spurs to his horse and galloped off.

On the morning of the day following Planchet's departure Bazin left for Tours and was given a week to carry out
his mission.

As was to be expected the four friends were on tenter-
hooks for the whole of the period of their servants'
absence. They spent their time listening to the gossip of
the camp, spying on the Cardinal and watching the
various messengers going in and out of his little house on
the dunes. The strain of waiting told on them, and
whenever they were summoned for some special duty
they would start and tremble. And they also had their
own personal safety to think of. Milady was like an evil
spirit which has only to appear to a man once to destroy
his peace of mind for ever after.

On the evening of the seventh day, just as the friends
were sitting down to supper at the Parpaillot inn, Bazin
entered, fresh and smiling as usual. He went up to
Aramis as arranged, held out a letter and said:

'Your cousin's reply, Sir.'

The four friends exchanged triumphant looks. Half
their task was already done, although it was the easiest
and the shortest half. Aramis took the letter, which was
addressed in a coarse and illiterate hand.

Aramis read the letter and passed it over to Athos.

'Look what she's written!' he said.

Athos shot a quick glance at the letter. Then, to allay any possible suspicions in the minds of the bystanders he started to read it aloud. It ran as follows:

Dear Cousin,
My sister and I interpret dreams very well, and are terrified of them. But let's hope we can say that your dream was just a nightmare.
Good-bye. Take care of yourself and write to us from time to time.
Marie Michon

But Bazin's return had relieved only half the four friends' burden. Days spent in anxious waiting seem interminable and to d'Artagnan that week seemed like a year. He forgot to take account of the uncertainty of sea-travel; in his anxiety he tended to overestimate Milady's power and to regard her as a fiend with supernatural attributes. He would start at the faintest sound, imagining that the Cardinal's men had come to arrest him; he pictured Planchet captured and brought back, and himself and his three friends seized and publicly confronted with him.

D'Artagnan's nervousness began to affect Porthos and Aramis. Only Athos remained calm and continued to behave normally.

When the fourteenth day arrived d'Artagnan and his two friends were so nervous that they could not stay still but kept wandering like lost souls up and down the road by which Planchet was expected to return. Athos gave them a good talking-to.

'You ought to be ashamed of yourselves,' he said. 'Three grown men letting a woman put the fear of God into them! What's there to be frightened of, anyway? Imprisonment? Possibly. But they'll get us out all right – they got Madame Bonacieux out, didn't they? Beheading? Why, we go up the line every day and risk worse than that. We might get a bullet through the thigh any

time and I bet the doctor would hurt us more lopping off
our legs than any headsman chopping off our heads. So
cheer up. In two, four, six hours at the most Planchet will
be here. He promised he'd be back and I've got great faith
in him. I think he's a first-rate fellow.'

'But suppose he doesn't turn up?' said d'Artagnan.

'If he doesn't turn up it'll mean he's been delayed,
that's all. He may have fallen off his horse; he may have
slipped on the deck of the boat and sprained his ankle; he
may have caught a chill. All sorts of things may have
happened. We must be calm. Come on, let's sit down and
drink. A glass of Chambertin will make us all feel better.'

'Yes,' said d'Artagnan, 'but it rather spoils a drink
never to be quite sure that it doesn't come out of Milady's
cellars.'

'You ungrateful devil, d'Artagnan!' said Athos. 'You
ought to be flattered. A lovely, exotic creature like her.'

'A woman of the best brand!' said Porthos, guffawing
at his own joke.

Athos suddenly began to tremble. Then he passed his
hand nervously across his forehead, got up and began
pacing up and down the room; even he seemed for a
moment to have lost his poise.

That day was to the four friends an eternity. But
evening came at last and the troops began to crowd into
the taverns. Athos had pocketed his share of the sale of
the diamond and spent the whole evening in the Parpaillot. De Busigny had entertained the four friends to dinner
and Athos had found in him a skilled dice player. The
two men were playing together when seven o'clock
struck, and the sound of the patrolling pickets echoed
through the camp. At seven-thirty the tattoo sounded
one full stop. D'Artagnan whispered to Athos:

'We're lost.'

Athos nudged him and, to put de Busigny off the
scent, said, pulling ten louis out of his pocket:

'You're right, I *have* lost!'

Then he added:

'Well, gentlemen, they've just sounded the tattoo. Let's turn in for the night.'

And he got up and left the Parpaillot, followed by d'Artagnan.

Aramis and Porthos went out shortly afterwards, arm in arm. Aramis was reciting verses under his breath and Porthos was tugging fiercely at his moustache.

Suddenly the four friends saw a figure running towards them through the shadows. And a voice which d'Artagnan recognized at once called out:

'I've brought you your coat, Sir. It's very cold this evening.'

'Planchet!' cried d'Artagnan, wild with excitement.

'Planchet!' echoed Porthos and Aramis.

'Yes, it's Planchet,' said Athos, 'and what's surprising about that? He promised to be back at eight o'clock and there's eight striking now. Bravo, Planchet, you're a man of your word. If ever you leave your master you can always be sure of a place with me.'

'Oh no, Sir!' said Planchet. 'I'll never leave Monsieur d'Artagnan.'

At that moment d'Artagnan felt Planchet slip a little note into his hand. He whispered excitedly to his three friends:

'I've got a reply in writing.'

'Good,' said Athos. 'Let's go home and read it.'

The four started off in the direction of the camp. D'Artagnan was so impatient to read the note that he broke into a run. But Athos took hold of his arm, held him back and forced him to set his pace by him.

At last they reached the tent. They lit a lamp; Planchet stood on guard outside while d'Artagnan tremblingly broke the seal and opened the long awaited letter. It contained only these four words in English:

Thank you. Be easy.

Athos took the letter from d'Artagnan and held it over the flame of the lamp until it was burned to a cinder. Then he called Planchet and said:

'Now, my lad, you can have 700 livres as reward. And consider yourself handsomely paid. You weren't risking much carrying a note like that.'

'Well, sir, I tried to make it as short as possible,' replied Planchet.

'Come on, Planchet, tell us the whole story,' said d'Artagnan.

'It'll take a long time, Sir,' replied Planchet.

'Leave it till later then,' said Athos. 'The tattoo's sounded and we'd be noticed if our tent was the only one with its light on.'

'Right,' said d'Artagnan. 'Let's turn in. Sleep well, Planchet.'

'It'll be the first good sleep I've had for a fortnight, Sir,' said Planchet.

'Same here,' said d'Artagnan.

'And here,' said Porthos.

'And here,' echoed Aramis.

'How about you, Athos?' inquired d'Artagnan.

'Well, if you must know, "Same here!"' said Athos.

Lord de Winter was as good as his word. Milady's crossing was delayed by her uncertainty whether or not to return immediately to the Cardinal and seek revenge on Athos. She eventually decided to bide her time and concentrate first on her mission in England. But by the time she reached Portsmouth, de Winter had prepared a reception for her. A young officer, John Felton, escorted her to de Winter's castle, where she was confined to a single room. Her brother-in-law confronted her with what he knew and guessed from Planchet's letter, and promised to have her deported to a penal settlement within a fortnight. He left her to be guarded by Felton,

first warning him that despite appearances she was a
fiend in human form: she would probably try to seduce
him; she may even try to kill him. She must not be
allowed to leave the room or write letters. Felton promised to carry out his orders. Milady, left alone in the
room, sank down in a vast armchair and started to
plan.

Meanwhile the Cardinal was growing alarmed. He was
daily expecting news from England but none came. La
Rochelle was now satisfactorily invested on land by the
besieging troops and at sea by an almost-finished dyke,
which would effectively prevent all ships from entering
the harbour. Ultimate success seemed certain and yet the
blockade might continue for many more months. This
was bad for the morale of the King's troops and irritating
for their commander.

In spite of the amazing example of fortitude shown by
the Mayor of La Rochelle the citizens had once mutinied
in favour of surrender. The Mayor had had all the ringleaders hanged. This measure had subdued all the worst
elements in the town, who thenceforth resigned themselves to the prospect of death by starvation, which they
considered a slower and less certain death than death by
strangulation, the fate reserved for heretics, which
would be theirs if La Rochelle were to be taken.

Mutinies inside and executions of spies outside the city
walls were the chief events of this period of stagnation.
Every day messengers sent by the people of La Rochelle
to Buckingham or by Buckingham to the citizens would
be captured by the besieging army and summarily dealt
with by the Cardinal, who always had them hanged. The
King usually attended these executions, for they helped
him to pass the time and bear the tedium of the siege. He
would come quite casually and choose a place from
which he could watch the operation in all its details. He
nevertheless constantly complained of boredom and

often talked of returning to Paris. If there was ever a
shortage of hangings His Eminence was hard put to it to
keep His Majesty amused.

The days passed and still the Rochellese held out. The
last spy captured had had a letter on him addressed to
Buckingham, telling him that the town was on its last
legs. But instead of adding, 'If you do not send help
within a fortnight we shall surrender', it said quite plain-
ly, 'If you do not send help within a fortnight we shall all
be dead from starvation by the time it arrives.' This letter
proved that the Rochellese were now relying entirely on
Buckingham. He was to be their saviour. If they ever
discovered for certain that Buckingham would fail them
they would immediately collapse.

So the Cardinal waited with the utmost impatience for
news from England, telling him that Buckingham would
not set sail. He knew Milady's extraordinary capacities,
her leonine courage and feline guile. She even frightened
him a little. Where was she now? Why had he heard no
news from her? Had she betrayed him? Was she dead?
He knew her well enough to realize that whether working as friend or foe she was not one to remain inactive.
What then was the explanation of her silence? He was
worried. And yet he felt he could trust her. He had
guessed that there were things in her past life from which
only his red robes could protect her, and that she would
be true to him because he was the only man powerful
enough to keep her foes at bay.

So he finally decided to carry on the campaign alone
and to regard anything else that would further his plan as
incidental good fortune. He gave orders for the com-
pletion of the dyke which was intended to starve La
Rochelle into submission. Meanwhile he pictured in his
mind's eye the distress of the inhabitants in the unfortunate city, which was holding out so valiantly. And he
remembered the maxim so often quoted by his political

predecessor, Louis XI, 'Divide and conquer', and saw how it could be applied to the present situation.

The Cardinal devised a scheme of throwing leaflets over the walls of La Rochelle which described the behaviour of the city's leaders as selfish, unjust, and barbarous. It was true that the leaders had a store of corn which they refused to issue to the population; they acted on the principle that it did not matter how many old men, women, and children died provided that the men who were defending the walls were kept healthy. So far no one had disputed this principle. But the leaflets attacked it. They reminded the citizens that these old men, women and children who were being allowed to die were their own fathers, wives and sons, and suggested that it would be more just if all the population were made to suffer equally, for then any edict passed would be in the interests of the community as a whole.

These leaflets had the effect which their author hoped for. They persuaded large numbers of the population to open negotiations with the King's armies. But just as the Cardinal was beginning to enjoy the fruits of his scheme and to congratulate himself on its success a citizen of La Rochelle managed to slip through the royal lines and enter the city. This man came from Portsmouth with news of a magnificent English fleet, manned, equipped and ready to set sail within a week. Buckingham had sent a special message by this man to the Mayor to say that the Grand Alliance against France was about to declare itself and that France herself would shortly be invaded simultaneously by the armies of England, Austria and Spain. This letter was read aloud in all the squares and copies of it were posted up at every street corner. Even those who had begun negotiations with the enemy now broke them off and decided to hold out until help came.

This untoward event restored all Richelieu's previous

misgivings and forced him once more to turn his attention to England.

It was the Cardinal's habit to ride through the camp and the surrounding districts unescorted and as simply dressed as any private in his army. He would inspect the constructions on the dyke which progressed very slowly in spite of the fact that he had summoned engineers from every corner of France to work on them. If on these excursions His Eminence ever met any musketeers of Monsieur de Tréville's company, he would ride up and scrutinize them closely. Having assured himself that they were none of our four friends he would ride off and turn his attention to solving some fresh strategical problem.

One afternoon, a prey to deadly boredom, frustrated in his efforts to negotiate with the town, still without news from England, the Cardinal left the camp without any object except to escape from it. He was accompanied only by two trusted members of his household, Cahusac and La Houdinière. He rode along the seashore, finding the vastness of the ocean in harmony with the vastness of his plans. Then he turned inland and rode along for about an hour, finally arriving at the top of a hill from where he could see a certain distance round him. Suddenly he caught sight of a party of seven men sprawling on the grass behind a hedge, about thirty yards away. Four of these men were our musketeers. One of them had a letter in his hand, which he was apparently reading aloud to the other three, who had their heads close to his. All four looked highly conspiratorial. Their three servants were seated a little way off, busy uncorking a demijohn of Collioure wine.

As we have said, the Cardinal was in a depressed mood. And when he was depressed nothing irritated him more than to see others enjoying themselves. He always imagined that the things which depressed him were the very things which made the rest of the world

laugh. The sight of the little party laughing and talking
behind the hedge annoyed him and, signing to Cahusac
and la Houdinière to halt, he dismounted and walked
towards them. He hoped that the sound of his footsteps
would be muffled by the grass, that the hedge would
hide him, and that he would be able to approach to
within earshot of these men and overhear their talk.
When he was about ten feet from the hedge he recognized d'Artagnan's Gascon brogue, and was convinced
that the other three were Athos, Porthos and Aramis.
This conviction made him all the more anxious to find out
what they were discussing. A crafty look came into his
eyes and he tiptoed lightly up to the hedge and stood
listening. But he had managed to catch only a few words
which gave him no clue when someone behind the hedge
suddenly shouted out:

'Officer!'

The Cardinal was startled and the musketeers at once
looked up. The shout had come from Grimaud.

Athos raised himself up on one elbow, glared at him
and said:

'Did I hear you speak, rascal?'

Grimaud said not another word but merely pointed in
the direction of the hedge to announce the presence of
the Cardinal and his escort.

The four musketeers at once got up and saluted him.
His Eminence was furious.

'Is it usual for Musketeers to post sentries to guard
them?' he said. 'Are you expecting a land attack by the
English, playing at being officers, or what?'

In the general panic Athos alone of the four kept his
head. He replied:

'Your Eminence, when Musketeers are off duty they
drink and gamble and rank as officers in the eyes of their
servants.'

The Cardinal retorted angrily:

'Did you say servants? They look more like sentries to me.'

Athos replied calmly:

'You'll agree, Sir, that if we hadn't posted the men there you'd have passed without our knowing and we'd have missed an opportunity of thanking you for your kindness in appointing us all to the same regiment. D'Artagnan here was just wondering when he'd be able to thank Your Eminence. Now's your chance, d'Artagnan.'

D'Artagnan went up to the Cardinal and tried to stammer a few words of thanks. But he faltered under the Cardinal's stern gaze. The latter was in no way appeased by Athos' attempt to smooth matters over and was still determined to discover what the four men were doing.

'That's all very well, gentlemen,' he said. 'But I don't like to see private soldiers behaving like officers just because they happen to belong to a crack regiment. Army regulations apply to you as much as to anyone else.'

Athos replied:

'Yes, Sir. But I don't think we've infringed army regulations. We were off duty and thought we could do as we liked. If you've some special duty for us, Sir, we're at your service. We've come armed, as you see, so we're ready to report at a moment's notice.'

And he pointed to their four muskets which were piled in a corner of the field. D'Artagnan now broke in:

'We'd have stood to attention at once, Sir, if we'd have known it was you coming up with such a small escort.'

At this the Cardinal frowned angrily. He replied:

'D'you realize the impression you four fellows give, always together, always armed and always guarded by your servants? You look as though you were plotting.'

Athos replied:

'And so we are, Sir. And so we were the other morning

in the St Gervais bastion, as Your Eminence probably noticed. We're plotting against the Rochellese.'

The Cardinal replied, still frowning:

'Politicians, eh? Yes, I don't doubt there's a lot going on in those heads of yours. I wish I could read them as easily as you were reading that letter you stuffed away so hurriedly when you saw me.'

Athos flushed angrily and strode up to the Cardinal.

'You seem to suspect us of something, Monseigneur,' he said. 'Is this a cross-examination, Sir? If you do suspect us, please say so. Then we shall know where we stand.'

The Cardinal replied:

'And what if I am cross-questioning you? I've cross-questioned others before you and they've had to answer.'

'Yes, Sir, that's why I'm asking you to put straight questions to us, so that we can give you straight answers.'

'Very well. What was that letter you were just going to read, Monsieur Aramis?' said the Cardinal. 'And why did you hide it away when you saw me?'

'It was a letter from a woman, Monseigneur.'

The Cardinal was convinced that the four men had in fact been plotting. But he also realized that the odds were four to three against him. So to save his face he did a quick mental somersault, suppressed his anger and said with a smile:

'All right, all right! You're first-rate young fellows, all of you. I forgive you. After all you're quite entitled to guard yourselves seeing how well you guard other people. I haven't forgotten the night you escorted me to the Red Dovecote inn and back. And if I were in danger now I'd ask you to escort me again. But I'm in no danger, so stay where you are and finish your drink and your letter. Good-bye, gentlemen.'

So saying he called to Cahusac to bring up his horse, leapt into the saddle and rode off. The four young men stood silent and motionless, watching his retreating figure until it disappeared from sight. Then they turned and looked at each other. Porthos, Aramis, and d'Artagnan were badly shaken. They knew quite well that the Cardinal's friendly farewell had been a pretence and that he was still very angry with them. Only Athos smiled cynically.

At last Porthos exclaimed:

'That Grimaud of yours was damned late warning us!'

He was thoroughly unnerved and determined to vent his spleen on somebody.

Grimaud was about to apologize but Athos signed to him to keep quiet.

'Would you have handed over the letter, Aramis?' asked d'Artagnan.

'If he'd insisted on seeing the letter I'd have held it out with one hand and run him through with the other.'

'I was expecting you to do that,' said Athos. 'That's why I got between you and him. His Eminence had no right to talk to us like that. You'd think he'd only had to deal with women and children all his life.'

D'Artagnan said:

'I admire you, Athos. But you must admit we were in the wrong.'

'What d'you mean, in the wrong?' replied Athos. 'Damn it all, who does this air belong to and the ocean over there? And the grass we're lying on? And that letter from your mistress? To the Cardinal? Of course not! That fellow thinks the whole world belongs to him. You were all standing there gaping like idiots; you looked as though the Bastille were looming in front of you and the earth about to open and swallow you up. Can being in love be called plotting? You're in love with a woman whom the Cardinal's imprisoned. You want to get her out of his hands. That's a personal matter between you and him. That letter's one of your trump cards. Why show your hand to your opponent? Let him guess it if he can. Aren't we trying to guess his?'

'Yes, Athos,' said d'Artagnan. 'That's true enough.'

'Well then, let's forget the whole incident, and let Aramis go on with the letter from where he left off when His Eminence interrupted him.'

Aramis pulled the letter out of his pocket. The three friends gathered round and the lackeys continued uncorking the demijohn.

'You'd only read a line or two,' said d'Artagnan. 'So start again from the beginning.'

'Very well,' said Aramis. And he read:

My dear Cousin,

I think I shall soon be leaving for Béthune where my sister has sent our little servant girl to the Carmelite Convent. The poor child is resigned to this move. She knows she can't live anywhere else with safety to her soul. But if our family affairs are soon settled in the way we hope I think she'll risk damnation and return to those friends she longs more than ever to see, now that she knows they still think of her.

Meanwhile she is not too unhappy. But she would like a letter from her lover. I know it's difficult to smuggle goods of that kind through barred windows. But I think I've already proved to you, dear cousin, that I am quite clever at that sort of thing, and I'll see that it's delivered safely.

My sister thanks you for your kind messages. She was very anxious for a time but is slightly more cheerful now. She has sent her agent to the place in question to see that nothing terrible happens.

Good-bye, dear cousin. Write as often as you can, that is to say whenever you think you can do so safely.

All my love,
Marie Michon

'I'm very, very grateful to you, Aramis,' cried d'Artagnan. 'Dear Constance. At last I've had news of her. She's alive. She's safe in a convent at Béthune. Where exactly is Béthune, Athos?'

'On the borders of Artois and Flanders. When the siege is over we might visit it.'

'It oughtn't to be long now,' said Porthos. 'They hanged another spy this morning; the fellow had a message on him that the Rochellese were now eating shoe leather. I suppose when they've finished the leather they'll get to work on the soles, and after that I don't quite know what they'll live on, unless they start eating each other.'

'You weren't thinking of putting that letter back in your pocket, were you, Aramis?' asked Athos.

'For God's sake don't,' said d'Artagnan. 'That letter must be burned. I doubt if we'll be safe even then. The Cardinal's probably invented a way of making cinders talk.'

Meanwhile the Cardinal continued his melancholy ride. From time to time he muttered to himself:

'I must have those four men on my side.'

30
BÉTHUNE

It took Milady only one day to find a chink in Lord de Winter's armour, and another four days to widen this chink until she could not only escape, but also execute the plan she and the Cardinal had hatched in the Red Dovecote inn.

John Felton was a Puritan. Milady made a convincing show of being a Puritan herself. When Felton was persuaded of this, it took Milady little time to convince him also that she had been imprisoned by her brother-in-law at Buckingham's orders, because Buckingham had ravished her and she had threatened to expose him. Thus, by playing the wounded innocent, she not only made Felton fall in love with her, but also fanned his religious fanaticism.

In mid-August Felton helped her to escape to France. She left him in England to assassinate Buckingham. Meanwhile there had been no new developments in the La Rochelle campaign. The King was still tremendously bored, perhaps even more so than usual. He decided to go and spend the St Louis festival at St Germain, and asked the Cardinal to grant him an escort of twenty musketeers. The Cardinal, who was sometimes as bored as the King himself, gladly agreed to His Majesty's departure, and it was arranged that he should return on about 15 September.

Monsieur de Tréville heard of the King's decision from the Cardinal, and at once prepared for the journey. He knew how keen the four friends were to return to Paris, though he did not know why, and therefore detailed them to form part of the King's escort.

The four friends' keenness to return to the capital was due chiefly to their concern for the safety of Madame Bonacieux. Athos, Porthos, and Aramis had overheard the Cardinal tell Milady to return at once to France after her mission and to go to the Carmelite Convent at Béthune. By a most unfortunate coincidence this was where Madame Bonacieux had been sent on the Queen's order, after her release from the Nantes prison. The friends calculated that if Lord de Winter had not succeeded in putting his sister-in-law out of harm's way while she was in England, she would have returned to France by now and would shortly be arriving at the convent in Béthune. They dreaded to think of Madame Bonacieux's fate when Milady, her mortal enemy, discovered her there. In their concern for her safety they

had agreed that Aramis should write again to Marie
Michon, the seamstress in Tours with the grand connections, to persuade the Queen to allow the young
woman to leave the convent and go into hiding either in
Lorraine or Belgium. Aramis had not had to wait long for
a reply. About a week after writing he received the
following answer:

My dear Cousin,

*Here is my sister's authority to remove our little servant girl from the
convent at Béthune, which you think is an unhealthy district for her.*

*My sister sends you this authority with her best wishes for your
success; she is very fond of the girl and hopes to be able to help her later.*

My love,

Marie Michon

To this letter was attached a written authority from the
Queen herself which ran as follows:

*The Superior of the Béthune Convent will please deliver the novice
who was received into the convent on my recommendation into the
charge of the bearer of this note.*

The Louvre, 10 August 1628   *Anne*

We can understand how amused Aramis' three friends
were at his pretence of kinship with this seamstress who
referred to the Queen as her sister. Aramis blushed
scarlet once or twice at Porthos' coarse innuendoes; then
he got angry and declared that if the subject were ever
referred to again he would refuse to employ his 'cousin'
as intermediary in the plot. So the name Marie Michon
was never again mentioned by any of the four friends;
they were thankful to have got what they wanted from
her, an authority to remove Madame Bonacieux from the
Béthune convent.

The royal party left on 16 August and eventually
reached Paris on the night of the 23rd.

The first four to be granted leave were, of course, our
four friends. Monsieur de Tréville did Athos the ad-

ditional favour of giving him two days' extra leave, and generously added two extra nights as well, by post-dating the period of leave to the 25th, although the four men actually set off on the evening of the 24th.

On the evening of the 25th they reached Arras. D'Artagnan had just dismounted at the Golden Harrow inn to drink a quick glass of wine when a man rode out of the courtyard where he had been hiring a remount, and started off at the gallop on a fresh horse in the direction of Paris. Although it was August he was wearing a heavy cloak and a wide-brimmed hat. Just as he was riding out of the main gate into the street the wind blew his cloak half open and lifted the brim of his hat. The stranger immediately caught hold of his hat and pressed it down low on his forehead, but not before d'Artagnan, who had been observing him closely, had caught a glimpse of his face. The young man went very white and dropped his glass of wine.

'What's the matter, Sir?' cried Planchet. 'Gentlemen, gentlemen, come quick; my master's fainting!'

The three others came running up. They found d'Artagnan not fainting at all but running towards his horse. They stopped him at the gate.

'Where the deuce d'you think you're going?' said Athos.

'It's the fellow himself,' cried d'Artagnan, pale and trembling with rage. 'Let me get at him!'

'What fellow?' asked Athos.

'That blackguard, my evil genius. I always meet him when there's trouble brewing. You know, the fellow who was with Milady when I met her for the first time, the fellow I was after when I had the row with Athos, the fellow I saw talking to Bonacieux in the street, the day we left for England. The fellow from Meung, in fact. I recognized him when the wind blew his hat up. It was him all right!'

Athos frowned.

'The devil it was!' he said.

'Come on, all of you!' cried d'Artagnan. 'Let's ride after him. We'll catch him!'

'Listen, d'Artagnan,' said Aramis. 'He's going the opposite way to us. He's got a fresh horse and ours are worn out. If we followed him we'd ride our horses to death and never get near him.'

At that moment a stable-boy ran out into the road, calling after the stranger.

'Hi, Sir! You've left something behind. This note dropped out of your hat. Hi, Sir! Hi! Hi!'

D'Artagnan went up to the boy.

'I'll give you half a pistole for that note, my lad,' he said.

'Most happy, Sir, I'm sure,' replied the boy. 'Here it is.'

And he ran back into the courtyard, delighted at this unexpected piece of good luck.

D'Artagnan unfolded the note while his friends waited for him to read it to them.

'Well?' they asked.

'There's only one word written on it,' said d'Artagnan.

'Yes,' said Aramis. 'But it's the name of a town.'

Porthos read out:

'Armentières.'

'Armentières?' he went on. 'Where's that? I've never heard of it.'

'And it's her handwriting!' cried Athos.

'We must guard this note with our lives,' said d'Artagnan. 'Perhaps we'll find that half-pistole of mine wasn't misspent after all. And now let's be off again.'

The four young men leaped into the saddle and galloped off in the direction of Béthune.

All great criminals are known to enjoy long periods of

prosperity, during which they seem to flourish in their
wickedness and even to be guided by some star, which
helps them to surmount all obstacles and to defy the
deadliest dangers. Then suddenly an angry Providence
intervenes and strikes them down. Thus it was with
Milady. The sloop which carried her from England ran
the gauntlet of the battleships of two nations and arrived
safely in Boulogne. When she had disembarked at Portsmouth she had posed as an Englishwoman who had been
driven out of La Rochelle by French persecution. Now,
disembarking at Boulogne, she posed as a Frenchwoman
whom the English, in their hatred of France, had been
persecuting at Portsmouth. Besides this alias Milady had
two assets as effective as any passports – personal attrac-
tion, and some hundreds of pistoles to scatter among
greedy officials.

She was granted an interview with the Governor of the
port, who immediately fell a victim to her charm and
exempted her from the usual Customs formalities.
Milady in fact stayed in Boulogne only long enough to
post one letter. It was addressed to:

His Eminence
 The Cardinal Richelieu
  At the Camp of La Rochelle

and ran as follows:

Monseigneur,
 Rest assured that the Duke of Buckingham will not leave for France.
                                    Lady de . . .
 P.S.   In accordance with Your Eminence's orders I am starting at
once for the Carmelite Convent at Béthune, where I will await your
further pleasure.

Having dispatched her letter her Ladyship set forth
that same evening. She spent that night at an inn. At five
the following morning she set out again, and three hours
later arrived at Béthune. Here she asked to be directed to

the Carmelite Convent and drove straight to the main gate.

The Mother Superior came out to meet her. Milady showed her the Cardinal's written authority, and the Reverend Mother ordered a room and breakfast to be prepared for her.

By now Milady had driven all her past experiences from her mind as a nightmare. Her thoughts were entirely fixed on the future and she looked forward to the glorious prospects in store for her as a reward for her bold stroke. She had served the Cardinal well and had not allowed her complicity in the damnable plot to be even suspected. Her life with its eversurging passions and ambitions was like a sky swept by stormclouds, inky black or fiery red, which pass and leave only destruction in their wake.

After breakfast the Abbess came to pay her respects to her new guest. Convent life offers few distractions, and the Reverend Mother was anxious to make Milady's acquaintance. Milady, for her part, wanted to make a good impression on the Abbess, no difficult task for a woman of her talents.

She now set to work to entertain the good Abbess with tales of the worldliness of the French Court, which formed such a startling contrast to the King's outward display of godliness.

By degrees Milady turned the conversation to the subject of the Cardinal. But now she had to tread warily, for she did not know whether the Abbess was a Royalist or a Cardinalist. At first she steered a prudent middle course, while the Abbess was even more cautious, confining herself to bowing low every time her visitor mentioned His Eminence's name.

Then she began to talk about the Cardinal's reign of terror. To this the Abbess said nothing but merely lowered her eyes and crossed herself, which seemed to confirm Milady's view that she was more Royalist than Cardinalist. She continued to embroider her theme until at last the Abbess was provoked to speak.

'I know very little about these things,' she said. 'But out of touch as we are with Court affairs and cut off from this world's problems we do come to hear of some very sad instances of what you describe. We've actually got a novice at the convent now who's being persecuted by the Cardinal.'

'The Cardinal doesn't only punish people for crimes,' said Milady. 'Certain virtues are more obnoxious to him than the worst vices.'

'Forgive me if I say I'm surprised to hear you talk like that,' remarked the Abbess.

'Why?' asked Milady innocently.

'It's not usual to hear the Cardinal spoken of like that. You must be a friend of His Eminence since he sent you here. And yet . . .'

The Abbess paused.

'And yet I criticize him, you mean?' prompted Milady.

'Well, you haven't said anything to his credit, have you?'

Milady sighed.

'The fact is, Reverend Mother, I'm not his friend at all,' she said. 'I'm another of his victims.'

'Then how d'you explain his letter recommending you to me?'

'It's merely an order sentencing me to a form of imprisonment. He'll be sending his secret agents for me soon.'

'Why didn't you escape?'

'Where could I have gone? The whole world's within the Cardinal's grasp if he takes the trouble to stretch out his hand. If I were a man I might have managed it. But what can a woman do? Did that novice of yours try to escape?'

'No, you're right; she didn't. But with her it's different. I fancy some love-affair's keeping her in France.'

Milady sighed again.

'If she's in love then she's not altogether unhappy,' she said.

The Abbess observed Milady with increasing interest.

'So now I've got another victim of oppression on my hands,' she said. 'In that case we'll do all we can to make you happy. Besides, you've got a fellow sufferer here, the young novice I was telling you about. She's clearly the victim of some Court intrigue. She's a good, kind soul. I'm sure you'll enjoy her company.'

'What's her name?'

'She was recommended to me by someone very influential as "Kitty". I've never troubled to ask her her other name.'

'Kitty!' exclaimed Milady. 'Are you sure?'

'I'm sure that's the name she goes by. Yes, Lady de Winter. Why? D'you know her?'

Milady had started involuntarily at the name of 'Kitty'. She now controlled herself and replied:

'No. I don't know her. I have a close friend of the name of Kitty, but she's a very different person. The coincidence of the two names being the same struck me. That was all.'

Milady smiled inwardly at the thought that the young novice might be her former maid. On having the girl thus recalled to her mind she felt a sudden wave of anger against her. Her desire to take revenge on her was so strong that for a moment she forgot herself and allowed a spiteful look to cross her face. But in a flash she regained her composure and gave the Abbess a sweet smile.

'And when shall I have the pleasure of meeting this young woman?' she asked. 'From your description I already feel attracted to her.'

'You can meet her this evening, this afternoon, if you

like,' replied the Abbess. 'But you told me you'd been
travelling for four days and that you were on the road at
five this morning. You need a rest. Go to bed and try and
sleep. We'll wake you at lunchtime.'

Milady decided to follow the Abbess' advice, although
she could well have done without sleep, elated as she
was by the prospect of this new adventure; to her intrigue
was the spice of life. But in the last fortnight she had lived
through so many crises that, strong as was her consti-
tution, her mind needed rest. So she asked the Abbess to
leave her and lay down on her bed, lulled by secret
thoughts of revenge which the recollection of Kitty had
roused in her. She remembered how the Cardinal had
promised her almost complete freedom to carry out her
schemes if she succeeded in her mission. She had succeeded; she would therefore be able to revenge herself on
d'Artagnan.

One thing alone appalled her, the recollection of her
husband, the Comte de la Fère, whom she had believed
dead and who had returned to her in the shape of Athos,
d'Artagnan's best friend. But then it occurred to her that
if he were d'Artagnan's friend he had probably been
involved in the various plots which had enabled the
Queen to outwit the Cardinal; as d'Artagnan's friend he
was the Cardinal's foe, and could therefore be included
in any plans of revenge against d'Artagnan. All these
fantasies were as balm to Milady's spirit; lulled by these
thoughts she soon fell into a peaceful sleep.

She was wakened by a gentle voice calling her from the
foot of the bed. She opened her eyes and saw the Abbess
and a young woman with fair hair and a fresh complexion, who was gazing at her with a look of kindly inquiry
on her face. The new arrival was a complete stranger to
her. The two women eyed each other closely as they
exchanged the usual formal compliments. Both were
beautiful but in different ways. Milady rejoiced to see

that she was vastly more distinguished-looking than the young novice and had more poise, though she admitted that the nun's habit which her rival wore would not show a woman at her best.

The Abbess introduced them. Then, her religious duties calling her, she begged to be excused and went out, leaving the two women together.

The novice was about to follow the Abbess out of the room for, as Milady was in bed, she concluded she did not wish to be disturbed. But Milady called her back.

'Don't go, my dear!' she exclaimed. 'I've only just got to know you. I was hoping you'd stay with me a little while. I'm relying on you to keep me company for at least some part of my stay in this place.'

'I shall be delighted, Lady de Winter,' replied the novice. 'I only thought that this was a bad time, as you were asleep when we came in and you must be tired.'

'After a sleep it's nice to have a pleasant surprise on waking. You're the pleasant surprise in this case. Let me enjoy you in comfort.'

And she took the novice by the hand and motioned her to an armchair which was beside her bed. The novice sat down.

'Oh dear, how unfortunate this is!' she exclaimed. 'I've been here six months and my life's been almost unbearably dull. Now you arrive. I was thrilled at the idea of having you to talk to. And now I hear I'm to leave the convent at any moment.'

'Leave the convent?' cried Milady.

'Yes, at least I hope so,' replied the novice, her eyes shining with a joy which she was at no pains to conceal.

'I gather you've got into the Cardinal's bad books,' said Milady. 'That would have been an added bond between us.'

'So what the Reverend Mother told me was true!' cried the novice. 'You're another of that wicked priest's victims!'

'Hush!' said Milady. 'Don't talk of him like that even in here. You never know who's listening. All my troubles arose from my once saying more or less what you said just now in front of a woman whom I thought was my friend and who informed on me. Was that how you got into trouble?'

'No,' replied the novice. 'I got into trouble through being loyal to a woman I loved, a woman I'd have given my life for, whom I'd give my life for even now.'

'Didn't she stand by you?'

'For some time I was wicked enough to believe she'd turned against me. Then a few days ago I discovered my mistake, for which I thank God. I'd have been miserable if she really had deserted me. But you, Lady de Winter, surely you're a free agent; you could easily get out of here if you wanted to.'

'Where could I go? I've got no friends and no money, and I don't know this part of France at all.'

'I'm sure you'd never lack for friends!' cried the novice. 'You're so beautiful and I'm sure you're good too.'

Milady smiled a sad, sweet smile.

'Even so I'm alone and the victim of oppression,' she said.

The novice replied:

'Lady de Winter, we must trust in God's mercy. Sooner or later God rewards us for the good we've done in this world. Perhaps God has brought you and me together so that I can help you. If I get out of here I've got powerful friends who'll work for me. When they've finished fighting my battles I'll get them to use their influence for you.'

Milady pricked up her ears at this. She hoped that by continuing the conversation along these lines the novice would be provoked into committing some indiscretion. To stimulate her further she now remarked:

'When I said I was alone I didn't mean that I hadn't also got powerful friends. But strong as they are, they're frightened of the Cardinal. Why, even the Queen daren't do anything which might interfere with his plans, and I know for a fact that, good as she is, she's often had to sacrifice people who've done her yeoman service because the Cardinal demanded their heads.'

'No, Lady de Winter,' replied the novice. 'The Queen may appear to sacrifice these people but she doesn't really. The more victimized they are the more she thinks about them, and often when they've given up hope they suddenly find she'd been working for them in secret all the time.'

'Yes, I can well believe that,' said Milady. 'The Queen is so good.'

The novice replied enthusiastically:

'So you know her then? You know our great and good Queen? You must know her to talk of her like that!'

Milady replied evasively:

'I haven't the honour of knowing her personally. But I know a great many of her intimate friends. I know Monsieur Putange, I knew Monsieur Dujart in England, and I know Monsieur de Tréville.'

'You know Monsieur de Tréville?' cried the novice.

'Yes. Quite well, in fact.'

'Oh, how exciting!' cried the novice. 'I'm sure we'll soon discover we've got lots of friends in common. In fact at this rate we'll soon be good friends ourselves. If you know Monsieur de Tréville you must have been to his house.'

'Often,' replied Milady.

She had embarked on her policy of lying, saw that it was succeeding and decided to pursue it. She was by now thoroughly enjoying the conversation.

'When you were in Monsieur de Tréville's house you must have met some of his musketeers,' continued the novice.

'All who visit him regularly.'

'You don't happen to know a gentleman of the name of Athos?'

Milady went as white as the sheets on which she was lying, and so far lost her composure as to start up in bed, seize the novice by the hand and stare at her, wide-eyed with fear. The unfortunate girl exclaimed:

'What on earth's the matter, Lady de Winter? Have I said something to offend you?'

'No, no,' replied Milady hastily. 'You see I did happen to know Monsieur Athos at one time and it seemed so strange to meet someone who also knew him.'

'I know him very well,' said the novice, 'and I know his friends too, Monsieur Porthos and Monsieur Aramis.'

Milady became more and more alarmed.

'Do you?' she replied. 'So do I.'

'As good and true a set of men as you could find,' continued the novice. 'If you know them why don't you appeal to them to get you out of trouble?'

Milady was struggling hard to control her emotion. To gain time she remarked quickly:

'When I said I knew them I didn't mean I knew any of them personally. I know of them through a friend of theirs, Monsieur d'Artagnan.'

It was now the novice's turn to start, go pale and stare at Milady in alarm.

'You know Monsieur d'Artagnan?' she cried. Then, noticing a strange look on Milady's face, she added coldly:

'Excuse me, Lady de Winter, but may I ask what exactly Monsieur d'Artagnan is to you?'

'Why, a . . . a friend, of course,' stammered Milady in great embarrassment.

'You're lying to me, Lady de Winter,' said the girl. 'You've been his mistress.'

'No,' retorted Milady, 'on the contrary, it's you who've been his mistress.'

'I!' exclaimed the novice.

'Yes, you. I know who you are now. You're Madame Bonacieux.'

The young woman shrank back and stared at the older woman in terror and surprise.

'Don't trouble to deny it,' said Milady.

'Very well, Lady de Winter,' answered the novice. 'I admit it. I love him. Are we rivals?'

A light of maniac rage suddenly shone in Milady's eyes, which at any other time would have frightened the younger woman out of her wits. But now she was entirely concerned with her jealousy. With a firmness surprising in one so gentle she repeated:

'Lady de Winter, I insist on knowing whether you've been Monsieur d'Artagnan's mistress!'

'No, never!' cried Milady in a tone of such scorn that it was obvious she was speaking the truth.

'Very well, I believe you,' said Madame Bonacieux. 'But why did you cry out like that?'

Milady had by now recovered her poise and presence of mind. Quick as a flash she said, in answer to Madame Bonacieux's question:

'What? You mean to say you don't understand?'

'How could I?' replied the girl. 'What do I know about your relations with Monsieur d'Artagnan?'

'Well, I'll explain the whole thing. It's perfectly simple. Monsieur d'Artagnan, being my friend, took me into his confidence.'

'Oh?'

'Yes. He told me everything. How you'd been kidnapped in the summer-house at St Cloud, how miserable he and his friends had been and how they'd searched everywhere but lost all trace of you. So you can imagine my surprise when I suddenly realized who you were, after the many hours we've spent discussing you. You, the woman he loves more than anything in the world and whom he'd persuaded me to love before I ever knew you! So I've found you, dear Constance! I've met you at last!'

And Milady stretched out her arms to embrace Madame Bonacieux. The poor girl was completely convinced by Milady's explanation, and having a moment ago eyed her askance as a rival now saw in her a sincere and devoted friend. She laid her head on her shoulder and cried:

'Oh, forgive me, forgive me! You see I love him so.'

For a moment the two women clung to each other. Had Milady's sinews been as strong as her feelings Madame Bonacieux would not have come out of that embrace alive. But since she could not strangle her she smiled at her.

'You dear, sweet, pretty child!' she said. 'How wonderful it is to have found you! Let me look at you!'

And she held her at arm's length and did, in fact, gaze long and searchingly at her.

'Yes, it's you all right,' she went on. 'I recognize you exactly from his description.'

The poor girl had no suspicion of the frightful thoughts that were passing through Milady's mind, of the cruel impulses that lay behind that pure brow and those limpid blue eyes, in which she read only affection and pity.

'And in any case my sufferings are nearly over now,' continued Madame Bonacieux. 'Tomorrow, possibly tonight, I shall see him again and then the past will be forgotten.'

Madame Bonacieux's last words startled Milady out of her reverie.

'What's that you say?' she exclaimed. 'Tomorrow?

Possibly tonight? Whatever do you mean? Are you expecting news of him?'

'I'm expecting him himself.'

'Monsieur d'Artagnan? Here?'

'Yes.'

'But that's impossible! He's with the Cardinal at La
Rochelle. He can't return to Paris till the siege is over.'

'It sounds incredible, I know. But I say that a man like
my d'Artagnan can do anything!'

'I wish I could believe you but I can't.'

In her excitement at the thought of seeing her lover
again the young woman was now so ill-advised as to take
a letter out of her bodice and hand it to Milady, saying:

'Just read this!'

Milady glanced at the letter.

'Madame de Chevreuse's writing,' she muttered to
herself. 'Very interesting. I always suspected they were
getting information from that quarter.'

She read rapidly through the letter, which ran as
follows:

My dearest child,

*Get ready. You'll be seeing 'our friend' soon. He's coming to remove
you from the prison where we had to hide you for your own safety. Get
ready to leave at once, and never lose faith in us again.*

*Our young Gascon has just given us further proof of his devotion and
courage. Tell him they're very grateful to him in certain quarters for his
warning.*

'Yes, yes,' said Milady. 'The letter's clear enough. But
what do they mean by "his warning"?'

'I don't know for certain, but I suspect he warned the
Queen of some fresh villainy on the part of the Cardinal.'

'Yes, that's probably what it is,' said Milady.

She returned the letter to Madame Bonacieux and laid
her head back against the pillows.

At that moment they heard the sound of a horse

galloping down the road. Madame Bonacieux rushed to
the window crying:

'It couldn't be him already!'

Milady lay motionless in her bed, paralysed with fear.
Such a rapid succession of surprises had robbed her of
her usual presence of mind.

'Could it be him!' she echoed faintly.

And she lay rigid, her eyes wide and staring.

'No, alas, it's not him!' called Madame Bonacieux from
the window. 'It's a man I don't know. He looks as though
he's making for the convent. Yes, he's reining in his
horse; he's stopped at the door; he's ringing the bell.'

Milady sprang out of bed.

'You're certain it's not d'Artagnan?' she said.

'Quite.'

'Perhaps you didn't get a proper look at him?'

'Oh, I'd know him at once. I'd know him from the
feather in his hat or the edge of his cloak.'

Milady began dressing hurriedly.

'Never mind,' she exclaimed. 'The man, whoever he
was, stopped here, you say?'

'Yes. And he's come into the house now.'

'He's obviously come either for you or for me.'

'You look terribly upset, Lady de Winter. Do keep
calm.'

'I wish I had your courage, my dear. But I know the
Cardinal. I know he'll stop at nothing.'

'Hush,' said Madame Bonacieux. 'Somebody's coming
up the stairs.'

The next moment the door opened and the Reverend
Mother appeared.

'A gentleman's called asking for a lady who's come
from Boulogne,' she said, addressing her new visitor.
'Have you come from Boulogne?'

'Yes, yes, I have,' replied Milady. 'It must be me he
wants.'

Then, struggling to keep calm, she asked:

'Who is the man?'

'He won't give his name, but he says he's under orders from the Cardinal.'

'You're sure he wants to see me?' asked Milady.

'He wants to see the lady who's come from Boulogne.'

'Well then, show him in, Reverend Mother.'

'Oh dear, oh dear!' wailed Madame Bonacieux. 'I do pray it's nothing bad for you.'

'It doesn't look too hopeful,' said Milady.

'Well, I'd better leave you now to see this gentleman, whoever he is,' said the girl. 'But if I may I'll come back when he's gone.'

'Of course you may, my dear. In fact I hope you will.'

The Mother Superior and Madame Bonacieux left the room.

Milady remained alone. She stood motionless, staring at the door. A few seconds later she heard the sound of spurs jingling on the stone stairs and of footsteps approaching. Then the door opened and revealed a man standing on the threshold. When Milady saw him she gave a cry of joy. It was the Comte de Rochefort, the Cardinal's private spy.

31

THE FEMALE AND THE MALE

Milady and Rochefort cried out simultaneously:

'So it's you!'

Milady went on:

'Where have you come from?'

'La Rochelle. And you?'

'From England.'

'And Buckingham?'

'Dead or seriously wounded. I'd got nothing out of him and was just leaving England when some fanatic murdered him.'

'What an incredible piece of luck!' said Rochefort, smiling ironically. 'His Eminence *will* be pleased! Have you told him?'

'I wrote to him from Boulogne. But what's brought you here?'

'His Eminence was concerned about you and sent me to find out if you'd got here all right.'

'I arrived yesterday.'

'What have you done since?'

'Quite a lot. I haven't wasted my time.'

'I'm sure of that.'

'Guess who I've met here?'

'I can't imagine.'

'The young woman the Queen rescued from prison.'

'What? You mean young d'Artagnan's mistress?'

'Yes. Madame Bonacieux. You remember the Cardinal had lost track of her.'

'That's another stroke of luck which pairs well with the first. Fate seems to be on the Cardinal's side.'

'You can imagine my surprise meeting her like that,' said Milady.'

'Does she know who you are?'

'She knows my name but nothing about me.'

'She doesn't connect you with any of her troubles?'

Milady smiled.

'On the contrary. I'm her best friend,' she said.

Rochefort replied with a laugh:

'My dear Lady de Winter, no one but you could have worked a miracle like that.'

'It was lucky I did make friends with her,' replied Milady. 'What d'you think's happening tomorrow?'

'I've no idea,' said Rochefort.

'They're coming to take her away from here. They've got the Queen's written authority.'

'Oh! And who's "they"?'

'D'Artagnan and presumably his friends.'

'Those devils again! I can see we shall have to put them in the Bastille after all.'

'Why didn't you do that long ago?'

'You may well ask. I can't think why, but the Cardinal's got a soft spot for them.'

'Has he indeed? Well, I can tell him something which will harden his heart. D'you know, Rochefort, that those four men eavesdropped on his conversation with me at the Red Dovecote inn, and that after he left me one of them came up to my room and took my safe-conduct pass from me by force! Tell His Eminence that. Tell him, too, that those men got news through to Lord de Winter that I was coming to England and again all but succeeded in checkmating me, as they did in the affair of the diamond tags. Tell the Cardinal all that. And tell him that of the four only two are really dangerous, d'Artagnan and Athos. Tell him Aramis is Madame de Chevreuse's lover, and that it would be good policy to leave him alone. We know his secret and he might be useful. Tell him the fourth man, Porthos, is a pompous ass, not worth troubling about.'

'But surely those four fellows are away on the campaign!'

'I thought so too. But I saw a letter from Madame de Chevreuse to Madame Bonacieux – the little goose actually showed it to me herself – from which I gathered that none of them are at the siege at all, but all on their way to this convent to remove her.'

'The Devil they are! What had we better do?'

'What did the Cardinal want me to do?'

'He wanted you to give me a full written or verbal report which I was to take back to him at once. When he knew what you'd done he'd decide what you were to do next.'

'Does he want me to stay here?'

'Yes, here or somewhere fairly near.'

'Can't you take me with you?'

'No. His Eminence said definitely not. You might be recognized if you went anywhere near the camp, and if it was known that you were there he'd be compromised, especially after what's happened in England. You must stay either here or in this neighbourhood. If you're not going to stay here you must tell me where you'll be, so that I shall know where to find you when I've got fresh orders for you.'

'I may not be able to stay on here, Rochefort.'

'Why not?'

'I told you. My enemies may be here at any moment.'

'Yes, of course. But if you go little Madame Bonacieux may escape, and that'll annoy the Cardinal.'

Milady smiled her crafty smile.

'Don't worry about that,' she said. 'Remember I'm her best friend.'

'Yes, I forgot. As far as she's concerned, then, I can tell the Cardinal . . .'

'Not to worry.'

'Will he know what that means?'

'He'll guess.'

'Very well,' said Rochefort. 'And now what must I do?'

'Leave at once. I think the news I've given you's well worth taking back.'

'My post-chaise broke down just as I got into Lilliers.'

'Good!'

'Why good?'

'I need your chaise myself,' said Milady.

'And how am I to do the journey?'

'You can ride back.'

'D'you realize it's over 500 miles from here to La Rochelle?'

'That won't kill you.'

'Very well, I'll ride. And what about the chaise?'

'When you pass Lilliers send it and your servant here,' said Milady. 'And tell your servant he's to take orders from me in future.'

'Right.'

'I imagine you've got an authority from the Cardinal on you?'

'I've got my full warrant.'

'Show it to the Abbess and tell her someone will be coming for me either today or tomorrow and that I'm to be put in the charge of the man who comes in your name.'

'Very well.'

'Remember to speak badly of me to the Abbess.'

'Why?'

'I'm supposed to be one of the Cardinal's victims. I've got to go on pretending that for the little Bonacieux creature's benefit.'

'Of course. And now will you write a full report of everything you've done?'

'I've told you everything I've done. You've got a good head. Repeat the things I said back to me and memorize them. It's dangerous to write things down; reports get lost.'

'True. But you must tell me where I can find you again. I don't want to waste time searching all the neighbouring villages.'

'No, of course not. Let me think a moment.'

'D'you want a map?'

'Oh no, I know this district thoroughly. I was brought up here.'

'Well, where will you be waiting?'

'Let me think. Ah, I know the very place – Armentières.'

'What's that? A village, a town, or what?'

'A small town on the river Lys. From Armentières I'd only have to cross the river to be out of the country.'

'Excellent. But you won't cross the river unless you're forced to, will you?'

'No, that's agreed,' replied Milady.

'If you do have to cross it how shall I find you?'

'Can you manage without your servant for a while?'

'Yes.'

'Is he trustworthy?'

'Absolutely.'

'Let me keep him for a time. Nobody knows him. If I do cross the river I'll leave him behind and he'll bring you on to where I am.'

'And for the present you'll stay at Argentières?'

'Armentières,' corrected Milady.

'Write that place down for me to make sure I don't forget it. There's nothing compromising in the name of a town, surely?'

'Well, let's hope not.'

And Milady sat down and wrote 'Armentières' on a half sheet of paper.

Rochefort took the sheet from her, folded it and slipped it into the lining of his hat.

'Don't worry,' he said. 'I'll do what children do, repeat the name over and over again to myself as I go along in case I lose the paper. And now is that all?'

'I think so.'

'Let's see if I've got everything right . . . Buckingham dead or seriously wounded; your talk with the Cardinal overheard by the four musketeers; Lord de Winter told about your going to England; d'Artagnan and Athos to go to the Bastille; Aramis, Madame de Chevreuse's lover; Porthos a pompous ass; Madame Bonacieux found again;

my chaise and servant to be sent to you as soon as possible; I'm to speak badly of you to the Abbess to gull her; you're going to Armentières on the banks of the Lys. Is that right?'

'Rochefort, your memory's phenomenal! And there's just one thing more. I've noticed some charming woods just beyond the convent garden. Tell the Abbess to allow me to walk in those woods. You never know; I might have to make a quick escape by some side door if those fiends descended on me suddenly.'

'You think of everything.'

'And you, you've forgotten one thing.'

'What's that?'

'To ask me if I need money.'

'Of course. How much do you need?'

'Every sou you've got on you.'

'I've got about 500 pistoles.'

'And I've got another 500. 1,000 pistoles ought to do me all right. Give me your 500.'

Rochefort handed her the whole sum.

'Thank you, Rochefort,' said Milady. 'And now when are you leaving?'

'In about an hour. I'll send my servant for a post-horse and meanwhile get myself something to eat.'

'Excellent. Well, good-bye, Rochefort.'

'Good-bye, Lady de Winter.'

'My respects to the Cardinal,' said Milady.

'And mine to the Devil,' retorted Rochefort.

They smiled at each other. Then Rochefort turned and left the room.

An hour later he was galloping out of the town. Five hours later he was in Arras.

We have already heard how d'Artagnan recognized him, how alarmed the four friends were to see him and how his presence in the district brought home to them the need to reach Béthune without delay.

32

A Drop of Wine

Hardly had Rochefort left the room when Madame Bonacieux reappeared. To her surprise she found Milady looking quite cheerful.

'Oh dear!' she exclaimed. 'So your worst fears have been realized! The Cardinal's sending for you this evening or tomorrow morning.'

'How do *you* know that, dearest?'

'I heard his messenger saying so.'

'Come and sit over here, near me,' said Milady.

'Very well.'

'Now I'll just make sure no one's listening,' said Milady.

'Why all this secrecy?'

'You'll see.'

Milady got up, walked to the door, opened it, glanced down the passage and then came back and sat down beside Madame Bonacieux.

'I see he played his part well.'

'Who?'

'The man who called here, who pretended to be the Cardinal's envoy.'

'What? Wasn't he really that?'

'No, he was only pretending to be.'

'So he's not . . .'

'He's not what he said he was,' replied Milady, lowering her voice. 'Far from it. He's actually my brother.'

'Your brother!' exclaimed Madame Bonacieux.

'You're the only one who knows this, my dear, so keep it very dark. If you repeat it to a single soul I shall be lost and you too, perhaps.'

'Good Heavens! How awful!'

'Listen. I'll tell you what happened. My brother was coming to rescue me, and take me away from here, by force if need be. On the way he ran into the Cardinal's envoy, who was also coming for me. My brother followed him. When they reached a lonely part of the road my brother drew his sword and told the messenger to hand over his papers. The man tried to defend himself and my brother killed him.'

'How terrible!' cried Madame Bonacieux with a shudder.

'There was nothing else to be done, was there? My brother then decided to get me out of here not by force but by a trick. He took the messenger's papers and rode on. When he got here he pretended to be the Cardinal's agent himself. He deceived the Abbess completely and told her His Eminence would be sending a carriage for me in an hour or two.'

'I see. And the carriage will be your brother's carriage?'

'Exactly. And I've got something else to tell you. That letter you got, you think Madame de Chevreuse wrote it, don't you?'

'Yes. Why? Didn't she?'

'It's a forgery.'

'A forgery?'

'Yes. A trap to make sure you don't try to resist when the Cardinal's men come for you.'

'But d'Artagnan's coming!'

'Don't you believe it! D'Artagnan and his friends are campaigning at La Rochelle.'

'How d'you know that?'

'On his way here my brother ran into a party of the Cardinal's men dressed as musketeers. They saw he'd seen through their disguise and that spoilt their game. They were coming here dressed like that. They'd have called you to the door. You'd have taken them for friends, gone off quite happily with them and been taken back to Paris a prisoner.'

'Good Heavens! Is that really true? You're saying the most terrible things, Lady de Winter. I didn't know such villainy existed. I feel quite dazed by all these intrigues. If I hear much more I shall go mad.'

Milady suddenly started.

'Listen!' she said.

'What is it?'

'I hear a horse trotting down the street. That must be my brother going off. I must wave good-bye to him. Come and stand beside me.'

Milady opened the window, and she and Madame Bonacieux watched Rochefort riding past.

'Good-bye, George dear!' called Milady.

Rochefort looked up, saw the two women at the window and without drawing rein waved a friendly farewell.

'Good, kind George,' said Milady to her companion as she closed the window. On her face was a look of tenderness tinged with sadness. She went and sat down in her armchair and appeared to be lost in thoughts of an entirely personal nature.

'Dear Lady de Winter,' said Madame Bonacieux, 'forgive me for interrupting you, but what d'you advise me to do? I seem to be in a terrible fix. You've got more experience than I. Can't you suggest something?'

'Of course I may be wrong and d'Artagnan and his friends may really be coming for you,' replied Milady.

'Oh, that would be too wonderful!' cried Madame Bonacieux. 'I wouldn't deserve such happiness.'

'In that case,' continued Milady, 'it would be merely a question of who got here first. If your friends arrived first you'd be saved; if the Cardinal's men got here first you'd be lost.'

'Yes, yes. It would be all up with me then. I couldn't

expect any mercy from them. What am I to do? Oh, what am I to do?'

'I can think of one possible way out for you.'

'What's that?'

'You could hide somewhere close by and wait to see who arrived.'

'But where?'

'I know a place. When my brother's carriage comes for me I'm going off in it to hide somewhere a few miles from here and wait for my brother to join me. Why don't you come too? We'll hide together and watch what happens.'

'But they won't let me leave the convent. I'm virtually a prisoner here.'

'The Abbess thinks I'm being taken away on the Cardinal's order. She's not likely to suspect you of wanting to come with me.'

'No, I suppose not.'

'The carriage will be waiting at the door with my brother's servant as outrider. You'll step on to the footboard to give me a good-bye kiss. I'll tell the servant beforehand that when he sees you there he's to sign to the coachman to whip up the horses. You'll jump in and we'll gallop off.'

'But suppose d'Artagnan does come?'

'We'll find out all right.'

'How?'

'I'll send my brother's servant back to Béthune. He's completely trustworthy. He'll disguise himself somehow and take cover where he can see the convent. If he sees the Cardinal's men arrive he'll keep hidden; if he sees Monsieur d'Artagnan and his friends he'll go up to them and bring them to us.'

'Does he know them by sight?'

'He does indeed. He's seen Monsieur d'Artagnan often enough at my house.'

'Of course. I was forgetting. Well, that sounds a

very good plan. But don't let's go too far away from here.'

'A seven or eight hours' drive would get us to the frontier. That would be a good place to wait. If anything went wrong we could be out of the country at a moment's notice.'

'And what shall we do between then and now?'

'Wait.'

'And if they come?'

'My brother's carriage will get here first.'

'Suppose I'm at the other end of the building when it comes for you? Suppose I'm at lunch or supper?'

'I think we can get round that.'

'How?'

'Tell the Abbess you want to see me as much as possible, and would like to have your meals with me.'

'D'you think she'd allow that?'

'I can't see why not.'

'Marvellous! Then we'll never be separated for a moment.'

'That settles that, then. Now go down and ask the Abbess's permission. I've a slight headache and while you're seeing the Abbess I'll take a walk round the garden.'

'Where shall I find you?'

'Come back here in an hour. I'll be back by then.'

'Very well. I'll meet you here in an hour. Oh, how good you are, Lady de Winter! I'm so grateful to you!'

'Nonsense, my dear! It's only natural I should be interested in you; you're so pretty and attractive and you're the friend of one of my oldest friends.'

'Dear d'Artagnan!' whispered Madame Bonacieux. 'He'll be so grateful to you!'

'I hope so indeed. And now let's both go down.'

'You're going into the garden?' asked the novice.

'Yes.'

'Follow that passage. You'll find a little staircase at the end which'll take you to it.'

'Thank you, my dear.'

The two women exchanged affectionate smiles and parted.

Milady's headache was no sham. She had not yet perfected her plans and her brain was in a whirl. She saw her scheme in main outline but needed quiet and solitude to work out the details.

The most important thing was to carry off Madame Bonacieux to some safe place and there, if need be, use her as a hostage. Milady was beginning to have doubts about the outcome of this terrible duel, for she realized that her enemies were as relentless in their pursuit of her as she was in her resolve to take revenge on them. And as one feels the approach of a storm, she sensed that the final clash was near, and that it would be terrible indeed.

Her main concern, therefore, was to carry off Madame Bonacieux, for to hold Madame Bonacieux was to hold d'Artagnan. He loved the little draper's wife with all his heart, and Milady knew that she would be a powerful weapon with which to negotiate if things went wrong. Madame Bonacieux trusted her and would go with her. Once she had her in Armentières she could easily convince her that d'Artagnan had never come to Béthune. In a fortnight at the most Rochefort would be back, and she could spend the intervening time thinking out the best means of settling her account with the four friends. She would not be bored. Not for a moment! She would have what her mind at present most craved for, leisure to devise and perfect a scheme of revenge.

As she sat thinking Milady also made a mental note of the design of the garden. Like a good general she visualized defeat as well as victory, and laid her plans accordingly.

About an hour later she heard a gentle voice calling her

from the cloister door. It was Madame Bonacieux. She told Milady that the Abbess had agreed to everything and that they were to have supper together that very night.

As they were walking down the cloisters they heard a carriage drawing up at the gate. Milady stopped to listen.

'Did you hear that?' she asked.

'Yes, carriage wheels.'

'That's my brother's carriage.'

Madame Bonacieux suddenly put her hand to her heart.

'Oh God!' she exclaimed. 'My heart's beating so fast I can hardly walk. I feel stifled.'

'Courage! In a quarter of an hour you'll be free. Just think of that! And remember that what you're doing you're doing for his sake.'

'Yes, yes, for his sake! Thank you for saying that! I feel quite brave again now. Go to your room and I'll join you in a moment.'

Milady ran upstairs to her room, where she found Rochefort's servant waiting for her. She proceeded to give him his orders. He was to wait with the carriage at the convent gate. If the musketeers happened to arrive before they themselves had left he was to drive off at a gallop, circle round the convent, make for the little village of Festubert which lay beyond the wood, and there wait for Milady. She herself would meanwhile escape through the garden and, knowing the district thoroughly, would make for the village on foot. If, however, the musketeers did not appear everything was to be carried out as arranged. Madame Bonacieux was to get into the carriage on the pretext of saying good-bye to her friend, and they would then drive off with her.

At that moment Madame Bonacieux herself came in. To remove all suspicion from her mind Milady repeated the last part of her orders to the servant in front of her. She then made a few inquiries about the carriage and was told that it was a three-horse chaise driven by a postilion, and that Rochefort's servant would act as outrider.

When the servant had left the room Milady said:

'You see everything's perfectly arranged. The Abbess suspects nothing and thinks I'm being taken away on the Cardinal's order. The servant will pass on my orders to the coachman. Now eat and drink something to build up your strength. Then we must be off.'

Madame Bonacieux mechanically ate a few mouthfuls of chicken and sipped a little wine. Milady poured herself out a glass of the wine and said:

'Drink it down as I do. It'll do you good.'

She was raising the glass to her lips when she suddenly went rigid and stood for a moment transfixed. She had heard the sound of horses' hoofs in the distance. The sound grew louder, and now she fancied she heard horses neighing. At this all her exultation vanished, and she was like a sleeper woken from a dream by a thunderclap. She went deathly pale, put down her glass and ran to the window, while Madame Bonacieux got up trembling from her chair and stood with one arm resting on the table to support herself. Milady, watching from the window, could as yet see nothing. But the sound of the galloping horses grew louder.

'O God!' said Madame Bonacieux. 'What's that noise?'

Milady replied in a hard, cold voice:

'It's either our friends or our foes arriving. Stay where you are. Don't come to the window. I'll tell you what I see.'

Madame Bonacieux remained standing by the table, pale and speechless.

The sound of the galloping hoofs grew ever louder; now the party of riders could not be more than two hundred yards away. But still Milady could see nothing as a bend in the road hid them from her sight. But the noise was now so distinct that one could have counted the horses by the clip-clop of their hoofs on the cobble-stones.

Milady was watching and listening intently. The waning light was still strong enough to enable her to identify anyone coming along the road.

Suddenly at the bend of the road she saw braided cloaks and plumed hats glinting in the twilight. She counted first two, then five, then eight riders. One of them was about two horses' lengths ahead of the others. When Milady saw the leader of the party she gave a cry of rage. It was d'Artagnan.

'O God!' cried Madame Bonacieux. 'What's the matter?'

'The Cardinal's Guards!' cried Milady. 'Eight of them. We must escape at once. There's not a moment to lose.'

'Yes, yes, we must escape,' echoed Madame Bonacieux.

But she seemed unable to move and stood rooted to the spot with terror.

The two women heard the riders dismounting under the window.

'Come on!' cried Milady. 'We can still escape through the garden. I've got the key. But hurry! If we're not away in five minutes they'll get us.'

She seized Madame Bonacieux by the arm and tried to drag her out of the room by force. The unfortunate girl tried to walk to the door, but after a couple of steps sank helplessly to her knees. Milady now tried to lift her up to drag her through the door, but the effort was too great. At that moment they heard the sound of carriage wheels rattling down the street; seeing the musketeers arrive Rochefort's postilion had, as arranged, whipped up the horses and driven off. They then heard three or four pistol shots.

'For the last time, are you coming?' screamed Milady.

'Don't you see I'm too weak to move?' cried Madame

Bonacieux. 'I can't walk a step. Save yourself; don't worry about me.'

'Leave you here alone!' exclaimed Milady. 'Never!'

Suddenly she stood stock still and a livid light of rage flashed in her eyes. She then ran over to the table, took a ring off her finger, removed the stone from its setting with her nail and dropped a little red pellet from the ring into Madame Bonacieux's unfinished glass of wine. The pellet dissolved at once. She then took the glass, held it to the young woman's lips and said commandingly:

'Drink this. It'll give you back your strength.'

Madame Bonacieux mechanically drank down the wine. With a smile of devilish glee Milady replaced the glass on the table.

'That wasn't how I'd pictured taking my revenge,' she muttered. 'But it's better than nothing.'

Then she turned and fled from the room.

Madame Bonacieux watched her go but could make no move to follow her. She was like someone in a dream who knows himself pursued, yet cannot escape.

A few minutes passed. Then Madame Bonacieux heard a loud hammering at the convent gate. She expected every moment to see Milady return but Milady did not appear. She herself was still kneeling in a hunched attitude on the floor, trembling in every limb.

At last she heard the grinding of bolts on the floor below and realized that the nuns were opening the convent gate to the callers. Then came the noise of boots and spurs on the stone staircase; then a confused murmur of voices, which grew gradually louder. Suddenly she fancied she heard someone calling her by name and the next moment she gave a cry of joy, sprang to her feet and ran over to the door; she had recognized the voice of her beloved d'Artagnan.

'D'Artagnan, d'Artagnan!' she called. 'Is it you? I'm here!'

'Constance, Constance!' called the young man in reply. 'In Heaven's name, where are you?'

The next moment the door of the cell opened or rather yielded to a powerful impact and half a dozen men burst into the room. Madame Bonacieux had collapsed into an armchair and was lying there, as though paralysed.

D'Artagnan was holding a still smouldering pistol in his hand. He threw it into the corner of the room and fell on his knees before his loved one. Athos put his pistol back into his belt, and Porthos and Aramis, who both had drawn swords in their hands, sheathed them.

'Oh d'Artagnan, dearest d'Artagnan!' exclaimed the young woman. 'You've come at last. You haven't deserted me after all; you've really come!'

'Yes, yes, Constance. I've found you at last.'

'*She* kept telling me you wouldn't come. But in my heart of hearts I knew you would. I somehow didn't want to go away with her. Thank God I stayed behind!'

While the lovers had been talking Athos had sat down calmly in a corner of the room. But at the words 'she' and 'her' he sprang to his feet in alarm.

'She? Who d'you mean?' asked d'Artagnan.

'My good friend, my companion here. She wanted to help me escape from the Cardinal's agents. She mistook you for Cardinalists and escaped herself a few minutes ago.'

D'Artagnan went as white as the nun's veil which covered his beloved Constance's head.

'Your companion, your good friend?' he stammered.

'Yes, the woman whose carriage was at the gate just now. She said she was a friend of yours, d'Artagnan, and that you'd told her everything about us.'

'What's her name?' cried d'Artagnan. 'Don't you know her name?'

'Yes, of course I know her name. The Abbess told

me. How funny! I can't remember it. I feel quite
stupid suddenly and there's something wrong with my
eyes.'

D'Artagnan turned to his friends.

'Come here, quick, all of you,' he called. 'Her hands are
icy cold. She's ill. Good God, she's fainting!'

Porthos started shouting for help at the top of his voice
while Aramis ran over to the table to fetch a glass of
water. He stopped dead, however, when he noticed
Athos standing by the table with a look of horror on his
face, staring dazedly at one of the wine-glasses and
muttering to himself:

'No, no, it's impossible. God wouldn't allow that; it's
too vile!'

'Water, water!' shouted d'Artagnan.

Athos kept repeating brokenly:

'Poor soul, poor soul!'

D'Artagnan covered his beloved's hands with kisses.
At last she opened her eyes.

'She's coming round,' cried the young man. 'Oh thank
God, thank God!'

Athos said, pointing to the empty glass on the table:

'Madame Bonacieux, for God's sake tell me whose
glass that is.'

Madame Bonacieux replied faintly:

'That's my glass.'

'That glass has had wine in it,' went on Athos. 'Who
poured it out for you?'

'She did.'

'Who do you mean? You must know her name.'

'Ah yes, I remember now,' replied Madame Bonacieux.
'Lady de Winter.'

A single cry of horror rang through the room. All four
men had cried out together but Athos' voice rose above
the rest.

At that moment Madame Bonacieux turned a ghastly

leaden colour; a sudden spasm seized her and she slid from the armchair on to the floor.

D'Artagnan, realizing that she was dead, let her fall from his arms, gave a groan of despair and collapsed at her side, as pale and lifeless as she.

The three other men were standing by. Porthos started to weep, Aramis stood with bent head, and Athos crossed himself.

At that moment a figure suddenly appeared in the doorway. It was a man, a stranger. He looked pale and harassed and almost as distressed as the three who had just seen Madame Bonacieux die. He took a quick look round him, staring sharply first at the dead woman and her lover lying unconscious beside her and then at the other three occupants of the room, who were standing motionless with bent heads.

'If I'm not mistaken,' he said, addressing the last-named, 'that's Monsieur d'Artagnan over there, and you gentlemen are his three friends, Monsieur Athos, Monsieur Porthos and Monsieur Aramis.'

The three musketeers turned and stared at the new-comer in surprise. They said nothing in reply to his greeting, but all seemed to recollect having seen him before. The stranger continued:

'I suspect that you gentlemen, like myself, are in quest of a certain woman.'

He added with a ghastly smile:

'That corpse there makes me think she must have passed this way not so very long.'

Still the three friends said nothing. But the stranger's voice, like his face, seemed familiar, and they all thought they remembered having met him before, though they did not know when or where.

'I see you either don't or won't recognize me, gentlemen,' went on the stranger. 'And yet I think I'm right in saying you saved my life at least twice. So if you'll allow

me I'll introduce myself. I'm Lord de Winter, that
woman's brother-in-law.'

The three friends gave a start of surprise. Then Athos
walked up to de Winter and held out his hand.

'We're delighted to see you, Lord de Winter,' he said.
'Please consider us your friends and join us.'

At that moment d'Artagnan regained consciousness.
He pushed Porthos and Aramis aside, knelt over the
dead woman, took her in his arms again and laid his head
on her breast. Athos walked up to him and put his hand
affectionately on his shoulder. At this d'Artagnan broke
down and began to sob, upon which Athos, to give him
courage, said gently:

'D'Artagnan, be a man. Only women mourn the dead.
Men avenge them.'

At this d'Artagnan looked up.

'If you're out for revenge I'll go with you to the ends of
the earth,' he said.

Seeing that his friend had taken heart again Athos
signed to Porthos and Aramis to summon the Abbess.
When she arrived, Athos turned to her and said:

'Reverend Mother, please take charge of this poor
woman's body. She was once an angel on earth; now
she's an angel with God in Heaven. Care for her as
though she were one of your own sisterhood. One day
we'll return and say prayers at her grave.'

At this d'Artagnan laid his head on his friend's
shoulder and broke into stifled sobs.

'Weep, young lover,' said Athos. 'Would I could weep
with you.'

And with a father's tenderness and the understanding
of one who has himself suffered, he took his sorrowing
friend's arm and led him gently from the room.

All five men now left the convent, followed by their
servants, and walked down the road towards the town,
leading their horses by the bridle. The town was only a

few hundred yards away and the men stopped at the first inn they saw. D'Artagnan said:

'Aren't we going after that woman?'

'Later,' replied Athos. 'I've got some things to see to first.'

'But she'll get away, Athos,' objected the young man. 'You'll see she'll get away. God help us! And it'll be your fault.'

'I take full responsibility for her,' replied Athos.

D'Artagnan had such trust in his friend that he said no more. The little party now entered the inn.

Porthos and Aramis exchanged glances, for they did not share d'Artagnan's confidence in Athos' word. Lord de Winter thought that the musketeer had spoken as he had merely to ease d'Artagnan's grief.

Athos interviewed the innkeeper, discovered that he had five rooms to let, rejoined his friends and said:

'I suggest, gentlemen, that we all go to bed now. D'Artagnan needs to be alone to weep, and the rest of us to sleep. And don't any of you worry about plans, I'll see to everything.'

De Winter protested:

'I can't help thinking that if we're going to take action against this woman I should be the one responsible. After all, she is my sister-in-law.'

'And she's my wife,' said Athos.

At this d'Artagnan started and felt a chill run down his spine. He knew that Athos would not have betrayed his secret had he not been sure of revenge. Porthos and Aramis went very white. As for Lord de Winter he stared at the musketeer as though he were mad.

Athos continued:

'So you see you can all safely go to bed and leave me, as this woman's husband, to deal with her. Oh, there's just one thing, d'Artagnan. If you haven't lost it would you give me the slip of paper which fell out of that fellow's hat, with the name of the town on it.'

D'Artagnan's eyes lit up.

'Of course!' he said excitedly. 'I remember now; it's written in her handwriting.'

'Yes,' replied Athos. 'You see there is a God in Heaven after all.'

33

THE MAN IN THE RED CLOAK

Having promised his three friends and Lord de Winter that their common account with Lady de Winter would be settled, Athos cast off his habitual apathy and concentrated on the plan of campaign he had already vaguely outlined in his mind. He was the last of the five men to go to his room. He asked the innkeeper for a map of the district and sat poring over it for some time. He discovered that four roads led from Béthune to Armentières and immediately summoned the four servants.

When Planchet, Grimaud, Mousqueton and Bazin were standing before him he gave them all clear, precise instructions. They were to leave Béthune at dawn the next day and make for Armentières, each by a different road. Planchet, the most intelligent of the four, was to follow the road taken by the carriage which had driven off from the convent door as they had arrived, and which, as we know, was escorted by Rochefort's servant.

All four were to be at Armentières by eleven next morning. If they had discovered where Milady was hiding three of them were to remain and keep watch on her movements, while the fourth was to return to Béthune to report to Athos and act as guide to the four friends and Lord de Winter.

Having received their orders the servants themselves retired to bed.

Athos now got up from his chair, put on his sword and cloak and left the inn. It was already nearly ten o'clock, and at ten o'clock in the evening country lanes were in those days almost entirely deserted. But Athos was obviously searching for someone who could give him some information.

At last he met a belated passer-by. He went up to him and said something in a low voice. The man was evidently alarmed, for he started back and stared at Athos in surprise. After a moment, however, he recovered himself and pointed in a certain direction. Athos offered him half a pistole to come with him and show him the way, but the man refused.

Athos started off in the direction shown by the peasant. But after walking a little way he reached a crossroads and was again in doubt which way to go. The crossroads seemed the most likely spot for an encounter, so he waited here a few minutes. Sure enough a night watchman soon came along. Athos asked him the question he had asked the peasant and the night watchman showed the same alarm and surprise. But he, too, pointed in a certain direction and likewise refused Athos' offer of money to accompany him.

Athos again set off and soon reached the furthermost suburb of the town. Here he again seemed in doubt which road to take and stopped for the third time. Fortunately at that moment a beggar happened to approach him and ask for alms. Athos offered him a crown to accompany him to his destination.

The beggar hesitated a moment; then, seeing the glint

of the silver coin in the darkness, he agreed and started to walk ahead of Athos to show him the way. He led him a few hundred yards to where a side road branched off the main street. Here he stopped and pointed to a small, gloomy-looking house standing by itself. Athos started to walk towards it, while the beggar, having been paid his fee, made off in the opposite direction.

When Athos reached the house he had to walk round it to find the door, which was scarcely visible against the dingy red of the walls. No light filtered through the cracks in the shutters. No sound came from inside the house to betray the presence of a living soul. The house itself was as dark and silent as a tomb.

Athos knocked once, twice and then a third time. After the third knock he heard faint footsteps approaching the door. Then the door was half-opened and Athos, peering in, saw a man standing on the threshold, a tall fellow with a pale face and black hair and beard. The musketeer said something to him in a low voice. The man seemed to hesitate; then he pulled the door full open and signed to his caller to enter, closing the door behind him.

Athos was now face to face with the man whom he had come so far and taken such pains to find. His host led him into a laboratory where he had been busy piecing together the bones of a skeleton with wire. He had already assembled the body, but the head still lay separate on a table. Everything in the room revealed that its occupant was a natural scientist. There were bottles containing various species of reptile, all labelled; there were large, black, wooden crates filled with dried lizards which glittered like emeralds. Clumps of scented wild herbs, which doubtless contained therapeutic properties known only to the initiate, hung down from the ceiling in all four corners of the room. And there was not another human soul in the house; the man evidently lived alone, without family or servants.

Athos took a quick look round him. Then, at his host's invitation, he sat down opposite him and started to explain the reason for his visit and what he wished the man to do. But hardly had he stated his request than the man started back in alarm, shaking his head violently to show that he would have nothing to do with it.

At this Athos took a sheet of paper out of his pocket and handed it to his host, who noticed on it two lines of handwriting, a signature, and a seal. When he read the writing his attitude at once changed, and he nodded to Athos to show that he would now do as he was bid and take orders from him. After thanking him Athos bade him good night and walked back along the road by which he had come. When he reached the inn he retired to his room and locked the door.

The next day at dawn d'Artagnan knocked on his door to ask for orders for himself and his three friends.

'Just wait,' replied Athos.

A few moments later a man called at the inn with a message from the Abbess that Madame Bonacieux's funeral would take place that day at noon. As for the murderess nothing more had been heard of her. But footsteps which were clearly hers had been found in the garden, the garden gate had been found locked and the key missing. It was fairly obvious, therefore, that she had escaped that way.

At the hour appointed Lord de Winter and the four friends arrived at the convent. The bells were ringing out a full chime and the chapel door was open; only the wrought-iron gate into the chancel was closed. The murdered woman's body, dressed in novice's robes, lay exposed in the middle of the chancel. The nuns were assembled on either side of the chancel, behind iron gates which opened on to the convent. From here they took part in the service and sang in unison with the priests, hidden from the eyes of the lay congregation.

At the chapel door d'Artagnan felt his courage fail again; he turned round to look for Athos, but his friend had disappeared.

Faithful to his mission of revenge Athos had asked to be taken into the garden. There he had seen the footsteps mentioned by the Abbess, had followed them to the gate which led from the garden into the wood, had asked to have the gate opened and had plunged straight into the forest.

Now all his suspicions were confirmed. The road which the carriage had taken skirted the wood. Athos walked some distance down this road, his eyes fixed on the ground. At intervals along the road he noticed faint bloodstains which he realized must have come from a wound inflicted either on the man who was acting as outrider to the carriage or on one of the horses. After he had gone about two miles and was within a hundred yards of the village of Festubert he noticed a bloodstain considerably larger than the others; here, too, the surface of the road had been trodden down by the horses. Between the forest and this tell-tale spot on the road, a little behind the patch of trampled-on ground, Athos noticed the same small footsteps which he had seen in the garden. Here the carriage had obviously stopped; here Milady had come out of the forest, been picked up by the coachman and outrider and driven on.

Satisfied by this discovery, which confirmed all his previous conjectures, Athos returned to the inn, where he found Planchet waiting impatiently for him.

There was only one inn in Armentières, the Hôtel de la Poste. Planchet had called there, pretending to be a servant on the lookout for a job. Ten minutes' conversation with the host had revealed to him that a lady travelling alone had arrived in the village at eleven o'clock the previous night and had taken a room; she had

hen summoned the innkeeper and told him that she was
staying some time in the neighbourhood.

That was all Planchet wanted to know. He had hurried
to the place where he and his three associates were to
meet, had found all three waiting for him, taken them
back to the inn, posted them where they could watch all
the entrances to the building and then returned to report
to Athos. Just as Planchet was finishing his tale the three
friends came in. They all looked grim, even the gentle
Aramis.

'Well, what d'you want us to do?' asked d'Artagnan.

'Wait,' said Athos.

At this all three young men went up to their rooms.

At eight o'clock that evening Athos gave orders for the
horses to be saddled and told his friends and Lord de
Winter to get ready to start. All four were ready in a
moment, with their arms inspected and primed.

When Athos went down he found d'Artagnan already
in the saddle.

'You'll have to wait a bit, I'm afraid,' said Athos. 'One
of the party hasn't turned up yet.'

His four companions looked at each other in surprise;
who could the missing man be?

At that moment Planchet brought up Athos' horse and
the musketeer leapt lightly into the saddle.

'Wait for me here,' he said. 'I'll be back in a few
minutes.'

And he rode off at the gallop.

He returned a quarter of an hour later, sure enough
accompanied by a man in a mask, with a long red cloak
wrapped round him.

Lord de Winter and the three musketeers looked at
each other with raised eyebrows. All were equally in the
dark as to who this mysterious stranger might be. But
they accepted him without question, vouched for as he
was by Athos, who was in charge of affairs.

At nine o'clock the little cavalcade with Planchet at its head set out along the road taken by the carriage. The six men riding along in silence in the twilight appeared sinister. They were all sunk in their own thoughts and looked stern and solemn, like avenging angels or emissaries of Fate.

It was a dark and stormy night. Heavy clouds scudded across the sky, veiling the light of the stars. The moon was not due to rise till midnight. From time to time flashes of lightning would reveal the road winding white and desolate ahead of the party of riders. Then all would be in shadow again.

Lord de Winter, Porthos and Aramis had all in turn tried to talk to the man in the red cloak. But each time they questioned him he merely bowed and said nothing. They therefore assumed that he had some good reason for not wishing to speak and soon ceased to pester him.

The storm was gradually increasing in violence; the flashes of lightning followed one another rapidly; there were loud claps of thunder and the wind began to whistle across the valley, preluding a hurricane.

D'Artagnan had taken off his hat and not put on his cloak. He enjoyed the sensation of the rain streaming down his face and buffeting his body, cooling his fevered nerves.

The six riders were nearing their goal, when they saw a man step out from behind a tree. It was Grimaud. He told them that Milady had left Armentières, and he led them to her new hiding-place, a little house on the banks of the river about a mile away, where Mousqueton and Bazin were watching.

The little house was surrounded by a quickset hedge about three feet in height. Athos leapt over the hedge and stepped right up to the window, which was shutterless but had curtains drawn tightly across it. He climbed on to

he stone sill, from where he could see over the curtains
nto the room.

A lamp was burning in the room and in its rays Athos
saw a woman wrapped in a dark cloak seated on a chair
near the dying embers of a fire. She had her elbows on the
able in front of her and was resting her head in her
hands, which were as white as ivory. Athos could not see
her face, but as he stood watching her he smiled grimly.
There could be no doubt. It was the woman they were
looking for.

At that moment one of the horses neighed. Milady
looked up, saw Athos' pale face pressed against the
window and cried out.

The musketeer saw that she had recognized him. He
pressed his elbow and knee against the window until the
panes splintered and the frame collapsed. Then, like the
Spirit of vengeance, he sprang into the room. Milady
ran to the door and opened it. On the threshold stood a
figure even sterner and more threatening than Athos –
d'Artagnan.

Milady again gave a cry and shrank back into the room.
D'Artagnan, fearing that she might have some secret way
of escape, drew his pistol from his belt. But Athos called
out:

'Put that pistol away, d'Artagnan. This woman has to
be tried, not murdered. Patience! You'll soon be even
with her. Come in, the rest of you!'

D'Artagnan, awed by Athos' stern manner, obeyed.
And now Porthos, Aramis, Lord de Winter, and the man
in the red cloak followed him into the room.

The four servants were posted to guard the door and
the window.

Milady had fallen back on to her chair and was holding
her arms out in front of her as though to banish this
terrifying vision. When she caught sight of her brother-
in-law she gave another cry and stammered out:

'What do you want, all of you?'

Athos replied:

'We want Anne de Breuil, known first as the Comtesse de la Fère, and then as Clarice, Lady de Winter.'

Milady was dumbfounded.

'Yes, that's me!' she said. 'Why do you want me?'

'We want to try you for your crimes,' said Athos. 'You'll be free to plead your cause and to prove yourself innocent if you can. Monsieur d'Artagnan, I call on you first to bring your charges against this woman.'

D'Artagnan stepped forward.

'Before God and men,' he said, 'I charge this woman with having poisoned Constance Bonacieux, who died last night.'

He turned to Porthos and Aramis, who said in one voice:

'We bear witness to that.'

D'Artagnan continued:

'Before God and men I charge this woman with having tried to poison me with wine which she sent from Villeroy with a forged letter, written to make me believe the wine came from my friends. God protected me, but another died in my place, a man named Brisemont.'

Porthos and Aramis replied again:

'We bear witness to that.'

'Before God and men,' continued d'Artagnan, 'I further charge this woman with having incited me to murder the Comte de Wardes. No one present can bear witness to this charge, but I myself swear to the truth of it. That is the sum of my charges against this woman.'

So saying d'Artagnan went and stood beside Porthos and Aramis in the corner of the room.

'Lord de Winter, will you bring your charges next,' said Athos.

De Winter stepped forward in his turn.

'Before God and men,' he said, 'I charge this woman with having caused the murder of the Duke of Buckingham!'

'The Duke of Buckingham murdered!' cried the four musketeers.

'Yes, murdered,' replied de Winter. 'When I got your warning letter I had this woman arrested and put her in the charge of a man I thought I could trust. But she seduced him; she persuaded him to do this thing; she even put the knife into his hand. And now Felton's to die to atone for this fiend's crime.'

The others standing round felt a thrill of horror at this disclosure of outrages unknown to them.

'I have a further charge to bring,' said Lord de Winter. 'My brother, who made this woman his sole heir in his will, died within three hours of signing it of some mysterious illness, which left purple marks all over his body. Confess, Clarice, how did my brother die?'

'How vile!' cried Porthos and Aramis.

Lord de Winter continued:

'This woman murdered Buckingham, she murdered Felton, she murdered my brother. I demand redress against her and declare that if I don't get it from you here I shall take action on my own.'

Lord de Winter now took his place beside d'Artagnan, Porthos, and Aramis, leaving room for the next accuser to step forward and bring his charge.

Milady was sitting with her head buried in her hands, making frantic efforts to collect her thoughts. But mortal dread had seized her, numbing her wits.

Athos now stepped forward. As he gazed at his former wife he shuddered as a man shudders at the sight of a snake.

'Here's my charge against this woman,' he said. 'I married her when she was a girl, against my family's wishes; I gave her my name and a share in all my worldly goods. One day I discovered she was branded, marked with a fleur-de-lis on her left shoulder.'

At this Milady sprang to her feet and cried:

'I defy anyone to find the court which imposed that wicked sentence on me. And I defy anyone to find the man who executed it.'

At this a voice called out:

'Silence, everybody! I alone can answer that challenge!'

The speaker was the man in the red cloak, who now himself stepped forward.

'Who's that man? Who's that man?' cried Milady in a voice choked with fear.

Everyone was staring at the man in the cloak, for to all but Athos he was a stranger. Athos, too, now looked at him in surprise, for even he did not see how the man could be personally concerned in this terrible drama.

The man walked slowly up to Milady until only the table separated them. Then he took off his mask and stood looking at her. His face was pale and framed in thick black hair, beard and whiskers, and his expression and manner were deadly calm. Milady stared back at him for a moment in silence. Then she suddenly sprang to her feet, shrank back against the wall and cried in a voice hoarse with terror:

'No, no! It can't be! It's a ghost – an evil spirit! Help! Help!'

She now turned her face to the wall and began threshing against it with her arms, as though she were trying to beat a passage through it.

All the others present turned to the stranger and said:

'In Heaven's name, who are you?'

'Ask that woman,' replied the stranger. 'She recognizes me, as you see.'

Milady whipped round.

'The headsman of Lille, the headsman of Lille!' she shrieked.

She was now half-crazed with fear and clung to the
wall to prevent herself falling.

Everyone stood aside, leaving the man in the red cloak
alone in the middle of the room. Milady, who was
standing with her back pressed to the wall, cried out in
abject terror:

'Don't kill me, don't kill me! Have pity!'

The stranger waited for a moment. Then he said:

'You see! She does recognize me. Yes, I'm the public
executioner of the town of Lille. And here's my charge
against this woman.'

All eyes were fixed on him and everyone waited spellbound to hear what he had to say.

'I knew this woman when she was a girl,' he began.
'She was as beautiful then as she is now. She was a nun at
the Benedictine convent of Templemar. There was a
young priest, a simple, honest fellow, who officiated in
the convent chapel. This woman made up her mind to
seduce him and succeeded. She'd have seduced a saint.'

He paused and continued:

'Both of them, priest and nun, had taken vows which
were sacred and irrevocable. Their relationship couldn't
have gone on without bringing disaster to both. She
eventually persuaded him to leave the district with her.
But they needed money to help them start life in another
part of France where they could live in peace. And they
were both penniless. So the priest stole the Communion
plate from the church and sold it. But both were caught
and arrested just as they were leaving the district.

'A week later this woman seduced her gaoler's son and
escaped. The young priest was sentenced to ten years in
irons and to branding. I was at that time the public
executioner of Lille. I had to brand the convict, and the
convict, gentlemen, was my own brother!

'I vowed then that this woman, who'd ruined his life,
who was more than merely his accomplice, having

incited him to commit the crime, should at least share his punishment. I suspected where she was hiding, went after her, found her, bound her hand and foot and branded her with the very iron which I'd used on my brother.

'I then returned to Lille. The day after my return my brother also managed to escape. I was accused of aiding and abetting him, arrested and sentenced to detention in his place until he gave himself up again. My brother never discovered this till later. He'd gone to rejoin this woman, and together they'd fled to Berry, where he managed to procure a small living. He passed this woman off as his sister.

'The lord of the manor and patron of my brother's living met this woman and fell in love with her, so deeply in love that he proposed to her. She didn't hesitate, but left the man whose life she'd ruined and married the man whose life she was destined also to ruin. She became the Comtesse de la Fère.'

At this all eyes were turned on Athos, for of the five men present three knew that this was the musketeer's real name. Athos nodded to show that all the stranger had said was true. The stranger now continued:

'At this my brother became desperate and almost mad with grief. He returned to Lille, and on hearing that I'd been imprisoned in his place gave himself up and that very evening hanged himself in his cell. When his corpse had been identified the authorities released me.

'That, then, is the charge I bring against this woman; that's the crime for which I branded her.'

Now Athos spoke:

'Monsieur d'Artagnan,' he said, 'what punishment do you demand for this woman?'

'Death,' replied d'Artagnan.

'And you, Lord de Winter, what punishment do you demand?'

'Death,' replied Lord de Winter.

'And you, Monsieur Porthos and Monsieur Aramis, you're the judges in this case. What punishment do you call for?'

The two musketeers replied sternly.

'The punishment of death.'

Milady gave an unearthly shriek, sank on her knees, dragged herself across the room and fell prostrate before her judges.

Athos passed sentence on her as she lay there.

'Anne de Breuil,' he said. 'You've wearied God and men with your crimes. If you've ever prayed in your life, pray now, for you've been found guilty and are to die.'

When Milady heard this and knew that she had no more hope she staggered to her feet and tried to speak. But she could make no sound. And now she felt a strong hand – the executioner's hand – seize her by her hair and start to drag her away. Seeing it was useless to resist she turned and walked quietly out of the house.

Lord de Winter, d'Artagnan, Athos, Porthos and Aramis walked out behind her, followed by the four servants. The room was left empty with its window broken and its door creaking on its hinges. The smoky lamp still flickered near the hearth, shedding a small circle of light and casting sinister shadows on the walls.

34

THE EXECUTION

It was nearing midnight; the moon, now in its last quarter and reddened by the last traces of the storm, was rising behind the little town of Armentières, whose houses and tall, slender steeple were outlined against its faint glow. The river Lys lay opposite, its waters swirling like molten lead; on the far bank the dense forest rose black against a stormy sky swept with thick copper-edged clouds, which cast a sort of midnight twilight on the scene. To the left stood an old, disused windmill, from whose ruins came at intervals an owl's screech. The meadow land which bordered the road on either side was dotted here and there with low, stunted trees, like mis-shapen dwarfs squatting on their heels to spy on belated travellers.

From time to time broad, jagged streaks of lightning would illumine the whole landscape, curving scimitar-like over the dark mass of forest, and seeming to cleave the sky. The wind had dropped; the air was sultry; nature lay under a pall of deathly silence; the ground was wet and slippery and the grass and wild flowers smelled sweet after the recent rain.

Two of the servants had hold of Milady, each by one arm, and were urging her forward. The executioner walked behind her, and behind him Lord de Winter, d'Artagnan, Athos, Porthos and Aramis walked abreast. Planchet and Bazin brought up the rear.

The two servants were leading their prisoner towards the river. She was speechless; only her eyes spoke, and they spoke eloquently enough, as she cast beseeching looks at each of her judges in turn.

At one moment Milady and her two guards found

themselves some way ahead of the rest of the party. She whispered quickly to them:

'1,000 pistoles for each of you if you'll help me to escape. If you let your masters have their way with me I've some friends nearby who'll make you pay dearly for my death.' Grimaud was shaken and Mousqueton began to tremble. But Athos had heard Milady speak and walked quickly up to her and her escort, followed by Lord de Winter.

'Send Grimaud and Mousqueton back,' he said. 'She's been talking to them. They're no longer to be trusted.'

Lord de Winter called Planchet and Bazin, who took the places of the other two.

When the procession reached the river bank the executioner went up to Milady and began binding her hands and feet. Suddenly she broke her prolonged silence and cried out:

'Cowards! Murderers! Ten of you butchering one wretched woman! Take care! If I'm not rescued now I'll be avenged later!'

Athos replied coldly:

'You're not a woman! You're not human at all! You're a fiend escaped from Hell and we're sending you back where you belong.'

'Who are you to set yourselves up?' she cried. 'Who are you to appoint yourselves my judges? Remember, anyone who touches a hair of my head's a murderer himself!'

'Executioners can kill without murdering,' said the man in the red cloak, tapping his broadsword.

Milady gave an unearthly shriek and fell on her knees. The headsman half lifted her in his arms and began to drag her over to the boat.

'O God!' screamed Milady. 'Are you going to drown me?'

Her screams were so dreadful that d'Artagnan, who had at first been the most eager in pursuit of her, now sank down on the stump of a tree, groaned and put his hands to his ears to block out the sound. He was the youngest of the men present and his heart failed him.

'I can't look on at this horrible sight,' he said. 'I can't stand by and watch her die like this.'

Milady heard him and a ray of hope came to her. She cried out:

'D'Artagnan, d'Artagnan, remember I loved you! Remember our hours of perfect happiness together!'

D'Artagnan got up and started to walk towards her. But Athos drew his sword and stood barring his way.

'One step more and it'll be over my dead body,' he said.

D'Artagnan fell on his knees and began to pray. Athos said sternly:

'Headsman, do your duty!'

The headsman replied:

'With all my heart, Sir. For, as I believe in God, so I believe in my right to perform my official duty on this woman.'

'So be it then,' said Athos.

He now approached Milady.

'I forgive you,' he said, 'for the wrong you've done me, for wrecking my life, for bringing shame on me, for defiling my love for you, for destroying my hope of salvation by causing me to despair. Die in peace.'

Lord de Winter now approached the prisoner in his turn.

'I forgive you for murdering my brother,' he said, 'for murdering the Duke of Buckingham, for being the cause of Felton's death, and for your attempts to murder me. Die in peace.'

D'Artagnan now spoke.

'Forgive me, Lady de Winter,' he said, 'for rousing your hatred by my blackguardly conduct. I in return forgive you for murdering Constance Bonacieux and for your savage attacks on me. I forgive you and pity you. Die in peace.'

'I'm lost!' said Milady. 'I'm going to die!'

She had spoken softly, half to herself, but Athos overheard her.

'Yes,' he said. 'You're lost. You're going to die.'

At this Milady rose to her feet and cast a last swift, despairing glance round her. She saw no help anywhere, heard no reassuring voice, saw no friendly face. She was surrounded by enemies.

'Where am I going to die?' she asked.

'On the far bank of the river,' replied the headsman.

Whereupon he motioned her into the boat and was preparing to step in after her when Athos handed him a purse of gold.

'Take this,' he said. 'It's your fee for the execution. Let the prisoner see that we're acting officially as judges.'

'Very well,' said the headsman. 'And now let her see that I'm doing what I'm doing not for money but because I consider it my duty.'

And he threw the purse into the river.

The boat, with the headsman and his prisoner, now started off towards the left bank of the Lys. The rest of the party remained on the right bank; they had fallen on their knees and were praying.

The boat glided slowly along the ferry rope in the shadow of a dark cloud which at that moment hung over the water, intercepting the moon's pale glow. The watchers saw the boat reach the far bank and the two figures silhouetted black against the reddish gleam on the horizon.

On the way across Milady had managed to untie the rope which bound her feet. The moment the boat touched ground she sprang ashore and tried to flee. But the grass was wet and when she reached the top of the bank she slipped and fell on her knees.

Did some superstitious fear now assail her? Did she feel that Heaven and Fate were against her? Or what prompted her to remain motionless on her knees, with her head bowed and her hands folded in front of her, making no further attempt to save herself?

Now the watchers on the far bank saw the executioner slowly raise his arms; they saw the blade of his broadsword glint for a second in the moonlight; they saw his arms fall again; they heard the hiss of the scimitar passing through the air and the victim's shriek; and then the truncated body collapse under the blow, go inert and roll sideways.

And now the executioner took off his red cloak, spread it out on the ground, laid the body in it and then the head, knotted the four ends of the cloak together, hoisted it on to his shoulder and stepped back into the boat.

When he reached the middle of the river he stopped the boat, lifted up his burden, held it over the water and called out in a loud voice:

'I deliver you to God's justice. May His will be done!'

Then he dropped the corpse into the deep, swirling waters, which opened to receive it and closed over it again.

35

A Messenger from the Cardinal

Three days later the four musketeers returned to Paris. Their period of leave was up and they went that same evening to report their return to Monsieur de Tréville. The Captain greeted them heartily.

'Well, gentlemen,' he said, 'did you enjoy your leave?'
Athos had just enough self-control to stammer out:
'Enormously, Sir.'

On 6 September the King left Paris, faithful to his
promise to the Cardinal to return to La Rochelle. In
the interval he had heard the news of the Duke of
Buckingham's murder and was overjoyed.

One day the King had halted on the route to fly his
falcons and the four friends had, as usual, gone to drink a
glass of wine in a neighbouring inn. As they were sitting
drinking a rider drew rein at the door of the inn and
ordered a glass of wine to be brought out to him. He was
exhausted and covered in dust, having ridden all the way
from La Rochelle at full gallop. While waiting for his wine
he happened to glance inside the room where the four
friends were seated.

He gave a start of surprise and called out:
'Hullo, there, Monsieur d'Artagnan! It is Monsieur
d'Artagnan, isn't it?'

D'Artagnan looked up and also gave a start of surprise.
The stranger was none other than his evil genius, his
acquaintance of Meung, of the Rue des Fossoyeurs and of
Arras. He at once drew his sword and rushed to the door.
This time, however, the stranger did not attempt to flee,
but dismounted and walked up to him.

'Ha, Sir!' said the young man. 'So we meet at last!
You're not going to escape this time!'

'I've no intention of escaping, Sir,' replied the stranger.
'On the contrary, I was looking for you. I arrest you in the
King's name.'

'What's that?' cried d'Artagnan. 'What did you say?'

'I said I arrest you in the King's name. You must
surrender your sword at once and not try to resist. If you
do I warn you it'll be the worse for you.'

D'Artagnan lowered the point of his sword but did not
yet surrender it.

'Who are you?' he asked.

The stranger replied:

'Chevalier de Rochefort, Cardinal Richelieu's equerry. I've orders to take you back to His Eminence at La Rochelle.'

Athos had meanwhile come out of the inn and joined them. He said:

'We're all on our way back to La Rochelle now, Sir. You must take Monsieur d'Artagnan's and our word for that.'

'I've orders to have him brought back to camp under escort.'

'We'll act as his escort, Sir,' said Athos. 'You can trust us to bring him back safely.'

Then his face darkened and he added sternly:

'You can also trust us not to hand him over to you.'

De Rochefort glanced behind him and saw that Porthos and Aramis had come out and were standing between him and the inn door. He realized that he was completely at the mercy of these four men.

'Gentlemen,' he said, 'if Monsieur d'Artagnan will surrender his sword to me and give me his word of honour not to escape, I'll consent to your escorting him straight to His Eminence's quarters.'

'I give you my word, Sir,' said d'Artagnan. 'And here's my sword.'

'It really suits me better this way,' said de Rochefort. 'I'm not returning to camp myself. I've got to go on to the north.'

'If you're going to meet Lady de Winter,' said Athos coldly, 'you're going on a fool's errand. You won't find her.'

'Why? What's happened to her?' asked Rochefort sharply.

'Come back to the camp and you'll find out.'

Rochefort thought for a moment. Then he remembered that they were only a day's journey from Surgères, which

was the town agreed on as the meeting-place for the King
and the Cardinal, and decided to follow Athos' advice
and return with the royal party. This plan had the added
advantage of enabling him to keep an eye on the prisoner
himself.

Shortly afterwards the King took the road again with
his escort. At three in the afternoon of the following day
the party arrived at Surgères where the Cardinal was
awaiting His Majesty. Monarch and minister greeted one
another effusively, and exchanged congratulations on
the lucky stroke of fate which had rid France of the
formidable enemy who had been stirring up Europe
against her. Whereupon the Cardinal took leave of the
King, inviting him to come next day to inspect the
fortifications on the dyke, which were now completed.
He had heard from Rochefort that d'Artagnan had been
arrested and was keen to cross-question him.

When the Cardinal returned that night to his house on
the La Pierre bridge he found d'Artagnan and his three
friends standing at his door. D'Artagnan was swordless,
but the others were all armed. This time he had the whip
hand of them. He looked at them sternly and signed
imperiously to d'Artagnan to follow him into the house.

'We'll wait for you, d'Artagnan,' said Athos, just loud
enough for the Cardinal to hear.

His Eminence frowned, seemed to hesitate for a
moment, and then walked on without a word.

D'Artagnan entered the house behind him, and
Rochefort followed d'Artagnan. Sentries were posted on
either side of the door.

The Cardinal went into the room which he used as
his office and signed to Rochefort to show the young
musketeer in. Rochefort obeyed and then retired.

D'Artagnan was now alone with the Cardinal. It was
his second interview with the great man and he confessed afterwards that he was certain it would be his last.

Richelieu remained standing with his elbow on the mantelpiece; there was a table between him and the young man. He said:

'You've been arrested by my orders, Sir.'

'So I was told, Monseigneur.'

'D'you know why?'

'No, Monseigneur. There's only one charge I could be arrested on, and that Your Eminence doesn't yet know.'

Richelieu stared hard at d'Artagnan.

'Oh?' he asked. 'And what d'you mean by that?'

'If Your Eminence would be good enough to tell me first what crimes I'm charged with I'll tell you what I actually have done.'

'You're charged with crimes that have cost bigger men than you their heads, Sir,' said the Cardinal haughtily.

'What in particular?' asked d'Artagnan calmly.

'You're charged with corresponding with enemies of the State, with intercepting State documents and with attempting to frustrate your general's plans.'

D'Artagnan suspected that all these charges had been brought by Milady.

'Yes, and who brought these charges against me, Your Eminence?' he asked. 'A woman branded by the law of the land, a woman who married one man in France and another in England, a woman who poisoned her second husband and who once tried to poison me.'

The Cardinal stared at the young man in amazement.

'What are you saying, Sir?' he cried. 'What woman do you mean?'

'Lady de Winter,' replied d'Artagnan. 'Yes, Lady de Winter. I don't suppose Your Eminence knew anything about her crimes when she brought those charges against me.'

'If Lady de Winter's committed the crimes you accuse her of she shall be punished,' said the Cardinal.

'She has been punished, Monseigneur.'

'Who punished her?'

'We did.'

'Is she in prison?'

'She's dead.'

The Cardinal was dumbfounded.

'Dead?' he repeated. 'Did I hear you say she was dead?'

'She made no less than three attempts on my life, and I forgave her. But then she killed the woman I loved, so my friends and I captured her, tried her and sentenced her to death.'

D'Artagnan then related the events of the past few days; how Madame Bonacieux had been poisoned in the Carmelite Convent at Béthune, how they had tried Milady in the little house by the river, and how she had been beheaded on the banks of the Lys.

The Cardinal was not easily impressed. But even he shuddered at this gruesome tale. Then, as though some thought had struck him, the expression on his face, previously stern and anxious, suddenly cleared and he looked quite cheerful again. In gentle tones which contrasted strangely with the threat implied in his words he now said:

'So you all took the law into your own hands? Didn't it occur to you that you had no official right to judge and condemn this woman, and that when you punished her you were committing murder yourselves?'

D'Artagnan replied:

'Monseigneur, I won't try and justify my conduct to you. I'll submit to whatever punishment Your Eminence decides on. I'm not so attached to this life that I'd mind much leaving it.'

The Cardinal smiled and there was a note almost of affection in his voice as he said:

'I know you're brave enough, Monsieur d'Artagnan. So I can tell you here and now you'll have to stand trial and may be found guilty.'

'I might reply that I already have my official pardon in my pocket, Sir. But I won't. I merely say to Your Eminence: "Yours to command, mine to obey."'

'Your pardon?' echoed the Cardinal in astonishment.

'Yes, Monseigneur.'

'Signed by whom? The King?'

There was a hint of scorn in Richelieu's voice as he said this.

'No,' replied d'Artagnan. 'Signed by Your Eminence.'

'By me? What are you talking about? Are you mad?'

'I expect you'll recognize your own handwriting, Sir,' replied the young man.

Whereupon he drew from his pocket the precious scroll of paper which Athos had taken from Milady by force and which he had handed over to d'Artagnan for safe keeping.

His Eminence took the scroll and proceeded to read it aloud slowly, stressing every syllable.

It is by my order and for the benefit of the State that the bearer of this note has done what he has done.
3 December, 1627   Richelieu

Richelieu sat lost in thought, screwing the scroll of paper round in his hand. At last he looked up and fixed his eagle eye on d'Artagnan. When he saw his honest, open, intelligent look and realized from the tears which were coursing down his cheeks how greatly he had suffered during the past month, he was struck for the third or fourth time by the brilliant possibilities in store for this youth of twenty, and saw what treasures of energy, courage, and resource he would provide for a man who knew how to handle him. He compared the qualities of the young man in front of him with Milady's diabolical genius, her sinister intrigues and many crimes, and knew in his heart of hearts that he was on the whole thankful to be rid of such a dangerous accomplice.

He now slowly tore up the scroll of paper which d'Artagnan had so generously handed over to him. The young man thought to himself:

'I'm lost!'

The Cardinal walked over to the table and without sitting down added two lines to a sheet of parchment, two-thirds of which were already written on. Then he set his seal to it.

'That's my death sentence,' thought d'Artagnan. 'He's sparing me the boredom of the Bastille and the slow agony of a trial. It's really very good of him.'

The Cardinal handed him the paper and said:

'I've taken one signed warrant from you and am giving you another in exchange. The name's missing on this commission; write it in yourself.'

D'Artagnan took the paper rather gingerly and shot a quick glance at it. It was a lieutenant's commission in the Musketeers. He was quite overcome and fell on his knees before the Cardinal.

'Monseigneur,' he said, 'from now on my life's yours. I'll be loyal to you always. But this honour . . . it's too much. I don't deserve it. I've got three friends all of whom deserve it more than I.'

The Cardinal was delighted to have won over this recalcitrant spirit to his side. He patted him familiarly on the shoulder.

'You're a good lad, d'Artagnan,' he said. 'You can do what you like with that commission. The name's left blank, as you see. But don't forget you were the one I meant it for.'

'I won't forget, Monseigneur,' replied the young man. 'I'll never forget. Please believe that.'

The Cardinal now called out:

'Rochefort!'

The equerry, who was probably listening behind the door, was in the room in a flash.

'Rochefort,' said the Cardinal, 'you see Monsieur d'Artagnan here – from now on I'm numbering him among my friends. So make it up, you two. Shake hands and behave yourselves in future, if you value your heads.'

Rochefort and d'Artagnan shook hands rather half-heartedly, but the Cardinal kept his eyes fixed on them to see that they did so. They then left the room together. In the passage outside they said almost in one breath:

'We'll be seeing each other again, won't we?'

'Whenever you like,' said d'Artagnan.

'We'll get a chance soon enough,' said Rochefort.

At that moment the Cardinal opened the door and looked out.

'What were you saying, gentlemen?' he asked.

The two men at once gave each other forced smiles, shook hands again, bowed to His Eminence and walked out of the house.

The musketeer rejoined his friends.

'We were beginning to be worried about you,' said Athos.

'You needn't be,' replied d'Artagnan. 'I'm not only a free man – I'm actually in favour!'

'Tell us about it.'

'Yes, this evening. For the time being we'd better separate.'

That evening d'Artagnan called at Athos' billet. He found him drinking a bottle of Spanish wine, a duty he performed religiously every night. He described in detail his interview with the Cardinal. Then he pulled the commission out of his pocket and handed it to his friend.

'Here's something that falls to you by right, Athos,' he said.

Athos glanced at it and then smiled his sad, gentle smile.

'As Lieutenant Athos I should appear presumptuous,'

he said. 'As Lieutenant Comte de la Fère I should appear undignified. No. You keep that commission; it was meant for you. Damn it, you've paid dearly enough for it.'

D'Artagnan now left Athos and went to call on Porthos, whom he found pirouetting in front of the glass in a brand new, magnificent embroidered coat.

'Oh, so it's you, my lad,' said the big man. 'How d'you think this coat suits me?'

'Very well indeed,' answered d'Artagnan. 'But I've come to offer you something which'll suit you better still.'

'What's that?' asked Porthos.

'A commission in the Musketeers.'

D'Artagnan then described his interview with the Cardinal and, taking the commission out of his pocket, said:

'Porthos, just write your name on that. And when you're my officer don't be too harsh with me.'

Porthos glanced at the paper. Then, to d'Artagnan's great surprise, he handed it back to him:

'I'd have liked that very much,' he said, 'but it's too late now. My mistress' husband died while we were on our trip to Béthune and his whole fortune reverts to his widow. If I marry her I shall have the use of it. It's too good a chance to miss. As a matter of fact I was just trying on the coat I'm going to wear at my wedding. You take the commission, old boy. You thoroughly deserve it.'

The young man now called on Aramis. He found him on his knees at a *prie-dieu*, his forehead resting on an open Book of Hours. He described his interview with the Cardinal and, pulling the commission out of his pocket for the third time, said:

'You take this, Aramis. You're our guiding light. You deserve it more than anyone for your good sense and good staff work in our many adventures.'

'Thanks for the offer, d'Artagnan,' replied Aramis.

'But, alas, our last adventure sickened me of soldiering once and for all. I've made up my mind at last. When the siege is over I'm joining the Lazarists. You take the commission, d'Artagnan. A soldier's life suits you. You'll make a first-rate officer.'

D'Artagnan was exceedingly grateful to his friends for their kindness. He walked back to Athos' rooms treading on air. He found his friend still sitting at the table holding up his last glass of Malaga to the lamp.

'Well,' he said, 'the other two also refused the commission.'

His friend replied:

'The fact is, d'Artagnan, no one deserves it as much as you.'

Whereupon he took up a pen, wrote the name 'd'Artagnan' on the commission and returned it to him.

'Now I'll have no friends any more,' said the young man. 'I shall have nothing but bitter memories.'

'You're young,' replied Athos. 'Your bitter memories will soon change into happy ones.'

EPILOGUE

After Buckingham's death there was no more talk in England of sending a fleet to the help of the Rochellese, and the town surrendered after a year's siege. The capitulation was signed on 28 October 1628. In December of the same year the King made a triumphal entry into Paris, as though he had returned from a victorious campaign, not against Frenchmen, but against an external enemy.

D'Artagnan took his commission in the Musketeers. Porthos left the army and married Madame Coquenard in the course of the next year. The much-coveted coffer was found to contain 800,000 livres. Mousqueton was given a magnificent livery and got what he had longed for all his life – the right to sit on the box of a gilded coach.

Aramis went on a trip to Lorraine, after which he disappeared entirely and none of his friends heard another word from him. They learned later from one of Madame de Chevreuse's intimate friends that he had embraced what he had always maintained was his true vocation and retired to a monastery, though which monastery no one ever discovered. Bazin became one of the institution's lay brothers.

Athos remained in the King's service until 1633, with d'Artagnan as his officer. In 1633 he went on a trip to Roussillon, after which he, too, left the army on the pretext that he had just inherited a small property in the Blaisois. Grimaud retired with him to the country.

D'Artagnan fought three duels with Rochefort and wounded him three times. The third time he said to the equerry, as he helped him to his feet:

'If we have another fight I shall probably kill you.'

The wounded man replied:

'In that case it would be better for us both to forgive and forget. Damn it all, in some ways I've been a good friend to you. If I'd said a word to the Cardinal after our first fight I could have had your head chopped off.'

Upon which they shook hands, this time in genuine friendship and without any reservations. Rochefort got Planchet posted to the Piedmont regiment as a sergeant.

Monsieur Bonacieux went on living in moderate contentment, quite in the dark as to his wife's fate and not greatly concerned about it. One day, however, he was rash enough to write a letter to the Cardinal to remind him of his existence. The Cardinal sent one of his household begging him to call on him at once and promising to see that thenceforth he lacked for nothing. At seven in the evening of the following day the little draper set out for the Louvre. From that day to this no one in the Rue des Fossoyeurs has seen or heard of him. Rumour has it that his generous patron has been keeping him housed and fed at his own expense in one of the King's castles.

Some of the many other Puffin Classics

THE LOST WORLD
Sir Arthur Conan Doyle

Journalist Ed Malone is looking for an adventure, and
that's exactly what he finds when he meets the eccentric
Professor Challenger: an adventure that leads Malone
and his three companions deep into the Amazon jungle,
to a lost world where dinosaurs roam free and the natives
fight out a murderous war with their fierce neighbours,
the ape-men.

KING SOLOMON'S MINES
H. Rider Haggard

The magnificent story of three men who trek north to the
remote interior of Africa in search of a lost friend. And
how at the end of their perilous journey they find, not
just the missing adventurer, but the spectacular diamond
mines of Solomon!

TREASURE ISLAND
R. L. Stevenson

Jim Hawkins had no idea when he picked up the oilskin
packet from Captain Flint's sea chest that here lay the key
to untold wealth – a treasure map. When Jim sails on the
Hispaniola as cabin-boy, with the awesome Long John
Silver as ship's cook and the rest of the shifty crew, he
embarks on an adventure unrivalled for excitement and
suspense.

THE PRINCE AND THE PAUPER
Mark Twain

Tom Canty and Edward Tudor look alike, but their lives could hardly be more different. For Edward is Prince (and heir to the throne), whilst Tom is a miserable pauper. Until one day fate intervenes and for a while each must see how the other lives . . .

THE CHILDREN OF THE NEW FOREST
Captain Marryat

England in 1647: the country is divided as Cavaliers and Roundheads fight bitterly to decide who should rule. The four Beverley children lose their parents in the war and are forced to go into hiding. Ill-prepared for a life on the land, and always at great risk of discovery, they set about hunting and housekeeping with great spirit and courage.

OUR EXPLOITS AT WEST POLEY
Thomas Hardy

The story of two boys who discover how to divert the course of an underground river and play havoc with the lives of the local Somerset villagers. But it's their own lives that are finally most in danger!